CS

Trial and Error

CRIME CLASSICS

Trial and Error

HOW CAN A MURDERER PROVE HIS OWN GUILT?

ANTHONY BERKELEY

ABOUT THE AUTHOR

Founder of the prestigious, and still flourishing, Detection Club, Anthony
Berkeley Cox (1893-1971) was one of the most innovative crime writers of the
so-called 'golden age' and beyond. He used the pseudonyms Anthony Berkeley
and Francis Iles, and in both guises he explored the psychology of crime.

This edition published in the UK by Arcturus Publishing Limited
26/27 Bickels Yard, 151–153 Bermondsey Street, London SE1 3HA

This edition published in Australia and New Zealand by Hinkler Books Pty Ltd
45-55 Fairchild Street, Heatherton Victoria 3202 Australia

Cover artwork by Duncan Smith
Typesetting by Couper Street Type Co.

AD002222EN

Printed in Canada

CONTENTS

Prologue

SYMPOSIUM

" 'The sanctity of Human Life has been much exaggerated,' " quoted Ferrers. "Just think what courage it took to say that, to a crowd of confirmed sentimentalists—professional sentimentalists, some of 'em."

"And you believe it's true?" asked the Rev. Jack Denney.

"Of course it's true."

"Ah well, I suppose it's part of your profession as a journalist to be cynical." The clergyman smiled and sipped his port.

Ferrers smiled suavely back, touching the elegant bow of his black tie. He was not a journalist, unless the literary editor of one of London's oldest and most dignified literary weeklies could be so described; and he recognised the jibe hidden in the meiosis. He and Jack Denney were old antagonists.

"Just as it's part of your profession as a parson to be sentimental, Jack," he returned provocatively.

"Perhaps, perhaps." The clergyman refused the challenge.

On the other side of the table a soldier and a retired Indian civilian were discussing the New Youth.

Major Barrington, a tall, good-looking man with a clipped grey moustache, had retired from the regular army soon after the war to take up a diplomatic appointment and not long ago had married one of the comparatively New Youth, so that he might be expected to know something about the genus. Dale, the civilian, having returned from India with a prewar mind, was frankly bewildered by them; they seemed to speak almost a different language from the Old Youth whom he had known.

He had caught an echo from the other side of the table and used it to help his own argument. " 'Sanctity of human life'!" he snorted, ruffling the grey hair which tumbled over his forehead like a sheep dog's. "There you are. A sign of the times. Just what I was saying. They're so fond of their own precious skins nowadays that nothing else counts in comparison. But of course they have to wrap it up in some high-sounding phrase like 'the sanctity of human life.' "

"I will say for 'em, they're careful for other people's skins as well as their own," defended the major. "I don't think it's all selfishness, you know."

Mr Todhunter, like a good host, saw his opportunity to make the discussion general. He poked forward his small round bald head, which was balanced on the top of his gaunt frame rather like a potato that has been left out of its sack, and peered through his glasses at the civilian.

"Then you agree with Ferrers, Dale, that the sanctity of human life has been much exaggerated?" he asked.

"Oh well, I didn't say quite that, you know."

"But you implied it," pointed out Ferrers. "Be a man and admit that you meant it too."

"Well, all right. Perhaps I did."

"Of course. Any sensible man must. It's only sentimentalists like Jack here who pretend to believe that the life of some stupid oaf is a sacred thing. Eh, Major?"

"I think you want to draw the net a bit closer," opined the major. "I won't argue for or against plain stupidity; but if you'd said, stupidity of the kind that's a danger to other people, I'm with you every time."

"There you are, Jack, you see." Ferrers smiled his eighteenth-century smile and sketched an unconscious little bow. Ferrers was perfect eighteenth century. "The major's a brave man, as a soldier ought to be. It takes a brave man to say straight out what all of us think: that the best thing that can happen to the stupid motorist, for instance, is that he should get killed—as quickly as possible, up against a telegraph pole—for the benefit of all the rest of us. But you think his life, which he uses to our danger, is sacred?"

"I do, certainly." The Rev. Mr Denney leaned his rotund little form comfortably back in his chair and smiled at his neighbour with that bland conviction of being in the right, against all proof and all logic, which is so exasperating to those foolish enough to argue with the clergy.

Major Barrington twiddled the stem of his wineglass. "I wasn't thinking so much of the foolish motorist. But take the case of a statesman johnny who's going to plunge his country into war. Say that he alone can prevent it and he won't. He's going to cause the loss of hundreds of thousands of lives, sacred or not, as you like. And supposing some patriotic assassin comes along and wipes him out from the best motives. Well, would you say that was a wicked thing to do? Would you still think the statesman's life a sacred thing, in itself, irrespective of how he was going to use it?"

"Good old army," murmured Ferrers courteously. "He's got you there, Jack."

"Do evil that good may come?" The clergyman twiddled the stem of his wineglass. "Well, that's a very old problem, isn't it?"

"No doubt," agreed Ferrers. "But let's hear your views on it."

"I've often thought, you know, that that was really the best way to stop war," put in a diffident voice from the other end of the table. "I mean, threaten one or two of the leading statesmen with assassination if they declared it. But of course you'd have to make them believe that you meant it."

"That implies a very low opinion of statesmen," smiled the clergyman.

"Well, I think we all have that nowadays, haven't we?" suggested Mr Ambrose Chitterwick with the same diffidence.

"Yes," said Mr Todhunter, "but I'm inclined to agree with you, Major, that it's the way in which a life may be used, rather than the actual fact of existence itself, that may constitute the sacred element. And that raises an interesting point. What is the best use to which a life may be put?"

The others listened politely, as one does to one's host; but the general feeling obviously was that the question had not done Mr Todhunter justice.

"Surely," suggested the clergyman, "there can't be any doubt about that."

"You mean, in the service of humanity?"

"Certainly."

"Yes, of course. But service in what particular direction? There are two, you see: to some extent, positive and negative. I mean, the bestowal of benefits or the removal of menace. And would it be better to aim at benefiting the whole of humanity or a very large body such as a nation, which must be a hit-or-miss affair, or concentrate on a much smaller group of people with a correspondingly greater chance of achieving something?"

"Dear me, you're opening up very large questions there."

"But rather academic?" suggested Ferrers.

The others looked as if they had understood what the questions were.

"Academic?" repeated Mr Todhunter. "Not at all. I'll give you a concrete instance if I can. Let me see. Yes. Take the case of a man whose doctor has given him only a few months to live. He——"

"I seem to have met some such situation before," laughed Ferrers. "And I'll tell you what inevitably happens. Rendered reckless by this knowledge of his approaching end, the man, who by the way is generally a feeble, henpecked, downtrodden fellow, suddenly develops powers hitherto quite unknown to himself, engages in a desperate struggle with a super-villain, knocks out his gang singlehanded, falls in love with an incredibly beautiful girl whom he at first believes to be a member of the gang and then discovers chained to the wall in a cellar with the water up to her chin, is unable to marry her because of his coming death—and discovers at the last minute that the doctor was wrong all the time. Is that what you mean?"

"Yes, of course the situation has been used often enough in fiction," agreed Mr Todhunter with a polite smile. "Nevertheless it must happen still more often in real life. After all, there are many incurable diseases. And supposing, for the sake of my concrete instance, that there is such a man and that he wishes, in the few months that remain to him, to do the best that he can for his fellows: to dedicate these last months, we may say, to some great service on their behalf. What do you think would be the best thing he could do?"

Mr Todhunter had addressed his question rather vaguely to the company at large rather than to any particular member, and answers came with tolerable promptitude from each.

"Shoot Mussolini," said Major Barrington without hesitation. "He's a great man, I'm convinced; but he's a menace to the whole world."

"No, Hitler," corrected the Indian civilian. "Hitler's the real menace. Besides, I've always found Jews very decent fellows. Though a better job still might be to wipe out all the leaders of the military party in Japan. Our own fellows are too contemptible to be worth bothering about."

"Personally, I don't believe in political assassination," said Ferrers. "Wiping out Hitler wouldn't necessarily destroy Hitlerism. These movements have to play themselves out. No, I think if I were in that situation I should be inclined to eliminate some perhaps quite insignificant person who was deliberately making the lives of a small group of persons intolerable. On balance, I believe that the sum total of benefit would be greater than in wiping out some dictator who is really only the mouthpiece of a movement."

"I agree," said Mr Chitterwick, as if thankful at being helped towards a decision. "Unless of course there was some definite case at hand of a statesman who was personally manoeuvring his country into war and whose removal would avert it."

Mr Todhunter looked at the clergyman. "And you, Denney?"

"I? Well, you can hardly expect me to join in this general call for violence. I would offer myself to the research department of a hospital for dangerous experiments which could not be carried out on anyone not under expectation of speedy death. And I'm convinced I should be more use to my fellow creatures than any of you blood-and-thunder merchants."

Mr Todhunter looked acutely interested. "That is quite a new idea," he said.

No one seemed to notice that Mr Todhunter himself had put forward no view of his own.

"You're wrong as usual, Jack," bantered Ferrers. "For one thing no hospital would make use of you, I can promise you that; the outcry, if an experiment proved too dangerous, would be far too serious to risk. And in any case you'd be little or no use. There must be precious few experiments, if any, for which a human being is indispensable and no animal would do."

"Are you sure of that?" asked Mr Todhunter seriously.

"I'm positive."

The clergyman shrugged his shoulders. "Well, the whole question's only academic."

"Of course," agreed Mr Todhunter at once. "Nevertheless, don't you think it's interesting that out of five people voting, four are for elimination; what I called the negative direction: benefiting through removal of an existing evil rather than increasing the supply of good. In other words, murder. Which seems to bring us back to where we started, the sanctity of human life."

Mr Todhunter poured himself out another glass of port and circulated the decanter. Mr Todhunter had no wife and was therefore at liberty to sit over his dinner table just as long as he pleased; and there were in any case this evening no ladies to join.

With the second circulation of the decanter the attitudes of the others became more relaxed. A pleasantly academic subject for argument had been found, the port was good, and the absence of impatient ladies elsewhere seemed a goodly thing.

"Very well," said Ferrers. "To bring the wheel full circle, I'll repeat that 'the sanctity of human life has been much exaggerated.' And this time I'll ask anyone who disagrees to tell me what sanctity there is in the continued existence of the worst type of moneylender, of a blackmailer, of a syphilitic seducer of young girls, of a Jack-in-office who curries favour with a stupid employer by throwing out on the street decent, hard-working men with wives and families—" Ferrers's voice had become unusually bitter. He looked round the table and seemed to collect himself. "Yes, if you like, even of incurable lunatics of the idiot type. Well, Jack?"

"You mean, you'd set yourself up as a judge of life and death?" counterthrust the clergyman.

"Why not? I should make a very good judge."

"And your aim would be to eliminate these people, rather than reform them?"

"If I considered them unreformable."

"So you'd be not only a judge of life and death, but of the potentialities for good and evil of the human soul itself?"

Ferrers refused to be intimidated. "Certainly. They're not so difficult to size up as you're suggesting."

"I wish I had your confidence."

"Ah, but then you're handicapped professionally, you see. You have to believe—or pretend to believe—that the souls of blackmailers, usurers and seducers are redeemable. I don't. And even if they were, the process would be too long and costly to be worth it, so far as the rest of the community is concerned."

"And you still think that the greatest good a man can do, in such a case as I put forward, is to eliminate a source of evil?" put in Mr Todhunter with his usual earnestness.

"Source of misery or injustice," corrected Ferrers. "I'm not concerned with abstract evil. Yes, I do. In fact I'm convinced. In anything from a political system to the human body the bad must be cut out before the good can be increased. To go about the job the other way round is to nullify your work. You agree with me, Major?"

"I do, yes. Yes, I think that's sound enough."

"Absolutely," pronounced the civilian.

Everyone looked at Mr Chitterwick, who blushed.

"Yes, I—I'm afraid I must agree too. It sounds distressing, in a way; but we must take things as they are, not as we would prefer them to be."

"Then that seems one point established," Mr Todhunter summed up. "With its corollaries it amounts to this: that the sanctity of human life has exceptions and that the greatest good a man could do is to eliminate a selected evildoer whose death must fulfil the condition of changing misery into happiness for a larger or smaller group of persons. That is the general opinion?"

"With one dissentient," said the clergyman firmly. "You've made out a very specious case for murder, but there's one insuperable answer to it: murder can never be justified, in any circumstances at all."

"Oh, come, sir," objected the major. "That's not an argument, is it? It's merely an assertion, incapable of proof. I mean, I might just as well say that sometimes murder can be justified. It's a dead end."

Ferrers's eyes twinkled. "Do you mean to say, Major, that you haven't yet discovered that nine tenths of Jack's arguments are only assertions? What else can a poor parson do when he's called upon to defend what no one can prove? He can only fall back on repeating what he considers to be axioms. And if we don't accept them as axioms of course there's a dead end."

"You'd be a better man if you did accept some of them, Lionel," retorted the parson amiably.

"I doubt it. But of course you have to say so."

"Yes," said Mr Todhunter. "Then what it all amounts to is that the man with only a few months to live can't do anything better than commit a murder, of the type defined. You really believe that?"

"I'm not going to run away from a nasty word," Ferrers smiled. "Whether you call it murder or elimination, that's what I believe."

"A man in such a position would be well placed to commit a righteous murder, wouldn't he?" hazarded Mr Chitterwick. "I mean, if he timed it properly there would be no fear of the strongest practical argument against murder—the hangman."

"Yes, that is perfectly true," said Mr Todhunter with interest. "But if we decide on murder, what kind of murder is he to commit? Two of you seemed to be in favour of a political murder, with the idea of benefiting the whole world, or at any rate a whole nation, and two preferred the private murder. It would be interesting to hear the arguments on either side."

"Oh, I withdraw Mussolini," Major Barrington offered. "I didn't make the suggestion very seriously. Besides, it's more than I'd care to do, to take the responsibility of deciding whether a Mussolini or a Hitler doesn't fulfill some need in the world today, if only on the principle that things have got to be worse before they can be bettered. In other words, like Ferrers, I don't believe in political assassination."

"And you, Dale?"

"Well, if the major withdraws Mussolini I'll withdraw my candidate. Though I must say I'd like to see every dishonest politician in this country shot."

"Would there be any left?" smiled Ferrers.

"Oh, come now," protested the clergyman. "There'd be Stanley Baldwin."

"And his pipe."

"Of peace, yes."

"Peace at any price—even fifteen hundred million pounds. Yes, and his pigs. Well, they'd be useful to fill up the vacancies in the cabinet. We should never notice the difference."

"Oh yes, we should," grinned the major. "Pigs wouldn't sign outrageous agreements with French prime ministers and let us down with a thud all over the world and then have to be publicly disowned. Pigs would have their uses."

"Yes," said Mr Todhunter. "Then the idea now seems to be that the private murder is to be preferred to the political assassination. Well, it would be interesting to hear what kind of private person would confer most benefits on his fellow creatures by dying."

"A newspaper proprietor who deliberately deceives his readers to further his own ends," suggested the major.

"Wouldn't that mean all newspaper proprietors?" asked Mr Chitterwick with unwonted cynicism.

Ferrers looked pained.

"Oh, we'll except the _London Review_ of course," the clergyman told him. "We all know that the _London Review_ stands alone in the newspaper world. Lionel wouldn't be working for it otherwise."

"The _London Review_ isn't a newspaper," Ferrers pointed out.

"Well, my vote would be for a really vindictive anonymous letter writer," said Dale. "No one does more harm, and no one is more difficult to bring to justice."

"Except a blackmailer, don't you think?" supplied Mr Chitterwick.

"Well, you ought to know something about murder, Chitterwick," Ferrers said. "Two, isn't it, that you've been mixed up in?"

"Well, yes, I suppose so, in a way," agreed Mr Chitterwick uneasily. "But..."

"No, no. All in confidence. Between friends and so on. Guaranteed not for publication. Come on."

Protesting, Mr Chitterwick was bullied into relating one or two of his experiences.

The decanter circulated for the third time.

Mr Todhunter allowed the discussion to drop. Any further attempts to keep it going would, he felt, look suspicious. In any case he had learned what he wanted to know.

For Mr Todhunter had been told by his doctor a week ago that he could not possibly live for more than a few months; and he had called together this carefully chosen group of assorted persons to advise him, all unwittingly, what to do with the time that remained to him.

And greatly to Mr Todhunter's surprise, it appeared that he had been advised, with remarkable unanimity, to commit a murder.

PART I

Picaresque

MR TODHUNTER IN
SEARCH OF A VICTIM

CHAPTER I

When Mr Lawrence Todhunter learned from his doctor that he was suffering from an aortic aneurism and must not expect to live for more than a few months, his first feeling had been one of incredulity.

"Well, how old are you?" asked the doctor, seeing his unbelief.

"Fifty-one," said Mr Todhunter, buttoning his shirt again over his bony chest.

"Exactly. And you've never been very fit."

"Of late years," agreed Mr Todhunter solemnly, "no, certainly not."

The doctor swung his stethoscope. "Well, what can you expect? Your blood pressure's been too high for years. If you hadn't followed my directions so carefully, you'd have been dead long ago." The doctor, an old friend, spoke with what seemed to Mr Todhunter unseemly callousness.

He produced what was intended for a cynical laugh but which sounded to his own ears more like a cackle of rather cheap bravado. "Yes, but to be told that one can't last longer than a few months . . . I mean, it's a situation that seems to belong to romantic fiction rather than real life."

"It happens often enough in real life," returned the doctor drily. "After all, there are plenty of incurable diseases, apart from the kind of thing that you're suffering from. And there's always cancer. The body must give out sooner or later. It's an exceedingly complicated mechanism, you know. The wonder is that all its parts continue to function as long as they do."

"You seem to regard death very lightly," observed Mr Todhunter not without resentment; and by "death" he meant "my death."

"I do," retorted the doctor with a little smile.

"Eh?" For a moment Mr Todhunter was quite taken aback that anyone could regard death lightly, and in particular his own death.

"I said, I do. No, no, I'm not a religious man. At least, not religious in any orthodox way. I just happen to believe quite firmly in survival."

"Oh!" said Mr Todhunter, somewhat blankly.

"I also believe that this present life on the physical plane is a ~~confounded~~ nuisance; and the sooner we're out of it the better. To ask for sympathy for a dying man seems to me tantamount to asking sympathy for a man coming out of prison into freedom."

"The deuce it does," remarked Mr Todhunter, staring. "I must say, for a man who likes good claret as much as you do, that sounds a bit thick."

"A prisoner must have his consolations. Sympathy," continued the doctor, warming to his subject, "on behalf of those left behind in prison, yes. They have a personal loss; though their feeling ought to be one of envy rather than grief. But in your case, my dear fellow, even that is absent. You have no wife, no children, not even any close relatives. You're extremely lucky. You can walk out of prison with an untroubled mind."

Mr Todhunter, who did not consider himself at all lucky, grunted a little angrily.

"However," relented the doctor, "if you don't see it that way, I suppose we must try to keep you in prison as long as we can; though I must say I wish I had your chances. Frankly, you remind me of that poor old chap in Madame Tussaud's who was released from his cell in the Bastille by the mob and never got over it."

"Don't talk such ███████ nonsense," said Mr Todhunter wrathfully.

"You mustn't get angry," advised the doctor. "That's the first thing. No strong emotions, please, or you'll be shot out of prison straight way. Likewise, no violent exertion. Walk slowly, never run, rest every second step going upstairs, no excitement, be on your guard all the time against any sudden strain. It'll be a drab life, but you can prolong it that way if you really want to. We can't cut down your diet much further, or I'd do that too. In any case, the aneurism is almost bound to burst within six months—well, a year at the outside—however careful you are. You asked me to be frank, you know."

"Oh yes, I did," Mr Todhunter agreed bitterly.

"Rest as much as you can," the doctor went on. "Avoid all alcohol. No smoking. Heaven help you, if I were in your shoes I'd run straight home from here and arrive there dead. Made your will, I suppose?"

"I never knew," said Mr Todhunter with distaste, "what a ███████ old ghoul you are."

"Nothing of the sort," retorted the doctor indignantly. "Ghoul be blowed! That's just your infernal conventionality, Todhunter. You always were a conventional old stick. It's the accepted thing to be sorry for the dying—yes, in spite of religion which teaches us that anyone who isn't a scoundrel is going to be a whole lot better off dead—so you think I ought to be sorry for you; and when I tell you I envy you instead, you call me a ghoul."

"Very well," said Mr Todhunter with dignity. "You're not a ghoul. But I can't help wondering whether your unselfish anxiety for my welfare can have coloured your diagnosis. In other words, I think I'd like a second opinion."

The doctor grinned and drew a slip of paper towards him. "You won't get me rattled that way. By all means have a second opinion, and a third, and a fourth. They'll only confirm me. Here's an address for you. A very sound man, perhaps the soundest for this kind of thing. He'll soak you three guineas, and you'll jolly well deserve it."

Mr Todhunter slowly put on his coat.

"I wonder," he said with reluctance, "whether you're not really such an ass as you sound?"

"You mean, whether there's something in what I've been saying? My boy, there's a whole lot in it. In my opinion the case for survival is proved—scientifically proved. And what does that give us? Well, no state can be lower, and consequently more unpleasant, than the physical one. That means that any subsequent state must, for the ordinarily decent person, be considerably more pleasant. It absolutely follows therefore that——"

"Yes, yes," said Mr Todhunter and took his leave.

2

Feeling slightly unreal, Mr Todhunter took a taxi to Welbeck Street. Although well able to afford it, this was actually the first time he had ever taken a taxi from Richmond, where he lived, to the West End; for Mr Todhunter was as careful in matters of money as in matters of health. But the occasion seemed to demand a taxi this time.

The specialist took his three guineas and confirmed the doctor's diagnosis, and prognosis, too, in every detail.

Shaken, Mr Todhunter took another taxi. He was a cautious man and seldom made up his own mind on any point until he had canvassed the views of at least three other people. He therefore caused himself to be driven to a second specialist, who could not conceivably be in a league with either of the other two men. When this third opinion proved in complete agreement with theirs, Mr Todhunter allowed himself to feel convinced.

He took a taxi back to Richmond.

3

Mr Todhunter was a bachelor.

The state was his own choice; for in spite of his complete lack of anything which might be expected to rouse a lady's passion, it had often been hinted to him that he should change it. Not that Mr Todhunter was repellent to the other sex. His nature, which he was unable to disguise under a cloak of cynical disillusion, was a singularly sweet one. Mr Todhunter was in fact one of those unfortunate persons who court disappointment after disappointment by always believing the best of their fellow creatures. No amount of enlightenment had ever convinced Mr Todhunter that his friends could ever be capable of ignoble actions. He knew that in a way grown men can bully children, that apparently decent women do write exceedingly indecent anonymous letters and that there must be a great deal of unpleasant behaviour in this far from perfect world. But it was always other people who behaved in these strange ways, never Mr Todhunter's own friends or acquaintances. To these Mr Todhunter automatically credited his own high standards; and if emphatic evidence to the contrary were ever offered him, Mr Todhunter with much indignation ignored it.

This trait of his was apparent at once to any woman over thirty, and they naturally looked on Mr Todhunter as the heaven-designed husband. Younger women might have looked askance at his gaunt, bony frame, his bald little head which poked forward on his shoulders to address them, and his dusty coat collar, no less than at his old-maidish fussiness, his concern with his own health, his indifference to their attractions and even his slightly obtrusive scholarship. They might have looked so askance, had not Mr Todhunter possessed something which outweighed any lack of appeal to the passions and any number of dusty collars, namely, a very snug little private income.

It was this snug little income which allowed Mr Todhunter to live in a comfortable house in a chosen street in Richmond, looked after by a housekeeper, a housemaid and a man to do the boots, the garden and the furnace.

Not that Mr Todhunter lived in complete complacency in all this comfort. His conscience troubled him, making him feel at times quite guilty that he should thus be indulged when over two million of his fellow countrymen were existing only on pittances. Not even the fact that the government, by direct and indirect methods, relieved him of at least half his income for the purpose of benefiting his own nationals and killing those of other countries, could assuage Mr Todhunter's qualms. Not content therefore with reflecting that out of his eleven or twelve hundred a year he was maintaining directly in tolerable comfort one housekeeper, one housemaid and one elderly man, that he must be maintaining elsewhere in irksome idleness at least one able-bodied but thwarted worker and his family, that he was maintaining a substantial portion of one unknown civil servant, probably superfluous, and that he was giving to the country each year at least half a dozen shells and perhaps a vital part of a machine gun or two—not content with all this, Mr Todhunter was accustomed to devote such other gleanings from his income as he could save to certain private charities of his own preference and to the ready hands of anyone who turned up at his front door with a tale of hard luck.

Returning now from his consultation with the second specialist, Mr Todhunter sank down into an armchair in his library just in time for tea. Tea was served to Mr Todhunter in his library precisely at fifteen minutes past four each day. If it arrived at fourteen minutes past four, Mr Todhunter would send it away again with instructions for it to return at the proper time; if it had not appeared by fifteen and a half minutes past four Mr Todhunter would ring his bell and raise gentlemanly hell. Today, since Mr Todhunter was unprecedentedly absent, tea was a full five minutes late: and Mr Todhunter, slumped in his chair, said not a word.

"Coo!" as the house-parlourmaid observed to the housekeeper two minutes later. "And me expecting to have the sugar basin thrown in me face, as you might say. He's had bad news, mark my words."

"That'll do from you, Edie," replied Mrs Greenhill austerely.

But Edie was right, and both of them knew it. Nothing less than bad news could have made Mr Todhunter overlook such a lapse.

4

In Mr Todhunter's mind strange thoughts were coursing.

They continued to course for the next week, becoming stranger and stranger.

It had taken him just three days, spinning it out as long as possible, to make sure that his affairs were in order; and of course they were. After that there had seemed to be nothing to do but sit about and wait and never hurry upstairs. This seemed to Mr Todhunter a morbid as well as a boring business.

It was then that the strange thoughts began first to invade Mr Todhunter's mind; for after another three days he had decided that he could sit about no longer. He must do something. What, he did not know. But something. And something, if possible, out of the ordinary. Mr Todhunter began to feel, not without surprise, that he had really been excessively ordinary all his life, and if this drab record were ever to be broken now was the time. In fact Mr Todhunter, most conventional of men, began for the first time in his life to experience a strange, unholy urge to do something spectacular, just once, before he passed out.

Unfortunately the only spectacular deeds that he could remember on the part of others seemed so futile. Hadn't someone once thrown herself under the hooves of the Derby horses in order to prove that women ought to have the vote? Hadn't people been thrown out of the public gallery of the House of Commons for being spectacular at the wrong moment? And of course there was Moseley, most spectacular of all and—dear, dear, dear!—most futile. Though of course there was Lawrence of Arabia too. But Lawrence's chances were not likely to come anyone else's way.

What, then, Mr Todhunter began to ponder with increasing frequency as he sat in his comfortable library in Richmond and stroked his long fingers together—what, then, was it possible for a man in his position to do of a nature sufficiently startling to satisfy this strange new urge towards self-assertion but which would yet not involve the lifting of any heavy logs, the running violently up any stairs or the consumption of alcohol? There seemed no answer.

Nor was there anything in Mr Todhunter's previous life to suggest an answer.

Mr Todhunter had always lived what is called "a sheltered life." First of all he had been sheltered by his mother; then by a kindly regulation which forbade the enlisting of semi-invalids in the British army during the late European War and so prevented Mr Todhunter from attending that function—much against his will but, one could not help feeling, much to the British army's benefit; then, at the very private school where he had felt himself impelled to work at one period in order to avoid the self-reproach of idle uselessness, he had been sheltered by the young gentlemen themselves who, ragging fiercely any other master whom they could, yet had enough of the Proper Spirit to realise that ragging Mr Todhunter would be just about on a sporting par with standing a baby of two in boxing gloves up against the school champion. Since his mother's death some years ago Mr Todhunter had been most efficiently sheltered by his elderly housekeeper; and always he had been sheltered from the only really unbearable tribulation of this world by an adequate private income. So far as previous experience went, therefore, Mr Todhunter simply had none to help him.

As to contact with the great world, this was limited on Mr Todhunter's part to a few middle-aged or elderly cronies with whom he played bridge one or two evenings a week when there was no good music to be listened to through his earphones, to the Children's Clinic where, at the dictates of conscience, he spent half a dozen repellent hours every week doing voluntary work connected with the scrofulous skins of the youthful Richmond poor, and to his visit each Wednesday afternoon to the literary offices of the *London Review;* for Mr Todhunter, whose tastes were scholarly, had a sound if somewhat finicky critical intellect and contributed a column each Friday to the book pages of the *London Review* upon some suitable volume of biography or historical research. Indeed these Wednesday visits to Fleet Street and the happy half-hour he spent in the editor's room fingering the dozens of books awaiting review or chatting with Ferrers himself made up the high spots of Mr Todhunter's life.

It was therefore at this juncture that Mr Todhunter, following his usual habit, decided to consult the views of others. In this case, however, the consultation must be surreptitious. He therefore invited a carefully selected group of men to dinner and, over the port, cunningly introduced his subject. The unanimity with which his guests, all of them men of impeccable correctitude, had settled upon murder as the solution of his problem, had come as a shock; and Mr Todhunter was not at all sure that the Rev. Jack Denney, that well-known and popular cricketing parson, would not have joined with the others if he could have forgotten his cloth after another round of the decanter sufficiently to say what he really thought as a man.

Mr Todhunter had been shocked; but he had also been impressed. Murder had never entered his head at all. Some vague deed of an unspecified benevolent nature had been in his mind, the only clear thing being that it must be of benefit to his fellow creatures. But now that he came to consider it, murder filled this particular bill quite admirably. The removal of some human menace to the peace or unhappiness of the world would be a deed as useful to mankind as any, and what could be more spectacular?

This being so, had his advisers been right in recommending him to steer clear of political assassination?

Mr Todhunter may have been in the habit of consulting other people before he made up his mind, but this does not mean that his subsequent decision coincided with the advice he received. Very often he was convinced in exactly the opposite way. This of course does not make the advice any less helpful. On this very important matter, however, Mr Todhunter found himself unable to decide.

There were excellent academic arguments. For an altruistic murder his situation was ideal. Indeed in his more glamorous moments, during the evenings, for instance, sipping very slowly his one glass of port, which, in defiance of his doctor, he continued to allow himself, Mr Todhunter was able to see himself as dedicated to a great cause—the man who could alter history, the ruthless servant of humanity. That was most interesting and great comfort to a man with only a few months to live. But in practice . . . well, murder is a nasty business. And when Mr Todhunter remembered what a very nasty business it was, he would cast around once more for some other form of coup by which he could benefit his fellow creatures in a particularly striking way. And he would not be able to find one.

And so by degrees Mr Todhunter did come to accept the idea of murder. It took him two or three weeks, and his thoughts went round in many circles before they came to rest. But once there they remained. Murder it was to be.

Or rather, political assassination. For on this point, too, Mr Todhunter had practically made up his mind. After all, as a benefit to mankind a political assassination, if one can find just the right candidate, is practically unbeatable; and there was certainly no lack of suitable candidates. Whether it came to rubbing out Hitler or bumping off Mussolini or even putting Stalin on the spot, the progress of humanity would receive an equal jolt forward.

Having arrived thus at the stage of considering himself a dedicated shotgun in the hand of humanity, Mr Todhunter determined to take further advice. It was essential that he should not be wasted; his aim must be directed truly and firmly at the most worthy objective. It was necessary therefore to take the very best opinion on the matter. And, considering the question in all its aspects, Mr Todhunter could imagine no better opinion than that of Mr A. W. Furze. He therefore rang up Mr Chitterwick, who claimed some slight acquaintance with Furze, and with much cunning arranged for an introduction to that gentleman.

Three days later the introduction materialised into an invitation to take lunch with Mr Furze at his club. Mr Todhunter accepted with gratitude.

CHAPTER II

Furze rubbed his massive head.

"Do I understand, then," he said carefully, "that you are offering to murder anyone whom I recommend?"

"Tee-hee," cackled Mr Todhunter. "Well, if you put it so bluntly, yes."

"It's best, I think, to have these things quite plain."

"Oh, undoubtedly, undoubtedly."

Furze ate a few more mouthfuls with a thoughtful air. Then he glanced round the club dining room. The walls were still there, the elderly waiters, the baron of beef on the cold table, everything seemed quite normal except his guest.

"Then let me sum up what you've told me. You're suffering from an incurable disease. You've only got a few more months to live. But you feel quite fit. You want to use the situation to do some good in the world, of a kind that a man not in your position could hardly do. And you've come to the conclusion that a judicious murder would best meet the case. Is that correct?"

"Well, yes. But as I told you, the idea was not mine; I had a few men to dinner a few weeks ago and put the case to them, of course in a hypothetical way. Except for a clergyman, they all agreed on murder."

"Yes. And now you want my advice whether to go out to Germany and assassinate Hitler?"

"If you'd be so good."

"Very well, then. Don't."

"Don't?"

"Don't. For one thing, you'd never get near him. For another, you'd only make bad worse. Hitler isn't nearly so impossible as his successor might be. And the same applies to Mussolini, Stalin and even Sir Stafford Cripps. In other words, keep off dictators, actual or potential."

Mr Todhunter seemed inclined to argue. "Don't you think that the man who shot Huey Long did more good for America than Roosevelt himself has?"

"Perhaps I do. And Sinclair Lewis has pointed the moral. But that was an isolated case. The movement collapsed with Huey Long's removal. Hitlerism wouldn't collapse if Hitler were killed. In fact the Jews in Germany would probably find themselves worse off still."

"That," said Mr Todhunter reluctantly, "is more or less what these fellows said the other night."

"They showed sense. By the way, Chitterwick doesn't know all you've been telling me?"

"Oh no, not a thing. He believed, like the others, that we were discussing a supposititious case."

Furze permitted himself to smile. "Don't you think that if they'd known it was a real case, they wouldn't have advised murder quite so readily?"

"Oh, I'm sure of that," Mr Todhunter grinned, not without a touch of malice. He took a very small sip of claret. "You see, it was just because I knew I shouldn't get a genuine opinion otherwise that I pretended it was a supposititious case."

"Yes, quite so. And Chitterwick suspected nothing when you asked him for the introduction to me?"

"Why should he suspect anything? I told him I'd always admired your work and would like to ask you to lunch and have a talk. Instead of which, you very kindly asked me."

"Well," said Furze, "the thing I don't understand is why the devil you want my advice at all. This is the sort of thing a man has to worry out for himself. Why ask me to take the responsibility of advising you on anything so crazy?"

Mr Todhunter leaned across the table, his head poised in front of his bony shoulders, more like that of a tortoise than ever.

"I'll tell you," he said earnestly. "Because I'd formed the opinion that you aren't afraid of responsibility. Nearly everyone is. I am myself. And furthermore, I believed that anything a little crazy, as you describe it, might appeal to you."

Furze gave a sudden shout of laughter, startling a waiter. "By Jove, I believe you're right there too."

"And thirdly," pursued Mr Todhunter seriously, "because you're one of the few people I know of who are really doing some good in the world."

"Oh, nonsense," Furze contradicted. "There are plenty of people working in a quiet way, without any thanks or recognition. You'd be surprised."

"I should," said Mr Todhunter drily. "In any case, I know through Chitterwick what you've been doing ever since the war, for the Middleman's League-oppressed middle classes and so on. And I know how much solid good you've done, if all these things like insurance for blackcoat workers and so on that they've been putting through Parliament lately are chiefly due to you, as Chitterwick says. So you seemed to me the obvious person to advise me on my own position and tell me if there's any way I can use it for the general good,"

"That's all nonsense of course. There are dozens of us working on this tack alone and still more trying to get things done on sensible lines for the unemployed. There's plenty of altruism about still, thank heaven, though goodness knows how long it will last. But as for your own case, if you really want me to advise you. . ."

"Yes?" said Mr Todhunter eagerly.

"Go off and have as good a time as you can and forget all about Hitler and everyone else."

For a moment Mr Todhunter looked disappointed, and his head drew back as if into its shell. Then once again it shot forward.

"Yes, I understand. That's your advice. And now tell me what you'd do if you were in my place."

"Ah," said Furze, "That's quite different. But I think, if you don't mind, that I won't. After all, I've never met you before, have I? I'm sure Chitterwick is quite right in all he says of you, but I really can't put myself in the position later of having been an accessory before the fact."

Mr Todhunter sighed. "Yes, I quite see your point. And of course the idea sounds quite fantastic. It was very good of you to listen to me at all."

"Not at all. Most interesting. You'll have cheese, won't you? The green cheddar here is usually quite eatable."

"No, thank you. I'm afraid cheese invariably disagrees with me."

"Really? That's a pity. By the way, are you interested in cricket? I was at Lord's last Wednesday, and--"

"How very odd. So was I. A magnificent finish, wasn't it? And that reminds me, you and I once played against each other."

"Is that so?"

"Yes. I was in the Valetudinarian team that came down to Winchester the year you were keeping wicket, during the war."

"The old Crocks? Were you really? I remember that match very well. Then you must have known Dick Warburton?"

"Very well indeed. We went to Sherborne the same year."

"Oh, you were at Sherborne? I've got a young cousin there now."

There are persons, ill informed and ignorant, who aver that public-school career never did any good to anyone. How wrong is this idea may be gathered from the case of Mr Todhunter which is now being cited. For after about ten minutes of this sort of thing Mr Todhunter, reverting to the main issue, posed his question once more.

"No truthfully, Furze, what would you do in my place?"

And this time he received an answer.

For Furze, mellowed by the public-school spirit, rubbed his massive head once more and delivered himself as follows:

"Well, don't be influenced by anything I say, but I think that if I were in your position I should look round for someone who was making life a burden to half a dozen people, whether out of malice of just wrongheadedness—a blackmailer, say, or some rich old bully who will neither die nor hand out a dime in advance to a pack of semistarving descendants—and . . . well, as I said, these things don't bear talking about."

"Dear me, this is very odd," cried Mr Todhunter, much struck. "That's exactly what those fellows the other night advised."

"Well," grinned Furze, "*verb. sat.,* no doubt, *sap.*" Then he remembered that his guest was a man under sentence of death and cancelled the grin.

As for all this earnest talk about altruistic murder, Furze never took a word of it seriously. And that is just where Furze made a big mistake.

2

For Mr Todhunter took it very seriously indeed.

He had been impressed by Furze and was ready to attach much more weight to his advice than to the advice of his own friends; as indeed one usually is in the case of strangers. In any case Mr Todhunter now abandoned political assassination as his gesture; and could they have known it, no doubt Hitler and Musolini would have breathed more freely in consequence.

But he was still a Man with a Mission. The only problem now was to find an adequate subject for treatment.

How that treatment was to be applied Mr Todhunter did not for the moment wish to consider. From such gruesome details his mind shrank. Perhaps, too, his instinctive caution kept him from a frank realisation of all the unpleasantness which murder involves. Up to this point Mr Todhunter was regarding the whole thing in an entirely academic way, and the word itself remained to him little more than a word. On the other hand, he did go so far as to congratulate himself, not without astonishment, upon the qualities of pluck and decision which he must possess which Mr Todhunter had hitherto never dreamed might be his. The realisation that they were, gratified him a good deal.

Academic though Mr Todhunter's purpose might be, one thing he realised quite clearly: he must have a victim.

Not without some reluctance Mr Todhunter roused himself to go forth and look for one, walking very carefully on account of his aneurism.

3

However bravely one may be determined to commit a helpful murder, it is not so easy to find a victim. One cannot very well approach one's friends and say:

"Look here, old fellow, can you tell me anyone who ought to be murdered? Because I'm prepared to do the job."

And even if one did, the chances are that the friend would not be able to assist. After all, the number of people whom the average person would like to see murdered is very small; and when these are winnowed down to the number who actually deserve murdering, the result is surprisingly often negative.

Enquiries therefore have to be exceedingly circumspect. Mr Todhunter's personal feeling was that a nice juicy blackmailer would suit the bill best, but here again there are difficulties, for blackmailers are elusive creatures. Unlike almost any other person today, they seek no publicity. And if one asks one's friends point-blank whether, by any chance, they are being blackmailed, they would almost certainly resent it.

Mr Todhunter did think at one time that he had got on the track of a promising writer of anonymous letters, but the malice of the lady whom the victim roundly named as their author was directed against one person alone, and the final proof rested in the office of the king's proctor, who seemed wishful to shield her; so on the whole Mr Todhunter thought he had better not oblige.

By the end of a month Mr Todhunter was becoming so worried that several times he quite forgot to take his digestive tablets after a meal. Here he was, all ready to commit murder, and there was simply no response to his unspoken appeal. And time was getting on. Soon he would be so busy expecting to die at any moment that he would simply have no time to spare for murdering. It was most disturbing.

In this dilemma Mr Todhunter at last decided, having thought it over for several hours, to invite Mr Chitterwick round for an evening's conversation and quietly pump him.

4

"Even in July," remarked Mr Todhunter affably, 'it's sometimes nice to see a fire."

"Oh, certainly," agreed Mr Chitterwick, stretching out his plump little legs to the blaze. "The evenings are really quite chilly."

Mr Todhunter prepared to be cunning.

"I thought that was a highly interesting discussion we had at dinner last month," he said in a careless voice.

"Oh yes, extremely. About the pollination of fruit trees, you mean?"

Mr Todhunter frowned. "No after that. About murder."

"Oh, I see. Yes, of course. Yes."

"You belong to a Crime Circle, don't you?"

"Yes, I do. We have some quite distinguished members," said Mr Chitterwick with pride. "Our president's Roger Sheringham, you know."

"Oh yes. Now I expect," said Mr Todhunter still more carelessly, "that in the course of your discussions you hear of a good many people who ought to be murdered?"

"Ought to be murdered?"

"Yes, you remember we were discussing last month people who ought to be murdered. I expect you come across a good many?"

"No," said Mr Chitterwick in a puzzled voice. "I don't think we do, really."

"But you're aware of several blackmailers, no doubt?"

"No, I can't say that we are."

"Not even any dope kings or white slavers?" asked Mr Todhunter a little wildly.

"Oh no, nothing like that. We only discuss murder, you know."

"You mean; murders that have been committed already?"

"Yes, of course." Mr Chitterwick looked surprised.

"I see," mumbled Mr Todhunter, much disappointed. He looked gloomily at the fire.

Mr Chitterwick shifted in his chair. He had disappointed his host, though he could not quite understand how, and that made him feel remorseful.

Mr Todhunter was brooding gloomily on Hitler once more, as the only man whom he knew really to deserve being murdered. Or Mussolini, of course. Those Abyssinians . . . the Jews . . . yes, it would be a great gesture. Someone might even put a statue up to him after he was dead. That would be nice. But his death would probably come from being trampled under the heavy boots of infuriated Nazis, like that assassin at Marseilles. No, that would not be so nice.

He turned back to his guest.

"Don't you know a single person who ought to be murdered?" asked Mr Todhunter with disapproval.

"Well—er—no," Mr Chitterwick had to apologise. "I'm afraid I don't." He wondered why his host should appear to set so much store by his acquaintance with potential murderees but hardly liked to ask.

Mr Todhunter frowned at him. He felt that Mr Chitterwick had accepted his invitation on false pretences.

He felt, too, that he might just as well give the whole idea up, now as later. Mr Todhunter was not prepared to advertise his services in the daily press as a benevolent murderer to those in need, and short of some such drastic step it seemed that those services would never be required. He found himself both relieved and, at the same time, curiously disappointed.

5

One goes forth to seek something and finds it not; one returns home and finds the object of one's search being handed to one by some kind friend on a platter.

It was on a Tuesday evening that Mr Todhunter decided, on the failure of Mr Chitterwick, that he must abandon his great plan. It was on the very next afternoon that Ferrers, the literary editor of the *London Review* handed him, in the most casual way, exactly what he wanted. While Mr Todhunter had been searching the highways and byways for a suitable victim, it seemed that one had been lurking complacently all the time right in his path.

It was a chance question of Mr Todhunter's which brought the matter to light. Before going to Ferrers's room to select his book for review he had strolled down another passage to pass the time of day with an old friend of his on the staff, one of the leader writers, to whom in point of fact Mr Todhunter's own slight connection with the *London Review* was due. The man was not in his room, and there was another name on the door.

"By the way," said Mr Todhunter when he had deposited his ancient brown trilby hat on a file of newspapers in Ferrers' big room overlooking Fleet Street, "by the way, is Ogilvie away ill? He's not in his room."

Ferrers looked up from the copy he was cutting, blue pencil in hand. "Ill? Not he. He's the latest to go, that's all."

"To go?" repeated Mr Todhunter, mildly puzzled.

"Sacked! Poor old Ogilvie's been sacked, to put it frankly. They handed him a cheque for six months salary yesterday and told him to clear out."

"Ogilvie sacked?" Mr Todhunter was shocked. Ogilvie, with his big head, bulging with solid brain, and his calm, penetrating pen, had always seemed an integral part of the *London Review.* "Dear me, I thought he was a fixture here."

"It's a damned shame." Ferrers, usually discretion in trousers, spoke with unwonted heat. "Just shot him out, like that."

One of the fiction reviewers was turning over a huge pile of new novels on a table by the window. "Why?" he asked.

"Oh, these blasted internal politics. Too complicated for you to understand, young fellow."

The fiction reviewer, who happened to be three months older than his literary editor, grinned amiably. "Sorry, boss." He was under the delusion that Ferrers disliked being called "boss."

"Look here," asked Mr Todhunter. "About Ogilvie. Why did you say he had to go?"

"Internal reorganisation, my boy," Ferrers told him bitterly. "And do you know what that means?"

"No," said Mr Todhunter.

"Well, so far as I can make out it means sack all the men with any guts and retain the spittle-lickers. That's a fine thing for a paper like this, isn't it?" Ferrers was genuinely proud of the *London Review* and its reputation for solid, old-fashioned dignity, honesty and decorum, which he had fought hard to maintain even after the weekly had passed into the control of Consolidated and Periodicals Ltd., who were now its unworthy owners.

"But what will Ogilvie do?"

"God knows. He's got a wife and family to look after somehow."

"I suppose," said Mr Todhunter, now much worried, "that he'll get a job somewhere else without much difficulty?"

"Will he? I doubt it. He's no chicken, old Ogilvie. Besides, it doesn't do a man any good to be sacked from Consolidated Periodicals. Remember that, by the way, young fellow," added Ferrers to the fiction reviewer.

"You pay me a little more and I wouldn't give you so many chances," retorted the fiction reviewer.

"What's the good of paying you any more? You'd never write the kind of review I want."

"If you mean, write a column of unctuous praise every week on behalf of your biggest advertisers, all full of nice, fat quotable sentences, no, I wouldn't," said the other nastily. "I've told you before, I'm not that kind of reviewer."

"And I've told you before, young fellow, that you'll come to a bad end. You have to take things as you find them in this world."

The reviewer made a rude noise and turned back to his novels.

Mr Todhunter opened the doors of the big bookcase in which the nonfiction books were kept, but for once his eye did not light up. He was one of those unfortunate people who, against all reason, feel a kind of responsibility for those in distress or trouble; and the present plight and future predicament of Ogilvie were worrying him already. Mr Todhunter felt that he ought to do something about it.

"It was Armstrong who dismissed Ogilvie?" he asked, turning back to Ferrers. Armstrong was the new managing editor of Consolidated Periodicals Ltd.

Ferrers, who had got busy with his blue pencil again, looked up patiently. "Armstrong? Oh no. He's got no say in that kind of thing at present."

"Lord Felixbourne, then?" Lord Felixbourne was the owner.

"No. It was . . . Oh well, I suppose I ought not to talk about it. But it's a dirty business."

"Any chance of you being next, Ferrers?" asked the fiction reviewer. "I mean, it would be rather jolly if we could have a literary editor who'd let me say, just once a month or so, that a novel is bad when it is."

"You say what you like, don't you? I don't interfere with you."

"No, you merely cut out all my best bits." The fiction reviewer strolled across the room and stood behind his editor's shoulder. He uttered a wail of despair and stabbed at the copy on the desk. "Oh, my lord, you haven't cut that paragraph, have you? But, good heavens, man, why? It isn't even rude. It only amounts to saying that——"

"Listen, Todhunter. This is what Byle's written: 'If this were Mr Firkin's first novel there might be some excuse for this turgid spate of words, curdled with cliches like cream with clots, for it might only mean that he had not thought it necessary to find out how to handle his tools before using them; but by his sixth attempt Mr Firkin should at least have learned his English grammar. For the rest, if there is any meaning hidden away under the deluge of his verbosity, I could not find it. Perhaps those of my colleagues who, impressed no doubt by Mr Firkin's powers of drooling on to any given length without saying anything at all, have bestowed such generous praise on his earlier books will oblige with an explanation of why this one should ever have been written. Or is that a secret known only to Mr Firkin's publishers?' And he says it isn't even rude. What would you do in my place?"

Mr Todhunter gave his deprecating, almost guilty little smile. "Perhaps it is a little outspoken."

"I'll say it is," agreed Ferrers and drew two more large blue crosses over the offending paragraph.

The reviewer, a man of violent passion, stamped with rage. "I can't understand you. Damn it, Todhunter, you ought to back me up. Of course it's outspoken. And why ▓▓▓▓ shouldn't it be? It's time something like that was said about Firkin. The man's reputation is absurdly inflated. He's not good at all; ▓▓▓▓ he's bad! And he gets all this sickening praise because half the reviewers can't be bothered to plough through his stuff at all and so find it easier to praise than criticise, and the other half really do think that inordinate length is a sign of genius, instead of being impressed as they should be by a man who can say just twice as much in a quarter of the space. Or else they know that the public likes value for its money and confuse value with verbiage. ▓▓▓▓ It's time someone pricked the bubble, isn't it?"

"That's all very well, young fellow," replied Ferrers, unperturbed by this outburst. "But there are ways of pricking it without using an axe. After all, you don't need a butcher's cleaver to burst a bubble. If I printed that, I should get a dozen letters from dear old ladies the next morning saying how unfair it is to attack poor Mr Firkin's book that he'd worked so hard to write, when he'd never done anything to you, and can't I get a reviewer with no axe of his own to grind."

"But I haven't any axe to grind!" foamed the reviewer.

"I know that," soothed Ferrers. "But they don't."

Mr Todhunter picked a book almost at random from the shelves and crept out of the room. As he went, he heard Mr Byle's excited voice behind him:

"Very well, I resign. Curse your old ladies. I don't care a hoot about them. If you won't let me review honestly, I resign."

Mr Todhunter was not impressed. Mr Byle resigned with fair regularity every Wednesday afternoon, if he happened to see his copy in process of being cut. If not, he forgot what he had written and remained happy. In any case the difficulty pleaded so feelingly by Ferrers of finding another reviewer worthy of the *London Review* at such short notice invariable caused Mr Byle to soften his heart and agree to remain for just one more week, and the process was then repeated all over again.

The first requisite for a literary editor is tact. The second and third are tact too.

6

Mr Todhunter was acting with unusual cunning.

He wanted to find out more about Ogilvie's dismissal; and though Ferrers would not tell him, Mr Todhunter thought he knew where he might pick up a little gossip. He therefore made his way to the assistant editor's room.

Leslie Wilson was a sociable young man with literary intentions of his own. He shared a room with the musical editor, but the latter was rarely in it. To Mr Todhunter's invitation that he should come and drink a cup of tea in the restaurant at the top of the building he agreed with pleased promptitude. Young Wilson had respect for few people outside Ferrers and the editor in chief, but Mr Todhunter, with his slightly spinsterish manners and donnish mind, had always impressed him; though Mr Todhunter, who was by way of being alarmed himself before Wilson's competence and youth, would have been much astonished to hear it.

They took the lift, and Mr Todhunter disposed his lightly covered bones on a hard chair. To the waitress he was firm upon the matter of China tea, with so many spoonfuls to the pot and no more. Wilson professed his eagerness to eat and drink exactly what Mr Todhunter thought of eating and drinking.

They then discussed the book pages for eight minutes.

At the end of that time Mr Todhunter introduced the name of Ogilvie and was gratified to notice a distinct reaction on the part of his companion.

"It's a damned shame," said young Wilson hotly.

"Yes, but what is the cause of his being dismissed so unexpectedly?" Mr Todhunter poured out the tea with care and pushed the sugar basin across to his guest. It was early, and the two had the room to themselves. "I should have thought he was such a competent man."

"He is competent. One of the best leader writers we've ever had. That hasn't anything to do with his going."

"Dear me, then what had?"

"Oh, it's all part and parcel of the same game. Ogilvie got the boot because he wouldn't knuckle under to Fisher."

"Fisher? I don't think I've heard of him before. Who is he?"

"He's a nasty piece of work," replied the assistant literary editor without discretion. "As nasty as they make 'em. His real name's Fischmann. American German Jew, with a dash of anything else unpleasant thrown in. And he's just making merry hell of this place."

In response to Mr Todhunter's enquiries Wilson told the whole story. It was not a nice one.

The *London Review* had recently passed out of the hands of kindly, tolerant old Sir John Verney into those of Lord Felixbourne, the chairman of Consolidated Periodicals Ltd. Lord Felixbourne believed in pep and vim, but he had the sense to realise that one of the *London Review*'s greatest assets was its freedom from the prevalent vulgarity of the English press, and he approved its old policy, which had been to keep a course between the pompous tediousness of the *Spectator* and that tone of common pertness which is the popular press's version of the American tabloids. Indeed Lord Felixbourne quite understood that it was just this policy which gave the *London Review* the surprisingly large circulation it had, for it attracted as its readers most of those whose minds still remain decent and who are yet bored by too solemn a tone at their Saturday breakfast tables.

But this was not enough for Lord Felixbourne. The policy was to continue, but the men who had made it were to go—or reform. There was a saying in Fleet Street that an appointment on the *London Review* meant a job for life. No one was ever sacked; few reprimands were ever administered; the staff was trusted. It was this condition of affairs that the new proprietor wished to change. Lord Felixbourne had found that the threat of instant dismissal at the first, smallest error kept a journalist on his toes. He was a kind man, but he believed sincerely that his toes were the members on which a journalist should be, not on any other more comfortable part of his anatomy. He had made a speech to this effect to the staff of the *London Review* when he first took over control. That a serious weekly is not the same as a daily newspaper did not seem to have occurred to him.

The staff of the *London Review* had not been seriously perturbed. They knew their jobs, and they knew, too, that they did them as well as the staff of any other weekly journal—and, in the general opinion, a good deal better. Proprietors like to let off a little hot air occasionally; but the circulation was going up steadily, the paper had as good a reputation as any in Europe, earthquakes might happen in Patagonia but not in the serene offices of the *London Review.*

The staff were wrong. Lord Felixbourne was a kindly man and it would have distressed him very much to carry out the purging himself. He therefore imported Mr Isidore Fischmann, at considerable expense, from the United States and gave him full powers to do it instead. The whole of Consolidated Periodicals Ltd. was placed at his mercy. Mr Fischmann showed his mettle before he had been in the place a week by sacking the editor of the *London Review* himself.

Young Wilson was quite fair. He admitted handsomely that it had been quite time old Vincent retired. He was a relic from Victorian journalism; he was hopelessly out of date; he was a bit of a joke. But the decent thing would have been for Lord Felixbourne to persuade him into resigning and then settle a nice fat pension on the old man, not have him more or less kicked out of the place by this Fischmann fellow, with a cheque for a year's salary in his pocket and not a penny more. When asked why he had not recommended even a pension, Fischmann had replied that the old man had been grossly overpaid for years and ought to have saved enough three times over to last him for the short remainder of his life. As a matter of fact, the old man had; but that was neither here nor there. A nice fat pension to editors retiring for reasons of old age (and no editor had ever retired from the *London Review* for anything else) was a part of the journal's tradition.

The staff was upset. But their disapproval was as nothing compared with the perturbation which overtook the whole building during the next three months; a perturbation verging in some cases on panic. For dismissals became as common as primroses in Devon. A storm had struck Fleet Street and the staff of Consolidated Periodicals Ltd. were scattered before it as cigarette ash before an electric fan.

The whole trouble, opined young Wilson, still trying to be fair but becoming more and more red every minute, the whole trouble was due to the fact that Fischmann was the wrong sort of man for the job. Young Wilson quite admitted that a slight gingering up of the *London Review*'s staff would have been a perfectly sound thing; while a change to a rather more definite policy need not have incurred any real risk of stunting, which had been the

Old Gang's bogey. But Fischmann had lost his head completely.

Crazy with power, he was sacking people now throughout the whole building, not on any question of efficiency or lack of value, but on nothing more nor less now than an attitude of independence to himself. Things had reached such a pitch that the most useless fellow could obtain the editorship of one of the minor periodicals in the firm's control so long as he was prepared to join the band of Fischmann's toadies; sooner or later the best man must go if he kept up his attitude of independence. Even hostility was not required; a mere reluctance to touch his hat to Fischmann in the corridor was almost enough now to earn the dismissal, at twelve hours notice, of the best man in Fleet Street.

"But I can't believe that anything like that can be happening here," protested Mr Todhunter. "One hears of these absurd affairs in the popular newspapers, but surely not in the *London Review*."

"Ask Ferrers, ask Ogilvie himself, ask anyone," countered Wilson.

"I did ask Ferrers," admitted Mr Todhunter, "and he refused to tell me."

"Oh well." Wilson smiled rather engagingly. "Ferrers thinks it's best to keep these things to ourselves. Besides, Byle was there, wasn't he? He's a bit inclined to go up in the air over any question of what he calls 'abstract justice,'" said Wilson with tolerance, having just been very much up in the air himself over this question of thoroughly practical injustice.

Some such thought occurred to Mr Todhunter as he wondered vaguely what justice might be when not abstract; but of course justice can be perfectly practical, and injustice usually is.

Mr Todhunter liked Wilson. It was one of his chief joys on Wednesday afternoons to stand and laugh guiltily in a corner when Wilson, lacking his chief's gift of suave authority, was cornered by an irate Byle wanting to know why his choicest denuciations had been blue-pencilled or accusing the staff of walking off with the books in their pockets that he particularly wanted to review. Wilson's wriggling, "Oh, come now, I say—draw it mild!" gave him much malicious pleasure; for the young man had so obviously not yet learned the necessary art of prevaricating convincingly.

What Wilson said therefore upon the present state of affairs Mr Todhunter found himself compelled to accept, and the knowledge distressed him. The thing seemed so alien to the whole spirit of the *London Review*. For Mr Todhunter, like everyone else connected with it, took a peculiar pride in the dignity and traditions of the paper and was proud to work for it.

"Dear me, dear me," he murmured, his small bony face showing his concern. "But doesn't Lord Felixbourne know what is going on?"

"He does—and yet he won't. He's given this chap a free hand, you see, and he just won't go back on it."

"But apart from the injustice, if things are really as bad as you say a great deal of real hardship is surely being caused too? I don't imagine that all these men are going to find other jobs quite at once. And no doubt some of them have wives and families like Ogilvie."

"That's just the ~~~~~~~ part," Wilson almost shouted. "Half of them won't ever get a job again. They're too old. Ogilvie himself may, because he's exceptionally good; but I doubt if even he will. I tell you it's enough to make a cat cry."

Mr Todhunter nodded. A sudden thought had struck him so forcibly as to make him catch his breath and remember his aneurism; for in the emotion of the preceding ten minutes he had quite forgotten it.

"Mind you," Wilson was going on, "I don't say that not a single one of the chaps didn't deserve to go. There are one or two who won't be missed at all. But the other dozen . . ."

"It's really as many as that?" Mr Todhunter spoke a little absently. He was wondering what young Wilson would say if he were to tell him, straight out, that in another three or four months he would be dead. Mr Todhunter had an absurd longing to make the confidence and soothe himself with Wilson's inarticulate sympathy.

"Quite as many. More. And there'll be a dozen more before the little devil's through. Armstrong doesn't care. Fischmann put him there, and he licks Fischmann's boots clean every morning when he comes to the office. That's a fine thing for a firm like this. Good God, we might be the *Daily Wire*."

Mr Todhunter shot his head forward and fixed his glasses on the young man's face.

"And what would happen if Fischmann were dismissed himself?"

Wilson laughed harshly. "He won't be. There's no one to do it but himself, and I don't quite see that happening."

"Well, we'll say if he had a serious illness and had to resign. Would Lord Felixbourne appoint someone else—possibly even someone worse?" asked Mr Todhunter, thinking of Hitler and movements that have to play themselves out.

"There couldn't be anyone worse," replied Wilson. "No, but seriously, I think Felixbourne wouldn't be sorry. At any rate I'm pretty sure he wouldn't appoint anyone else to the same job. We'd be left to ourselves again. And without Fischmann, Armstrong wouldn't last long. Then with a decent man like Ferrers running the *London Review* we could make something of the old rag once more."

"Ferrers?"

"Oh yes. He'll be the next editor. Been marked out for it for years, and Felixbourne at least has the sense to recognise one good man when he sees him. In fact he'll probably be managing editor soon—boss of the whole concern. That's why Ferrers hasn't been sacked like the others, because you can be pretty sure he doesn't kowtow to that little swine. And that," added young Mr Wilson candidly "is the only reason I'm still here, because I told our Mr Fischmann pretty well what I thought of him the first week he was here; and Ferrers stopped me from getting the sack. God knows how."

"And if Ferrers were made managing editor," said Mr Todhunter carefully, "would he do anything about the men who have been unjustly dismissed?"

"Of course he would," cried the young man indignantly. "Ferrers is a dam' decent chap. The very first thing he'd do as editor would be to bring 'em all back again. And what's more, Felixbourne would let him too."

"I see," Mr Todhunter nodded thoughtfully. "Er—these notices of dismissal, are they sent out at any time or on a special day?"

"Saturday mornings. Why?"

"Oh, nothing," said Mr Todhunter.

CHAPTER III

Mr Todhunter was not going to murder Fischmann (to call the man by his real name) without careful enquiry first. As has been shown, it had never been Mr Todhunter's habit to commit himself to any course of action without consulting a great number of people as to the advisability or not of his intentions, and he was going to make no exception in such a matter as murder. Having allowed his mind to be made up concerning the deed, he had now to assure himself that the proposed victim was up to sample. One must, in short, make sure.

The first step in making sure was to pay a call at Ogilvie's flat in Hammersmith, and this Mr Todhunter did on the day following his conversation with Wilson.

Mr Todhunter found Ogilvie in his shirt sleeves, writing furiously. Mrs Ogilvie, a small, rather faded little woman, tittered for a moment and then vanished. Mr Todhunter politely asked Ogilvie how he was.

"Not at all well," said Ogilvie with gloom. He was a large, fleshy man, as the husbands of small, faded wives so often are; his heavy face bore now an expression even more serious than usual.

"I'm very sorry to hear that," said Mr Todhunter, taking a chair.

"This business has upset me a great deal," pronounced Ogilvie. "You've heard, of course, that I've left the *London Review*?"

"Yes, Ferrers told me."

"It's brought on my indigestion very badly."

"Worry always brings my indigestion on too," agreed Mr Todhunter, perhaps with more sympathy for himself than for his friend.

"I haven't been able to touch meat since It Happened."

"I have to be very careful about meat too," said Mr Todhunter with gloomy relish. "In fact my doctor says—"

"Even tea—"

"Only one small glass of port—"

"It's very upsetting," said Ogilvie heavily, "after all these years."

"What are you going to do now?"

"What can I do? I shall never get another job."

"Oh," said Mr Todhunter uneasily, "don't say that."

"Why not? It's true. I'm too old. So I've begun a novel. After all," said Ogilvie, the cloud of depression lifting a little, "William de Morgan didn't begin writing his novels till he was over seventy."

"And you can write, at any rate . . . But what are your private feelings about the matter, Ogilvie? I understand your dismissal is only one of many."

"It's appalling," asserted Ogilvie solemnly. "Upon my word, I think the man must be a lunatic. Apart from my own case, his actions have been quite unjustifiable. It seems that he's determined to get rid of every good man in the place. I simply can't understand it."

"Perhaps he is mad, in a way?"

"I'm not at all sure that he isn't. That seems to me the only way of accounting for it."

"In any case," said Mr Todhunter carefully, "quite apart, as you say, from your own case, it's your conviction that this man Fischmann is a menace to the happiness of a great many persons, without adequate justification or even excuse?"

"I certainly do. He's caused a great deal of misery already, and he's going on to cause more. I know of several hard cases of men he's dismissed without the faintest reason so far as their work goes, who have wives and families and not a penny saved. What they're going to do I can't imagine. Luckily we're not in that position, but the outlook is serious enough for us. Really, Todhunter, it's pitiable that one man—one swollen-headed crook, rather—should be able to reduce a hundred people to such a state of abject terror as they are reduced to every Saturday morning. It's enough to make one a Communist."

"Ah yes," nodded Mr Todhunter. "Saturday morning." He ruminated. "The man ought to be shot," he said at last in real indignation.

"He ought, indeed," agreed Ogilvie; and somehow the well-worn phrase seemed to have been used by the one and accepted by the other more literally than is generally the case.

2

On any Saturday morning the huge building occupied by Consolidated Periodicals Ltd. is a centre of activity. A couple of months ago this activity had been not unpleasurable. Enlivened by thoughts of leisure ahead, assistant editors of the bright weeklies in which Consolidated Periodicals specialised would stop for a chat with the lady secretaries past whose desks their way took them; art editors would pause to exchange a quick story with film reviewers; even editors would swing their umbrellas with a more jaunty air, for the editors at Consolidated Periodicals are not a haughty lot of men.

But on this particular Saturday morning, as indeed for the last five Saturday mornings, there were no such pleasant interludes. Assistant editors dashed past secretaries with a frown of preoccupation, as if intent only upon reaching their desks; art editors and film reviewers alike wore expressions intended to convey that work and the firm's interests were the only preoccupations of their minds; and editors walked delicately and with reluctance. There was indeed a hum of activity throughout the warren of offices, but its note was sharp now with fear. In one or two of the cubbyholes in which the main work was carried on the note was even shrill with something very like hysteria.

Very soon rumours were spreading.

On the third floor young Bennett, assistant editor of the *Peepshow*, had hardly settled himself at his table, exceedingly conscious of arriving there ten minutes late, when the door opened and the tall figure of Owen Staithes, the art editor, came into the room.

"Oh, about those blocks for the centre page, Benney," he began loudly and then, as the door closed behind him, changed abruptly to a lower tone. "Not got yours?"

"Not yet. Has anyone?"

"Not that I've heard. It's a bit early yet."

"He usually sends them round about eleven."

"Yes." Staithes fiddled with the coins in his pocket. He looked worried. "Damn these Saturday mornings. I've got the wind up, badly." Staithes was married and had a small son.

"Oh, you're safe enough."

"Am I? What about poor old Gregory last week? It's my belief he wants to be rid of all us art editors."

"But you're doing Greg's work. He couldn't leave the *Housewife* as well as the *Peepshow* without an art editor."

"God knows what he could do." Staithes kicked moodily at the leg of Bennett's table. "Seen Mac yet?"

"No. I say, I was ten minutes late."

"The devil you were. Did you run into him?"

"No. But I had to pass his door and it's my belief he can see clean through it. I'm expecting a chit at any minute."

"Don't be an ass. . ... Oh, hullo, young Butts."

Young Butts, so known to distinguish him from his uncle, the editor of *Film Fancy*, sidled in with an uneasy grin.

"Hullo, chaps. I say, is it true that Fletcher's got his?"

"Fletcher? Surely not." Staithes looked surprised. "What would the *Sunday Messenger* be without Fletcher?"

"You might just as well have asked a month ago what it would be like without Purefoy, or what the *Film Trader* would be without Fitch. Dash it, Fitch founded the thing and ran it for twenty years at a pretty useful profit; but that didn't save him."

"It's the devil," muttered Staithes.

There was a knock at the door and a girl looked in, pencil and notebook still in her hands. She was a pretty girl, but the men looked at her as if she were Medusa herself.

"Mr Bennett, Mr Fisher wants to see you at once in his room."

Bennett stood up awkwardly. "Me-me?" he stammered.

"Yes." A look of sympathy crossed the girl's face. "Perhaps I oughtn't to tell you, but Mr Southey's just told Mr Fisher he saw you come in a quarter of an hour late this morning."

"Oh ▓▓▓▓" groaned the young man. "That's torn it. All right, thanks, Miss Merriman," he added with an attempt at jauntiness. "Tell the little rat to get his cup of cold poison ready, and I'll be along to drink it."

The girl went out, and the others looked at each other.

"▓▓▓▓▓▓" burst out Staithes. "Southey used to be a decent chap once. It's a bit thick seeing decent fellows turned into skunks and taletellers and toadies just because they're afraid of losing their jobs."

"You're right, Owen," said young Bennett. "And what's more, I'm going to tell him so. So long, you chaps. Wait for the condemned man here."

Bennett was out of the room only five minutes. While he was away Staithes and young Butts exchanged no more than three sentences.

"Southey's married, you know," said the latter.

"Well, so am I," retorted Staithes. "But I'm ▓▓▓▓▓ hanged if I'll come down to that sort of level."

"Then you'll be getting yours," replied young Butts simply.

Bennett, when he came back, wore a slightly bewildered air.

"No," he said in reply to the question on the others' faces. "No, I haven't been sacked. He said if it had been anyone else he'd have sacked me, but he thought—what the blazes did he think?—that I was a good man really, or some rot. And he asked me to lunch."

"*Lunch?*"

"Yes. I think he's mad."

The other two exchanged a long glance.

"Then you didn't tell him what you thought of him?"

"Under the circs," said Bennett, "no."

Once more there was a knock at the door. "Mr Staithes?" said the office boy. "Couldn't find you in your own room, sir. Sorry, sir," he added awkwardly. "We'll all be sorry, sir."

Staithes took the envelope with barely a glance.

"Thanks, Jim . . . Well, Benney, I think I'll tell him myself. It won't do any good, but it won't do any harm. I may give him a clout as well."

He went out.

"I told him only two-three minutes ago he'd be getting his," said young Butts.

"And how the blazes," demanded Bennett savagely, "does Fisher think we're going to run the *Peepshow* without an art editor? That's what I want to know."

"Ask him at lunch," suggested young Butts, lounging out of the room.

As Bennett sat down once more at his desk Mr Todhunter uncoiled himself from the chair in which he had been partially concealed behind a filing cabinet.

"I beg your pardon," he said courteously, "my name's Todhunter. Wilson, of the *London Review,* asked me to let him know whether you could lunch with him today."

Bennett turned slightly glazed eyes on him. "Today? No, not today."

"I'll tell him," promised Mr Todhunter and escaped into the passage. He did not wonder at that time why Bennett's eyes looked so curiously glazed, but he was surprised that the young man should not have asked him how long he had been there and how much he had overheard.

On the stone stairs leading down to the street Mr Todhunter shook his head several times. His mind might not have been quite made up even yet, but he had reached the stage of wondering where he could buy a revolver and what formalities had to be observed first.

Someone coming up the stairs bumped into him. Vaguely Mr Todhunter realized it was young Butts.

"Sorry," said young Butts.

"Yes," said Mr Todhunter absently. "Er—can you tell me where I could buy a revolver?"

"A *what*?"

"It doesn't matter," mumbled Mr Todhunter in confusion.

3

Mr Todhunter bought a revolver, with surprisingly little difficulty, at a gunsmith's in the Strand. It was an old army revolver, a heavy weapon firing a .45 bullet, and the salesman assured him it was no more than shop soiled; it had never been used in action. He promised to give it a good cleanup during the next day or two, for Mr Todhunter could not take the weapon away with him. There were forms to be filled out, for registration in the usual way; and Mr Todhunter could not obtain possession until a firearms certificate had been issued.

It is doubtful whether the authorities, in devising this means of delaying a bargain of this kind, were actually influenced by the consideration that it is better not to allow an angry man to walk into a shop and walk straight out again with a lethal weapon; but whether they did or not, the effect upon Mr Todhunter was salutary. For by the time the revolver was actually delivered, which was nearly a week later, Mr Todhunter had had time to think things over. And by the very process his indignation had lessened. Similarly the notion that he, Lawrence Butterfield Todhunter, had actually planned to murder in cold blood a complete stranger, out of really nothing more than sheer officiousness, had grown correspondingly more fantastic.

To put it shortly, Mr Todhunter had determined, days before the revolver was even delivered, that he would be shut of the whole affair; and, looking at the unpleasant weapon when it arrived, he considered himself lucky to have come to his senses.

That was on the Friday morning.

Precisely at fifteen minutes past six the next evening Edith brought into the library the usual copy of the *Evening Mercury,* neatly folded on a salver. The headline on the front page caught Mr Todhunter's eye even before he had taken the paper into his hands. The result, for the next half an hour, was something like chaos.

"Heaven bless us," panted Mrs Greenhill to Edie when they had cleared away at last the hot water, the cold compresses, the ice, the sal volatile, the brandy, the drops, the basins, the towels, the eau de cologne, the hot-water bottles, the blankets, the burnt feathers and everything else, useful or useless, that two distracted women could frenziedly collect for an employer with a face like chalk and blue lips. "Heaven save us all, that was a near thing, I'm thinking."

"I was sure he was a goner," squeaked Edie, much impressed. "Coo, didn't he look awful? Proper gashly, and no mistake."

"Edie," said Mrs Greenhill, dropping her bulk into an inadequate kitchen chair, "go and get me a teaspoonful of that brandy out of the dining-room cupboard. I need it."

"Won't he notice?" asked Edie doubtfully.

"He won't grudge it me," said Mrs Greenhill.

Edie turned back at the door. "And fancy him not letting us call the doctor when he come round. You'd have thought he'd have been hollering for him down the phone the minute he could stand, wouldn't you?"

"There's bin something different about him lately," nodded Mrs Greenhill, fanning herself with a tea cosy. "I've noticed it meself."

"Yes, ever since that day tea was late and he never said a word. Don't you remember me passing a remark about it at the time? And he don't seem to read so much as he used to. Seems to sit for hours scraping his finger tips together. Thinking, I suppose. Coo, fair gives me the creeps, it does, to go in there and see him at it. And the way he looks at me sometimes. Upon my word, I sometimes think—"

"That'll do, Edie. You run along and get me that brandy. Mr Todhunter ain't the only one in this house to feel queer at this blessed moment."

Mr Todhunter, however, was no longer feeling queer. Having expected to die at once and now, to his secret astonishment, feeling quite recovered, with aneurism still intact, he was reading the paragraph under the startling headline.

4

The paragraph stated, quite simply, that Mr Isidore Fisher, the American efficiency expert at present engaged in reorganising the business of Consolidated Periodicals Ltd., had been run over by a lorry in Fleet Street outside the offices of Consolidated Periodicals Ltd. on his way to lunch and killed instantly.

Four days later the inquest revealed the full story,

Mr Fisher had not been alone. His companion had been a young man, also employed by Consolidated Periodicals Ltd., by the name of Bennett, and the two had been on their way to lunch together.

Mr Fisher and Bennett, it seemed, had been crossing Fleet Street, with Bennett on the side of the oncoming traffic. They had passed behind a stationary bus, and Bennett had seen the lorry bearing down on them. He had drawn back, but his body must have masked the lorry from the view of Fisher, who was talking animatedly at the time, and he had continued forward. Bennett had caught his arm and tried to pull him back, but it had been too late. The lorry was not travelling unduly fast, and Bennett had had no difficulty in saving himself with ordinary care and attention.

The driver of the bus corroborated this evidence from Bennett and the lorry driver. He had witnessed the accident, and it had seemed to him that when Fisher did see the lorry he had appeared to jump forward right into its path rather than backward. The bus driver had seen people do that kind of thing before: seemed to think they stood a better chance running forward than jumping back. He considered that no one but Fisher was to blame.

A verdict of accidental death was thereupon returned, all parties being exonerated except the dead man, who could not answer back.

In his library Mr Todhunter studied the short report with the closest attention. So straightforward was the affair and so usual the type of accident that there was really no reason why Mr Todhunter should have jumped to the conclusion that he did about it. Nevertheless his conviction amounted to a certainty. Right from the very first moment of seeing the headline Mr Todhunter had known, beyond all explanation but with complete conviction, that Fischmann's death had been no accident. That hand which had been outstretched to save him . . . it had never been intended to save. It had not pulled, that hand. It had pushed.

Bitterly and remorsefully Mr Todhunter blamed himself.

By his weakness, by his cowardice, he had turned that nice young Bennett into a murderer. The revolver had been in his possession for over twenty-four hours before Fischmann died. It had been intended for use on Fischmann, at once. Had its owner not been a useless, pusillanimous creature, young Bennett would not now have to go through life with the load of murder burdening his soul. He, Mr Todhunter, could have saved him from that and had failed.

Mr Todhunter held his bald head in his hands and groaned over his own uselessness: he who had planned to be of such use.

Why Mr Todhunter should have been so certain that young Bennett pushed Fischmann under that lorry the second time they were to lunch together, there is no explaining. Nobody else ever dreamed of such a thing.

As a matter of fact Mr Todhunter had been perfectly right.

CHAPTER IV

Fischmann was out of the way.

In spite of his remorse, Mr Todhunter could not help feeling a certain selfish relief. He had not wanted to kill Fischmann. He had not wanted to kill anyone, however unpleasant. He was not of the stuff of which killers are made. Mr Todhunter realised all that now. He knew he had only been deceiving himself. It was a depressing reflection, and yet there were compensations. Peace was what Mr Todhunter really wanted for himself after all, and now he could have it. He had made his gesture, and its bluff had been called. Good.

As his relief grew Mr Todhunter even abandoned with equanimity the Italian and German nations to their fates and prepared for a peaceful passing.

Yet for all that, life seemed now excessively flat.

It was himself that Mr Todhunter had been bluffing. It was he, and probably no one else, who had once foolishly imagined himself capable of great things. And after all, when one has wound oneself up (as one imagines) to tremendous, magnificent action, it is bound to have a depressing effect to find the mainspring under one suddenly turn, as it were, into a piece of chewed string. It is like a high jumper who, taking an enormous run to clear the bar, finds on arriving there that it has been placed, not six feet above the ground, but six inches.

Nevertheless, though life might now be flat, it was restful. Mr Todhunter grew less irritable, his frayed nerves joined themselves together once more, he sat out in his garden again by day, he began to sleep better at night.

"Seems to have done him good, that attack of his," opined Edie to Mrs Greenhill. "Been ever so bobbish since, he has."

"Well, let's hope he don't get no more of them," said Mrs Greenhill devoutly. "Gave me a nasty turn, that one did, and that's a fact."

It was, in short, only after he seemed to have allayed his mental indigestion and settled down once more to the old, comfortable routine of his life, and indeed had already begun to look on the strange urges and compulsions that had stirred in him as a kind of temporary aberration due to shock, that the chance encounter befell Mr Todhunter which was to jerk him out of that routine once more and alter not only the short life remaining to him but the lives of several other people too.

The meeting took place at Christie's. It was Mr Todhunter's pleasure to go occasionally and watch the treasures of the world changing hands. On this occasion a seventeenth-century mazer was up for sale. It had belonged, since it was made, to an obscure little church in Northamptonshire. The early English tower was now in danger of collapsing, as early English towers will; and the incumbent had decided that a substantial tower was more useful to his church than a silver bowl and had therefore obtained the necessary permission to transmute the metal into cement.

Mr Todhunter had a school friend, a certain Frederick Sleights, to whom he was wont to refer in a somewhat deprecating way as "that chap Sleights." The deprecation was due to a fear on Mr Todhunter's part that in referring to Mr Sleights at all he might seem to be claiming acquaintance with the Great; for Mr Sleights wrote novels and, in the opinion of Mr Todhunter, very good novels too. This opinion was, however, not shared by the public at large, few of whom had ever heard of Mr Sleights; so that Mr Todhunter's deprecation, while well intentioned, was scarcely needed.

Frederick Sleights and Mr Todhunter would dine occasionally at each other's houses, and it was inevitable that they should sometimes meet strangers there. These strangers invariably passed straight out of Mr Todhunter's mind the instant their backs were turned towards the front door; for Mr Todhunter had an atrocious memory for names and faces and even for individuals. It seemed, however, that Mr Todhunter himself did not pass so readily out of the minds of others; for, while he was happily examining the mazer on its green baize cloth prior to the sale, a voice at his side accosted him by name and, when Mr Todhunter looked courteously baffled, reminded him that they had met last year at Sleights's.

"Farroway!" repeated Mr Todhunter with well simulated enthusiasm, staring at the trimly bearded face of the little man at his side. "Of course I remember. Naturally." And indeed the name of Farroway, in connection with that neat little pointed beard, did now seem in some way familiar.

They discussed the points of the bowl and moved on to an early Georgian teapot.

Gradually recollection filtered into Mr Todhunter's mind. Farroway, yes. This must be Nicholas Farroway, the author of—what was the thing called?— *Michael Staveling's Redemption* or some such dreadful title, and a dozen other novels with equally repellent names. Popular stuff. Mr Todhunter had read none of them of course. But he did seem to remember now meeting the man and rather liking him. Or at any rate thinking that he was not so bad as his books must be. There was a gentle, almost wistful air about him, an un-ostentatiousness which one did not quite associate with a popular novelist. Sleights had said something afterwards about Farroway being quite unspoiled in spite of his success. Yes, and hadn't the fellow made some complimentary reference to his own reviews in the *London Review*? Yes, now Mr Todhunter came to think of it, he had. Yes, yes; quite a good chap, Farroway. Mr Todhunter did not at all mind spending an hour or so in Farroway's company.

Mr Todhunter and Farroway looked at each other.

"Thinking of making a bid for anything?" they asked simultaneously.

"You answer first," suggested Mr Todhunter.

"Me? Oh no." Farroway looked round him somewhat vaguely. "I'm just watching the prices. I—I happen to be rather interested."

"In prices?"

"Oh well, in all this kind of thing. And you?"

Mr Todhunter chuckled. He suffered from a dry, donnish form of humour, extremely irritating to other people, which consisted in telling wild untruths with a perfectly serious face; and the more the victim appeared to believe him, the more firmly would Mr Todhunter elaborate his fiction. In consequence, until one knew him very well it was impossible to know when Mr Todhunter was speaking the truth and when he was not.

"Well," said Mr Todhunter gravely now, "I rather thought of having a shot at that Calchester mazer, you know. That is, if the bidding doesn't go too high."

It was obvious, to Mr Todhunter's fiendish pleasure, that Farroway had swallowed this preposterous statement whole. He looked at Mr Todhunter with undisguised respect.

"You collect?" he asked in the kind of reverent voice in which the B.B.C elocutionists read poetry.

Mr Todhunter waved a desiccated claw. "Oh well, only in a very small way," he replied modestly. Mr Todhunter had once bought at an auction a silver sugar basin and cream jug which happened to match exactly his own family George III teapot, and he felt that this act might entitle him to answer as he did.

"Ah," said Farroway thoughtfully and said no more.

They continued their progress round the hall.

Mr Todhunter was mildly interested. Farroway had seemed so much impressed on hearing that he was a collector that Mr Todhunter could not help feeling it odd that he should have dropped the subject so quickly, almost abruptly. On the other hand there had been a hint of suspense about that "Ah" as if the subject had only been temporarily shelved and was to be brought up again at some more favourable opportunity. But why in any case should it matter to Farroway whether he was a collector or not?

No doubt, Mr Todhunter decided, Farroway was a collector himself and wished to exchange gossip with another of the same kidney; but even so it was strange that he should not have plunged into the subject at once.

Mr Todhunter was sufficiently intrigued to make a couple of absolutely safe bids for the mazer when its turn came, just in order to support the fiction with his companion, and perfunctorily bewailed the fact that, when the bidding rose above six thousand pounds, the price was getting beyond what he cared to spend.

Farroway nodded. "It's a lot of money," he said.

His tone caused Mr Todhunter to look at him sharply. There was a quality of sheer envy about it which was quite startling. Had the man got some sort of a money complex which brought him here just for the satisfaction of hearing large sums change hands? And yet a popular novelist like Farroway must be making a very large income, ten thousand a year at least. It all seemed to Mr Todhunter rather queer.

No less queer was it, when the two finally strolled into the street, that Farroway should begin quite obviously and rather clumsily to pump Mr Todhunter as to his worldly circumstances. Without ever actually saying anything which could be quoted against him afterwards, Mr Todhunter amused himself by implying with much subtlety that his establishment in Richmond was just about four times as big as it really was, and his income to match, that his tastes were thoroughly expensive and even that he was not without influence in the financial world, a friend of Money Barons and a crony of Commercial Peers. Indeed, so favourable did Mr Todhunter find the opportunity for the exercise of his gift of the *suggestio falso* that he was in some danger of overdoing it.

Mr Todhunter had no idea that this time the retribution which lies in wait for all practical jokers, however subtle, was grinning behind his back. In fact, had he but known it, the laugh this time was decidedly on Mr Todhunter. For if, on this one single occasion, he had failed to indulge this elfin humour of his, a great deal of subsequent trouble might have been spared him. He would indeed have actually had the peaceful end to which he was even then looking forward, instead of the far from peaceful death which was in store for him. He would never have seen the inside of a condemned cell. He would never— But there is no need to elaborate. Retribution awaited Mr Todhunter at last.

It was a simple question of his companion's which put the wheels of fate in motion.

"Are you doing anything now?" asked Farroway.

Mr Todhunter could not recognise his chance. There was nothing to warn him that if he replied firmly that he had an urgent appointment in the City and must leave for it at once, he might still have been saved. Instead he replied, like any other sucker falling for Destiny's confidence trick:

"Nothing in particular."

"Perhaps you would come and have some tea with me? The—my flat is quite close."

Mr Todhunter in his foolishness saw only an opportunity for further enjoyment.

"There's nothing I should like better," he replied courteously.

Just behind him Fate put away her gold brick, tucked the forged bond out of sight and stuffed the bogus balance sheet into her pocket again. The sucker had sucked.

2

Mr Todhunter's first impression of Farroway's flat was that he must have totally misjudged its owner. He looked in a puzzled way round the room in which he had been left alone. No, he would certainly never have thought Farroway the kind of man to decorate his piano with Chinese embroidery and put a hoop skirted doll over the telephone. Farroway was a small man, but he was neat and trim in a thoroughly masculine way. No one would have suspected him of such effeminate taste, and such downright bad feminine taste at that. Mr Todhunter was mildly astonished.

The flat was really palatial. The room in which Mr Todhunter was now somewhat uneasily sitting, with its wide windows and view over the Park, would not have disgraced a country house so far as size went; and from the large hall into which the front door opened Mr Todhunter had seen two long, broad passages leading, each with half a dozen doors. The rent of such a place must be enormous. Even a popular novelist would find his resources squeezed, to fit his style of living to such surroundings.

Meditating thus, Mr Todhunter was surprised by the return of his host, accompanied this time by a young and handsome man.

"My son-in-law," said Farroway. "Vincent, have you had tea?"

For some reason the young man, who looked as if he would normally have aplomb enough for a dozen, appeared embarrassed.

"No, I was waiting for—you." The pause before the last word was very slight but it was perceptible.

"Then ring." Farroway spoke more drily than such a simple request appeared to warrant.

There was a pause, which continued long enough to be awkward.

Mr Todhunter was thinking that to have a son-in-law, Farroway must be married, and this therefore accounted for the feminine air of the room. But even so it seemed strange that a woman in the position of Farroway's wife should have such appalling taste or indeed that Farroway should allow her to exercise it if she possessed it.

Farroway, who had been staring at the carpet, looked up at his son-in-law—literally, for the latter topped him by four inches or more, a blond, curly haired young cross between Apollo and a rowing blue, quite improperly handsome, thought Mr Todhunter.

"Did Jean say when she'd be in?"

The young man did not alter his abstracted gaze towards the window. "I haven't seen her," he said shortly. He was leaning back against the mantlepiece and smoking a cigarette with an air of detachment so pronounced as to something very like defiance.

Mr Todhunter was not a perceptive man, but even he could not fail to be aware that there was something wrong here. The feeling between the two men seemed to amount almost to enmity. And whether the unknown Jean might be Farroway's wife or his daughter, there was surely no reason why his own son-in-law should appear to resent the mention of her name.

Farroway seemed to be catching the resentment.

"Has your firm given you the afternoon off, Vincent?" he asked with a distinct edge in his usually gentle voice.

The young man stared at him haughtily. "I happen to be here on business."

"Really? For Fitch and Son?" The sarcasm was almost crude.

"No. Private," replied the young man very curtly.

"Indeed? Then I won't enquire further. Nevertheless, Mr Todhunter and I—"

"All right," interrupted the young man rudely. "I was just going in any case."

With a brief nod in the direction of Mr Todhunter he stumped out of the room. Farroway drooped into a chair in a spiritless way and wiped his forehead.

Mr Todhunter, who had been growing more and more embarrassed, remarked rather foolishly:

"What an extremely handsome young man."

"Vincent? Yes, I suppose he is. He's an engineer. With Fitch and Son. Big firm—something to do with steel construction work. Ferroconcrete, I believe it's called. Not brilliant, but quite sound at his job. He married my elder daughter." Farroway wiped his forehead again, as if the recital of this short biography had been almost too much for him.

Mr Todhunter was spared the necessity for comment by the entrance with tea of an extremely pretty maid, her daintiness enhanced by the almost musical-comedy style of her uniform, with its too-short black silk skirts, too-small, too-frilly apron, and over-elaborate cap.

"Tea, sir," she remarked in a voice that was distinctly pert.

"Thank you, Marie," Farroway replied listlessly. Then as the maid reached the door he added: "Oh, Marie, I'm expecting a telephone call from Paris. If it comes through, call me at once."

"Yes sir. Very good," replied the girl and minced daintily out of the room. Mr Todhunter almost expected her to pause in the doorway and kick a saucy heel.

Mr Todhunter ventured a question: "I hope I may have the pleasure of meeting your wife?"

Farroway looked at him over the teapot. "My wife's at home."

"At home?"

"In the north. We live in Yorkshire. I thought you knew." Farroway spoke in a dull voice, pouring out the tea in a mechanical way. Since the exit of the Greek god he seemed to have relapsed into a kind of listless melancholy. "Milk and sugar?"

"One very small lump of sugar first, please, then the tea, and then a very little milk, please," replied Mr Todhunter with precision.

Farroway stared in a helpless kind of way at the tray. "I'm afraid I put the tea in first. Does it matter?" He glanced uncertainly at the bell, as if wondering whether to ring for a fresh cup.

"Not at all, not at all," replied Mr Todhunter politely. But his opinion of Farroway, which had been sinking ever since he entered the room, dropped a further couple of inches. A man who does not know better than to put in the sugar first and the tea after, is even worse than a man who allows his wife to smother her piano in embroidery and dress her maid like something out of a Cochran revue.

"No," he went on with forced brightness, "I don't think I knew you lived in the north. Then this is just a pied-à-terre for you in London?"

"Well, in a way." Farroway seemed a little embarrassed. "That is, it isn't really my flat. Or rather . . . at least, I use it when I'm up. That is to say, I have a bedroom here. I have to be up in London a great deal, you see. Business and—and so on. And both my daughters live in London."

"Of course." Mr Todhunter wondered why the man should evidently feel it necessary to make excuses to a semi-stranger for his presence in London.

"My younger daughter isn't even married, you see," continued Farroway almost feverishly. "I find it advisable to keep an eye on her at times. My wife quite agrees with me."

"Of course," repeated Mr Todhunter, his wonder growing.

"The stage, you know," said Farroway vaguely and took an absent bite of the piece of wafer-like bread and butter which he had been waving a little wildly in the air.

"Oh yes? Your daughter's on stage?"

"Felicity? No, I don't think she is. At least, I'm not sure. She *was*, of course. But I believe she's left it. She told me she was going to when I saw her last. But I haven't seen her for some time now."

If Mr Todhunter had not been a very well-brought-up man, he would have stared at his host. He was convinced by now that the man was a little mad, and he did not care for mad persons. With growing uneasiness he took a small iced cake, although iced cakes invariably upset him.

While he was wondering how to get away, Farroway said in a completely different tone:

"By the way, did you notice that exquisite little oil which was put up just after the big Lawrence? It was supposed to be attributed to one of the Ostades, but it didn't seem to me like their style at all. I shouldn't be at all surprised if it wasn't an early Frans Hals. I very nearly had a shot for it. I would have done, if I could have afforded the chance."

A lucid interval, thought Mr Todhunter, and proceeded to encourage it. "Certainly I remember it," he said without very much truth. "Let me see, how much did it fetch?"

"Twenty-four pounds."

"Oh yes, of course, yes. Most interesting. Yes, it's quite possible." Mr Todhunter did have time for a fleeting surprise that a man with Farroway's income should think he could not afford twenty-four pounds for a picture, but he was too anxious to keep the conversaton on rational lines to dwell on it.

For ten minutes the two discussed objects of beauty and value, and Farroway presented a perfect picture of the alert and intelligent connoisseur. His lethargy had fallen from him, he spoke with firmness and precision.

Then a faint ringing could be heard, and Farroway cocked an eager ear. "That sounds like my telephone call," he remarked.

A moment later the musical-comedy maid appeared in the doorway. "Paris on the line, sir," she said with a bright smile and a coquettish little flounce of her brief skirts which seemed to be directed as much at Mr Todhunter as at anyone.

Mr Todhunter modestly looked away as his host excused himself. If there was one thing Mr Todhunter detested and dreaded, it was coquettish advances on the part of the other sex. Fortunately he had been bothered with them very little.

Left alone again, Mr Todhunter rubbed the freckled top of his small bald head and polished his pince-nez, as he debated whether to await the return of his host or escape there and then while the way was clear. The advantages of the latter course were obvious, while on the other hand a natural curiosity (and if anything Mr Todhunter had more than his share of natural curiosity) urged him to stay and draw the conversation back to Farroway's private affairs; for that something was very queer about those affairs was as obvious as the polished gleam on Mr Todhunter's own cranium.

These reflections had lasted no more than half a minute when they were interrupted by voices outside the door of the room in which Mr Todhunter was sitting.

There had been the sound of a heavy door closing, as it might be the front door, and then a deep feminine voice spoke with cold and clear enunciation:

"I pay you to answer the bell at once, Marie; not to keep me waiting outside."

3

Mr Todhunter unashamedly cupped a bony hand round his ear.

The tone of the voice had been so unpleasant, with a grating edge in spite of its deepness, that Mr Todhunter's attention was riveted, and he listened as hard as he could.

The maid's reply was indistinguishable, but the newcomer's words carried clearly.

"I'm not interested in Mr Farroway's telephone calls. Perhaps I'd better remind you, Marie, that you're here to attend to me, not to Mr Farroway. I've noticed lately that you don't seem to understand that. You'd better not let me have to speak to you about it again."

There was the low, deferential tone of the maid's apology, and the next thing Mr Todhunter heard was a sharply irritated:

"Gentleman? What gentleman?"

Before Mr Todhunter had time to squirm, the door was flung open and the owner of the voice swept (there was no other word for it) into the room. Mr Todhunter shambled hurriedly to his feet.

She was a magnificent creature, there was no doubt about that: tall, slim, with dark brown hair, exceedingly soignée and opulently dressed, and she knew how to wear her furs. This alone was enough to disconcert Mr Todhunter as the lady gazed at him with cold and hostile enquiry; but what completed his discomfort was the curious aspect of the lady's eyes. These were dark brown, large and lustrous; they were even beautiful. But they were too large, in Mr Todhunter's opinion. They seemed to him naked, indecent eyes; and his own weak light blue ones found themselves attracted in a kind of stare of fascination.

If I look at them for long, Mr Todhunter found himself thinking rather wildly, I might become hypnotised, and that would be exceedingly awkward. But he was unable to look away.

"Good afternoon," said the lady, and her tone was not a welcoming one.

"Good afternoon," mumbled Mr Todhunter, still gazing in a fascinated way at those outsize orbs. "I—er—should apologise . . . this intrusion . . . had no idea . . . Mr Farroway . . ." He subsided into helpless silence.

"Mr Farroway appears to be entertaining himself on the telephone. Perhaps we had better introduce ourselves."

"My name is Todhunter," apologised Mr Todhunter.

"Indeed?" The lady did not offer her own. Instead she looked at Mr Todhunter with cold dislike, as if his name had added the last drop to her cup of annoyance, and proceeded to undo her furs. Mr Todhunter wondered whether he ought to take them from her and put them down somewhere or whether this would not be adjudged correct. The lady solved his problem by flinging them petulantly into one chair and herself into another.

"You are an old friend of Mr Farroway's, Mr Todhunter?"

"Oh no." Mr Todhunter seized eagerly on this conversational straw, letting himself down gingerly onto the extreme edge of a very large armchair. The lady's gaze had been fixed with an expression of acute distaste upon his trousers, which were creaseless, baggy and indeed quite deplorable. Mr Todhunter was thankful to be able to fill some of their bagginess up with his knees.

"No, no. Not at all. In fact I've only met him once before. We ran into each other this afternoon at Christie's."

"Indeed?" The lady's tone enquired as plainly as plain speech why on earth Farroway should have collected this piece of human jetsam to come and litter up her exquisite flat. Her gaze was fixed now on his waistcoat. Glancing furtively down towards the point of impact, Mr Todhunter perceived a large smear of egg. He could not even remember when he had had egg last. It was all very awkward.

"Well!" The lady tore off her hat, flung it onto a couch and followed it up with her gloves and bag.

Mr Todhunter squirmed afresh. For this time her tone had asked him, very definitely, how soon he proposed to get up and go and whether it would not be a good thing to do it at once. It would indeed, thought Mr Todhunter desperately, if only he could find the correct words to do it with; but these eluded him. He sought for them unhappily and found that he was staring at his hostess in a positively rude way. Under the protest of her lifted eyebrows he transferred his hot gaze out of the window.

At this juncture, when Mr Todhunter was beginning to feel that he could bear life not a moment longer, Farroway returned. Mr Todhunter swayed towards him and scrambled to his feet.

"I must be going," he blurted out.

For the first time the lady looked at him with approval.

"No, no," protested Farroway. "You must make Jean's acquaintance properly now she's back."

"You know I have to rest now before the theatre," observed the lady coldly.

"Yes, of course. Of course. But a few minutes won't make much difference. And I want you to know Todhunter."

Mr Todhunter looked at Farroway with annoyance. He did not want to be kept. Also there had been a ring of false heartiness in the man's voice which Mr Todhunter found distasteful.

Unaware apparently of the feelings he was rousing, Farroway elaborated his theme.

"Sit down, Todhunter. Marie will be bringing cocktails in a minute. Yes, dear, I met Mr Todhunter at Christie's this afternoon. There was a fine old mazer bowl up for sale, and--"

"Really, Nick, you *know* how these details of your eternal sales bore me."

Farroway flushed. "Yes, dear. But the point is that Todhunter here intended to have a shot for the bowl. He was going up to six thousand for it; but he didn't get it nevertheless. It fetched eight. Still—six thousand, eh? That's a lot of money."

"It is—for a silly old bowl. Were you really going to spend as much as that, Mr Todhunter?" The lady's tone was no longer cold. Her voice almost cooed out the question; her enormous eyes shone on Mr Todhunter with benevolence.

"Oh well, I don't know," mumbled Mr Todhunter, aware that his foolish little jest had come home to roost and not quite sure what to do with it. "Well—er—good-bye."

"Oh, but you mustn't go yet," protested the lady. "You must stay and have a cocktail with me, Mr Todhunter. Positively, I insist."

"I expect you know what Jean's like when she insists," chuckled Farroway. "There's no option, I assure you."

"Ha, ha," muttered Mr Todhunter, who had no idea at all what Jean was like when she insisted and did not know why he should be expected to have one.

Farroway must have noticed something in his guest's expression, for he uttered an exclamation of incredulity. "I don't believe you know yet who Jean is. Jean, I don't believe Todhunter's recognised you."

"Well, you can't expect everyone in the world to recognise me at first glance, you know, Nick," replied the lady with magnanimity.

"She's Jean Norwood, Todhunter," cried Farroway, as one introducing a lion hunter's prize catch.

"Good gracious," politely replied Mr Todhunter, who could not remember ever having heard of a Jean Norwood in his life.

"You never recognised her?"

"No, I must confess I didn't."

"Such is fame!" said Farroway and struck a tragic attitude which Mr

Todhunter thought exceedingly silly. "Still," he added, "no doubt it works the other way too. Ask Jean if she recognised you as Lawrence Todhunter, the eminent critic of the *London Review*."

"You write then, Mr Todhunter?" kindly asked Miss Norwood.

Mr Todhunter was understood to mumble that he did.

"Just for a hobby, I suppose?"

"Well-er-yes."

"You must write me a play," pronounced Miss Norwood, whose benevolence towards Mr Todhunter seemed to be growing with every minute.

"Don't be quite foolish, darling," implored Farroway. "Eminent literary critics don't write plays, not even for great actresses like you."

"I'm sure Mr Todhunter would write me a play if I asked him," protested Miss Norwood playfully, laying a long, slender and super-manicured hand over the one which Farroway had rested on her shoulder. "Wouldn't you, Mr Todhunter?"

Mr Todhunter grinned in a sickly way.

"Ah, cocktails." Farroway's voice again held the false heartiness which had grated on Mr Todhunter before. "All right, Marie. Put them down there." He jumped up and busied himself with the shaker. "Darling?"

"Thank you, darling." Miss Norwood accepted a pale green cocktail which to Mr Todhunter's sherry loving eye appeared quite repellent, sipped it and pronounced verdict. "That idiot of a girl hasn't put in enough lemon juice. Ring, Nickie."

Marie appeared, was reprimanded and retired with the shaker for additional lemon juice. Farroway apologised for keeping Mr Todhunter waiting. Mr Todhunter explained with some diffidence, for it sounded more feeble than tragic, that he was unable to drink cocktails by doctor's orders. He also added that he must go now.

"Not until you've fixed a date to come and have lunch with me," at once said Miss Norwood. "We'll get rid of Nicholas and just have a cosy lunch here and a chat by ourselves. I adore meeting new people, and I've never met an eminent literary critic before."

Mr Todhunter found himself promising to take lunch with Miss Norwood next Tuesday without fail, one o'clock sharp.

Miss Norwood looked at him wistfully. "Yes, how nice it must be to be able to afford a hobby like that; I mean, making a hobby of one's profession. Not that I don't adore the theatre, of course, and I wouldn't do anything else, however rich I was. But for a man it must be delightful."

"Yes, quite," murmured Mr Todhunter uneasily.

"You know, Mr Todhunter," pursued Miss Norwood, "I should never have taken you for a rich man. I mean, a *very* rich man."

"Oh?" Mr Todhunter cackled dismally "Why not?"

"Well, I don't know. You don't *look* like one somehow," replied Miss Norwood, her soulful gaze passing from the egg on Mr Todhunter's waistcoat to the bagginess of Mr Todhunter's trouser knees.

"Well, I'm not one," asserted Mr Todhunter manfully. "You—it's all a mistake, I assure you."

Miss Norwood shook an arch finger at him. "That's what you rich men always say. After all, I don't blame you. There must be so many people wanting to help themselves to a slice of it."

"They wouldn't stand much chance with Todhunter," interposed Farroway in jovial tone. "There are no flies on him, I can assure you. You ask him about his connections in the City."

"I will next Tuesday at lunch," said Miss Norwood sweetly and with that allowed Mr Todhunter to depart, which he did thankfully, pausing on the pavement outside to mop his forehead.

As he mopped, Mr Todhunter was firmly determined on one thing: that next Tuesday he would have a sick headache, an infectious disease of peculiar malignity or be, if necessary, dead. But he would not be lunching with Miss Norwood.

That, as it happens, is just where Mr Todhunter was wrong.

CHAPTER V

Mr Todhunter had caught a glimpse of an alien world: a world of luxury and elegance, of exquisite scents, exquisite women, cocktails, flowers and musical-comedy service. To Mr Todhunter, with his Richmond outlook, this world had seemed not very attractive and definitely alarming. He looked round his own library-sitting room. Compared with Miss Norwood's it was dingy, drab and hideous, but to Mr Todhunter it was good.

Mr Todhunter was glad to have had a glimpse of a world of which he had often heard but never quite believed in; but he wanted no more than that glimpse.

As for Jean Norwood, Mr Todhunter had now identified her, much to his own satisfaction. Beginning with the theory that she must be an actress, he had pursued investigations in the theatre announcements of his *Times;* and there sure enough was Jean Norwood, the star apparently of *Fallen Petals* at the Sovereign Theatre. Mr Todhunter, who had a household rule that all newspapers must be kept for three months before being disposed of, sent Edie for the *Sunday Times* pile and succeeded in finding the notice of the play. From it he learned, reading between the words, that Miss Norwood's particular line was popular high-brow stuff, that she was an actress-manager and that *Fallen Petals* would probably keep the suburbs busy for months trooping up to the West End to see it.

"Well, well!" said Mr Todhunter.

It happens often that a name never heard before crops up two or three times immediately after one has first become cognisant of it, or a person never seen before is met again at once after the first introduction. It may be that one is more alert to recognise, or it may be just coincidence. In any case both these phenomena occurred to Mr Todhunter during the four days following his meeting with Farroway.

The first person to mention Jean Norwood's name to him was a young woman, a distant cousin, who came to take tea with Mr Todhunter on the Saturday of that week end. Mr Todhunter was not at all averse from the company of the young; especially the female young, so long as he felt quite safe and at his ease with them. He liked to listen to their artless prattle and cackle at them with a great pretence of sardonic disillusion; though to tell the truth, the young were probably a great deal more disillusioned than Mr Todhunter himself. It was therefore his custom to seek out obscure family connections and make their acquaintance. The young men often borrowed his money, which Mr Todhunter lent readily, for he had strong family feelings; the girls would come down to Richmond, pour out Mr Todhunter's tea for him and tell him all the family gossip—much of it about people he had never heard of and most of it about people he had never met, but none the less interesting to him for that.

Scarcely had the young third cousin of this Saturday afternoon set foot in Mr Todhunter's trim little garden than she came out with her news.

"Such a thrill, Lawrence. Whom do you think I met at a party last week?"

"Really, I've no idea, Ethel." Privately Mr Todhunter thought Ethel Markham a rather crude and rather foolish young suburban woman. She was secretary to a firm of dress designers in Oxford Street, and Mr Todhunter could never understand why they paid her as much money as she affirmed that they did.

"I thought it was going to be a deadly stuffy party too. But it wasn't. Jean Norwood came along after the theatre. And if you'll believe it, she seemed to take quite a fancy to little me. What do you think of that?"

"Poisonous woman," threw out Mr Todhunter.

"She's not; she's charming. Really sweet. One of the sweetest women I've ever met."

"Indeed? I thought her poisonous." Mr Todhunter cackled wickedly.

His cousin stared at him. "What do you know about her?"

"Oh," said Mr Todhunter very casually, "I was round at her flat for a cocktail the day before yesterday. There are pink bows on her piano," he added with distaste.

"Rot! Jean Norwood hasn't a pink-bow mind."

"Well, it may only have been Chinese embroidery, but that's just as bad. And her maid—Marie, you know—looks like something out of a musical comedy."

"Lawrence! You're pulling my leg, ~~you know~~. You've never been in Jean's flat in your life."

"I assure you I have, my dear girl. And what is more I have an invitation to lunch there next Tuesday week which, by the way, I do not intend to accept. And you will oblige me, Ethel," added Mr Todhunter severely, "by not referring to Miss Norwood by her Christian name unless you are already on familiar terms with her. That is a practice peculiar to the more repellent types of suburban youth and to the still more repellently vulgar newspapers, and I don't care to hear it from any relative of mine."

"I always said you ought to have been born a hundred years ago, Lawrence," responded the young woman without rancour. "And the other sex at that. In fact what you ought to have been is a spinster aunt. I can just see you with your hair screwed up in a bun and ghastly boned stays."

"Tush!" said Mr Todhunter, annoyed.

The other person to mention Miss Norwood was a neighbour, a solid, walrus-like man who occasionally escaped from a shrewish wife to drink Mr Todhunter's whiskey and sit in companionable silence with the spare pair of earphones clamped over his head. Mr Todhunter had a passion for Bach and would interrupt any engagement or activity to sit by his wireless when Bach was on the air. But for some reason obscure to his friends, and perhaps obscure to Mr Todhunter himself, he would not have a loud speaker or anything but an old-fashioned crystal set.

This man, after an unbroken silence of thirty-eight minutes, produced the information that he and his wife had been last week to see Jean Norwood at the Sovereign. Mr Todhunter, with a writer's sensitiveness, noticed that it was not *Fallen Petals* the couple had been to see, but Jean Norwood. Probably they had never noticed the name of the play. Quite certainly they had no idea who had written it and thus given Miss Norwood her chance.

After seven minutes more silence the visitor followed this up with the remark that he knew a man who knew Jean Norwood. Fellow of the name of Battersby. This chap said she was a delightful woman; just the same off the stage as on; do anything for anybody; always looking for young actresses and helping them; heart of gold.

"Gold," nodded Mr Todhunter. "Yes. . . . I'm supposed to be lunching with her next Tuesday," he added.

His visitor took his pipe out of his mouth and stared at him. "Good God!" he said reverently.

Mr Todhunter was not ill pleased.

He was, however, puzzled.

Here were the impressions of two persons that Miss Norwood was a lady of charm and sweetness, whereas Mr Todhunter's own conviction had been that she was a rude word. A just man, he considered the problem. Had he perhaps been prejudiced? Had he allowed the feeling of inferiority which the luxurious flat might have produced in him to sway his judgment to the detriment of its owner? But no. His feeling had not been altogether one of inferiority. He had been impressed, perhaps against his will, but he had never wavered in his opinion that 267 Lower Putney Road, Richmond, had been an infinitely better place in which to dwell; and it had not been a defiant opinion either, but a genuine one.

No again. The woman had been unmistakably hostile, cold and rude. Then Farroway had come in and told her, almost crudely, that he, Mr Todhunter, was a man of wealth; and instantly her attitude had changed. That was not very nice. She had a reverence for money quite evidently. An unsympathetic person became at once sympathetic to her with the knowledge that he was rich; a bore would become interesting; a nondescript might become—well, might become her lover, thought Mr Todhunter uncomfortably, knowing very little about these things and disliking what he guessed. For Farroway, though he might be a writer of popular appeal, as a man was undoubtedly nondescript. Yet there he was, installed apparently in that exquisite flat, in the capacity of . . . what? He bored her, plainly; but she tolerated him. Almost ironically she had echoed his endearing names. Mr Todhunter, feeling slightly disgusted, could have no doubt that they were on "terms." And Farroway must have been a man of wealth—positively must have been. Yet now he was almost touting for the chance to sell Mr Todhunter expensive antiques on commission; for if that had not been the object of his advances, what else could have been?

There's something very queer going on here, decided Mr Todhunter, remembering the wife in the north of England and the almost forgotten daughters. Very queer indeed.

And then came the third of those coincidences which happen so often and make us wonder whether they really are coincidences at all or whether everything is part of one great Plan, including our own insignificant selves.

An elderly cousin of Mr Todhunter (on his mother's side) was in the habit of doing his part towards the family solidarity by sending Mr Todhunter a blue pass every year for the Royal Horticultural Society's annual exhibition at Chelsea. Mr Todhunter knew nothing at all about horticulture outside the wild orchid, of which for some utterly disintegrated reason he was able to name and identify twenty-seven varieties, but he had a general feeling of benevolence towards all flowers and a feeling of satisfaction and repose in their presence; and so to Chelsea each year he duly went. Nor this year did he allow his aneurism to rob him of this mild pleasure but took it there for an airing, albeit walking with circumspection and sitting down whenever he found a chair vacant, which was not very often.

It was, then, in the space of that triangle formed by the rock gardens, the formal gardens and the ladies' cloakroom, and actually behind the largest potted rhododendron that he had ever seen, that Mr Todhunter caught sight of a woman whose face seemed somehow familiar to him, flirting with a man whom he was sure he had seen somewhere before. The woman was slender and very elegant, and she wore her white fox fur with an air; the man was young and quite indecently handsome. That they were flirting was evident, for the lady's French-gloved hand rested on that of her companion, and even while Mr Todhunter stared at them, wondering where he had seen them before if ever, the young man tried to kiss her. Moreover the way she repulsed him showed even Mr Todhunter that it was opportunity which she considered lacking and not inclination.

Really, thought Mr Todhunter with exasperation, I don't believe my memory's as good as it was. I'm sure I've seen those two somewhere before.

"I say—look!" obligingly remarked an eager feminine voice behind him. "That's Jean Norwood, surely. Yes, it is. Isn't she *lovely?*"

Mr Todhunter resisted a strong impulse to turn round and reply: "No, madam. She is not lovely, for that implies that she is lovesome; and she is, in point of cold fact, a perdition cat. And what is more, I *am* going to lunch with her next Tuesday, just to find out what her dirty little game is and why she is flirting thus blatantly with her silly, middle-aged lover's handsome son-in-law."

2

That was on a Wednesday. Mr. Todhunter, having thus made up his mind to interfere, proceeded to utilise the days at his disposal before the appointment.

His first move was to ring up Farroway at the flat, the telephone number of which had been pressed upon him, and offer him lunch on Friday; an offer that was instantly, not to say eagerly, accepted.

"What a pity Jean isn't here," remarked Farroway before ringing off amid effusive thanks. "She'd have liked a word with you. But she's down in Richmond."

"Richmond?"

"Oh yes. That's where she lives, you know."

"I didn't know," said Mr Todhunter.

At lunch Farroway wanted to talk about antiques and some of the remarkably good things, going dirt cheap, onto which he could put his host; but Mr Todhunter kept the conversation steadily on Miss Norwood and/or the Farroway family. The lunch lasted a long time, for Mr Todhunter had reluctantly decided upon an exceedingly expensive restaurant to suit his role of wealthy dilettante, which he considered it convenient to maintain, and he was at least determined to get some small portion of his money's worth by spinning the meal out as long as possible, to the visible annoyance of the high priest in charge of this temple of food and his acolytes; an annoyance which was by no means allayed by the parsimonious tip with which Mr Todhunter, frightened of being frightened into over-tipping, finally rewarded their mostly unnecessary services.

In the course of these two and a quarter hours, then, Mr Todhunter learned many new and significant facts.

He learned that Miss Norwood lived for the most part in a small mansion on the riverbank at Richmond, using the flat only as a pied-à-terre for resting in the afternoons or when feeling too exhausted after her performance to face the drive back to Richmond.

"Poor girl, she works ~~so very~~ hard," remarked her admirer in what Mr Todhunter thought was the most unctuously fatuous voice he had ever heard. "The theatre's a ~~deuced~~ hard life, Todhunter, I can tell you. And the nearer the top you are, the harder it is. I had no idea, before I met Jean, how these women work. At it all day long, one thing and another, from morning to night."

"Indeed yes," nodded Mr Todhunter with sympathy. "When not giving interviews to the newspapers about the loss of their pearls, I understand, they are writing testimonials for toothpaste and face-cream firms. It must be a very exacting life... By the way," added Mr Todhunter politely, "does Miss Norwood find the competition in the testimonial business from professional peeresses nowadays rather trying?"

"It's musical-comedy stars who do that sort of thing, not serious actresses like Jean," replied Farroway, hurt.

Mr Todhunter apologised and resumed the questioning which, in his own mind, he considered to be not a little adroit.

He learned a great deal more about Miss Norwood. He learned the name of her manager at the Sovereign; he learned that she was the lessee of the theatre herself; he learned that she would have had no difficulty in finding the money for any new play, so anxious were the playboys of the City to finance her, but that she always financed her own; he learned that out of her own sweet kindness of heart she had given Farroway's youngest daughter, Felicity, a part in no fewer than three consecutive plays, until it became so patent that the poor girl couldn't act for little green apples that not even Jean could risk the reputation of her casts by continuing to include Felicity.

"Dear, dear, how sad for the poor girl." Mr Todhunter seemed quite distressed over Felicity's failure.

"Yes, the child was thoroughly upset. In fact she said some exceedingly foolish and ungrateful things, considering the chances she'd been given. The artistic temperament, I suppose; and all the worse when there's nothing to warrant it. If indeed there is such a thing at all as the artistic temperament. I've never been bothered with one myself, thank heaven," said Farroway, not without complacence. "And in my opinion it's only a high-sounding name for infernal selfishness—a name and an excuse."

But Mr Todhunter had no intention of being led aside into a discussion of the artistic temperament. He wanted to know what kind of foolish, ungrateful things Felicity Farroway had said, and asked her father as much.

"Oh, I don't know." Farroway pulled his neat little beard and looked vague. Mr Todhunter noticed his hands. They were as white and small and fine as a woman's, with long, sensitive fingers. A real artist's hand, thought Mr Todhunter, and yet he only writes popular romances.

"You don't know?"

"No—well, you know, the usual sort of thing. Abuse of the benefactor, biting the hand that fed her, anybody's fault but her own; and chiefly, of course, that she was a great actress but was being kept out of her rightful place by jealousy. You know. All the hackneyed complaints of disgruntled failure. Poor girl, I'm afraid we had rather a quarrel over it. My fault, I expect. I shouldn't have taken her seriously."

"So she's left the stage?"

"Oh yes. She wouldn't get another job after Jean had had to get rid of her from the company for incompetence. These things get around, you know."

"I suppose she's gone back home?"

"Well . . . no." Farroway hesitated. "As a matter of fact I believe she's got another sort of job. Though to tell you the truth, I haven't seen her since our little tiff."

"What sort of a job could a girl like that get, I wonder?" enquired Mr Todhunter artlessly, toying with the baked custard he had ordered to the undisguised horror of the high priest. Incidentally, Mr Todhunter did not consider it cooked nearly so well as Mrs Greenhill cooked it at home.

Farroway, however, had drunk far too many of the cocktails which Mr Todhunter had cunningly pressed upon him, and far too much champagne later, to resent this curiosity about his private affairs. Indeed he seemed quite eager to talk about them now that the antique hurdle had been safely leaped.

"Well, Viola (that's my elder daughter) told me that the silly girl has got a job in a shop Somewhere. Quite unnecessary. Her mother would have been very pleased to have her at home. She wouldn't accept an allowance from me either. Positively refused. Felicity always was very independent," said Farroway indifferently. He did not seem to care much what had happened to his daugher or why. "I say, this is really an excellent champagne, Todhunter."

"I'm glad to hear you like it. Let me offer you another bottle." Mr Todhunter himself was drinking barley water (for the kidneys).

"No, no, I couldn't manage another alone, really." Mr Todhunter with calculated recklessness summoned the high priest and ordered another bottle. "And don't ice it this time," he added, emboldened perhaps by the barley water. "This gentleman likes his champagne served properly: cooled, but not iced."

The high priest, who like most of his kind knew a little about wines but not enough, departed champing with rage. Mr. Todhunter felt better.

With the second bottle of champagne Mr Todhunter made more discoveries. He learned the name and address, in Bromley, of Farroway's married daughter; he learned that Mrs Farroway had never understood Farroway; he learned that Farroway had not seen Mrs Farroway for seven months; and he learned that Farroway had not written a novel for over a year and had no immediate hope of beginning one.

"I can't seem to get down to it somehow," Farroway lamented. "I hate the job anyhow, turning out slushy tripe for suburban library subscribers. Always did hate it. But in those days I could do it. Had the knack somehow. Now I don't believe I could, not since I came up against the real thing."

"The real thing?" queried Mr Todhunter.

"Jean," replied Farroway solemnly, "has opened up a new emotional world to me. I had never lived until I met her. I must have been half dead all my life: stifled, numbed, blanketed, any metaphor you like. Now that I know what love really is, I can't go on writing about what it isn't."

Mr Todhunter, half repelled and half fascinated by Farroway's confidences, now definitely maudlin, did his best to encourage his guest by remarking:

"I've never been in love."

"You're lucky, Todhunter. You're lucky, ole man. Love—love's just plain hell. I wish ~~to God~~ I'd never met Jean. Don't you ever meet a woman you'll fall in love with, Todhunter, ole boy. Love's hell. Yes. Interesting, extremely. But hell."

With this final frankness Farroway staggered to his feet, wiped the beads from his chalk-white face and demanded in a loud voice:

"Where's the lavatory?"

Three acolytes, assisted by the high priest in person, led him hastily out of the now almost empty room.

Mr Todhunter occupied his absence by thoughtfully jotting down such of the names and addresses and other material facts as he could remember.

When Farroway returned, twelve minutes later, he appeared completely sobered, but wished to get away at once.

"About those majolica plaques we were mentioning," he said as they retrieved his own smart grey hat and wash-leather gloves and the appalling, shapeless, grease-ridden object which Mr Todhunter was content to wear on his head and which the superior young man behind the counter handled as if he wished the management supplied a pair of tongs for such emergencies. "About those plaques, the man you want to see is Herder, of Vigo Street. He knows more about majolica than anyone in London. He'll tell you all you want to know, and considering that his guarantee of genuineness is absolutely cast iron, his prices are very reasonable. Look here, I've just jotted down your name on my card as an introduction. He'll do his very best for you if he knows you're a friend of mine."

"Thank you," said Mr Todhunter, perfunctorily glancing at the card. On it Farroway had written: "To introduce Mr Lawrence Todhunter. Please tell him anything he wants to know. N.F."

Mr Todhunter put the card into his pocket.

3

During these days Mr Todhunter knew quite well that he was playing a game with himself. He was not going to interfere in Farroway's affairs; he knew that for certain. Farroway was nothing to him, nothing at all; and Farroway's family was still less. But it was amusing to pretend to oneself that one was going to interfere. It was amusing to pretend that one was a kind of deus ex machina with the power of solving all petty mortal problems with the final argument of the thunderbolt; the thunderbolt in this case being, of course, a bullet from the revolver which was still reposing idly in a drawer of Mr Todhunter's dressing table. Besides, it took the mind off one's aneurism.

So although he knew with such conviction that it was all going to lead nowhere, Mr Todhunter set about his enquiries and his careful analysis of Farroway's situation just as if he had never put the fantastic idea of altruistic murder away from him once and for all after the Fischmann fiasco.

Carefully, therefore, Mr Todhunter worked through the list of names and addresses in his possession, taking taxis everywhere on account of his aneurism and spending money with a recklessness which a year ago would have burst every artery in his body with horror. The lunch for Farroway alone had set Mr Todhunter back more than six pounds, and he just did not care a couple of fried kippers.

There were three people in particular with whom Mr Todhunter wanted to talk: Farroway's two daughters and the manager of the Sovereign Theatre. Arguing cunningly, Mr Todhunter decided that his best move would be to interview the married daughter in Bromley at once after the Farroway lunch, for her husband would certainly not be at home that afternoon but probably would be during the next two days. He therefore caused himself to be driven straight from the restaurant to Victoria Station and there took a train for Bromley.

The address given him indicated a house in the Grove Park district, and his taxi driver at Bromley Station told Mr Todhunter, in the pitying yet scornful way of those in possession of information to those without it, that he ought to have taken a train to Bromley North Station from Charing Cross, which would have cost him a much smaller taxi fare; on the other hand, opined the driver, it was doubtful whether there would be a taxi at Bromley North Station at all at this time of the day.

"Yes, well, step on the gas," observed Mr Todhunter, cutting short this interesting discussion of alternatives as he crept, carefully crouched, into the cab.

"Eh?" said the driver, startled.

Mr Todhunter thrust his head out of the window like a baleful old bird peeping out of its nest in some mountain crag. "I said, step on the gas."

"O.K.," responded the driver, and stepped.

The Vincent Palmers proved to live in one of the new roads which are rapidly linking up Bromley with its neighbours to the north. The taxi stopped outside a small, semidetached villa which did not look as if it had been built more than five years, and as he paid the driver Mr Todhunter conscientiously noted the trimness of the privet hedge along the front wall and the raggedness of the clematis clambering over the porch. As these two appeared to cancel out as evidence, Mr Todhunter was not quite certain what conclusion to draw.

Luck, however, was with him. The maid, correct in black and white, who answered his ring, informed him that Mrs Palmer was in and showed him straight into the sitting room, where Mrs Palmer was indulging in a nap on a big overstuffed couch.

She sprang up in mingled annoyance and embarrassment, a short, pretty girl of twenty-four or five, her brown hair rather charmingly disarrayed. Mr Todhunter's embarrassment, however, was so much greater than her own that the latter was swamped and, with it, her annoyance.

"How absurd of Elsie!" she laughed. "She came to me quite untrained two years ago, when we first came here, and it's useless to pretend I've trained her yet. However she did announce you. Mr Todhunter, I think she said?"

"Er—Todhunter, yes," mumbled Mr Todhunter, crimson to his rather naked, winglike ears, and already half regretting his impulsive visit. "Must apologise. . . unhappy intrusion. . . friend of y' father's. . . passing house. . . call. . ."

"Oh, you're a friend of Father's? How interesting. Do sit down, Mr Todhunter."

With great deliberation, to hide his shame, Mr Todhunter extracted Farroway's card from his pocketbook and handed it to Viola Palmer, who interrupted her hair-patting to peruse it.

"I see, yes. Well, what can I tell you, Mr Todhunter?"

Mr Todhunter extended a desiccated hand for the card and tucked it away in his pocketbook again. It was going to be very useful, that card.

"Errrm-hem!" Mr Todhunter cleared his throat, adjusted his glasses, put a hand on each bony knee and leaned forward in a way that he hoped was impressive. "Mrs Palmer, I'm exceedingly worried about your father."

Viola Palmer looked startled. "About Father."

"Yes," nodded Mr Todhunter. "Jean Norwood!"

"Oh!" The girl stared at him.

Mr Todhunter watched her anxiously. It had been hit or miss, thus to burst into his main theme without introduction, but if (thought Mr Todhunter) Bach could get away with it, why not he?

"My goodness, so are all of us!" exclaimed the girl. "It's—there's something really horrible in it. That woman's just a devil."

Mr Todhunter clapped his bony shanks with satisfaction. It had been hit, not miss. The girl had accepted him without question as an old friend of her father's, was going to ask no difficult questions and looked as if she might talk without reserve. As Mr Todhunter was anxious to find out whether she knew anything about her own husband's little antics, all this was very fortunate.

"A devil," he repeated. "Precisely. Exactly. That describes her very justly."

"And everyone says she is so sweet."

"They don't know her."

"Indeed they don't."

"What," propounded Mr Todhunter, "can be done about it?"

The girl shrugged her shoulders, "Goodness knows. It's no good talking to him of course. He always has an answer for everything, or else he just looks pathetic and helpless. I've tried, and so has Mother, but if anything I should think we've only made things worse. Poor Mother! It's dreadful for her."

"Yes indeed." Mr Todhunter, nodding violently, remembered himself and nodded gently. "It must be. She's still in the north?"

"Oh yes. It wouldn't be any good her coming down. She's got the sense to see that. Besides, I doubt if she's got the fare now."

"The fare?"

"Well, since Father cut off supplies, she's hardly a penny, you know. I send her what I can from time to time, but. . ."

"Good gracious, I didn't know it was as bad as that," exclaimed Mr Todhunter. "I knew he'd left her of course," he added with half truth, "but I didn't know he'd cut off supplies."

"Well, not formally. He just hasn't sent her anything, not a farthing since he left. And when she asks for some, he goes all pathetic and says he hasn't got any money himself. And all the time he's keeping that woman and paying the rent of that flat and squandering pounds and pounds on her. I think," said Farroway's daughter calmly, "that he's gone mad."

"In a way," agreed Mr Todhunter, "that is so. I'm sorry to say that in this respect your father seems to be really not quite sane. Great Infatuations," he added vaguely, "are often like that."

"Well, certainly there's no arguing with them," said the girl.

The peculiar bitterness in her voice caught Mr Todhunter's attention and he looked at her sharply.

"Ah!" he agreed as meaningly as he could. "Yes. You mean, of course . . . yes. I wondered if you knew."

"Of course I know," she replied in a voice between scorn and tears.

"And what are you going to do about that?"

"About Vincent? I don't know—*yet*"

"Do nothing for the time being," Mr Todhunter advised with earnestness. She looked at him. "Nothing?"

"Nothing. I—er—it's true that I know very little about these things, but I understand that at this stage intervention on the part of a wife, or open opposition, is often fatal. Things may adjust themselves, Mrs Palmer, or they may not. But please do nothing for a week or so. Does he know that you know?"

"I don't think so."

"Excellent. Then you will leave matters as they are for the time being?"

The girl thought. "Very well," she said a little wonderingly.

Soon afterwards Mr Todhunter took his leave. He carried away the impression of a personality much more forceful than that of Mrs Palmer's father. When she had said that she did not know what she was going to do—*yet*, Mr Todhunter had received the idea that when she did make up her mind, it would be to something drastic. Certainly young Mrs Palmer did not appear the kind of person to sit supinely by and let things drift.

Before he left Mr Todhunter asked and obtained the address of Farroway's other daughter.

Reviewing the interview on his way back to London, Mr Todhunter decided that it had been interesting but had added little to his knowledge of the situation.

4

This, however, was not the case with the two interviews which followed.

On that same evening Mr Todhunter sought out the manager of the Sovereign Theatre. His name was Budd, and he was a depressed-looking man of about fifty, with black hair and the kind of jowls which contrive to look always unshaven. It took Mr Todhunter some time and a great deal of tact to gain his confidence; but when that had been done the revelations which ensued would have startled Miss Norwood's worshippers.

"She's a bitch, Mr Todhunter," pronounced Mr Budd with a kind of gloomy zest. "You get her kind in the theatre often enough, but she's the worst specimen I've ever met. How I manage to stick her, I don't know. Well, a job's a job in these days, and even if she thinks she owns me body and soul in her theatre, I'm my own man at home." He swallowed quickly what was left of his double whiskey and rapped on the table for another. A very young waiter arrived at a run.

"Indeed?" said Mr Todhunter with interest. "Tell me about the type."

Mr Budd obliged, with details.

The two were sitting in the Foyer Club, whither Mr Budd had piloted Mr Todhunter "for a couple of quick ones" after the fall of the curtain at the Sovereign. Mr Todhunter, displaying Farroway's card, had pretended that he was collecting information to incorporate in an article which he was writing on the theatre in the *London Review*, and had implored Mr Budd's help. Mr Budd had been perfectly willing, if Mr Todhunter would wait till the curtain was down and everything fixed for the night. Mr Todhunter had waited and now, against all doctors' rules and in some agitation, was sitting well past midnight imbibing barley water in the small and shabby Foyer Club and listening to Mr Budd's growing indiscretions.

"It's genuine in a way. She really believes she's a great actress—the greatest since Bernhardt at least. And I expect in her heart of hearts she believes she could give Bernhardt a few tips. She's all wrong of course. She isn't a great actress. She just has the knack of getting hold of an audience. Not that she's a bad actress. In fact," conceded Mr Budd handsomely, "she's a pretty good one. But not great, no... Boy, get me another of the same. Here, Mr Todhunter, your glass is empty. Have a bit of a stiffener in it this time, for heaven's sake."

Mr Todhunter refused the stiffener with some difficulty, since Mr Budd seemed inclined to make a personal matter of it, and returned to the subject in hand.

"Yes, but as a woman, what is she like? She appears to have considerable professional charm. Does it extend into her ordinary relations with other people?"

"It does not," replied Mr Budd with firmness. "Jean's a devastating woman. I can tell you, every producer in London had a couple of quick ones in relief when he heard that she'd gone into management and he wouldn't be bothered with her tantrums any more."

"Tantrums?"

"Yes. They say she never let a single play that she was in run smoothly in rehearsal, ever since she got into the top line. Always had to be throwing her weight about: quarrelling with the producer, wanting her lines altered, objecting to this, that and the other person in the cast, making life hell for everyone."

"Then why," said Mr Todhunter wonderingly, "did anyone ever engage her?" It was a question that laymen have often asked before concerning the

Jean Norwood type of actress, and never has a satisfactory answer been received.

"Oh well," said Mr Budd vaguely, "she's a pull, you know; she's got a public. They had to have her." "But surely not at such a cost in time and trouble?"

"I remember," said Mr Budd, "I was with her once in *The Silver Penny,* in 1925. It was just after she'd made her name, and the public were eating her. She knew dam' well we couldn't do without her. Well, there was a kid playing the part of the maid. (You remember the show? No? It ran nearly a year.) Well, it was this kid's first West End part, and she was a bit nervous at rehearsal. Jean had it in for her for some reason or other. Well, one morning the kid gave Jean the wrong cue. Put in a line out of the second act or something when we were rehearsing the first. Jean swept-down to the front and said to old George Furness (he was producing) : 'Mr Furness, dismiss this girl and get a competent actress for the part or I'll walk out.' Well, there was no help for it. They argued with her, and the kid cried, but it was no use. The kid had to go."

"But it's outrageous," cried Mr Todhunter in great indignation.

"That's Jean though, all over," replied Mr Budd with gloomy relish. "Now poor old Alfred Gordon, who did manager for her before me . . ." Mr Budd related how Miss Norwood had made Mr Gordon's life unbearable, until the old man, faced with ruin and the prospect of never finding another job, had gassed himself in his little flat in Notting Hill Gate.

"He left a note, I happen to know, saying just what he thought of her, but they suppressed it at the inquest. That give her a jolt for a time. But it didn't last. Pretty soon she was taking hell out of us all again in the same old way."

"But why does anyone work for her?"

Mr Budd looked at his companion with a faint smile. "It's pretty plain you don't know much about the theatre, Mr Todhunter. Jobs aren't exactly easy to get, you know. Besides," added Mr Budd cynically, "anyone who can say they were in Jean Norwood's company for a couple of years has a pull. Any producer knows that someone trained by Jean will be pretty easy to handle. Besides, Jean only employs people who really can act. I'll say that for her. She's keen, and she will have the best. Though of course anyone who looks like being as good as she is doesn't last long. Well, after all," said Mr Budd frankly, "you couldn't expect her to let another girl act her off her own stage, could you? Like your friend Farroway's girl for instance."

Mr Todhunter sat up. "Felicity Farroway? She could act then?"

"You bet your life she could. Finest little natural actress I've ever seen. Wanted polishing, of course, and had to learn a bit of technique, but the stuff was right there. But Jean finished her, like she's finished dozens of others. Nobody'll dare to give her another chance now."

"Dare?" Mr Todhunter's indignation was rising again. "But surely other managers aren't *afraid* of Miss Norwood?"

Mr Budd stroked his blue jowls. "Well, I'm not so sure they're not, if you put it like that. But we're sheep in this profession, you know. Once the word gets around that Miss Dash can't really act for toffee and had to be sacked out of Jean Norword's last show for being too downright rotten, Miss Dash can go on calling on the agents for the rest of her natural, but no one's ever going to offer her a part again. And you can bet Jean did put it round, all right. And after all, the kid's got no pull."

"But why should Miss Norwood want to ruin the girl?" demanded Mr Todhunter.

"Because," replied Mr Budd succinctly, "she's a bitch, that's why. . .. Here, *boy*!"

5

So on the Sunday morning Mr Todhunter took a bus to the address in Maida Vale that Mrs Palmer had given him and in due course found himself interviewing a charming young woman with fair hair, blue eyes and a peachlike complexion, but none of the lack of character which so often goes with this combination, as if Nature, having worked pretty well skin deep, could not be bothered to go any further into the case. In this respect Felicity Farroway was as like her sister as both were unlike their father.

She received Mr Todhunter in a minute sitting room which tried hard to be modern by containing as little furniture as possible, but which was so small as to appear crowded by the minimum required for practical purposes. Having examined Mr Todhunter's invaluable card and dismissed to some retreat unspecified the rather stumpy stable companion who shared the flat with her, Miss Farroway settled Mr Todhunter and herself in the only two armchairs and prepared to be interviewed.

Mr Todhunter used the same opening which he had found so successful before, but this time he added an unfortunate tail to it.

"Miss Farroway, I am exceedingly worried about your father, and I feel sure that you must be too."

On this second occasion the result of his cunning made Mr Todhunter feel very uncomfortable; for Felicity Farroway first stared at him, then looked wildly round the room, then stared again and then burst straight into tears.

"Oh, dear me," observed Mr Todhunter, much distressed. "I didn't mean to upset you. Really, I apologise. . . I . . ."

"But don't you see?" sobbed Miss Farroway. "It's me who's responsible for the whole thing."

Mr Todhunter was so startled that he did not even notice this remarkable grammar. "You?" he said owlishly. "Responsible?"

"Yes! I introduced them."

"Oh, I see. Dear me, yes. How very unfortunate. But surely . . ."

"Yes!" repeated the girl vigorously. "I knew what she was like, and I knew Father. I ought to have been drowned for not foreseeing what would happen. Drowned!" She blew her nose unhappily into a piece of chiffon about the size of a rather small postcard.

"Oh, come," protested Mr Todhunter, feeling thoroughly guilty. "I don't think you need blame yourself, you know. I'm sure you . . ."

"You're a friend of Father's?"

"Well, yes, I—"

"You know everything of course?"

"I think so, but . . . Ah!" said Mr Todhunter cunningly. "Yes, suppose you tell me everything from *your* point of view, Miss Farroway."

"I don't know that the point of view matters much. It's the facts. And goodness knows, they're damnable enough. Well, Father came to see me at the theatre one day. Jean came into the dressing room I shared with another girl. I introduced Father. She was all over him of course; you know her smarmy way. She'd read all his books and thought they were just *too* marvellous; her favourite author; genius; when would he do her the honour of lunching with her? You know, all the usual gush. And Father simply lapped it up. He's very simple, you know. He really believes what people say to him.

"And the next thing was that I heard from Mother, very worried because Father was coming up to London from Yorkshire more and more often and she had an idea that he was seeing a good deal too much of Jean; did I know anything about it? Well, I thought that was a bit funny, because I hadn't seen Father at all. I was sure he hadn't been to the theatre, at any rate; so I said that what he had told her about the visits being on business was probably true. And the week after that he came up and never went back—nearly a year ago. And he hasn't been back since."

"But I understand he hasn't formally left your mother?"

"Formally, no. But practically, he has. I simply can't make it out. Jean's got her hooks into him, of course, but I should never have thought Father could have fallen with quite such a thud. The rest of us simply don't exist for him any more."

"Your sister—Mrs Palmer—thinks he is hardly responsible for his actions over the affair."

"Oh, you know Viola? Yes, temporary insanity, I suppose. But it's pretty beastly to watch. I mean, when it's your own father."

"Indeed yes." Mr Todhunter wondered whether his companion knew anything about recent developments. He put out a feeler. "But I understand the lady is showing signs now of other intentions?"

"You mean she's chucking him? Well, thank goodness for that. I only wonder she hasn't before. She must have sucked him pretty well dry by now. Who's the new victim?"

"Oh well," hedged Mr Todhunter, regretting his rashness. "I don't know, really. . . ."

Mr Todhunter was not a good dissembler. Within two minutes the information had been dragged out of him.

The girl was really shocked. Her chest rose and fell as she breathed quickly and shallowly; her eyes sparkled, more with anger than tears.

"Mr Todhunter, something—something must be done!"

"I agree," said Mr Todhunter earnestly. "I do indeed."

"That woman must have wrecked dozens of lives in her time. She's wrecked my career, I expect you've heard."

"Well, yes, I. . ."

"I really can act, you know," said the girl with complete simplicity. "But of course she had to get rid of me, once she'd got Father in tow. Anyhow that doesn't matter. The point is, she's not going to be allowed to wreck Viola's life. Vincent's a bit of an ass anyway, and I really believe that woman could get round the devil himself."

"Yes," said Mr Todhunter. "But how do you propose to stop it?"

"I don't know. But I will. You see if I don't. Mr. Todhunter, things are much worse than I let out to you just now. You see, I didn't know how much you knew. Mother's even having to sell the house and furniture because she can't get a penny out of Father. And she won't take him to court. I advised her to. I thought just the threat might bring him to his senses. But you know what Mother is."

"No—er—as a matter of fact I haven't that pleasure."

"Oh well, she's all stiff and proud and that sort of thing. She'd far sooner starve to death, in a thoroughly ladylike way, then do anything so vulgar as haul Father into any sort of court, even the divorce one. And of course he's trading on it. In a way, I mean, because, poor darling of an idiot that he is, he doesn't know what he *is* doing. I tried to get Mother to appeal to him on the grounds of Faith, but she won't even do that."

"Faith?" repeated Mr Todhunter, puzzled.

Miss Farroway seemed surprised. "Yes, you know. Faith. Oh, I see. You don't know. Well, Faith's my small sister. Thirteen. And Mother told me about a couple of months ago that our charming cook got drunk one day and blurted out to Faith the whole story. It's been a bit of a shock to all of us, but just fancy what it must have been to a sensitive child of thirteen. Mother could hardly get her to go to school the next day, she was so ashamed. And of course she's brooding over it and getting quite ill, Mother says. It's damnable, Mr Todhunter—damnable! And all because of that damned woman's vanity and greed."

Mr Todhunter was old fashioned enough still to feel mildly shocked at hearing oaths on the lips of pretty girls, but if ever there was an occasion on which such a thing was justified, it was this one.

"Dear me! Tut, tut!" he muttered inadequately. "Yes indeed. Dear me, no. I had no idea things were so bad. And your career too . . ."

"Oh, the career," said the girl impatiently. "Yes, that's annoying enough, but no real importance. What *is* maddening about that is the fact that as an actress I could have been earning just three times what I'm getting as a shop assistant, and so could have sent Mother about ten times what I'm able to send her now."

"Yes, that is so. Of course. Dear me, a shop assistant . . . I—er—understand it's very tiring work?" said Mr Todhunter vaguely. "Standing behind a counter. . ."

"Oh well," smiled the girl, "I don't exactly have to do that. I'm one of those superior young ladies in black frocks who lurk languidly in our smaller dress shops; only we don't call them 'dress shops' of course, we call them 'modistes.' Like this." She jumped up and gave an imitation of one of the young ladies in question dealing with a plump matron from the provinces, so humorously lifelike that Mr Todhunter, who had never been in a modiste's in his life, instantly felt that he knew all about them.

"Why," he exclaimed, "upon my word, you're as good as Ruth Draper." For Mr Todhunter, who went to see Miss Draper every time she was in London, this was almost extravagant praise.

Laughing a little, the girl sat down. "Oh no; Ruth Draper's unique. Though it's sweet of you to say so."

"Anyhow, you can certainly act," affirmed Mr Todhunter.

"Oh yes," agreed Felicity Farroway somewhat ruefully. "I can act, all right. And a fat lot of use that is to me—and to Mother."

"Yes," said Mr Todhunter, a little embarrassed. "And—er—that reminds me. You must allow . . . old friend of your father's . . . haven't pleasure of her acquaintance, but would esteem it a privilege . . . er . . . yes . . ." Subsiding into incoherence, Mr Todhunter drew out his chequebook and fountain pen and, blushing till his ears glowed, wrote out a cheque for fifty pounds.

"*Oh!*" gasped the girl, when Mr Todhunter handed it to her with a mumbled request that she send it on to her mother. "Oh, you *angel*! You sweet lamb! You perfect *pet*!" And, jumping out of her chair, she threw her lovely arms round Mr Todhunter's stringy neck and kissed him with the utmost fervour.

"Hey! Really! Well, dear me!" cackled Mr Todhunter in high glee.

Soon afterwards he refused with regret a most pressing invitation to stay to lunch (being his own housekeeper, he knew the difficulties of an unexpected guest when the shops are closed) and took his leave, not a little pleased with himself and not a little perturbed too.

CHAPTER VI

It must be admitted that during these days Mr Todhunter was thoroughly enjoying himself.

He was genuinely and quite altruistically worried about the Farraway situation, and the thought of that unhappy child in Yorkshire distressed him; but nevertheless the part he was playing gave him a good deal of pleasure. For one thing, it made him feel important. Mr Todhunter could not remember ever having been made to feel important before, and the sensation was by no means unpleasant. All these people—Viola Palmer, charming Felicity Farraway, even to some extent the gloomy Mr Budd—had all looked towards Mr Todhunter as though he could really *do* something. Mr Todhunter knew that in a mild and perhaps unconscious way he had encouraged this view. The knowledge made him feel slightly guilty but in no way spoilt his pleasure.

For if (he thought) I really were going to do something, it would no doubt turn out all wrong and leave everyone much worse off than before. How admirable therefore to savour the situation, even to reap the kudos, and yet to do no one any harm.

Such reflections made Mr Todhunter feel extremely detached and superior and still were able to leave him with the sneaking conviction that he could have done something very helpful had he liked. But of course he did not like. That had all been decided long ago. Much better to stand outside all these foolish imbroglios. A philosophic detachment combined with a sympathetic interest; that was the only correct attitude for a man in his position.

It was therefore still with the outlook of a professor of entomology studying an ant heap, and with no intention at all of becoming an ant himself and burdening himself with huge eggs to be carried about wildly for no apparent purpose, that Mr Todhunter presented himself at the Norwood-cum-Farraway flat on Tuesday He was not exactly looking forward to the meeting, for Miss Jean Norwood was the kind of person who made him feel as if his skin were crinkling all down his back, but he anticipated a certain amount of sardonic amusement in observing her efforts to enslave him. That an attempt would be made to enslave him Mr Todhunter was convinced. The technique was apparently the same as had already been employed in Farraway's case. Whether he was going to pretend to be enslaved or not Mr Todhunter was not certain, though he fancied that the role would be rather too difficult for him to sustain; it all depended how much his skin crinkled. But that he was going basely to deceive the lady and sustain the fiction of his great wealth Mr Todhunter was determined. He thought she deserved that at least.

He therefore arrived for lunch, malignantly looking his very worst (and that was saying a good deal), in the same misshapen old suit that Miss Norwood had wrinkled her pretty nose at before, wearing a hat so dilapidated and ancient that even a real professor might have realised that something was a trifle wrong with it, and with the same identical egg stain (unaccountably not yet removed) still decorating his waistcoat. Wealthy eccentricity was Mr Todhunter's theme, and he cackled maliciously to himself as he pressed the bell button and prepared to act the part as he conceived it.

2

Mr Todhunter had to admit afterwards that, whatever her shortcomings in other respects, Miss Norwood knew how to order a lunch. (It did not occur to him that Miss Norwood might never have ordered it at all but left everything to her thoroughly competent and extremely expensive cook.) The trouble was that, like the cocktails which preceded it, practically everything had to be refused by such a conscientious invalid as Mr Todhunter. When at last his hostess asked him in despair what he would really like, Mr Todhunter asked modestly whether he might be accommodated with a glass of milk and a rusk. That this was not a promising basis for attempted enslavement both hostess and guest could not but feel.

If, however, Mr Todhunter had conceived any highly coloured visions of an exiguously clad Miss Norwood languishing at him from a leopard-skin rug, he was disappointed. Nothing could have exceeded the decorum with which the proceedings after lunch were conducted. Miss Norwood, sipping her coffee, entertained her guest with a really intelligent commentary on contemporary theatrical matters; and Mr Todhunter, regretting that he had had to refuse coffee which smelt as good as this did, listened happily. To his surprise, he found himself quite at his ease. To his greater surprise, he found Miss Norwood quite a different person from the idea he had formed of her on his first visit. Not a single allusion was made to his supposed riches; gone were all the small coquetries and affectations which had jarred on him so when Farroway was present; here, one would have said, was a perfectly simple, charming and intelligent woman who was enjoying his company and perhaps might be hoping that he was enjoying hers. Mr Todhunter's caution, which had lasted all through lunch, slithered, slipped and melted. He relaxed; he unbent; he grew genial.

She *is* charming, he thought. Those people were wrong. This is no devil, but as natural and pleasant a lady as ever I've met. With a little time I might even fall in love with her myself.

He cackled.

"What are you laughing at, Mr Todhunter?" politely enquired his hostess.

"I was thinking that with a little time I might fall in love with you myself," replied Mr Todhunter.

The lady smiled. "Don't do that. It would be such a bore for me. I should never fall in love with you, and you can't imagine how deadly boring it is for a woman to have a man in love with her when she can't feel that way about him."

"It must be indeed," agreed Mr Todhunter earnestly.

Miss Norwood lifted her arm in the air and allowed the sleeve to fall back from it. She contemplated the slender white column with an absent air.

"Men are so odd when they're in love," she reflected. "They seem to think that the very act of being in love gives them certain proprietary rights; certainly the right to be jealous. At least they don't actually think it, because they can't think at all when they're in that state, poor dears."

"Ha, ha," cackled Mr Todhunter. "No, I suppose they can't. Well, I've never been in that state myself, I'm glad to say."

"You've never been in love, Mr Todhunter?"

"No, never."

Miss Norwood clapped her elegant hands. "But this is marvelous! I do believe you're the person I've been looking for—oh, I don't know how long. And I'd quite given up hope of ever finding him. Oh, do say it's true, Mr Todhunter."

"What's true?" asked Mr Todhunter affably.

"Why, that you and I can be just simple, ordinary *friends,* without any boring complications. Will you be friends with me, Mr Todhunter?"

"I sincerely hope I may be," Mr Todhunter replied with something like fervour.

"Good! Then that's settled. Now, what shall we do to celebrate? I can give you a box for *Fallen Petals* of course, and I shall. But that's so ordinary. Oh, I know! Let's make a blind promise, shall we? We'll each ask the other for a boon and promise to grant it, whatever it is. There, I call that a real thrill. Will you agree, if I do?"

"Do you mean, no reservations of any kind?" asked Mr Todhunter, his caution popping up its head again.

"Absolutely none. Have you the courage? I have." Miss Norwood really seemed quite excited. She leaned forward in her chair, her enormous eyes (which Mr Todhunter remembered with shame that he had once thought naked and indecent) alight with a childlike pleasure. "Have you, Mr Todhunter?" she repeated.

Mr Todhunter's caution made a final grab for the side, lost its hold and disappeared under the water.

"Yes," he said with a smile which on anyone else he would have considered just fatuous. Mr. Todhunter really was behaving very foolishly.

"Oh, how sporting of you! Very well, that's a bargain. We've promised, remember. Now, you ask me first."

"No, no," cackled Mr Todhunter inanely. "Ladies first. You ask me."

"Very well." The lady closed her lustrous eyes, placed the tips of her encarmined fingers together and considered. "Now, what shall it be? My first real friend. . . what shall I ask him?"

Suddenly caution, which Mr Todhunter had thought safely submerged, popped up an unexpected head and addressed him in blunt terms. "You adjectival fool, don't you see she's been playing a game with you? She's going to ask for a diamond necklace or something—and you, poor noodle, have undertaken to give it her. Didn't everyone tell you what she was?"

Horribly alarmed, Mr Todhunter clutched at the arms of his chair and wondered desperately how he could save the situation.

The lady opened her eyes and smiled at him. "I've decided."

Mr Todhunter gulped. "Yes?" he asked shakily.

"I ask you to dedicate your next book to me in these words, 'To my friend, Jean Norwood.'"

"Oh!" Mr Todhunter clutched at his handkerchief and wiped his forehead. Relief, not the agony which went before, had bespangled it with moisture. "Yes, certainly. Very glad indeed . . . great honour . . ." Mr Todhunter had once published, at his own expense, a critical study of the work of an unknown eighteenth-century diarist, whom he had acclaimed as the equal of Evelyn and Pepys. The book had sold forty-seven copies and the diarist was still unknown. There was no intention in Mr Todhunter's mind of ever publishing another, but he saw no need to tell Miss Norwood that.

"Now you!" Miss Norwood laughed delightedly. "Whatever it is, I'll grant it, you know. That's rather brave, I think—for a woman. But I always flatter myself I can judge character. Now, what is it to be?"

A sudden idea jumped into Mr Todhunter's mind. Without stopping to think, he said:

"Send Farroway back to his wife in Yorkshire."

Miss Norwood stared at him, her eyes widening till Mr Todhunter could hardly believe that any eyes could be so enormous. Then she laughed, simply and naturally.

"But my dear man, that's just what I've been trying to do for the last six months. I can't tell you how much I wish he'd do it. But he simply won't go."

"He'll do anything you tell him," said Mr Todhunter mulishly. "And you promised. Send him."

"I'll send him," laughed Miss Norwood lightly. "I promise you that. But I can't promise that he'll go."

"You can make him if you try. I ask you to make sure he goes."

Miss Norwood's fine eyebrows lifted for a second, then dropped. She smiled—a smile different from all the others that Mr Todhunter had seen. It was, as a matter of fact, a provocative, pleased, quietly triumphant, faintly deriding smile, but Mr Todhunter recognised none of that.

"Mr Todhunter," said Miss Norwood softly, "just why are you so anxious that Nicholas should retire back to the north? Tell me, between friends."

"Oh, come," protested Mr Todhunter. "Don't tell me you can't see that for yourself."

"Perhaps I can," murmured Miss Norwood, and her smile became a little intensified.

"Then you'll make him go?" asked Mr Todhunter earnestly.

"He shall go. I promise you," replied Miss Norwood with an earnestness matching Mr Todhunter's own.

"Thank you," said Mr Todhunter simply.

He beamed in happy relief upon his hostess. Mr Todhunter had quite decided now that Miss Norwood was a thoroughly maligned woman. It was the penalty, he supposed, of greatness. Jealousy, no doubt, and all that sort of thing. Anyone who really knew her could see at once what a sweet nature she had.

"But I think," remarked the maligned woman with an attractively wicked little laugh, "that you rather threw your opportunity away, Mr. Todhunter, didn't you? And it's not the sort of opportunity that occurs twice. I was quite in your hands, you know—well, I mean, I might have been."

"But that would hardly have been fair," replied Mr Todhunter roguishly.

Miss Norwood tilted her charming head. "Isn't all fair in war and—other things?"

Mr Todhunter cackled happily and felt the very devil of a fellow. For the first time in six weeks he had completely forgotten his aneurism.

Mr Todhunter always had thought the best of people.

3

It was past three o'clock when Mr Todhunter got up to leave, and he did so then with reluctance.

"It has been delightful, Miss Norwood," he said, shaking his hostess's hand. "I can't recall when I enjoyed a luncheon more."

"Oh, come," smiled the lady. "To my friends I'm Jean. 'Miss Norwood' sounds just too grim for words."

"And my name is Lawrence," crowed Mr Todhunter, apparently unaware that his hand was being held.

They parted with assurances of a further meeting in the very near future.

It was only as he was going down the stairs that Mr Todhunter recalled the delusion of which his hostess had been the victim. Something had been said about Miss Norwood visiting him next, in Richmond. She would expect a palace, and she would find—well, not a hovel but a semidetached Victorian house of quite revolting aspect. It was not fair to let her remain under the impression that he was a rich man. Not that it would make any difference to so generous a nature, of course, but . . . well, one simply did not deceive one's friends.

Mr Todhunter turned and sought the electric lift again.

It is a matter for question whether Miss Norwood's life might have been saved had Mr Todhunter been not quite so punctilious. Had he written his information, for instance, or even telephoned it, Miss Norwood would just have dropped him quietly, Nicholas Farroway would probably have returned in any case to the north, for, having come to the end of his cash, he was of little practical use and therefore interest to anyone in London, and Mr Todhunter would duly have died at the appointed time of his aneurism. But all this simple arrangement was shattered by Mr Todhunter's regard for the requirements of friendship.

For the door of Miss Norwood's flat stood just a little ajar when Mr Todhunter reached it. In point of fact the lock was defective and should have been put right that morning, and the locksmith, in failing to keep his promise to do so, had driven a screw into Miss Norwood's coffin as surely as if he had wielded the screwdriver with his own hands. Mr Todhunter was therefore able to hear only too clearly certain observations which Miss Norwood, in a voice very different from that in which she had addressed him, was calling through the open door of her bedroom to the maid, Marie, in the sitting room.

"Marie, for God's sake get me a glass of brandy, and quick. This off-stage acting's more exhausting than the real thing."

"Yes, madam." The maid's voice came pertly. "I thought you'd taken on a bit of a job this time, madam."

"What the hell do you mean by that?"

"Oh, nothing, madam. I beg your pardon."

"Get me that brandy."

"Very good, madam."

Mr Todhunter's hand, already raised to the bell push, dropped back to his side. He had not meant to listen, but there it was. He hesitated whether to ring or not.

Miss Norwood's voice came again.

"Oh, and Marie!"

"Yes, madam?"

"I'm not at home to Mr Farroway any longer, thank God! At least, not in Richmond. I suppose I'll have to be here for a bit, but . . ."

"Then we shan't be giving this place up after all, madam?"

"I think not, Marie. I think not." Even to Mr Todhunter's inexperienced ears Miss Norwood's voice sounded almost indecently complacent.

"I thought you were getting him nice and interested, madam. And I should think he's the sort that'd stump up the rent and not even ask for a latchkey, isn't he?"

"Damn you, Marie, who do you think you're talking to?" Miss Norwood's voice was suddenly shrill with rage. "Don't you know your place yet? I'll have to teach you a lesson one of these days, my girl. I pay you to wait on me, not to try to gossip about my private affairs."

"I beg your pardon, madam, I'm sure." Marie's voice held the perfunctory tone of one used to making a stereotyped apology.

Mr Todhunter turned away. He was a man of little experience but he was nobody's fool. At the present moment, too, he was in a temper so vile that it was touch and go whether his aneurism could stand the strain.

4

What upset Mr Todhunter as much as anything was the vulgarity of the little scene he had just overheard. Mr Todhunter was a bit of a snob. His snobbery, however, was not of the negative kind which consists merely of refusing to know persons of a lower social stratum than one's own. He believed that class, as well as the nobility, has its obligations; and one of the attributes of a "lady" was an inability to confide in her maids. Mr Todhunter had mistaken Miss Norwood for a lady, and it upset him to find out how far he had been deceived. So curiously constituted was Mr Todhunter that this really upset him more than the revelation that Miss Norwood considered him enslaved already by her charms and was confidently expecting to shift onto him from Farroway the responsibility for the rent of her palatial flat.

Meditating wickedly upon these matters in the safe anchorage of his library once more, Mr Todhunter found it simple enough to decide to have no more to do with Miss Norwood, with Farroway or with any of the participants in this sordid tragi-comedy; but there were some matters upon which he still found himself puzzled. Why, for instance, did Miss Norwood require anyone to pay her rents for her? As an actress-manager, with long run after long run to her credit and never a failure, was she not making quite enough money to pay her own rents? And was her behaviour not quite at variance with every canon of the legitimate stage? It was indeed more like the traditional behaviour of the musical-comedy chorus girl than the great and dignified figures of the drama proper.

From this point it was only a step to wonder if it were possible that he could be on the wrong lines altogether, so that by the time his tea arrived (at fifteen minutes past four to the second) Mr Todhunter was actually wondering whether he had really heard what he had heard and if so whether he had not read all kinds of horrible meanings into what might have been a perfectly innocent conversation. It was all very bewildering.

At this point, and while actually pouring out his second cup of tea, Mr Todhunter remembered Joseph Pleydell, the dramatic critic of the *London Review,* who was reputed not only to be the best judge of a play and a performance of acting in London, but to know more about stage folks than any man living. So great was Mr Todhunter's relief that he actually jumped up with his cup of tea only half poured, rang up Pleydell that instant on the telephone and for the first time in his life proffered an invitation for dinner that same evening without at least twenty minutes anxious consultation with Mrs Greenhill first upon ways and means. It was perhaps fortunate that Mr Pleydell, having to attend a first night as usual (a possibility which Mr Todhunter had quite overlooked) , was unable to come. Upon Mr Todhunter's urgent pleading, however, it was discovered that Pleydell lived in Putney, only half a mile from Mr Todhunter's house, and would therefore come along for a half-hour's chat after his play.

Mr Todhunter had made a lucky choice. At the interview which followed at around midnight that evening he learned all he wanted to know.

Jean Norwood, explained Mr Pleydell in reply to his host's questioning, was a curious and interesting type. She combined an inordinate avarice and greed in money matters with an almost morbid craving for public admiration. She had some small artistic feeling, but what she lacked here she more than made up in flair; for Jean Norwood was to the theatre what a certain type of popular novelist is to literature.

"Mediocrity passionately called to mediocrity, it's been defined," observed Mr Pleydell drily, "and it certainly pays. Jean Norwood is the mediocre mind in excelsis. She can feel precisely what the suburbs want in a play, and she can act in it precisely as they want her to. You know it's her boast that she's never had a failure."

"Then she must be a very wealthy woman?" suggested Mr Todhunter.
"No."

"But she must have made a great deal of money?"

"Oh yes."

"She's extravagant, then?"

"On the contrary, I told you, she's exceedingly mean. She'll never pay herself for anything that she can get some man to buy for her; and she's quite unscrupulous as to how she'll induce him to do so."

"Dear, dear," lamented Mr Todhunter. "But I don't understand."

Mr. Pleydell took a small sip of whiskey and soda and stroked his neat little pointed beard.

"That is precisely where the interest lies. Without it Jean Norwood would be a commonplace character; as it is, she is possibly unique, certainly on the English stage. The key to her complexity is her passion for the public's applause. To ensure that she stints her private expenditure to a remarkable degree—and, frankly, is willing to be the kept woman of any man who is both wealthy and discreet, for of course her public must not know anything about that. I really believe she's persuaded herself that she is sacrificing herself in this way to the public."

"But how? I'm afraid I still don't understand."

"Why, she uses very little of the money she makes in her theatre for private living; only the smallest sum necessary to keep up a certain position and dress her part. Out of her profits she first sets aside a sum to finance her next production, for she always puts on her own plays and up to a point she's a very sound businesswoman. The rest goes back onto the stage. That is to say, she throws away nearly all the money she makes—and there's a very great deal of it—in keeping her plays on long after they've ceased to earn money. To do that she'll sacrifice anything. I'm sure she'd live on bread and water if necessary."

"But why?" asked Mr Todhunter, bewildered.

"Because she can't bear to have anything approaching—well, not a failure because she never has that, but even anything that can't be called a stupendous success. Haven't you noticed that the Jean Norwood runs are becoming longer and longer? All records broken time and time again, and each record has to be broken all over again next time. It's fantastic. And as I say, she'll stick at absolutely nothing to break these records. Of course the press love it, and the public cheer the roof off each time a record's broken. It's become quite a game at the Sovereign. That's what she lives for: the public's cheers."

"How very odd," commented Mr Todhunter.

"Very odd. I shouldn't think there's ever been another instance of an actress in a really big position behaving off the stage like a professional courtesan, but that's what she does—and is. Though I give her the credit for having genuinely persuaded herself that her position is the same as that of the old temple prostitute and that she is serving the God of Art as devoutly as you like. But of course a woman like that could persuade herself of anything."

"Then what is your private opinion of her as a person?" asked Mr Todhunter with interest.

"A poisonous bitch," replied Mr Pleydell succinctly. "And a disgrace to a great profession," he added more temperately.

"Dear me. Is she," ventured Mr Todhunter, for he was about to use a word which has fallen into considerable disrepair, "is she a lady?"

"Neither by instinct nor birth, Her father was, I believe, a small tradesman in Balham; her mother had been in service. Both admirable people and still alive. But they never see their daughter nowadays; unless, of course, they like to pay for a ticket to the pit, Jean disowned 'em long ago, bless her. I believe she's invented a colonel in the guards, killed at Mons, and a poor but proud descendant of one of the earlier English reigning families (I'm not sure it isn't a Plantagenet) to take their places. Ah well, that's how things are."

"Has she," asked Mr Todhunter, "a single redeeming quality?"

"Well, no one's bad all through, you know, but I should think Jean comes as near it as anyone."

"Would you say," pursued Mr Todhunter, "that she does a great deal of harm to a great many people?"

"Undoubtedly I would. She does. But on the other hand she does a great deal of good. I mean, she provides a great many worthy people with considerable and wholesome pleasure."

"But anyone could do that."

"Oh no. A Jean Norwood is just as rare as an Ethel M. Dell—and, in her way, just as great a genius."

"Still," demanded Mr Todhunter, lured on by a morbid fascination, "would you say that on balance it would be a great deal better if she were dead?"

"Oh, a great deal," concurred Mr Pleydell without hesitation.

Mr Todhunter sipped his barley water.

5

"Well, *I*'m not going to kill the woman," decided Mr Todhunter as he reached out a bony arm towards the bedside lamp and snapped off the switch. "All that nonsense came to an end weeks ago, I'm exceedingly glad to say." And, having quite made up his mind on that point, Mr Todhunter fell tranquilly asleep.

PART II

Transpontine

THE MURDER IN
THE OLD BARN

CHAPTER VII

It amused Mr Todhunter very much to reflect upon the way in which he had been vamped. His eyes were open now, and he saw just how it had been done. He also saw, not without shame, how easily and thoroughly he had fallen into the trap, with all the blithe confidence of a rabbit walking into a snare. The net had been spread in his sight, and he had positively rushed to occupy a position fairly and squarely in the middle of it. If he had not happened, just by the merest chance pricking of a punctilious conscience, to turn back into the lift. . .

Mr Todhunter was annoyed with himself. He was still more annoyed with Miss Jean Norwood. But of course he was going to do nothing about that.

It is probable that Mr Todhunter never would have done anything had it not been for a telephone call he received shortly after his lunch with Miss Norwood. It was from Farroway's younger daughter, Felicity.

"Mr Todhunter," she began at once in tones of obvious agitation, "can you come up to my flat this evening? Mother's come up to London, and . . . oh, I can't explain on the telephone, but I'm really terribly worried. I've no possible excuse for bothering you with our troubles, except that I've simply no one else to consult. Could you possibly come?"

"My dear girl, of course I'll come," responded Mr Todhunter stoutly.

At a quarter past eight he summoned a taxi and caused himself to be driven, reckless of expense, to Maida Vale.

Felicity Farroway was not alone. With her was a tall, dignified lady with iron-grey hair and calm eyes. Mr Todhunter recognised her type of face at once. It was of the kind which had often sat with him upon the committees to examine infant welfare, provide milk for indigent school children and organise crèches, to which Mr Todhunter's sense of public duty reluctantly drove him.

Felicity introduced the lady as her mother. Mrs Farroway briefly apologised for bothering him and in a few quiet words thanked him for his cheque, out of the proceeds of which she had bought her ticket for London. Much embarrassed, Mr Todhunter obeyed an invitation to sit down and massaged his sharp knees. He felt that he was present on false pretences, and his conscience was again worried.

"Mother's come up to see to things for herself," Felicity Farroway explained somewhat crudely.

The elder woman nodded. "Yes. So long as it was a question of myself only

I did not care to interfere. I believe in the right of every individual to choose his own course of action, provided only that he does no actual harm to others; and so I was ready to let Nicholas go his own way. But Felicity has passed on to me the information you gave her about Vincent, Mr Todhunter, having first, I may say, had it fully confirmed by Viola, and I felt that I could stand by no longer. This Miss Norwood must not be allowed to wreck Viola's life."

Felicity nodded vigorously. "It's damnable. She ought to be shot. Viola's a pet."

Mrs Farroway smiled faintly at her daughter's violence.

"Felicity is full of wild schemes for having the woman arrested on some trumped-up charge, and—"

"Framed, Mother. It'd be quite easy. I bet she sails pretty near the wind as it is. Father may not have sold all your jewelry. We could easily find out if he gave anything to her, and then you could take out a summons against her for theft. Or we could plant (that's what they call it) a ring or something among her things and then swear she'd stolen it. . . . We *could*!" added the girl passionately.

Mrs Farroway smiled again, at Mr Todhunter. "I think we'd better stick to less melodramatic methods. Now, Mr Todhunter, you're a friend of Nicholas's, but you can take a more or less detached view of this regrettable business. I wonder if you can suggest anything."

Mother and daughter looked hopefully at their guest.

Mr Todhunter wriggled. He could suggest nothing; his mind was completely empty.

"I don't know," he began feebly. "Your husband seems to be quite obsessed, Mrs Farroway, if I am to speak frankly. I—I must say that I can't see anything short of—um!—rather drastic measures proving effective."

"I said so," Felicity cried.

"I'm afraid that is so," agreed Mrs Farroway calmly, "though I think we must stop short of 'framing'. But what measures? Measures on what lines? I'm afraid I know so little about this kind of situation or how to deal with it. Our life has been very quiet, in spite of Nicholas's reputation. It's a shame to drag you in like this, Mr Todhunter, but there literally is no one else. And you have probably heard," added Mrs Farroway with a rueful smile, "that a mother will sacrifice anyone to protect her children. I'm afraid it seems to be true, so far as you're concerned."

Mr Todhunter protested that he was only too anxious and eager to be sacrificed and did his utmost to produce a suggestion of some value. But in a matter of this kind Mr Todhunter was even more helpless than Mrs Farroway; and though a great deal of talk ensued during the next two hours, the only concrete conclusion was that Mrs Farroway had better not have a talk with her husband herself in case the interview only made him still more obstinate, or appeal to him personally in any way. And the corollary to that appeared to be that Mr Todhunter had better do so instead; for it was obvious to all three, including Felicity herself, that for Felicity to do so in her present mood would be as near disaster as made no matter.

Mr Todhunter therefore promised to do his best to probe in order to find out whether there was any weak spot in Farroway's feelings or any circumstances upon which an attack might be directed, and took his leave, feeling that he had been rather worse than useless.

This night he did not sleep so well. An exceedingly disturbing thought had occurred to him during his drive home. Mrs Farroway had said that a mother would stick at nothing in defence of her children. Mr Todhunter could not fail to remember the last occasion on which somebody had stuck at nothing. Was it possible that, just as young Bennett might have been already meditating murder during Mr Todhunter's last interview with him, the same intention had been forming behind Mrs Farroway's placid brow? Mr Todhunter could not rid his mind of the possibility, and it perturbed him exceedingly. For what, this time, was he going to do about it?

2

Mr Todhunter, having considered the matter with some care, decided that it would be useful to keep up his pose with Farroway of a wealthy dilettante; and if that was to be done, Farroway could not be asked to the modest home in Richmond. Nor did Mr Todhunter wish to conduct his promised interview again in a restaurant, where the clatter and bustle made it difficult for him to keep his thoughts fixed. Having therefore deliberated a little further, he rang up Farroway at the number which had been given him and, rather to his surprise finding Farroway at home, asked if he might call round in the morning on a matter of business. Farroway with undisguised eagerness pressed him to do so.

Somewhat shaken, for duplicity was new to him and therefore a strain, Mr Todhunter hung up the receiver, wiped his clammy brow and turned away to think up a tolerably convincing excuse for the call.

The address which Farroway had given him on the telephone proved the next morning to be that of a modest, very modest pair of rooms on a landing in a big gloomy house off the Bayswater Road; not even a flatlet, for it had no front door of its own. Marveling slightly, Mr Todhunter followed his host into a sitting room quite obviously furnished by the house owner and not by its present occupant.

Indeed Farroway seemed impelled to apologise for these dingy surroundings, for with an apologetic smile he remarked as he closed the door:

"Not much of a place, I'm afraid, but I find it convenient, you know."

"Oh yes. You're collecting the atmosphere for a novel, no doubt," replied Mr Todhunter politely.

"Well, in a way perhaps . . . I don't know. Yes. Er—sit down, Todhunter. Well now, what's the business?"

Mr Todhunter did not answer this question. Instead he decided to be tactless and said:

"I quite thought, you know, that the other flat Miss Norwood's—was really yours."

Farroway blushed. "Well, it is really. That is, I've lent it to Jean. It's useful for her to have a pied-à-terre in the West End where she can rest after matinees and so on. But yes, you're quite right; it is actually my flat. I—er—reserve a room there for myself, you know, but of course I don't occupy it much. Jean has a reputation to keep up, and it's astonishing how soon scandal gets round about an actress, even when there's nothing in it. . . . Nothing," added Farroway a little defiantly, "at all."

"Yes, yes, of course," soothed Mr Todhunter. The other's somewhat redundant, not to say feverish, explanations interested him. He wondered whether Miss Norwood really had kept her word, so lightly given, and denied to the unfortunate Farroway the use of his reserved room. "Have you seen Miss Norwood lately?" he asked blandly.

"Jean?" Farroway looked a little discomposed and glanced in a helpless kind of way round the room. "Oh yes. At least, not for a day or two. I've been rather busy, you know. Er—you lunched, there the other day, didn't you? How was she? Quite fit and all that? She's terribly delicate, you know. Her work is a great strain to her. I wonder sometimes that she's able to keep it up."

Mr Todhunter, repressing a wish to beat his host over the head with some blunt instrument, replied that when he saw her last Miss Norwood appeared perfectly fit and bearing up remarkably under the strain. He then prepared to burst his little bombshell; for, having spent a couple of hours in steady deliberation on the point, Mr Todhunter had at last made up his mind that a bombshell was after all the most effective weapon with which to open his attack.

"I saw your wife yesterday too," he said as casually as possible. "She seemed to be bearing up equally well, if I may say so."

There was no doubt of the bombshell's effect. Farroway went quite white.

"My w-wife?" he stammered.

Mr Todhunter suddenly felt that he had complete command of the situation. Farroway's nervousness had given him confidence. He marched straight forward without disguise or subterfuge.

"Yes. And that's the business I've come to see you about, Farroway. I am the bearer of an olive branch from your wife. She wants you to go back home with her and finish this wretched business once and for all; and I think you can rely on her to make no trouble if you do. She seems to me a very fine woman, and you've treated her abominably."

There was a long silence after Mr Todhunter had spoken. Farroway, who had looked for a moment almost dazed, slowly pulled out his case and lit a cigarette. Then he leaned back in his chair and seemed to brood. Mr Todhunter discreetly examined an engraving of a stag with a little girl caressing one of its horns which hung on the wall opposite him, and distracted himself by trying to guess what its title could be.

At last Farroway said in a dreary voice:

"You probably think I'm a cad, Todhunter?"

"I do," agreed Mr Todhunter, who had an unfortunate passion for the truth and could rarely refrain from speaking it.

Farroway nodded. "Yes. Almost everyone would. And yet . . . oh, I don't know, and I'm not excusing myself, but to judge an action one must know it inside out—know its volume, so to speak. You can only see the surface of this case. You ought not to draw conclusions until you can see it in the round."

Mr Todhunter, a little surprised, took refuge in a platitude. "There are always two sides to a question, if that's what you mean."

"It is, in a way. Look here, I'm going to tell you all about it. It'll be a relief for one thing. Self-analysis is dull work unless you can discuss your conclusions with another person. And secondly, if you're really the bearer of an official olive branch, I think you ought to know."

He reached mechanically for a box of matches and then, noticing that his cigarette was still burning, put it down again.

"First, let me say that Grace (my wife) has been splendid. Really magnificent. I don't think she actually understood the business from my point of view, but she's acted as if she had. Grace," added Farroway wistfully, "always has been an exceptionally fine woman." He paused. "Jean, on the other hand, is a common little bitch, as no doubt you've realised for yourself."

Mr Todhunter was startled. Farroway had spoken without emotion, in a dull, flat tone, and his words had been the last that Mr Todhunter had expected to hear.

Farroway smiled. "I see you have. You needn't mind agreeing with me. I've known exactly what Jean is for a long time now. Infatuation doesn't make you blind, as the popular novelists of my type pretend. The extraordinary thing is that it persists after one's eyes are wide open.

"Well, this is how the whole damned thing began.

"I was in London on business, about a year ago, and I called, quite casually, at the Princess to pick up Felicity one evening after the show. I thought I'd give her supper. Well, Jean happened to come into the dressing room just by chance, and Felicity introduced us. Rather pleasantly ironical, wasn't it? Daughter introduces father to his future mistress. That sort of thing doesn't tickle you? Oh, I always had an eye for irony. The trouble was, I could use it so seldom. The popular public doesn't care for irony, you know.

"Well, we chatted a little, and then I left with Felicity. Jean, I must honestly say, had made no impression on me. I realised that she was a striking woman, but I had seen other women of her type before and on the whole it didn't appeal to me. So I forgot all about her.

"Then, a fortnight later, I called at the Princess again, this time in the afternoon, after a rehearsal. Felicity, however, had left already, and instead I saw Jean. She was very amiable. Talked about my books and all that kind of thing. And not vaguely. She really had read 'em. I was flattered naturally. So when she asked if I wouldn't go round to her flat in Brunton Street (yes, she had a flat in Brunton Street then) and have a cocktail, of course I said I'd be delighted. I was delighted too. I stayed an hour or so, and we made friends. She—"

"Did she ask you to be friends with her?" Mr Todhunter interrupted.

"Yes, I believe she did. Why?"

"Did she ask you to be just simple ordinary friends, without any boring complications?" pursued Mr Todhunter with interest. "Did she say she believed you were the person she'd been looking for all her life and thought she'd never find?"

"As a matter of fact she did. Why?"

Mr Todhunter cackled suddenly. Then, remembering the solemnity of the occasion, cut off the cackle in mid-note and apologised instead.

"Nothing, nothing. I beg your pardon. Go on, please."

Farroway, looking for the moment a little uncertain, continued his saga.

"Well, that's how it began. When I say 'it' I mean a kind of visual obsession. After that, whatever I was doing, I saw her all the time. It was extraordinary. I just *saw* her. There was no longing nor passion nor anything like that. Certainly no desire.' Farroway paused and slowly stubbed out his cigarette. "But I couldn't shake off my visual memory of Jean. It held on day after day, till I became quite alarmed and began worrying. After a week of worrying I rang her up and called on her. Then I called again and again. Jean didn't seem to mind. I was terrified of boring her, but she always seemed really pleased to see me. After the third call I knew what the matter was: I wanted that woman more than I had wanted anything else in my life. The visual obsession had become a definitely physical one—ordinary, if you like.

"At the risk," said Farroway slowly, "of appearing a still worse cad, I have to tell you that Jean raised no particular objections. At the positive certainty of seeming to you a cad quite unspeakable, I have to add that she questioned me minutely first about my financial position; and my financial position, at that time, was thoroughly satisfactory. I can't help it. I know what Jean is, and it won't make her any different if I smooth over certain bumps in her spiritual make-up. It amuses me, too, if you like, to voice the precise truth about her just for once."

"Of course," said Mr Todhunter uncomfortably. Mr Todhunter, helpless devotee of truth as he was, yet found himself sufficiently human to be dis-composed by it on the lips of others.

"And that's how our liaison began," Farroway continued, taking not the least notice of Mr Todhunter's acquiescence or his discomposure. " 'Liaison.' A good, important word, that. It gives me pleasure to apply it to myself. But there's no other. An *affaire* with Jean Norwood deserves the term, or at any rate some Gallic euphemism. 'Affair' is too banal altogether.

"Well, I had no scruples. I said to myself, it was the best way of ending the matter. It was the only way, I pretended, to end the matter. At the same time I knew I was lying to myself. For if I had been, before, the accolyte of desire, I was now utterly the slave of my own mastership. Yes, it was the possession of her that really enslaved me to her; completely, irrevocably. You find that a psychological contradiction? Believe me, my dear fellow, that is the basis of all genuine feeling of a man for a woman. The pre-possession instinct; that's just animal. But the post-possession . . . love, infatuation, call it what you will, it's what differentiates us from the animals. And I envy the animals. Because it isn't amusing. Not at all.

"Almost before I knew what had happened Jean had become the centre of my existence. That's a cant phrase, but I mean it. She was. Other human beings—my family, everyone—had shifted to the periphery. She wanted money to keep her play on a week or two longer, to break a record. (It was *The Amulet*, if you remember.) I gave it to her. She merely admired a car in a shop window. I bought it for her. Then she found that flat. I took it, in my own name, for her. I knew I was ruining myself. I knew I was despoiling my family. I didn't care. I couldn't work to replace the money I was spending on her. Still I didn't care."

Farroway lit another cigarette, slowly, as if collecting his thoughts.

"You know the hackneyed dramatic situation. A girl wants to marry a young man. Her mother, with the best intentions, says she'll die rather than allow the girl to marry that particular young man. But she does marry him and everybody sympathises with her, even if the old lady actually dies of a broken heart. And why? Because love—sexual love—is above all other affections. That is an accepted axiom. But for some reason people don't apply it to love that arises after one's married. In that case the reasoning is different. People say then, 'Ah no, he should have stifled it.' They say that because they haven't gone through it themselves. What if he can't stifle it? They don't take that into account. Whereas if they'd gone through it themselves, they'd know that love—or lust or passion or obsession or infatuation or any damned unimportant name you like—simply can't be stifled when it's strong enough. There *is* such a thing as the fatal type. If you're lucky enough not to meet that type, your life goes on quietly, respectably, peacefully. If you do, it goes to pieces. You're done for."

As Farroway uttered this dictim in a flat, unimpassioned voice, Mr Todhunter could only nod. Having never met his own fatal type, Mr Todhunter could at least sympathise respectfully with the man who had, though the monologue was taking him far out of his own emotional depth.

"At first," pursued Farroway in the same rather dreary voice, "I struggled with myself. One does, you know. I called myself a weakling. I told myself it was ridiculous that this thing should be happening to me, of all people. I blamed myself for being more feeble than all the others whom I had despised for becoming infatuated with a woman. Then I saw that the ideas of strength and weakness were inapplicable; they had no relation to the state I was in. How can I illustrate it? Well, suppose you decide when bathing to stay under water for ten minutes. Are you a weakling if you give up after the first minute because you have no oxygen left in you? No. You can't help it. The ideas of strength or weakness don't apply. And that was my case.

"Of course I knew only too well what all this meant to my family. And I'm not a wicked man. I did feel for them. But what could I do? To give Jean up was impossible—just as impossible as for the finest swimmer in the world to stay under water for more than a few minutes. Of course I was making them miserable. I knew that and hated it. But I was miserable too. Partly because I felt for them and partly through jealousy. I never knew I was jealous by nature—I never have been before—but with Jean I became an Othello. I knew it was stupid and sordid, but there again I couldn't help myself. I was almost afraid that someone or something would deprive me of the very oxygen I was breathing.

"And with Jean I had good reason for being jealous. For if she hasn't been unfaithful to me so far, she will be. She can't help it, poor girl. She can't help wanting men, not for themselves exactly, but for exercising her power over them. And she can't help wanting money. Oh, I've no illusions. Has she—how shall I put it?—offered you any encouragement yet?"

"Yes," said Mr Todhunter.

Farroway nodded. "She knows I'm about squeezed dry. Poor Jean. She's just amoral, however much she wraps it up to herself and talks highfalutin nonsense about her art. There's no question of love. Jean simply never could love any man, because she loves only herself. She adores herself. It's an obsession with her. I don't suppose it's ever entered her mind to do anything for the sake of somebody else, because she can hardly conceive the existence of anybody else apart from her.

"You've heard of Sir James Bohum, the psychiatrist? Besides knowing his job, he's an extremely intelligent man. I met him once, at some dinner. Afterwards I got him to talk a little. I remember him saying that sex is the region least accessible to examination. We're beginning to know quite a lot about the hidden motives for our actions; but when it comes to sex we know less than paleolithic man did. The sexual choice in particular seems to have no reason and no explanation. Why does A lose his head and his reason over B? No one can say. It's merely a fact that has to be accepted without analysis or criticism. His love for C had a softening and ennobling effect on him; his love for B makes a madman of him.

"I told him my own theory of the fatal type, and he jumped at it. He said it looked like a chemical reaction. Taken by themselves, the two ingredients may be as harmless as you like, and they remain harmless in combination with all other substances. But mix the two together, and you get an explosion. With plenty of smoke and smell naturally. I asked him if it was possible to fight obsession, and he thought that the only way out was its sublimation into some other form—religion or something like that; but this can't be done deliberately; it must come of itself.

"And I know now that he's right. I can't do anything except wait. Perhaps a harebrained motorist will kill me. Perhaps Jean will have no more use for me and send me away. But as long as she still summons me, I shall go. On the telephone this morning I was really longing to say 'No!' But I couldn't. I was powerless. Or, of course, the Other Man will come along. That's bound to happen soon, and I'm dreading it. Because it will mean drama. If only Jean would die . . . that would be the best thing. But no such luck. She isn't obliging enough to do that.

"I've often thought of killing her of course. Oh, you needn't look so startled, Todhunter," said Farroway with a mirthless little laugh. "I suppose every man in violent love has meditated killing his beloved at one time or another. Usually over a trifle. But it wouldn't be a trifle in Jean's case. If ever there was a woman worth killing, it's she. Mind you, she's not wicked, in the sense that she doesn't actively wish to cause pain to others. But she's worse than wicked because she doesn't even notice the existence of those others. It's women of that kind—women and men—who are responsible for nine tenths of human suffering. Evil is rare. I'm inclined to think it's a pathological phenomenon. Indifference, that's what is terrible. . .."

Mr Todhunter waited, but Farroway seemed to have finished.

"I beg your pardon," he ventured, "but you said something about the telephone this morning. Do I understand that Miss Norwood rang you up and asked you to go round and see her?"

Farroway looked at him dully. "Yes. Why She always does if I stay away more than a day or two. Wants to know if I've forgotten all about her, and don't I love her any more, and all that sort of thing. The dog has to be kept on the lead, you see."

"Yes, I see," said Mr Todhunter. He did not add that what he saw was Miss Norwood's prudent intention to keep the one dog on its lead until the new one was safely leashed, in spite of all her promises to send it away for painless extermination.

He rubbed his bald head in some bewilderment. What he had just heard seemed to him the most complete expression of defeatism he had ever encountered. But it had been genuine. Whether one could struggle successfully against an infatuation or not, Mr Todhunter was cautiously not prepared to say, though he had an idea that it had been done. But Farroway obviously was a defeatist, and there was no struggle in him—except the physical struggle which might follow the advent of the Other Man. And what, in his present demented state of mind, he might do then, nobody could say.

3

Mr Todhunter drove back to Richmond in a bitter temper.

He had thought all that foolishness was behind him; he had never really liked the idea; now he positively detested and dreaded it. But conscience was too strong; now that the way had been so clearly shown him by which he might do a little good in the world before leaving it in a month or two's time, conscience would not allow him to shirk it. Cursing and swearing and exceedingly unhappy, Mr Todhunter faced the necessity of killing Miss Norwood just as soon as convenient.

CHAPTER VIII

Although he felt himself impelled to commit murder, Mr Todhunter saw no reason to advertise the fact. He thought of all those cousins and how distressed they would be to learn that there was a murderer in the family. Without being in the least ashamed of his intentions, Mr Todhunter yet felt that he owed it to the family to keep his deed as quiet as possible.

Somewhat at sea, therefore, Mr Todhunter expended a sum of money on the cheap editions of a great many detective stories in order to try to learn what was the best method of procedure in a case such as his. From these he gathered that so long as nobody saw you at the scene of the crime or near it and you left neither incriminating evidence of any sort nor fingerprints and had no possible motive for eliminating the victim you were absolutely certain to be caught in fiction but not so probably in real life.

Not altogether satisfied with this conclusion, Mr Todhunter expended a further sum on a number of works of popular criminology and, swallowing his horror of the semiliterate style in which the greater number seemed to be written, studied them diligently. From these it appeared that the most successful practitioners of the art of murder (that is to say, those who have blundered far enough as to allow themselves to be suspected in the end but had yet two or three previous and perfectly safe killings to their credit) were those who followed the method of disposing of the body, preferably through fire. This, however, Mr Todhunter had no intention of doing. To kill, as mercifully as possible, and then to get away with all speed was his hope. Certainly he was going to have nothing to do with the corpse once it was dead. It was therefore to the accounts of swift, silent killings, with subsequent lack of all means of identification, that he paid the closest attention.

And by degrees, almost to his regret and certainly to his fascinated horror, there began to form in Mr Todhunter's mind as the summer drew on the first glimmerings of a plan.

The first essential of this plan was that Mr Todhunter should make himself familiar not only with Miss Norwood's Richmond home, but also with her habits when staying there; and this without rousing suspicion or allowing any third person to remember later that such enquiries had been made. After duly considering this problem Mr Todhunter decided that his best informant would be Miss Norwood herself. On the other hand, he did not wish to have anything more to do with Miss Norwood officially, so that the connection between them should appear afterwards of the slightest. It seemed to him therefore that his best plan would be somehow to waylay Miss Norwood in the open, if possible when she was out walking, stroll beside her for a few minutes and ask his question and then depart with no witness to the encounter.

Feeling rather like the villian in a transpontine melodrama, Mr Todhunter duly lurked in the neighbourhood of Miss Norwood's flat at a time when she might be expected to have recovered from her rest and be on her way to the theatre for the evening performance. For two days he did not see her at all. On the third she emerged with Farroway and instantly entered a taxi with him, while Mr Todhunter turned hurriedly away; though not before he had been able to observe that Farroway's face was positively besotted with pleasure and that he looked like anything but a man who has just received his congé. On the fourth day Mr Todhunter's persistence was rewarded. Miss Norwood emerged alone and looked up and down the street as if for a taxi. At some risk to his aneurism, Mr Todhunter hurried towards her.

He was greeted by a brilliant smile and an eagerly outstretched hand.

"Mr Todhunter! I was beginning to believe you'd quite deserted me. You've been very naughty—very naughty indeed. Why haven't you rung me up about that box I promised you?" Miss Norwood, still holding Mr Todhunter's hand, pressed it in gentle reproach.

Mr Todhunter, finding this archness a little hard-to bear, tried to withdraw his hand, without success.

"Oh well, I thought you were going to ring me," he mumbled.

"Dear me! And did you think I had nothing to do but bother you on the telephone all day? If you only knew how busy I am. All day long and every day. That's just like you great financiers, isn't it?"

"What is?" asked the great financier.

"Why, thinking that no one is ever busy but yourselves. Still," relented Miss Norwood, "as you were coming to call on me at last, I suppose I must forgive you. But isn't it too bad I'm going straight to the theatre. If you wanted me to dine, I'm afraid it's out of the question."

With a manful effort Mr Todhunter snatched away his hand. Anxiety that someone might see them lingering thus on Miss Norwood's doorstep caused him to lose his head a little.

"No," he blurted out. "I'm dining at home. I just happened to be passing."

For a moment Miss Norwood looked disconcerted. Then she burst into a peal of laughter, which may or may not have sounded a little forced.

"Oh, you are refreshing. That's what I like about you. You're different. Most men would have jumped at the chance of saying they were coming to call on me, you know."

"Would they?" said Mr Todhunter obtusely. "Why?"

Miss Norwood's huge eyes narrowed slightly. "Why, because . . . oh, never mind why, if you can't see. Well, I mustn't keep you, then, Mr Todhunter. Though perhaps if you aren't in a *very* great hurry, you could spare just a few seconds to call me a taxi?"

"I'm not in a hurry at all," responded Mr Todhunter, more gallantly. "And I should be much honoured if you would allow me to escort you to the theatre."

"I'm afraid," said the lady coldly, "that would be a great bore for you?"

Mr Todhunter, suppressing a strong wish to shake her, summoned up a hypocritical smile. "I thought we were to be friends, Jean?" he asked, looking as fatuous as he could.

Miss Norwood melted instantly. "You still want to be? I was beginning to think . . . You know, Mr Todhunter, you *puzzle* me."

"Do I?" Mr Todhunter, in a fever to be gone, began to edge nervously along the pavement. Miss Norwood was compelled to follow him. "Er—how is that?"

"Well, I can't quite make you out. The other day, after lunch, I thought we understood each other so well. But today .. . you're *different.*"

"Am I?" said Mr Todhunter, quickening his pace. "I don't feel different. That is to say—er—my admiration for you has not decreased in any way."

Miss Norwood uttered another peal of laughter, causing Mr Todhunter to look round anxiously in case the attention of any passerby might have been attracted.

"No, no," laughed Miss Norwood. "You mustn't try to pay compliments. That isn't your line at all. Your line is blunt, brutal candour. That's what sweeps us poor weak women off our feet, you know."

"Is it?" Mr Todhunter removed his dreadful hat and surreptitiously passed a handkerchief over his pate. "Um . . . I didn't know. Er—you have a house in Richmond, haven't you?"

"Yes," replied Miss Norwood, a little surprised. "Why?"

"I live in Richmond too. I thought," said Mr Todhunter desperately, "as we lived in the same district, we might perhaps meet sometime."

"I should adore to. Why don't you come to lunch with me on Sunday? Or supper, if you like?"

"On Sunday?" This did not suit Mr Todhunter's book at all, and he hurriedly sought for an excuse. "Er—no, I'm afraid I can't on *Sunday,* but . . . that is, where exactly is your house?"

"It's on the river. Too sweet. The garden runs right along the bank. People climb out of punts and picnic on the lawn. Everyone tells me I ought to have it fenced off, but I think one should be generous, don't you? I mean, if it gives people pleasure to come and picnic on my lawn, I feel I ought to let them; so long as they don't do any actual *damage.* I ought to warn you, I'm quite a Communist. Are you terribly shocked?"

"Not at all. I'm a bit of a Communist myself," replied Mr Todhunter, disconcertingly but quite unintentionally so. To tell the truth, Mr Todhunter was unaccustomed to escorting lovely and extremely smartly dressed women on foot about the West End of London, and the glances which every single passerby threw at his companion were upsetting him. To his nervousness it seemed that everyone must recognise her and that the contrast between her exquisiteness and his own uncouthness must be so marked as to remain in each person's memory, with subsequent identification in the witness box. And yet, as Mr Todhunter well knew from his reading, taxicab rides are as easily traced as footprints in the snow.

He tried to concentrate on his purpose.

"Er—so your house is on the river? Mine isn't. But I often go on the river. I expect I've passed it frequently. Where exactly is it?"

Miss Norwood described its precise location, and Mr Todhunter, who knew the river fairly well, was able to recognise it without difficulty. He said as much.

"You often go on the river?" commented Miss Norwood. "Why don't you pick me up one day? I adore being punted."

"I should be charmed. Perhaps," said Mr Todhunter slowly, for an idea had just occurred to him, "if I happened to see you sitting in the garden one evening . . . ?"

"I'm at the theatre every evening."

"Oh yes, of course. I meant, one Sunday evening. . ."

"There's usually such a crowd on Sundays," sighed Miss Norwood. She glanced at her escort, and the crestfallen expression on his face made her take a sudden decision. The man looked hot. It was a pity for Miss Norwood that she could not read behind the expression to the cause of it, or she would certainly not have altered certain arrangements of her own to fit in with her new admirer's obvious wish.

"But as a matter of fact," she went on, "just as it happens, next Sunday evening I shall be quite alone. And when I'm alone in the evening, I always sit in my own special nook that I had made just to be alone in. It's a little corner with a few roses and lovely perfumed flowers, quite hidden from everywhere except a tiny view out over the river and backed by a long pergola that I had made out of the ruins of an old barn. It's just too, too perfect. So perhaps," continued Miss Norwood archly, "if you *were* to find yourself at a loose end next Sunday evening, Mr Todhunter, and *happened* to be on the river and thought you *might* like to see me and have a talk in the moonlight . . . well, all you'd have to do would be to land on my lawn and walk up through the garden, keeping just a little left, till you came to my corner— that's all."

"I hope very much," said Mr Todhunter, masking his jubilation with an excessive solemnity, "that I shall be able to be there."

Miss Norwood looked as if she would have liked something a little more definite than this, and for a moment a hard, calculating look came into her face. The next instant it had gone; but not before Mr Todhunter, who had happened to glance round at just that second, had had time to catch it.

"It would be nice," said Miss Norwood wistfully, "to be alone for once, just with a friend—a real friend . . . to talk . . . to open one's heart for once. . ."

"Yes," said Mr Todhunter, who privately thought that Miss Norwood was overdoing it a bit.

They were getting near the theatre now, and Mr Todhunter was becoming alarmed at the frequent admiring glances, and even salutes, to which his companion was becoming subjected. Indeed their walk was becoming something of a distinguished progress, and though Miss Norwood was evidently accustomed to this, Mr Todhunter was not. To all the glances she responded with a charming little bow, containing just the right mixture of friendliness and condescension, and for the salutes she added an exquisite smile.

Mr Todhunter gave way to panic.

"I'm sorry," he said abruptly. "I—er—just forgotten, most important appointment. Er—deal involving millions—that is, thousands. Must apologise, Er—next Sunday, I hope. Goodbye." And, turning suddenly on his heel, he left the most surprised lady in London on the pavement staring after his shambling retreat.

As he went Mr Todhunter became aware of a difference in the air around him. It was some moments before he realised that this was due to its freedom from the cloud of perfume in which Miss Norwood was apparently accustomed to envelope herself.

"Phew!" thought Mr Todhunter in high disgust. "The woman stinks."

2

Mr Todhunter had never been given very much to the habit of self-analysis, but in the next few days he did scrutinise quite closely the state of his feelings, firstly towards Miss Norwood and secondly towards the idea of killing her.

Rather to his surprise, he found that he seemed to have no natural objection to this course. His objection, when it appeared, was a civilised one and concerned murder in general. The application of reason at once showed him that the elimination of Miss Norwood from a world in which she was such an infernal nuisance to so many people was an act for which there could be, philosophically, nothing but approval. Of course this elimination must be painless. It would have been very much against Mr Todhunter's principles to inflict pain on any living creature, even Miss Norwood. But death was not pain. Mr Todhunter had no views on the afterlife, contenting himself only with the hope that there might be one and that it might prove less unpleasant than this one so often seemed to one afflicted with bad health; and he therefore was unable to pronounce any opinion as to whether he might be despatching Miss Norwood to a plane on which she might have to expiate her sins committed on this one or just into blank nothingness. Nor, in fact, did he care.

His meditations showed him, however, that much though he might commend the removal of Miss Norwood as an academically admirable deed, he would certainly never have undertaken it himself, absolutely never, had not he felt that to stand aside would be so dangerous as to be quite unjustified, Indeed Mr Todhunter resented not a little the ill fortune which had caught him up into this net of circumstance so that this time he could hardly help himself. For it seemed to him more than likely that, if he did not get in and murder Miss Norwood first, either Farroway or Mrs Farroway would do it instead; and though Mrs Farroway seemed no fool, Farroway undoubtedly was and would give himself away as sure as fate, thus bringing further sorrow on his unhappy family.

"Damn the fool!" bitterly observed Mr Todhunter to himself, not once but many times.

For though Mr Todhunter saw no moral or ethical objections to the forcible removal of Miss Norwood, he did not at all like the idea of performing the removal himself.

Nevertheless, impelled by those twin furies, duty and a relentless conscience, he got down the new revolver from its nest in his bedroom door and, handling it with some revulsion, oiled its exterior carefully all over, Mr Todhunter did not quite know why he oiled it, but felt it the right thing to do.

He did not, however, make arrangements to hire a punt for the following Sunday evening. Mr Todhunter was not such a fool as that.

3

What he did do was to find a lane which ran down to the river just two gardens away from that of Miss Norwood and with infinite precaution, both against being seen and to preserve his aneurism intact for another ten minutes (after that of course it did not matter), scale the fence which bounded it. Climbing another fence and yet another and pushing through a thick hedge, Mr Todhunter thus found himself, at exactly a quarter past nine on Sunday evening, in Miss Norwood's garden. His heart was thumping horribly, his mouth was dry and he was loathing his task as he had never loathed anything in his life.

In fact it is open to question whether Mr Todhunter was altogether in possession of his full faculties as he crept through the garden, mechanically following the directions that had been given him. His mind seemed to him, later, to have gone temporarily blank. He could remember continually feeling the revolver in his pocket to make sure that he had not dropped it and wishing desperately that the route to the old barn would go on prolonging itself indefinitely, to prevent him from ever getting there. He could remember, too, the look of the garden in the summer dusk, darker this evening than usual because of a great bank of cloud that had just come up, and listening with tense, indeed, almost distraught attention, every few steps, to make sure that no one else was about. And he remembered arriving at the long, open-fronted building, with roses clambering up its wooden beams, which he knew must be the fatal barn. And lastly he could remember, more dimly, his first glimpse of Miss Norwood lying back in a chair—alone, just as she had promised.

After that he preferred to remember nothing.

4

Mr Todhunter put the revolver back in his pocket. He looked round. Would anyone have heard the shot? The long, low building of the barn stood on a levelled platform halfway down the slope to the river. Behind it, dimly glimmering in the dusk, rose a bank planted with some kind of flowering shrub, thick and high. The house was not visible. Mr Todhunter stood holding his breath. There was not a sound. Even the usual noises on the river could not be heard. He was sure the shot could not have been heard.

He looked at Jean Norwood. She was still lying back in her elaborate swing chair, just inside the confines of the barn. Her face was turned sideways, both arms hung down limp from the shoulders. On the bosom of her too-elaborate white satin gown was a red stain, already big and still spreading.

Mr Todhunter forced himself forward and touched her forehead, then her chest. There was no doubt she was dead. With a feeling of nausea he peered at the scarlet stain. It had been a good shot—more luck, perhaps, than marksmanship?—it must have gone right through her heart. He wondered about the bullet.

With an effort he controlled his nerves and lifted the inert form a little forward. In the bare, smooth back was a horrible red hole which almost made Mr Todhunter faint on his feet. But he did not faint; for his eye had caught sight of a piece of dull metal actually lodged in the stuffed fabric of the chair. He drew it out and let the body slump back. It was the bullet, right enough, and scarcely misshapen for all that it was of lead and nothing harder. It must have gone clean through her without touching a bone. Mr Todhunter dropped it into his coat pocket.

He stood for a moment looking down at the dead woman. On her left. wrist was a bracelet, a costly affair of diamonds and pearls with a tiny oblong watch set in it. As if fascinated, Mr Todhunter slipped it over the unresisting hand and dropped it into his pocket along with the bullet. It would sound fantastic to say that he wanted a souvenir of the occasion, yet something uncommonly like that must have actuated the almost mechanical action.

He paused irresolutely. His mind was working again now, and he felt that there must be all sorts of things that ought to be done: safeguards to be taken, evidence to be suppressed, vital precautions of some sort or another.

He stood by the body, looking round. On a table close at hand was a tray with a decanter of brandy and two glasses. If ever Mr Todhunter had wanted a drink in his abstemious life it was now, but he dared not. To drop down dead here, beside Miss Norwood, would look very bad. The family would never get over such a scandal.

He picked one of the glasses up and wiped it carefully with his handkerchief. Glasses, he remembered with a touch of grim humour, always were wiped clean of fingerprints in detective stories. It would give the police something to puzzle over too.

He put the glass down, holding it carefully in his handkerchief, and was about to pick up the other when a noise outside startled him so severely as nearly to burst his aneurism there and then. It was only an owl hooting, but to Mr Todhunter it sounded like the siren of a police car.

"My nerves won't stand this," he muttered and fled, his heart thumping.

There was nothing more he could do by remaining, so far as he knew; and yet as he flitted, a gaunt shadow, through the dewy garden, he felt as if he must be leaving behind him the name of Miss Norwood's killer blazoned across the floor in letters of blood.

In the little lane he turned to the right and went down to the river. Taking the bullet from his pocket, he threw it out into the water as far as he could. Mr Todhunter's reading had taught him just how eloquent a bullet can become in the hands of a ballistics expert.

CHAPTER IX

Mr Todhunter slept badly that night. The vision of two dangling arms and a red stain across a white satin bosom haunted his vision as persistently as that of Miss Norwood in life had ever haunted Farroway's.

He still had the feeling, too, that certain things ought to be done.

Well, there was the revolver, for one thing. . . .

What Mr Todhunter actually did about the revolver was to pay a visit, very early the next morning, to Farroway. His idea was to find out whether Farroway had a revolver of his own and if so to substitute this one for it. Mr Todhunter did not consider that he would be involving Farroway himself in any risk by doing this. There were always alibis, and without doubt Farroway would have one. If not, Mr Todhunter was prepared to give him one.

Farroway, however, was in a state so distraught as to be of small use. He had had a visit from the police already, although the hour was not yet ten o'clock; and this, added to the lurid story in the paper, had almost put him off his balance. He wept openly, and Mr Todhunter, who was full of public-school traditions, felt exceedingly ashamed of him. However it did come out, in answer to Mr Todhunter's determined questioning, that Farroway had no revolver of his own and was in possession of an unimpeachable alibi, having spent the whole evening in a local pub till closing time, discoursing in a very maudlin state upon the popular taste in fiction. This interesting piece of news was, however, of little importance to Mr Todhunter without a revolver, and he therefore prepared to take his leave.

"Who could have done it, Todhunter?" weepingly implored Farroway in the doorway. "Who? And why? It's inexplicable . . . dreadful . . . poor little Jean."

"You were talking of doing it yourself only a few days ago," sternly reminded Mr Todhunter.

"Talking! Yes, we all talk. But that's as far as most of us get. But who could actually have *done* such a thing?"

Mr Todhunter escaped with some difficulty. If he had ever felt any regrets about Miss Norwood's sudden death, the sight and no less the sound of Farroway would have hardened him. Farroway must have been a decent, ordinarily self-reliant fellow once. It was pitiable that any woman should have reduced him to such a state as he was in now; deliberately, in order to get hold of his money. Yes, Miss Norwood had deserved death.

Mr Todhunter drove to Maida Vale.

Here he was ahead of the police.

Mrs Farroway opened the door to him. She said that Felicity was prostrated and unable to get up; they had read the news in their morning paper, and Felicity had instantly collapsed. She was, explained Mrs Farroway, very sensitive.

In the little sitting room the tall woman and her visitor exchanged a long, cautious look.

"Mr Todhunter," said Mrs Farroway, speaking slowly and deliberately, "I think I had better speak openly to you. It may be the only chance. I think—no, I'm *sure* you know who shot Miss Norwood. And . . . I'm afraid I know too."

Mr Todhunter felt his heart leap painfully. To his disgust his voice, when he spoke, was a harsh croak,

"What are you going to do about it."

"Nothing."

"Nothing?"

"No. All I know, officially, is that Felicity and I spent yesterday evening together here and we were, most fortunately," said Mrs Farroway with grim irony, "never out of each other's sight until we went to bed, at about half past eleven. And that's all I know."

"That," said Mr Todhunter with equal deliberation, "is all you need to know. Thank you. And. . ."

"Yes?"

Mr Todhunter turned away and stared out of the window. "Whoever did it, and why—don't presume to judge him, Mrs Farroway."

Mrs Farroway looked for a moment a little surprised. Then she nodded. "No, I don't. Who in any case," she added in a low voice, "am I to judge?"

Mr Todhunter, fearing that the scene might be in danger of becoming emotional, turned briskly round.

"Oh yes," he said, trying to speak as casually as possible. "There's one other thing. I wonder if you have a revolver here?"

Mrs Farroway started. "A—revolver? Yes, there is one here at the moment, as it happens. Vincent's. He brought it round—"

"May I see it?" interrupted Mr Todhunter. "The police may be here at any moment, and . . ."

"I'll get it," Mrs Farroway agreed. She had turned rather white, but her voice was unchanged.

She went unhurriedly out of the room, to return three minutes later with the weapon. Mr Todhunter took it gingerly, but it was not loaded. He drew his own out of his pocket and compared the two. They were of the ordinary Freeman and Starling army pattern and were identical. Mr Todhunter drew a big breath of relief.

Mrs Farroway looked on in surprise. "Where did you get the other?" she asked.

"That," said Mr Todhunter soberly, "is mine."

Mrs Farroway turned aside to stand by the window. There was an atmosphere of tenseness in the room which Mr Todhunter found most uncomfortable.

"Vincent says that the best defence," she said in a low voice, "is to know nothing; to have seen nothing, to have heard nothing, to remember nothing."

"Vincent?" repeated Mr Todhunter. "Oh, he rang you up."

"No. He came round here. An hour ago or more. Didn't I tell you? He was infatuated with her, too, as you know; though it will wear off now, of course, thank heaven. Naturally he was very much agitated. He kept saying that he was responsible for—for her death."

"Responsible?" Mr Todhunter frowned.

"I suppose he meant morally responsible. If he hadn't been mixed up with it, she'd never have been killed—that kind of idea."

"But he doesn't know who . . . um . . . shot her?" asked Mr Todhunter anxiously.

Mrs Farroway hesitated. "He may guess," she said slowly.

"Better if he didn't know for certain," Mr Todhunter mumbled. "In the circumstances."

Mrs Farroway nodded. "Much better."

Mr Todhunter had the feeling that all sorts of things were being said without being spoken. He pulled out his handkerchief and polished the top of his head. The situation was not an easy one. But after all, if one goes out to commit murder one can hardly expect easy situations afterwards.

A ring at the bell put an end to a silence which was becoming painful.

The two exchanged a frankly worried look, the thought of the police in the minds of both. Mrs Farroway hurried to open the door. Mr Todhunter, with a vague instinct of concealment, pushed both revolvers into his pockets, where they bulged quite obviously, and tried to look innocent

Voices could be heard in the hall. Then the sitting-room door opened again.

"It's Vincent," said Mrs Farroway.

Vincent Palmer, large and self-confident as ever but now plainly upset, strode into the room behind her. His eye fell upon the shrinking Mr Todhunter.

"Who's this man?" he demanded abruptly.

Mrs Farroway explained that Mr Todhunter was a friend of her husband's.

"I met you once," added Mr Todhunter, "if you remember, at . . ." His voice died away to a mumble as he realised the tactlessness of the reference.

"I remember. What are you doing here now?"

"Vincent, don't be silly, please," interposed Mrs Farroway calmly. "Mr Todhunter has come round to see if he can help us in any way."

"Well, he can't. We've got to manage this thing by ourselves. I'm sorry, Mr Todhunter, but. . ."

"That will do, Vincent." Mrs Farroway spoke with a calm authority which made Mr Todhunter glance at her in admiration. So, no doubt, had she been accustomed to handle unruly committees, "In any case, what have you come round again for so soon?"

The young man, quelled but not subdued, glanced in a hostile way at Mr Todhunter. "I came—for—for—"

"Your revolver? Mr Todhunter has it." Mrs Farroway hastened to deal with the thundercloud that leapt instantly to her son-in-law's brow. "Now, Vincent, please! Mr Todhunter thought it best to. . ."

The storm broke, muffled but alarming, "I don't care a damn what Mr Todhunter thought. Mr Todhunter will kindly keep his thoughts, and himself, out of the way. Give me back my revolver, please."

"Certainly, certainly," agreed Mr Todhunter without hesitation. He remembered that he had put his own revolver in the right pocket of his coat . . . or was it the left? No, the right, and the other in the left. He drew out the one from the right pocket.

Then he remembered that Vincent, too, must have an alibi before the exchange of revolvers could be made with safety.

"Please tell me this first," he said, disregarding the menacing hand already stretched out towards him. "It's important. Where were you between nine and ten last night?"

"It says in the papers," interposed Mrs Farroway, "that death is supposed to have occurred between a quarter to nine and a quarter past."

"Very well," amended Mr Todhunter. "Between eight-thirty and nine-thirty then?"

The young man was so taken aback that he answered.

"I . . . I was at home."

"Can you *prove* that?" asked Mr Todhunter earnestly-

"I suppose so," growled the other. "My wife was there."

"Anyone else?"

"No. The maid was out. We got the supper ourselves."

"Did you sit in the garden afterwards or in any place where other people might have seen you?"

"No, we didn't; we sat indoors. Look here, what the hell are you getting at? You talk almost as if I might be under suspicion myself."

"Everyone will be under suspicion, you young fool," snapped Mr Todhunter, his patience giving way before strained nerves. "Don't you realise that? You as much as anyone else—more, if your recent behaviour comes out. I don't suppose I was the only person who saw you at the Chelsea flower show, you know."

"The . . . Chelsea flower show?" stammered young Mr Palmer.

"Yes. Still, I suppose your alibi is as good as anyone else's, so I'll give you back your revolver. But one word of advice, young man. Don't talk to the police as you've spoken to me. It won't do you any good to put their backs up for nothing. Well, Mrs Farroway, I don't think I need stay any longer. If there's anything I can do for you, of course I shall expect you to call on me. And this young man here is perfectly right in the line he suggested to you. Just make sure, while you have him to yourself, that he too knows nothing, has seen nothing and can't remember anything."

And Mr Todhunter, having accomplished the object of his visit, handed the wrong revolver back to a young man who, subdued now as well as quelled, took it without hesitation as his own and did not even stop to examine it.

Not a little pleased with himself, Mr Todhunter made an excellent exit.

It was a pity, in a way, that Mrs Farroway should know the truth, as she undoubtedly did, but Mr Todhunter was convinced that it was safe with her.

2

Murder changes a man's mentality. He is a different being after the act from what he was before. It may be this fact that has tripped up so many murderers: they could not foresee into what kind of person they would change. Their whole trends of thought and feeling have undergone a revulsion, and for a time they are bewildered.

Mr Todhunter did not consider that he had committed murder; indeed, in his secret mind he knew very well that he had not. For that matter nobody calls the official executioner a murderer. Yet although for weeks Mr Todhunter had been making himself familiar with the idea, although he had gone over in his mind every detail, not once but a hundred times, till one would have said that the actual sight of real blood could add nothing to what his imagination had already depicted, yet now that the deed was a thing of the past he found himself almost more upset than before.

The confidence which he had shown in the flat with Mrs Farroway, the elation, even, with which he had taken his leave after the exchange of revolvers, rapidly disappeared. Mr Todhunter's mind was a-flutter. He worried deeply and unceasingly. The fact of death and the sight of the dead woman, even the knowledge that he had determined to mete that death out to her, had unhinged the system of his thoughts.

Yet to all appearances Mr Todhunter had no need to worry. The police never came near him. Mr Todhunter could not bring himself to read the newspapers, not even the accounts of the case in his own sober *Times*: anything to do with it now made him feel physically sick; yet it was obvious that the police were at a loss. Even though he did no more than glance reluctantly at the headlines, Mr Todhunter could gather that. There was no sign of an arrest of any kind, and least of all his own. Mr Todhunter began to feel sure he would die in his bed yet.

It seemed to him, too, that this would happen very soon. The strain and the insomnia from which he now constantly suffered were wearing him down. A week after the death Mr Todhunter looked as if he were fifteen years older.

It was not conscience. Mr Todhunter's conscience was perfectly clear. It was just sheer worry. Mr Todhunter had always been inclined to fuss over trifles; now he had something worth fussing over, and he did it full justice. Daily there increased in him a kind of semihysterical restlessness. He wanted to *do* something. He felt he ought to do something. But what? That he did not know.

He toyed with the idea of confessing. But what was the point? There was nothing to be gained by it. Besides, Mr Todhunter now quite violently did not want to go to prison. Before, he had really not cared very much whether he were caught or not. The idea of being imprisoned had seemed sardonically amusing to him, for of course he would be dead long before the date of execution came round. He would be able to observe his own trial for murder with complete detachment—a situation probably unique. He had only decided against it in the interests of the family.

But now all that was changed. He did not want to go to prison; he did not want to be tried; he did not want to be bothered at all. He wanted, if anything, to escape. Life still had its hold on him, and what was left of it he wanted to enjoy. He was not enjoying it at present, that was certain. He could not read, he could not play, even Bach had lost his spell. He felt in a kind of spiritual vice that was crushing the vitality out of him. He could remember nothing like the sensation since his first few miserable days at a preparatory school when he had first learned just how bleak life can be.

From all this Mr Todhunter longed to escape. He felt he ought not to go, but he felt, too, that he could bear the strain no longer.

One day he suddenly took a cab to the West End and booked a passage on a steamship cruising half round the world. The cruise was scheduled to last nearly four months, and Mr Todhunter knew that he would not come back from it alive. He was rather glad. It seemed to him a pleasant thing to die in luxury and comfort and be consigned to the warm waters of some tropical sea.

3

It was as if Mr Todhunter had been a bull confined in a tiny field surrounded by high hedges over which he could not see. While he was there he wandered round and round in circles, bellowing mournfully; but now that he had, so to speak, charged through the hedge and was in the spacious pastures beyond, life appeared a very different proposition. In other words, having taken his decision, Mr Todhunter found himself his own man again.

With all the old methodical care he made his preparations. The house in Richmond was to be kept in running order, with Mrs Greenhill as dominant housekeeper. It had been left in his will to two elderly and impoverished female cousins, and these Mr Todhunter thoughtfully installed in situ so that there should be no upheaval and bother for them in his absence. One or two items were added to his will. A visit was paid to his doctor, who annoyed Mr Todhunter as much as ever by persistently congratulating him on his approaching demise, the date of which, however, he was unable to name with any more accuracy than before, since it appeared that Mr Todhunter's aneurism had stood up to all this strain with astonishing fortitude and was in no worse condition than it had been four months before.

And lastly, having packed his bags and left nothing to chance, Mr Todhunter wrote out a careful account of the way in which he had murdered Miss Jean Norwood, added by way of proof that Miss Norwood's bracelet was in a certain locked drawer of the chest of drawers in his bedroom with the revolver, sealed up the document in an imposingly large envelope and deposited it with his solicitor to be handed over to Scotland Yard after his death.

This, Mr Todhunter considered, would round off the affair nicely. He had heard nothing from any of the Farroway family since his visit to Maida Vale and sincerely trusted that he never would. He had done what he could. The Farroways could now work out their own salvation for themselves.

In only one item did Mr Todhunter deviate from this decision; and the incident is perhaps worth recording as showing the new resolution which, after his black week, seemed to have descended upon him.

One day quite by chance he met Mr Budd, the manager of the Princess. It was, as a matter of fact, on the pavement in Cockspur Street just outside the offices of the shipping company which Mr Todhunter had been visiting in order to ask information upon a certain small point about which he could quite well have telephoned.

Mr Budd, looking bluer than ever about the jowls, recognised him at once, and greeted him with a degree of warmth which surprised Mr Todhunter. As a matter of fact it was just before closing time and Mr Budd, whose finances were temporarily low, was hoping to be asked to have the quick one for which there was just time—but not time for a return one.

Mr Todhunter did not particularly want to see Mr Budd or anyone who could remind him of Miss Norwood, but he was unable to cope with the exuberance which Mr Budd brought to his welcoming. Mr Budd, in fact, worked his hardest, but his luck was out. The vital five minutes passed, and there they were, still on the pavement. Resigning himself, Mr Budd invited Mr Todhunter into the Greenroom Club, and Mr Todhunter, unable to think up an excuse quickly enough, and indeed not sure whether he wanted one, suffered himself to be led. On such a hair hung the whole of Felicity Farroway's future.

For once inside, and Mr Budd having got off his chest his saga of woe (for of course the Princess was closed and Mr Budd with every expectation of being out of a job as soon as the lease had been transferred), the talk somehow veered round to a play which Mr Budd had just been reading and which, he averred, was a Pipper, a Peach and a Sure Thing,

"*She* told me to bung it back," recounted Mr Budd, "but I didn't. I just can't bear to let it go."

Mr Todhunter, not much interested, asked politely for explanations. From these he gathered that it had been one of Mr Budd's many tasks to read the dozens of plays showered by enthusiastic amateur playwrights upon Miss Norwood. Anything which he considered good enough he passed on to her to read, and the proportion amounted to something under one per cent.

"Hopeless!" pronounced Mr Budd with emphasis. "Ninety-nine out of a hundred of 'em. Just lousy. You'd think the poor goofs had never been inside a theatre in their lives."

But this particular play, it appeared, was the exception. It was by an unknown writer, a first play, and according to Mr Budd it would make a sensation—if it was ever put on.

"But there you are. I told you once we were sheep in this business, didn't I? Mr X.Y.Z. makes a success of a play; every manager in London's on his doorstep next morning asking for another. Miss A.B.C.'s never had a play produced in her life—and no manager in London's going to take the risk. . . But that isn't why *she* turned it down. She said it wasn't good enough, but that wasn't the reason either. She knew as well as I did that it's a pipper. No, she turned it down because she couldn't play the part. It's a young girl for one thing, and it'd need a darned good actress to carry it off for another. I will say that for Jean, she knew her limitations. Why . . ."

Mr Todhunter sat suddenly forward in his chair, looking like a great bird of ill omen about to swoop.

"You say this is a good play?" he interrupted.

"I do," agreed Mr Budd, a little startled.

"Would the part of the young girl suit Felicity Farroway?"

"Feli—Oh yes, I remember the kid. Mr Todhunter," said Mr Budd with admiration, "you've just about pit it. She could play any other actress in London off the stage in that part, properly produced. Yes, she's the girl for it. Now however did you think that one up?"

"I remember you telling me that she was a good actress."

"That's right. I remember now. You're a friend of the old man's. Poor old chap, just about knocked him up, this . . ."

"How much would it cost to put this play on with Miss Farroway in the leading part?"

Mr Budd looked doubtful. "It could be done for three thousand, easy. But look here, I'm not advising you, you know. It's a hell of a risk. Unknown actress, unknown playwright; you'd have everything against you. Mind you, if the public could be got in for a start you might have a chance, but—And who would you get to produce it? *I* should say Dane's the man, but . . . I say, you wouldn't be wanting a manager, would you?" asked Mr Budd, brightening.

"I'm going abroad in three days," said Mr Todhunter slowly. "I can't do anything in the matter myself. Would you be willing to undertake the full responsibility—settle with the author (and the contract must be approved by the Society of Authors, I stipulate that), engage Miss Farroway and a cast, choose a producer or whoever is necessary—provided I deposit a cheque for three thousand with you before I sail?"

"But you don't know me," almost wept Mr Budd. "You can't do a thing like that. I might hop off with the money, I might... you're barmy."

"Will you?" cackled Mr Todhunter.

"My bones and brisket," shouted Mr Budd, "you can bet I will. And if I don't make a fortune for you, it won't be my fault. Why . . . oh hell. *Boy!*"

4

Three days later Mr Todhunter sailed in the SS Anchusa. There had been no further developments in the Norwood case. The newspapers were openly accusing the police of being baffled, and the police seemed to be admitting that the newspapers were not far wrong. Mr Todhunter felt that he was out of the nightmare at last.

But that was where Mr Todhunter was immensely mistaken.

It was, in point of fact, in Tokyo that Mr Todhunter learned that Vincent Palmer had been arrested, nearly five weeks earlier, for the murder of Jean Norwood.

PART III

Detective

THE TOO-PERFECT
MURDER CASE

CHAPTER X

Mr Todhunter arrived back in England in late November, having travelled from Japan with all speed, just a week before the trial of Vincent Palmer was scheduled to open. This he learned from the English newspaper which he bought at Calais before embarking. It did not seem to him that an hour or two's further delay could matter very much, and he therefore drove from Victoria to Richmond to deposit his luggage and greet his cousins and Mrs Greenhill before driving to Scotland Yard.

It was about half past four when Mr Todhunter arrived, as he imagined, at the end of his journey, prepared for arrest and subsequent retirement from the world. He felt a little upset, but not at all panic-stricken. As for his aneurism, this seemed to be still in much the same state as when it had left England; certainly Mr Todhunter had taken all possible care of it during his tour, refrained from giving it any undue strain and sedulously withheld from it all alcohol. The voyage had done him good too. His mind was at rest now, and he had had no difficulty in keeping Miss Norwood out of it, except occasionally in dreams. The news of young Palmer's arrest had distressed him considerably, and he blamed himself for having gone abroad at all without foreseeing some such blunder on the part of the authorities; but of course that would all be put right now. If the red tape were not too strong, Palmer should be at liberty in time for dinner.

"I want," mumbled Mr Todhunter to the large policeman at the door of the Scotland Yard building, "to see the officer in charge of the Norwood case."

"That'll be Chief Inspector Moresby," replied the policeman in a friendly way. "Just fill in this form, sir, and state the business you wish to see him about."

Mr Todhunter, impressed by the friendliness, laid his shapeless hat on the table and duly filled in his form. The nature of the business on which Chief Inspector Moresby was to be troubled he stated as "important information concerning the death of Miss Jean Norwood."

The large policeman then invited Mr Todhunter to take a seat and withdrew.

Ten minutes later he informed Mr Todhunter that Chief Inspector Moresby would see him in a few minutes.

Half an hour later, in reply to a query of Mr Todhunter's, the policeman opined that Chief Inspector Moresby was a very busy man.

Twenty minutes after that Mr Todhunter was actually ushered into Chief Inspector Moresby's presence.

There rose to greet him from behind a severe-looking desk a burly man with a drooping walrus moustache, who shook Mr Todhunter's hand with great geniality, invited him to be seated and enquired what he could do for him.

"You're in charge of the—er—the Norwood case?" asked Mr Todhunter with care. He was not going to be put off, after all that waiting, with anyone less than the right man.

"I am, sir," agreed the chief inspector affably.

Mr Todhunter rubbed the top of his head. He had a hatred of the dramatic, but it seemed difficult to break his momentous news without being slightly dramatic.

"I—um—have been out of England recently. It was only a few weeks ago—in Japan, as a matter of fact—that I learned of Mr Palmer's arrest. It was—er—a great shock to me," mumbled Mr Todhunter.

"Yes sir," prompted the chief inspector with patience. "And why was Mr Palmer's arrest a great shock to you?"

"Why, because . . . that is, because . . . well, you see," floundered Mr Todhunter, not at all dramatically, "it was I who shot Miss Norwood."

The chief inspector looked at Mr Todhunter, and Mr Todhunter looked at the chief inspector. Rather to Mr Todhunter's surprise the other did not make an instant dive for handcuffs and clap them on the bony wrists which Mr Todhunter was already almost holding ready for them. Instead he said:

"Well, well. So you shot Miss Norwood, sir? Dear me, dear me." He shook his head as if to intimate that no doubt boys will be boys, but grown men should behave as grown men.

"Er—yes," said Mr Todhunter, a little puzzled. The chief inspector did not seem at all shocked. He did not seem even upset, although the whole of his case against Vincent Palmer must be clattering round his ears. He merely continued to shake his head in a slightly reproving way and pull at one end of his moustache.

"I want to make a statement," said Mr Todhunter.

"Yes sir, of course," soothed the chief inspector. "That is, you're quite sure you do?"

"Of course I'm sure," said Mr Todhunter, surprised.

"You've thought it well over?" persisted the chief inspector.

"I've been thinking it over all the way between Tokyo and London," riposted Mr Todhunter quite tartly,

"It's a serious thing, you know, accusing yourself of murder," pointed out the chief inspector in the kindliest way.

"Of course it's a serious thing," positively snapped Mr Todhunter. "So is murder itself. So is arresting the wrong man."

"Very well, sir." Almost resignedly, as it seemed to the astonished Mr Todhunter, the chief inspector pulled a pad towards him and prepared to take notes. "Now, what's this all about?"

"Oughtn't my statement to be taken down properly, for me to sign?" Mr Todhunter asked, remembering the textbooks.

"You just tell me about it first. Then if necessary we can put it down in statement form afterwards," suggested the chief inspector, as one humouring a child.

Somewhat haltingly Mr Todhunter began his story. It must be admitted that he told it badly, and that was only partly because he found it so difficult to tell at all. The necessity of leaving Farroway, and the whole Farroway family, out of the account was an added stumbling block.

"I see," said the chief inspector when Mr Todhunter had brought his tale to a diffident and somewhat lame close. So far as Mr Todhunter could judge, the chief inspector did not appear to have made a single note. "I see. And why did you determine to shoot Miss Norwood, sir? That wasn't quite clear to me."

"Jealousy," explained Mr Todhunter unhappily. Even to himself it did not sound altogether convincing. "I could not bear to—um—share her with others."

"Quite so. But had the question of sharing ever arisen? So far as I can make out, sir, you'd only met the lady once or twice. Had you on either of those occasions been—h'm—admitted to her favours?" queried the chief inspector delicately.

"Er—no. That is, not exactly. But. . ."

"You hoped, eh?"

"Quite so," agreed Mr Todhunter gratefully. "I hoped."

If the chief inspector thought privately that Mr Todhunter looked like anything in the world rather than an eager lover, or ever could look like one, he forebore to mention it.

"Then the actual question of sharing had never arisen, in point of fact, because you had never had a share, so to speak, yourself?"

"I suppose so."

"And you say you killed her before you could obtain the share? You killed her, in fact, while you were still hoping?"

"Well, if you put it like that," said Mr Todhunter doubtfully.

"I'm not putting it any way. I'm only repeating what you said, sir."

"We had a quarrel," said Mr Todhunter miserably. "A—um—a lovers' quarrel."

"Ah! A bit passionate, was it?"

"Very passionate."

"Shouted at each other and all that?"

"Certainly."

"And what time was that, sir?"

"I should think," said Mr Todhunter cautiously, "about a quarter to nine."

"And you shot her in the middle of the quarrel?"

"Yes."

"She didn't run up to the house or get away from you or anything like that?"

"No." said Mr Todhunter, puzzled. "I don't think so."

"Well, you'd have noticed if she had, wouldn't

"Certainly I should."

"Then how do you account for the fact that she spoke to her maid, *in* the house, at nine o'clock, sir? According to your version she was dead by then."

"I'm not giving you a Version,'" said Mr Todhunter angrily. "I'm telling you the truth. I may be mistaken over a matter of a quarter of an hour or so; that's of no importance. You can surely realise from what I'm able to tell you that in the main fact I'm right. For instance, I can give you an exact description of the scene as it was when I left it. Miss Norwood was lying . . ." Mr Todhunter gave as graphic a description as he could manage. "And there were two glasses on the table," he added triumphantly. "I wiped the prints off one but not the other."

"Why not the other?." awkwardly demanded the chief inspector.

"Because I lost my head," confessed Mr Todhunter. "I thought I heard a noise and escaped as quickly as I could. But the fact that I know that one of the glasses was wiped and the other not proves that I must have been there." For by this time Mr Todhunter had been compelled to realise that this idiot of a chief inspector was receiving his story with the greatest scepticism.

"Yes. No doubt." The chief inspector began to balance his pencil across one stubby finger in a way extremely irritating to Mr Todhunter. "Ever read the newspaper, Mr Todhunter?" he asked suddenly with great airiness.

"No. That is, yes. In the ordinary way. But not about this case."

"Why not about this case?"

"It was painful to me," Mr Todhunter said with dignity. "Having shot the woman I—um—loved, I had no wish to see the sensation that the Press was making of it. . . . Why?" asked Mr Todhunter in sudden alarm. "Was that information about the two glasses reported in the papers?"

The chief inspector nodded. "It was, sir. And so was everything else that you've told me. Every single thing."

"But I did it!" cried Mr Todhunter in high agitation. "Damn it all, I shot the woman. There must be some way I can prove it. Ask me questions. Ask me about some of the details that didn't get into the papers."

"Very well, sir." The chief inspector, stifling a yawn, proceeded to question Mr Todhunter about the exact situation of the barn in relation to the house, about a summerhouse that apparently stood somewhere near the barn and about similar topographical details.

Mr Todhunter, unable to answer, explained feverishly that he had only seen the place by night.

The chief inspector nodded and went on to ask him what he had done with the revolver after the shooting.

"It's in a drawer in—" Mr Todhunter clapped a hand to his forehead. "Ha! I can prove it!" he crowed. "Gracious me, I'm taking leave of my senses. Of course I can prove it. If you'll come back with me to Richmond, Chief Inspector, I can lay before you incontrovertible evidence, tangible evidence, of the truth of what I'm telling you. I have there a diamond bracelet which I actually took off Miss Norwood's wrist after she was—um—dead."

For the first time the chief inspector showed real interest. "A bracelet? Describe it if you please, sir."

Mr Todhunter did so.

The chief inspector nodded. "The bracelet that was reported as missing. And you say that it's in your possession?"

"I didn't know it was reported as missing, but it's certainly in my possession now."

The chief inspector pressed a button on his desk. "I'll send a sergeant back to Richmond with you. If what you say is true, sir, we shall have to go into all this seriously."

"What I say is true," returned Mr Todhunter with dignity, "and I should advise you very earnestly to take it seriously. You have an innocent man in prison. If you put him on trial, it will be a fiasco, in view of what I have to tell."

"No doubt, no doubt," returned the chief inspector equably. "But we'll look after that, Mr Todhunter."

To the sergeant, when he arrived a few moments later, the chief inspector gave his instructions; and, Mr Todhunter having been consigned to the newcomer's care, the two made their way downstairs. To Mr Todhunter's gratification, they entered a police car.

"I suppose I'm under arrest?" suggested Mr Todhunter, not without complacence, as the car pushed a cautious nose out into the traffic of Whitehall.

"Well, I wouldn't say that, sir," replied the sergeant, a taciturn person with the air of a drill sergeant.

It appeared that he would not say very much else, either, and the journey to Richmond was accomplished in almost complete silence, Mr Todhunter being filled with a strange mixture of elation and apprehension, and the sergeant wearing an expression like a stuffed sea lion, which might or might not have covered a complexity of emotions.

Mr Todhunter let himself into the house with his own key and, motioning to his companion to tread softly, led the way upstairs. The police car waited outside, presumably to conduct Mr Todhunter to prison. He wondered in a vague way whether he would have to walk out of the house between the sergeant and the plain-clothes driver, and if they would put gyves upon his wrists.

Selecting the right key with due deliberation, Mr Todhunter pulled open the drawer. There, in its nest under the handkerchiefs, was the revolver. Mr Todhunter pulled it out and handed it to the sergeant.

The sergeant broke it open and squinted down the barrel with an expert eye. "This gun's clean, sir."

"Well, I cleaned it of course," Mr Todhunter said testily, rummaging in the drawer.

"I mean, it's never been fired."

Mr Todhunter turned round and stared at him. "Never been ... but it *has*."

"This gun's never been fired, sir," repeated the sergeant stolidly.

"But . . ." A light broke on Mr Todhunter. "Bless my soul," he muttered. "Bless my soul!" He hesitated. "Er—are you at liberty to tell me this, Sergeant? Was a gun found in the possession of Mr Vincent Palmer?"

"It was, sir."

"And had that gun been recently fired? Please tell me. It's exceedingly important."

"Evidence was given before the magistrates that the gun in Mr Palmer's possession had been recently fired," replied the sergeant without emotion.

"Yes, and that was *my* gun," cried Mr Todhunter desperately. "I exchanged it surreptitiously for Mr Palmer's, the morning after. I—er—I was trying to get rid of the evidence, you see. I never thought he would be seriously suspected. It—it was culpable of me—criminally culpable. But that's what I did."

"Is that so, sir?"

"I can prove it. There was a witness. Mrs Farroway was there at the time. It was in Miss Farroway's . . ." Mr Todhunter's voice died away. The sergeant, that grim man, was actually smiling.

"Well, anyhow, what about that bracelet, sir?" smiled the sergeant.

"The bracelet, yes. Well there's no getting round that, at any rate," said Mr Todhunter almost defiantly and turned back to the drawer.

Two minutes later the contents of the drawer were on the floor. Three minutes after that the contents of all the other drawers had joined them there.

Finally Mr Todhunter could keep up the pretence of searching no longer.

"It's gone," he announced hopelessly. "I can't understand it. It—it must have been stolen."

"Gone, eh?" said the sergeant. "Well, and I must be going too. Good afternoon, sir."

"But I had it," cried Mr Todhunter shrilly. "It's preposterous. I shot the woman. You must arrest me."

"Yes sir," said the sergeant with remarkable stolidity. "But I don't think we'll arrest you just yet awhile. In fact, if I were you, sir, I wouldn't think any more about it."

One minute later Mr Todhunter, watching miserably from a window, saw the sergeant rejoin the driver of the police car. He also saw him touch his forehead significantly and jerk a thumb back towards the house. The sergeant's opinion was only too painfully obvious.

2

Ten minutes after the fiasco Mr Todhunter was ringing up his solicitor.

"The document you left with me?" said the latter, his voice a little surprised at the curtness with which Mr Todhunter cut short his greetings, but dry and efficient as ever. "Yes, of course I remember it. I have it still, yes. . . . You want me to do *what*?"

"I want you to take it round to Scotland Yard this minute," repeated Mr Todhunter loudly. "This minute, you understand. Ask for some high official— you'll know someone. Explain how the document came into your hands, and the precise date. If necessary take along a clerk to confirm it. Make the chap read it in your presence. Go though it with him if you like. And then please come along here to me."

"What is all this about, Todhunter?"

"Never mind what it's about," snapped Mr Todhunter. "Those are your instructions. It's a matter of vital urgency and importance, that's all I can tell you. Will you do it?"

"Very well," agreed the solicitor imperturbably. "No doubt you know what you're doing. Then I'll be at Richmond as soon as I can. Good-bye."

"Good-bye," said Mr Todhunter.

He hung up the receiver with relief. Benson was a sound chap. Benson could be relied on. If anyone could drum sense into the heads of those idiots, Benson could.

He sat down to await Benson's arrival.

It was nearly three hours before Benson came, neat and irreproachable in correct black coat and striped trousers. Mr Benson, senior partner in Benson, Whittaker, Doublebed and Benson, was the very model and pattern of a family solicitor.

"Well?" said Mr Todhunter eagerly.

With the privilege of a family solicitor, Mr Benson proceeded to speak his mind. He looked Mr Todhunter up, and he looked Mr Todhunter down, and he spoke.

"You're mad, Todhunter," said Mr Benson.

"I'm not mad," shouted Mr Todhunter. "I shot the woman."

Mr Benson shook his head and sat down without an invitation. "We'd better discuss this matter," he said, superimposing with some care one creased trouser leg upon the other.

"We certainly had," agreed Mr Todhunter savagely. "Whom did you see?"

"I saw Chief Constable Buckleigh, whom I happen to know slightly. I'm sorry now that I did. I assure you, if I'd known the contents of your precious document, I would never have gone there with it at all."

"You wouldn't?" sneered Mr Todhunter. "You think it of no importance to ensure justice being done?"

"On the contrary, I do, my dear fellow. And that's why I'm going to prevent you from doing anything foolish. I understand that you've been at Scotland Yard yourself this afternoon, trying to get yourself arrested. It's a pity you didn't consult me first."

With a great effort Mr Todhunter held himself under control. "You showed the man my statement?"

"I did, certainly. Those were your instructions."

"And what did he say?"

"He laughed. He'd heard about your visit already."

"It didn't convince him?"

"Certainly not."

"Nor you?"

"My dear Todhunter, you mustn't believe me so simple."

"What do you mean?"

Mr Benson smiled, a not uncomplacent smile. "You must remember that I drew up your new will before you sailed. I know of your interest in that particular family, I know that you expected to die very shortly, I know your quixotic nature and—"

"My nature isn't quixotic," interrupted Mr Todhunter loudly and rudely.

Mr Benson shrugged his shoulders.

"Look here," said Mr Todhunter more temperately, "do you honestly believe I faked the whole thing?"

"I'm quite sure you did," replied Mr Benson with a little smile. "As to that document, it is of course valueless. I read it carefully. It contains no information that you could not have got out of the newspapers and not a tittle of evidence.

You assert that you have the dead woman's bracelet, but you can't produce even that."

"Never mind the bracelet. That'll turn up. . . . Benson, whatever you may think, I'm speaking the truth. I admit I can't prove it, but I shot that woman."

Mr Benson slowly shook his head. "I'm sorry, Todhunter. . . ."

"You won't believe me?"

"I know you too well. I wouldn't believe you if you produced almost incontrovertible evidence. You couldn't shoot anyone, let alone a woman. So. . ."

"Well, I'm going to prove it," said Mr Todhunter violently. "If I don't, that chap Palmer is going on trial for a crime he never committed. I've got to convince the police—and you've got to help me."

Mr Benson shook his head again. "I'm sorry, I can't act for you in this."

"What do you mean?"

"What I say. I can't act for you. If you mean to go ahead with such a harebrained idea, you must obtain other advice."

"Very well," replied Mr Todhunter with dignity. "Then that's all there is to be said." He rose.

Mr Benson rose too. By the door he paused.

"I'm sorry, Todhunter. . . ."

"I hope you'll be sorrier still if an innocent man is hanged," said Mr Todhunter grimly.

3

Mr Todhunter sat alone in his library.

The two elderly cousins had gone to bed with much shaking of their frizzed old heads and wonderings whether the voyage had done dear Lawrence much good after all, he seemed so preoccupied and worried; and at last Mr Todhunter had the place to himself. His head looking rather like an ancient and time-stained ostrich egg as it poked forward on his shoulders, he set himself to consider the situation.

Mr Todhunter was, indeed, very much upset. He knew of course what the trouble was. His reading had shown him that after any particularly notorious crime has been committed the police are much bothered by unbalanced persons coming along and trying to confess to it. They had simply mistaken him for one of these lunatics. It was really excessively galling.

From the point of view of young Palmer it was tragic. He was innocent. It was almost inconceivable that he could be convicted. And yet . . . the police must have some kind of evidence, or they would never have arrested him. What could that evidence be?

Mr Todhunter's mind wavered helplessly from the mythical case against young Palmer to the actual case against himself, and his shockingly bad presentation of the latter. Had it been a mistake to pretend jealousy as the motive for the crime? But what else could he pretend? It was, perhaps, not vitally important to keep Farroway out of it, especially since the Farroway connection must now be known to the police; but the real motive was hopeless to put forward. Mr Todhunter knew, for every criminological volume he had read had told him so, that the police had no imagination. He had therefore decided long ago that to tell them the truth about the motive which had actuated him would be useless. They would never understand. They would never believe that a man would commit an absolutely academic, altruistic murder on behalf of a man and his family whom he scarcely knew at all. There was no getting away from it; put like that, the thing sounded fantastic. And yet it had not seemed at all fantastic in its gradual development.

But the jealousy theme . . . Mr Todhunter could not disguise from himself that he had not played the part well. He did not look like a passionately jealous lover. He did not even know what a passionately jealous lover feels like. Passionate jealousy seemed to Mr Todhunter just silly. No, the choice had not been a good one.

But what, in any case, was he to do now?

Mr. Todhunter felt a sudden spasm of alarm. Suppose his aneurism burst before he had persuaded the police that Palmer was innocent? Suppose Palmer was incredibly convicted . . . hanged horribly for a crime that he had never committed or dreamed of committing! The supposition was too dreadful. At all costs Mr Todhunter must keep himself alive until the truth was established. And to keep himself alive, he must not worry. But how the blazes was he to keep from worrying?

He had a sudden inspiration. A trouble shared was a trouble halved. He would take a lay confidant since Benson had proved useless—enlist a helper. Whom? Instantly Mr Todhunter knew the only person. Furze! He would see Furze tomorrow and put the whole thing before him. Furze had influence too. Furze would settle the whole ridiculous hash.

Much comforted, Mr Todhunter crept up the stairs to bed, pausing on each one to keep himself alive on behalf of young Mr Palmer.

4

"And you say you really shot this woman?"

"I did," averred Mr Todhunter solemnly.

Furze scratched his chin. "The devil you did! You know, I never for a moment dreamed you were serious."

"Of course not. It—um—sounded preposterous, no doubt. In fact," admitted Mr Todhunter, "I'm not sure that I really was serious then. The trouble was, I familiarised myself with the idea of committing murder. So when exactly the right case came along, I suppose I was already more than halfway over the stile."

"Interesting," nodded Furze, "There's no doubt that planning a murder is being halfway towards committing it. Perhaps that's why most of us stop short on the right side of the stile: we have the will, but we can't bother to work out the way. Still, about your case I don't know what's to be done."

"Something *must* be done," pronounced Mr Todhunter positively. "That fool of a solicitor of mine—"

The two were sitting in Furze's little office in Queen Anne's Gate. Mr Todhunter had been waiting in the anteroom when Furze arrived at ten o'clock.

"I'm afraid I'm interrupting your work," Mr Todhunter apologised now. "But the matter really is urgent, you know."

"I see it is. Deuced urgent. But what do you want me to do?"

"I thought perhaps you might be able to persuade the police . . ."

Furze looked thoughtful. "That's not so easy. The only thing that will persuade them is evidence. And that's just what you haven't got. I'll have a word with MacGregor. He's one of the assistant commissioners—belongs to my club. He might be useful. But otherwise . . . well, if we had that bracelet, we might be able to do something."

"I simply can't imagine what I can have done with that," admitted Mr Todhunter ruefully. "I could have taken my oath I'd put it in that drawer with the revolver."

"Well, you'd better concentrate your energies on finding that first of all. And it wouldn't be a bad thing to try to get some connected set of proofs for your story of what you did that night. It's plain that the police don't believe a single word of it. If you could manage to prove without question that you were in the Norwood woman's garden at all that evening, that would be a big point. Look here, why don't you call on Chitterwick?"

"Chitterwick?" repeated Mr Todhunter vaguely.

"Yes, he's done some good work in this line. Murder, you know."

"Murder? Oh, you mean finding the guilty person. Yes, of course. Yes indeed, I believe I remember seeing something about it. Dear me, yes, of course, I consulted him on the matter myself. My memory's becoming quite shocking."

"Well, you ring up Chitterwick and see if you can get him on the trail, and I'll sound Scotland Yard through MacGregor. I don't see what more we can do at the moment, but I'm sure something will come of it. I'm assuming, of course, that you're not suffering from a delusion of any kind. You really did shoot the woman?"

"There wasn't much delusion about it," returned Mr Todhunter with a little shiver, remembering that inert form and the red stain on that splendid white gown.

"Yes, well, knowing what I do, your story sounds more convincing to me than it probably did to the police and your solicitor," said Furze with his habitual candour. "And of course, if the worst comes to the worst, I can testify that you were meditating murder three months ago. And so can Chitterwick, to a certain extent."

"You don't think," asked Mr Todhunter anxiously, "that the worst will come to the worst?"

"You mean, that they'll hang this chap Palmer? No," said Furze cheerfully, "I don't think so for a moment. With the doubt that your story will throw on the case against him I should say that an acquittal ought to be fairly certain."

"Would you advise me to see Palmer's solicitors first or get in touch with Chitterwick?" asked Mr Todhunter humbly.

"Ring up Chitterwick and take him with you. That may make them take you more seriously. Of course you'll have to warn them that you can't prove a word of what you're saying, but that you're doing your best to collect proof; tell them you're ready to be called as a witness at the trial and ask them to cooperate with you in every possible way. They'll be ready enough to use you, even if they do think you're insane. Unless," added Furze thoughtfully, "counsel advises against calling you at all. Your story sounds so fantastic, you see, that it might do more harm than good. But that all depends how confident they are without it."

"Yes, I see; thank you very much," said Mr Todhunter and took his leave.

5

He did not, however, go first of all to the solicitors. He took a taxi up to Maida Vale to keep an appointment he had made before leaving Richmond.

The appointment was with Mrs Farroway.

It was three months since Miss Norwood's death, and as might have been imagined, Mrs Farroway had not allowed them to be wasted. Giving him a week or two to let over the worst of his trouble, she had firmly rejoined her husband, settled up his affairs and carried him back to the north; only to return immediately on the news of her son-in-law's arrest. But this time Farroway was not with her. He was, in fact, in the middle of a nervous breakdown at home. It had come upon him almost at once after he had got back, and in the opinion of Mr Todhunter, when he heard about it over the telephone, it was about the best thing that could have happened to him. At any rate it kept him out of the way and would prevent him from being called as a witness at the trial and, as would be the inevitable consequence, from showing himself up as a bit of a cad and a consummate fool.

Mrs Farroway therefore received Mr Todhunter alone; though Felicity, it was understood, was still in bed in a neighbouring room. The companion with whom she had shared the flat had lately been got rid of, it seemed, and the second bedroom was now Mrs Farroway's whenever she chose to occupy it.

Her first words to Mr Todhunter were not about the tragedy, but of gratitude for what he had done for her daughter.

"God bless my soul!" exclaimed Mr Todhunter. "I'd completely forgotten. The play, yes! Er—is it still running, then?"

"Still running?" Mrs Farroway laughed. "Really, you're a most unusual impresario. It's a success. A tremendous success. And so is Felicity. She's made for life, thanks to you. You really didn't know?"

"I—it escaped my mind to look out for the notices," apologised Mr Todhunter. "Besides, I was—um—in Borneo."

"Well, then, all I can say is that we're all very grateful to you, and Felicity will be coming in before you go to thank you herself. And I suppose you realise that you're making a small fortune?"

"A small fortune?" cackled Mr Todhunter. "Indeed, no, I didn't. Am I truly? How exceedingly gratifying. Well, well. That man—what was his name?— Budd, has managed well, then?"

"Mr Budd has been marvellous. He took a lease of the Princess itself from the executors, and . . . oh, but Felicity will tell you all this herself. Now sit down, Mr Todhunter, and tell me what you wanted to see me about."

Mr Todhunter disposed his uncouth length in a small chair and extended his legs. He put the tips of his fingers together and looked at Mrs Farroway over the top of them.

"You know, of course, that Vincent Palmer is innocent?" he began bluntly enough.

"Yes," Mrs Farroway replied steadily. "I know that,"

"In fact you know," Mr Todhunter said firmly, "that it was I who shot Miss Jean Norwood."

As if to quash any polite protest on Mrs Farroway's part, Mr Todhunter hurriedly waved for silence.

"The matter is too serious to beat about the bush, Mrs Farroway. We must speak openly. *I* killed Miss Norwood, for reasons which still appear to me excellent. I have never regretted it, nor shall I once this wretched trial has been successfully disposed of. But I want you to understand exactly how it came about that so unlikely a person as myself should have committed murder. It was this way."

Mr Todhunter then explained in full detail his version of the whole affair, from the moment he learned that he could live for only a few months longer until he heard casually from a fellow traveller in Tokyo that Vincent Palmer had been arrested. He blamed himself for the muddle over the revolvers, added an account of his visit to Scotland Yard, mentioned his anxiety lest the aneurism should burst prematurely and forestall his efforts to establish the truth and explained the steps he proposed to take in the immediate future.

"I want you," he concluded earnestly, "to tell your family what I have just told you; your daughters certainly, your husband, too, unless you think it advisable not to do so. It is only right that they should know; and not merely right but necessary—imperative. You understand?" And Mr Todhunter looked his hostess in the eye.

"I understand," said Mrs Farroway quietly. "I—" Then, to Mr Todhunter's inexpressible embarrassment, she burst into tears, jumped to her feet, seized Mr Todhunter's hand and kissed it and rushed out of the room. For a normally unemotional woman it was a remarkable display. But then, it was a remarkable occasion.

Mr Todhunter, feeling that his interview with Felicity could well be postponed to another day, bit his nails for a moment in indecision and then grabbed his hat and shambled on tiptoe out of the room, out of the flat and out of the building altogether.

6

"Dear me!" clucked Mr Chitterwick on the telephone. "Oh dear . . . Well, well, well . . . Yes, of course . . . Anything I can do . . . Yes, naturally . . . Dear, dear, dear."

"You'll come round at once then?" asked Mr Todhunter.

"At once, yes. Dear me, this is dreadful—dreadful." "Yes, isn't it?" said Mr Todhunter drily and hung up the receiver.

CHAPTER XI

"Dear, dear!" said Mr Chitterwick, "Dear, dear, dear! Dear, dear!"

Mr Todhunter looked at him with exasperation. Mr Chitterwick had been saying little else for the last half-hour. It did not sound very helpful to Mr Todhunter.

"The bracelet," repeated the latter now with scarcely hidden irritation.

"The bracelet, yes." Mr Chitterwick seemed to pull himself together. His round, pink, cherubic face settled itself into firmer lines. His plump little body visibly tautened for action. "The bracelet. Yes, undoubtedly we must find the bracelet," said Mr Chitterwick with great firmness.

The two were sitting in Mr Chitterwick's own special room at Chiswick. Mr Chitterwick lived with an elderly aunt who had once ruled his life with unremitting severity; but since he had achieved a certain notoriety of his own Mr Chitterwick had been emboldened to throw off his shackles and had even succeeded in acquiring a sitting room for his own particular use. Grumbling fiercely and unceasingly, Mr Chitterwick's ancient aunt had been cajoled or intimidated into allowing him, too, practically as much liberty as he wanted—which in any case was not very much.

Mr Chitterwick had called upon Mr Todhunter in Richmond and had heard the whole distressing story from its outset. He recalled of course Mr Todhunter's unsuccessful attempts to extract from him the name of a possible victim and, like Furze, found the affair not altogether impossible to believe. He had readily undertaken to do what he could towards helping Mr Todhunter in his remarkable dilemma.

The two had then paid a solemn visit to Vincent Palmer's solicitors, where they were received by a desiccated senior partner who seemed to take a great deal of convincing that Mr Todhunter was really in earnest. Having at last grasped that his visitor's supreme wish was to get into a dock—any dock—and there plead guilty to the murder of Miss Norwood, Mr Felixstowe (for such was the desiccated gentleman's name) had promised readily enough to do all he could to help Mr Todhunter attain this desire but had been depressingly pessimistic about his chances. Pointing out that in the absence of all evidence to the truth of a single word no jury would be likely to accept Mr Todhunter's tale and counsel for the prosecution would laugh it right out of court, he considered that in view of the certain severity of the judge's comments Mr Todhunter might well find himself faced with a prosecution for perjury. Mr Felixstowe had, however, promised to consult a number of people most carefully upon the advisability of calling such a possibly dangerous witness, had ventured a preliminary opinion of his own that it might possibly be better, all things considered, for Mr Todhunter before bursting his bombshell upon a sceptical world to await the verdict on Palmer which, without being optimistic, Mr Felixstowe opined might very well prove a favourable one, and, giving Mr Todhunter a hand like a piece of dried, cold fish, thanked him for coming. It had in fact been painfully plain that Mr Felixstowe had not believed a single word of Mr Todhunter's story and considered him at least a fool and possibly insane. Mr Todhunter did not seem to have much luck with solicitors. He had been so angry that his aneurism had been once more endangered.

His temper now, after listening to Mr Chitterwick clucking all the way from Lincoln's Inn to Chiswick, had scarcely improved.

"Er—lunch," said Mr Chitterwick, not without relief, as a gong boomed in the hall outside.

It was not usually the custom for Mr Chitterwick's aunt to take her meals in the dining room. She preferred a tray in the study where she passed most of her life, surrounded by her canaries and her collection of mosses; but on this occasion, supported by her companion, she made her appearance in the dining room just as Mr Chitterwick had been at some pains to arrange her tray exactly as she liked it.

"Huh! Begun already?" said Miss Chitterwick, sniffing the fragrant air. "Might have waited for me, I should think." She took no notice of Mr Todhunter at all.

The companion arranged her in a chair, a process which entailed much fussing with rugs and voluminous skirts.

"Er—this is Mr Todhunter, Aunt," said Mr Chitterwick when the arrangement had been completed.

"What's he want?" demanded Miss Chitterwick in return, without so much as a glance at Mr Todhunter.

"He's come to lunch. . . Aren't you staying, Miss Bell?" added Mr Chitterwick as the faded little lady who had accompanied Miss Chitterwick was slipping unobtrusively out of the room.

"Don't want her here," pronounced Miss Chitterwick. "Spoil the conversation, she would. The gurl can take a tray into your room for her. Can't trust her in mine. She'd have the place on fire before you knew where you were. Cut a bit off for her, Ambrose. Not too much. She don't want much food at her age."

With a sickly smile Miss Bell completed her exit. Mr Chitterwick began to carve.

"Committed a murder, have you?" suddenly said Miss Chitterwick, looking at Mr Todhunter for the first time.

"Er—yes," agreed Mr Todhunter, feeling like a small boy on the mat.

"Now, how did you know that, Aunt?" clucked Mr Chitterwick.

"Listened at the door," crowed Miss Chitterwick with relish. "Knew there was something up when you brought *him* here. Whom did you murder, Mr Snodbunting?"

"Really, Aunt!" deprecated Mr Chitterwick.

"I wasn't talking to you, Ambrose. I asked Mr Snodbunting a question, but it seems he's too high and mighty to answer it."

"I—er—I murdered a lady called Jean Norwood, an actress," hastily said Mr Todhunter.

"If she's an actress, she ain't a lady," Miss Chitterwick corrected him.

"My aunt hasn't—er—quite got used to modern ways," Mr Chitterwick twittered.

"Don't talk stuff and nonsense, Ambrose," riposted Miss Chitterwick, incensed. "I say 'gurl,' don't I? Not 'gairl' as my mother used to say. That's modern, ain't it? . . . Was she a lady, Mr Snodbunting?"

"No," said Mr Todhunter.

"There you are, Ambrose! Next time p'raps you won't try to be so sharp. Here, what's this? Duck? You know I can't eat duck."

"I'm sorry, Aunt. I—"

Miss Chitterwick thrust her plate in two yellow claws under Mr Todhunter's nose, shaking with rage. "Look what he's given me! Two little bits not fit to feed a pigeon. Just so as he could have more for himself. That's Ambrose all over. Mean!"

"I'm sorry, Aunt. I thought . . ." Hurriedly Mr Chitterwick laid another slice of breast on the outraged old lady's plate.

Mollified, she began to eat.

Mr Todhunter thought it best to avoid Mr Chitterwick's eye.

For a few minutes lunch progressed in silence. Then:

"Why'd yer shoot her?" demanded Miss Chitterwick, through duck.

Mr Todhunter offered a halting explanation.

"They goin' to hang yer?" enquired Miss Chitterwick with zest.

"I'm afraid not," mumbled Mr Todhunter.

"Wha'cha mean, you're afraid not? Should've thought it more likely you'd have been afraid they would. Hey, Ambrose? What's he mean?"

The two men looked helplessly at each other.

"You pulling my leg?" demanded Miss Chitterwick.

"No, no." Seeing nothing else for it, Mr Todhunter embarked on his story once more.

Miss Chitterwick heard him to the diffident end. Then she turned to her nephew.

"Ought to be in an asylum, *I* should say."

"Yes, Aunt," agreed Mr Chitterwick meekly.

"That's where they put people like him when I was a gurl."

"Yes, Aunt."

Mr Todhunter found himself stung into a certain defiance.

"I suppose you don't believe a word of what I've been saying?"

Miss Chitterwick looked at him with her shrewd old eyes. "Oh, Lawks, *I* believe yer. You're too big a fool to be a good liar."

"Yes, that's just what I think," chimed in Mr Chitterwick with relief. "I mean," he corrected himself hastily, "I believe Mr Todhunter too."

"But there's not many who will. And no wonder either," pronounced Miss Chitterwick.

"That—er—is precisely the trouble," lamented Mr Todhunter.

"You want to get yerself hanged?" asked Miss Chitterwick.

"I want to take the proper responsibility for what I've done and rescue an innocent man, madam," returned Mr Todhunter with dignity.

"More fool you, then," asserted Miss Chitterwick.

Mr Todhunter suddenly cackled.

"Yes, but anyhow, taking that for granted, what would you advise me to do in order to get myself hanged, Miss Chitterwick?"

"Oh, don't ask me. Better ask Ambrose. He's the high and mighty one about nowadays," replied Miss Chitterwick pettishly.

"But I am asking you."

"Oh, you are, are you?" Miss Chitterwick paused. "Well the noospapers call Ambrose a detective nowadays, it seems. I suppose they don't know what a guffin he is. So why don't you ask Ambrose to detect your murder for you? Lawks, any guffin—even Ambrose—ought to be able to do that when he knows who the murderer is—hey?"

"Detect it," echoed Mr Todhunter, much struck. "From the beginning. Exactly as in an unsolved case. Why, Miss Chitterwick, that's a very good idea."

Miss Chitterwick tossed her ancient head and bridled, but from the way in which the mauve ribbons trembled on her cap her nephew knew that she was pleased; though of course she would rather have died than admit it.

"Yes," continued Mr Todhunter. "Of course. That's exactly what we must do, Chitterwick. That is, if you will be good enough to spare the time. We must detect the murder together. We must—er—visit the scene of the crime, no doubt—"

"And try to find a witness who saw you there that night," chimed in Mr Chitterwick with enthusiasm, delighted because his aunt was pleased.

"And search for my footprints—"

"And fingerprints—"

"And prove that the case against Palmer is mistaken—"

"And enquire who was on the river that night—"

"And question my servants—"

"And find someone who heard the shot—"

"And prove my purchase of the revolver—"

"And draw out a correct timetable—"

"And trace my progress step by step—"

"And find the places where you broke through the hedges—"

"And—good gracious me, of course you're perfectly right, Miss Chitterwick. We must go about this matter in a methodical way and prove a convincing case against me. After all, you should be able to do that, Chitterwick, seeing that you know the murderer."

"That usual stumbling block is certainly absent," beamed Mr Chitterwick.

Mr Todhunter finished the last morsel of duck on his plate.

"Well," he remarked with a touch of his old sardonic humour, "well, I hope you really are a good detective, Chitterwick, for it seems that I am an unusually skilful murderer. I've baffled the police quite successfully. I only hope I shall not baffle you too."

"Surely," said Mr Chitterwick, "you won't be able to baffle us both together."

"Unless I've really committed the perfect murder."

Mr Todhunter cackled again. In spite of the gravity of the situation, the irony tickled him that he should be faced with so much difficulty in detecting the murder he had planned so long and so carefully.

2

The difficulty was a real one, for the case against Vincent Palmer was as strong as it was simple. Mr Todhunter and Mr Chitterwick had learned something of its details from the solicitors for the defence, and the main lines had of course appeared during the arguments before the magistrates.

It appeared that the young man had lied when he told Mr Todhunter, and the police, too, that he had been at home with his wife in Bromley on the evening of the crime. He had not only been in Richmond, he had been in the grounds of Miss Norwood's house—or so, at any rate, no less than three witnesses were ready to swear. These witnesses had heard the sounds of a quarrel, too, coming from the barn, voices shrill with anger.

Miss Norwood had then come running up to the house in a state of obvious agitation and, seeing her personal maid, had told her to tell the parlourmaid that no one else was to be admitted that evening. She returned to the garden and, a few minutes later, a shot was heard—by the maid, who at that time had her head out of a window and was listening hopefully for more quarrelling. (Mr Todhunter, remembering Marie, could well believe this.) She did not recognise the noise as a shot but thought it a motorboat misfiring on the river.

The glass which Mr Todhunter so unfortunately had omitted to wipe was the deciding factor in the case against Palmer. It bore fingerprints which were undoubtedly his. Witnesses may be mistaken, but here was definite proof that Palmer had not been in Bromley that evening but in Richmond; so definite that Palmer had been compelled to admit that he had been there. Why, then, had he lied, if it were not that he had shot Jean Norwood? That the revolver taken from him bore traces of having been recently fired was only needed to clinch the case.

In face of this evidence, Mr Chitterwick felt it necessary to point out that Mr Todhunter's coldblooded prudence in removing the fatal bullet had been a terrible mistake. The error about the revolvers would be easily cleared up, for the police would be able to establish with certainty which one had been purchased by Mr Todhunter through the records of the gunsmith at whose establishment it had been bought. But only the bullet could have identified which revolver had killed Miss Norwood.

Mr Todhunter could only bow his head and agree.

"You see," pointed out Mr Chitterwick as the two sat in his room again after lunch was over, Miss Chitterwick having been persuaded back to her own study and the care of Miss Bell, "you see, Palmer's own revolver appears to be useless as a means of identification. It was his father's army revolver, used in the war, and no record remains of its number and issue to him."

"Exactly," agreed Mr Todhunter, who had heard the solicitor make that very point. "But as to its having been used in the war that does not necessarily mean that it was ever fired, you must remember. It might never even have been out of England. The man at the shop where I bought mine pointed out that, though it was being sold as secondhand, it had never actually been fired; and he advanced that suggestion when I asked him how a revolver carried in the war could have escaped being fired. I suppose, by the way, they can tell whether a revolver has been fired or not?"

"An expert could tell, undoubtedly."

"Then," said Mr Todhunter triumphantly, "the sergeant who examined the revolver in my possession—that is, Palmer's revolver—was either no expert, or else his evidence exculpates Palmer; because he said that that gun had never been fired."

Mr Chitterwick rubbed his forehead.

"I find this confusion between the two revolvers extremely—er—confusing," he admitted.

"So do I," Mr Todhunter had to agree. "For instance when I exchanged the revolvers surreptitiously with Palmer, I must confess I had quite overlooked the fact that the police could identify mine by the gunsmith's register. Completely! It was damnably foolish of me."

"Then you can state positively that the revolver the police have—the one taken from Palmer—was the one you bought?"

"Undoubtedly. And I can only assume that it has not been identified as mine owing to the belief that the army revolver of Palmer's father was unidentifiable."

"But even so," muttered Mr Chitterwick, his plump round face puckered in a puzzlement, "even so it seems very remiss of the police. Quite unlike Moresby. A very conscientious, painstaking man, Moresby."

"You know him?" cried Mr Todhunter.

"Oh yes. Quite well."

Mr Todhunter uttered a harsh oath. "Then why didn't you say so before? He'll listen to you. We must go and see him at once."

"I'm extremely sorry. I—dear me, yes, perhaps I should have mentioned it," said Mr Chitterwick in distress. "Though indeed, as to listening . . ."

"Don't you see," pointed out Mr Todhunter with a great effort at patience, "that if the revolver in Moresby's possession is proved by the gunsmith's register to be mine, the case against Palmer is at end?"

"Shaken, yes." Mr. Chitterwick brightened. "Very considerably shaken. There are still the witnesses who saw him there, and—indeed, he now admits to having been there. But of course . . . yes, indeed. The sergeant asserted that the revolver in your possession had never been fired? Dear me, if that is true and the revolver can be proved to be Palmer's . . . why, yes, I really believe the police could be induced to withdraw the charge against him."

"Then the whole thing's at an end, even without the bracelet? We have our proof already?"

"So it would certainly appear," Mr Chitterwick

"Then we must go at once to Scotland Yard." Mr Todhunter shambled to his feet.

"Perhaps we ought to go to Richmond first and take that other revolver with us?" suggested Mr Chitterwick, bounding from his chair.

"No need," Mr Todhunter replied impatiently. "The police can come back with me again and collect it." To tell the truth, Mr Todhunter was looking forward quite childishly to another ride in that police car.

Mr Chitterwick acquiesced. Perhaps he felt himself a trifle overwhelmed by Mr Todhunter.

3

"Well, Mr Chitterwick, sir, what can I do for you? Why, you've got Mr—let me see, yes—Mr Todhunter with you."

"Er—yes," agreed Mr Chitterwick diffidently.

"Er—yes," mumbled Mr Todhunter.

"Well, sit down, gentlemen. Now, what is it?"

"Moresby," said Mr Chitterwick with great earnestness, "you've made a terrible mistake."

"So Mr Todhunter here told me yesterday," returned the chief inspector with unimpaired cheerfulness.

"But you really have. And we can prove it."

"What, found that bracelet, have you?"

Mr Todhunter was filled with a noble anger at the twinkle in the burly official's eye.

"No, we haven't found the bracelet, but—"

"But we can prove that you've got the wrong revolver," squeaked Mr Chitterwick excitedly. "Truly, Chief Inspector, you must listen to us. The revolver in your possession is Mr Todhunter's, and the one he has at Richmond is the young man Palmer's."

"Mr Todhunter said something like that to my sergeant yesterday," assented Moresby tolerantly.

"Well, we've come to give you the name of the gunsmith where Todhunter bought his, and you can prove the fact by his register."

Mr Todhunter nodded with severity.

"Now let's get this right, sir. You say that the number on the revolver in our possession is the number entered up in the gunsmith's register as belonging to the revolver sold to Mr Todhunter?"

"That's it, exactly."

"And that's the whole of your case?"

"Er—yes, I suppose so. But I think it's enough."

"Well, sir," said Moresby with benevolence, "you're wrong."

"What?"

"As soon as my sergeant got back yesterday he made enquiries on the matter. No need to bother with the gunsmith. He looked up the record of the firearms certificate issued to Mr Todhunter and verified that the number of the revolver sold to him is the number of the revolver now in his possession."

There was a short silence.

"Good God!" observed Mr Todhunter with inexpressible disgust. The disgust was for himself and no one else. A faint fear that had been present ever since the sergeant's visit had been verified. Mr Todhunter had blundered, and badly: in the confusion of the moment he had never exchanged those revolvers at all.

"Oh, just a moment, Mr Chitterwick, sir," said Moresby.

Mr Todhunter passed out into the cold stone passage alone.

4

"And the only evidence—the only incontrovertible evidence as to which revolver fired the fatal shot is now lying at the bottom of the Thames," lamented Mr Chitterwick.

Mr Todhunter did not answer. There was nothing to answer.

In silence the disconsolate pair pursued their gloomy way along Whitehall.

"What did he call you back for?" suddenly asked Mr Todhunter.

Mr Chitterwick looked embarrassed.

"What did he call you back for?" fiercely repeated Mr Todhunter.

"Oh well . . ." Mr Chitterwick wriggled. "He—that is, he advised me not to—to bother with . . ."

"Why? Why not?"

"He thinks you're mad," said Mr Chitterwick unhappily.

Mr Todhunter's aneurism was only saved by a miracle.

"But there's still the bracelet," Mr Chitterwick reminded him, just in time.

CHAPTER XII

"I hope sir," said Mrs Greenhill austerely and, as it seemed to the exasperated Mr Todhunter, for the thousandth time, "that you don't think *I* had anything to do with it."

"Of course not. If I did, Mrs Greenhill, I should have said so. We're simply trying to find out whether you have any information that can explain its disappearance."

"I hope, sir, that you don't think *I* had anything to do with it," repeated Mrs Greenhill woodenly,

"No, I told you I don't think that. But it's gone."

"So you say, sir. But I'm sure I never took it. And I'm surprised, sir, that you should think such a thing of me after so many years."

"I don't think so! But it's *gone*!" shouted Mr Todhunter.

Mrs Greenhill pursed her lips. Edie's sobs redoubled. The examination, conducted alternately by Mr Todhunter and Mr Chitterwick, had been in progress now for twenty minutes, nineteen of which Edie had spent in tears, protesting her innocence.

Mr Chitterwick waved his colleague's wrath aside.

"Now listen, Mrs Greenhill, please, and you too, Edie," he began in his most persuasive tones, "the point is—"

"Stop snivelling, Edie!" shouted Mr Todhunter, maddened beyond control by an extra large sniff and gulp from his wilting housemaid.

"I—I can't, sir," snivelled Edie. "Nobody's ever said such things to me before, I'm sure."

"Nobody has said anything to you, Edie," interposed Mr Chitterwick more sharply, "except that this bracelet has disappeared, which is a fact. If you make all this fuss over a mere fact, we shall soon begin to think there's something behind it, you know."

To Mr Chitterwick's surprise as much as anyone's, Edie did stop snivelling.

"Mr Todhunter thinks I took it," she said indignantly.

Mr Chitterwick hastily forestalled another outburst. "For God's sake, keep calm, Todhunter," he implored. "Remember, if you burst now—that is, your aneurism—goodness knows what may happen." He turned towards the guiltless pair and looked as severe as his benevolent countenance would allow. "You must remember, both of you, that Mr Todhunter is in a very precarious state of health, and if you persist in exasperating him in this ridiculous way by pretending that you've been accused of something that no one has accused you of, I wouldn't care to answer for the consequences."

"I was only saying that I wouldn't like Mr Todhunter or anyone else to think that I had anything to do with it," protested Mrs Greenhill, taken aback as though a tame budgerigar had suddenly nipped a large piece out of her ear.

"Well, no one does think that," beamed Mr Chitterwick, looking like a budgerigar once more. "So let's see what we can find out between us. Now the facts are these. When Mr Todhunter went away on his cruise he left a valuable diamond bracelet in the upper right-hand drawer of his chest of drawers. The drawer was locked. When he came back, the drawer was still locked, but the bracelet was not there. I've examined the drawer myself, and it shows no signs of having been forced. But on the other hand the lock appears to be a very simple one, and a skilled thief would have no difficulty in opening it. Now neither you, Mrs Greenhill, nor you, Edie," Mr Chitterwick continued to beam, "are skilled thieves, so that rules both of you out at once. You quite see that?"

There was a small chorus of gratified assent.

"Very well, then. Somebody else took it. That means, somebody who was not a member of the household. Now, Mrs Greenhill, just see if you can remember what strangers visited this house while Mr Todhunter was away,"

Mrs Greenhill and Edie looked at each other.

"Why, there wasn't anyone, sir. No stranger so much as set foot in the house all the time Mr Todhunter was away."

"Really? What, no one came to read the gas meter or see to anything connected with the electric light, or inspect the water connections or mend anything or clean anything?"

"Oh, those," said Mrs Greenhill in great surprise.

After five minutes patient questioning Mr Chitterwick was in possession of a rough list of meter readers, electricians and so forth, totalling seven.

"And that's all?"

"That's all, sir, so far as I can remember."

"I see. Well, if anyone else occurs to you, just let Mr Todhunter have a note of it."

"You don't think it can have been a burglar, sir?" asked Mrs Greenhill as they prepared to go.

"It's a possibility of course," Mr Chitterwick replied affably. "But I don't see a sign anywhere of a forcible entry having been made, and I'm quite sure that both you and Edie were far too careful to leave any windows open at night?"

"Oh no, sir. You can depend on that. Every window was shut and bolted before we went to bed every night. I saw to that myself."

"Exactly. Well, if there's nothing else you can tell us, I don't think we need keep you and Edie any longer."

The pair withdrew, and Mr Chitterwick shook his head.

"Not very helpful, I fear."

"That precious pair damned nearly killed me," snarled Mr Todhunter.

"Yes, yes. They were most exasperating. But there! No doubt they felt themselves in a very equivocal position."

"You don't think it was either of them?" asked Mr Todhunter hopefully.

Mr Chitterwick shook his head. "No, my impression is they are both of them quite honest. But.. ."

"What?"

"I wonder if the elder woman has a husband?"

"Mrs Greenhill? No, she's a widow."

Mr Chitterwick shook his head. "A pity. I believe with such a woman there is often a ne'er-do-weel husband in the background. That might have suited our investigations very well."

"Yes, but in the absence of a ne'er-do-weel husband," said Mr Todhunter impatiently, "what do you imagine has happened to that bracelet?"

"Dear me," said Mr Chitterwick, looking much distressed. "I'm afraid I can't say. The—the trail is cold, you see. We can investigate all these persons whom we know have been here. They may have had a moment to slip into your room, you see. I suppose," added Mr Chitterwick diffidently, "that you really did leave that drawer locked?"

"Of course I left it locked."

"Yes, of course, of course," Mr Chitterwick said hastily. "It was just. .. yes, of course."

"And how long," asked Mr Todhunter with sarcasm, "do you imagine it's going to take to enquire into the movements and problematical guilt of all those persons? A couple of months?"

"It would take time, certainly," Mr Chitterwick had to admit.

"Then let's pursue some other line," barked Mr Todhunter, whose nerves were wearing thin. "We've only got five days. Perhaps you're forgetting that?"

"No, no. Oh, no indeed. I assure you I'm not overlooking that."

"Well, damn and blast it," shouted Mr Todhunter. "I shot the woman! What sort of detective do you call yourself if you can't prove it in five days when I can tell you everything that happened, from A to Z?"

"Don't distress yourself, Todhunter," implored Mr Chitterwick. "I do beg of you not to distress yourself."

"Well, you'd be distressed in my position, wouldn't you?" croaked Mr Todhunter.

"I am distressed in any case," answered Mr Chitterwick, and from his face it was plain that he spoke the truth.

2

Mr Chitterwick dined with Mr Todhunter that evening, and afterwards they discussed the case for two solid hours, for the most part calmly. Such was Mr Chitterwick's power of soothing that not once was Mr. Todhunter's aneurism endangered. But unfortunately no conclusion was reached nor any very hopeful line of enquiry uncovered. By the time Mr Chitterwick left it had only been decided that the next morning, which was a Saturday, should be spent in traversing, in daylight, the route taken by Mr Todhunter on the fatal evening—and damn the owners of the gardens on the way if they objected!

At 10 a.m. punctually, therefore, on Saturday, December fourth, Mr Chitterwick presented himself in Richmond and the pair set forth. Their faces were stern and set; even Mr Chitterwick's cherubic countenance seemed to be trying to set itself into lines of relentlessness. With long, shambling strides Mr Todhunter strode along the pavement, and Mr Chitterwick trotted at his side, bouncing at every few steps rather like a large rubber ball,

At last Mr Todhunter turned, without hesitation, down a side lane and stopped before a certain place in a 6-foot fence.

"It was somewhere about here that I climbed over," he said.

Mr Chitterwick regarded the fence with surprise. "You climbed that? Good gracious me."

"I used to be a good climber. A fence like that presents no difficulties."

"Yes, but you might have killed yourself."

"I rather hoped," confessed Mr Todhunter, "that I should. But I didn't. One can't rely on doctors."

"You're not going to climb it now?" asked Mr Chitterwick anxiously.

"I am not. If you can find the place where I climbed over before, we will go round and find another way into the garden."

Mr Chitterwick looked doubtful. "I'm afraid there are hardly likely to be any traces remaining. It was so long ago." He stared at the fence in a vague and somewhat helpless way.

"I seem to remember that my foot slipped near the top," persisted Mr

Todhunter. "It might have scored the wood. We could at any rate examine the thing."

"Oh yes," Mr Chitterwick agreed readily enough. "We'll examine it, by all means."

They examined it.

After a few minutes Mr Todhunter could have been seen staring at a faint excoriation of the wood about a foot from the top of the fence. Mr Chitterwick joined him.

"That fits with your recollection," he said, but not too hopefully.

"It could have been made by the toe of a boot?"

"Oh, undoubtedly," said Mr Chitterwick, examining the mark more closely. "But it need not have been. I mean, there's no proof that this is where you climbed over."

"There may be marks the other side, where I landed," suggested Mr Todhunter, who appeared unusually sanguine now that the hunt was really up. "Footprints, perhaps. I jumped down, you see."

"After all this time? Well, it's possible, if there is no cultivated bed the other side, but . . ." Mr Chitterwick, generally so optimistic, was giving the impression that he considered their present quest not far from useless.

"We'll see if we can get into that garden without climbing the fence," pronounced Mr Todhunter.

They went a little further down the lane. A gate in the fence towards the river end proved to be luckily unbolted. Access to the garden was simple.

Mr Chitterwick had marked the top of the fence above the excoriation, and the two proceeded to examine the ground beneath it in the garden. A hedge of Lonicera nitida ran along the fence and for the distance of a foot or more beyond its roots the ground was hard and had obviously not been broken up for some time. Beyond this caked earth was a gravel path.

Hardly had they bent to their task before Mr Todhunter uttered an expression of jubilation. "What's that?" he asked, pointing a bony forefinger at an undoubted depression in the earth.

Mr Chitterwick plumped down on his hands and knees. "It is the mark of a heel, undoubtedly."

"Made by someone jumping off the fence?"

"It could have been," said Mr Chitterwick cautiously.

"What do you mean, it could have been? It was."

"Oh yes, undoubtedly," Mr Chitterwick agreed hurriedly." "Of course."

"Well, this is satisfactory, isn't it? We're finding what we wanted to find? If we have as much luck at the other hedges, we shall be able to prove the passage of someone across these gardens into Miss Norwood's, whereas it's known that Palmer came in through the front gates."

"Oh, undoubtedly." Mr Chitterwick began to beam, but the worried look did not altogether leave his face.

"Then what's troubling you?"

"Well, you see the only thing is, will the police accept that these marks were made so long ago, even if we are able to make a connected lie of them leading into Miss Norwood's garden? They may hold that they are—er—casual marks, and we have selected them arbitrarily."

"But we haven't."

"I'm only trying to put the police answer, "said Mr Chitterwick humbly.

Mr Todhunter snorted. "Come and see if there's anything to be found on the other side," he said and strode across the lawn.

Mr Chitterwick followed, not without a timorous glance or two towards the house whose privacy they were thus invading. Mr Chitterwick had all the Englishman's horror of committing trespass.

To cut half a morning's work short, it may be said at once that some indication of Mr Todhunter's passage three months ago was found at every barrier; or if not always a definite indication, something that could be interpreted as such—a broken shoot, a bent stem or the like, but no more footprints.

It was while they were examining the very last hedge of all, lining Miss Norwood's garden, that Mr Chitterwick's forebodings were fulfilled. A voice spoke behind them, harshly and loudly, causing Mr Chitterwick to jump nearly out of his overcoat and gravely imperilling Mr Todhunter's aneurism.

"Hey! What the devil do you two think you're doing here?"

A large man with one of those round, red, well-fed faces was looking at them with obvious displeasure.

Mr Chitterwick began to twitter incoherent apologies, but Mr Todhunter, having recovered his breath, took charge of the situation with firmness.

"I must apologise for this unceremonious intrusion, sir, but the matter is urgent. We are examining these gardens for clues."

"Clues? What clues?"

"It will not have escaped your knowledge," Mr Todhunter went on in tones of the greatest courtesy, "that a woman was shot a few months ago in the garden adjoining yours, and—"

"It will not, and I don't want anyone to be shot in this garden," interrupted the newcomer grimly. "Are you two members of the police? Because frankly you don't look like it."

"We are not members of the police force, no, but—"

"Then get out."

"But neither," continued Mr Todhunter suavely, "are we mere sensation hunters, as you have every right to think. This gentleman is Mr Ambrose Chitterwick, who has worked with Scotland Yard on several important occasions. My own name is Todhunter. We have every reason to believe, in fact we know, that an innocent man has been arrested for Miss Norwood's murder. We know that the real murderer approached Miss Norwood's garden through this one and through those between here and the little lane. Although the trail is, to speak technically, cold, we have already discovered important evidence to bear this out. We were examining your hedge to find the final proof of his passage into Miss Norwood's garden. Speaking personally, I am glad to see you, because we need an independent witness to the various small points of evidence we have discovered in case these are impugned later by the police, who will be naturally anxious to prove their case against the man they have arrested. We therefore invite you, sir, in the name of justice, to assist us in this and every other respect."

"Good God!" observed the stout man, while Mr Chitterwick looked with undisguised admiration at his companion and colleague. "You say this fellow Palmer's innocent?"

"I have the very best of reasons for knowing he is."

"What reason?"

"Because," said Mr Todhunter simply, "it was I who shot Miss Norwood."

The stout man stared. "You're mad."

"So the police say. But I assure you I'm perfectly sane. I shot Miss Norwood, and I can prove it to the satisfaction of any reasonable person; but not, it seems, to that of the police."

The stout man was still staring. "Well, you don't *sound* mad to me," he muttered.

"I'm not mad," repeated Mr Todhunter gently.

"Look here!" The stout man seemed to take a decision. "Look here, come up to the house. I'd like to talk to you about this."

"With pleasure. But may I have the honour of knowing your name, sir?"

"You may." The stout man looked at Mr Todhunter narrowly. "My name is Prettiboy. Ernest Prettiboy."

Mr Todhunter bowed. The name had conveyed nothing to him.

Mr Chitterwick, however, had uttered a slight yelp. "Not—not *Sir* Ernest Pettiboy?"

It was the stout man's turn to bow.

"I've heard of you, Mr Chitterwick," he added.

"Oh," cried Mr Chitterwick, "this is a piece of luck. This is a very great piece of luck indeed. Todhunter, this is Sir Ernest Prettiboy—the K.C. I beg you to tell him your story. This may make all the difference."

3

"This sounds an extraordinary tale," said Sir Ernest Prettiboy, K.C. He massaged the tight little black curls that covered his large head.

"It *is* an extraordinary story," Mr Todhunter agreed.

"But I believe it," pronounced Sir Ernest. His tone gave one to understand that the story was thereby made true.

Mr Todhunter thanked him politely.

"But what do you advise, Sir Ernest?" chirruped Mr Chitterwick anxiously. "I know this is most irregular. There should be a solicitor present. A consultation . . ."

Sir Ernest waved the irregularity aside. "We must consider what it is best to do," he said, not without weight.

"Yes, yes," agreed Mr Chitterwick gratefully, "That is just what I should propose myself."

Sir Ernest looked at Mr Todhunter and grinned. He was not a pompous man by any means, though occasionally the courtroom manner invaded him involuntarily.

"You're in the devil of a dilemma, my friend."

"I am," confessed Mr Todhunter. "It seems absurd that I should have so much difficulty in convincing the authorities that I shot this woman."

"Well, you must put yourself in their position. In the first place, I happen to know that no less than eight different people have already confessed to this murder. You can't be surprised if the authorities are getting a little sceptical.

"Eight?" echoed Mr Chitterwick. "Really! Ah, I see. She was a well-known figure. That would undoubtedly attract those who suffer from this curious kink."

"Exactly, in the second place, your story really has no more support than theirs. You were not able to bring forward one single item of proof to support it. I feel it was a pity that you should have gone to Scotland Yard so impetuously, without taking proper legal advice first. Any solicitor with criminal experience could have forecast the result."

"Yes, I see that now. I fancy I did think of doing so though my memory is so bad nowadays that I can't say for certain; but in any case my own solicitor, as I've discovered since, is quite useless."

"I can put you in touch with a good man. And I can tell you this. It was the biggest stroke of luck you've had yet to run into me during your trespassing expedition this morning, because I know something about this case. Living next door to the woman as I did, I had the police on my doorstep every day for a couple of months. And of course they didn't bother keeping any secrets from me. So I can tell you this: they have no doubt at all that they've got the right man."

"But it's ridiculous! I—"

"It's not at all ridiculous, from their point of view. The circumstantial evidence against this chap Palmer is very nearly as strong as circumstantial evidence can be—and that means wrought iron. Not cast iron; that's brittle."

"But his solicitor sounded sanguine," put in Mr Chitterwick.

"Yes. There are loopholes. But motive is covered, opportunity is covered and the means . . . by the way, tell me that bit about the revolvers again."

"Yes," nodded Mr Chitterwick, "I found this question of the revolvers a little puzzling."

"There was no exchange," mumbled Mr Todhunter with shame and explained his blunder again.

Mr Chitterwick chimed in with a further explanation of Mr Todhunter's error in throwing the fatal bullet away.

"Won't the absence of the bullet leave a gap in the chain of proof?" Mr Todhunter asked. "Without it they can't really prove that it was Palmer's revolver that killed her."

"There is that small gap, undoubtedly. But its value is nothing compared with the proof which the bullet would have given us that Palmer's revolver definitely did not fire the shot." Sir Ernest took another gulp from the tankard of beer which he had been holding throughout the interview. Mr Chitterwick also had a tankard. Mr Todhunter held a glass of lemonade.

Sir Ernest leaned back in his chair. The three were sitting in the K.C's study, and the massive legal volumes on the shelves all round them seemed to frown upon this unorthodox conference.

"Well, I think I understand your case. It's not an impossibility at any rate, though I think the police, not being professional psychologists, would find your motive hard to swallow—"

"That's precisely why I told them that I committed the murder out of jealousy," put in Mr Todhunter.

"Yes. But I feel," twinkled Sir Ernest, "that they would have even more difficulty in swallowing that. It really is a great pity that you didn't take advice. However, as I was saying, I believe your story, and we must see what can be done."

"You'll help us?" asked Mr Chitterwick eagerly.

"I couldn't reconcile it even with my professional conscience to stand aside and see what I thought might be injustice done. Besides," said Sir Ernest with a sudden grin, "it's going to be damned interesting and instructive. Now let me see whether I have any inside knowledge that might help. Yes—did you know that there are witnesses to the fact of a punt being moored at the bottom of Miss Norwood's garden at just about the time of the shooting that night? The police have been unable to trace the occupant."

Mr Chitterwick nodded. "There was a wireless broadcast for the person or persons to come forward."

"Was there? Oh yes, I believe there was. Well, anyhow, they haven't come forward. That seems a little odd to me."

"There might be reasons," ventured Mr Chitterwick.

Sir Ernest winked. "Oh yes. And I suppose there were. But the really interesting thing is that one witness swears that the punt, when he passed it in a skiff, was empty."

"Oh!" Mr Chitterwick looked puzzled. "But does this have any bearing on the case?"

"Possibly not. Only . . . supposing there was somebody else in the garden that night. There would be an exceedingly valuable witness, don't you think?"

"Oh, I see. Yes indeed. You think the person—or persons—might have landed?"

"How else could the punt be empty?"

"Yes, of course," agreed Mr Chitterwick, as if annoyed with his own stupidity. "But how could we trace them if the police have failed?"

"There," confessed Sir Ernest, "you've got me beat. There was nothing," he added to Mr Todhunter, "that led you to suspect that anyone else might have been in the garden while you were there?"

"Nothing," said Mr Todhunter firmly. "It was nearly dark. Besides, I was in a state of considerable agitation."

"Yes, of course. Well, we must put that point aside for the time being. Now you tell me that you've found some evidence, even after all this time, that somebody did make his way from the lane through these gardens. I think we'd better go out and verify that."

Not without pride Mr Todhunter and Mr Chitterwick led their new ally down the lane and showed him the mark on the fence where Mr Todhunter had climbed over; and thence, making their way through the other gardens without any more ado than before, the footprint, broken twigs and all the rest of it in the various hedges. This time, however, they did not remain in Sir Ernest's enclosure but pushed through into Miss Norwood's own garden. The house, Sir Ernest was able to tell them, had not yet been let; the police had finished with it, and they had the place to themselves.

"We'd better look at the scene of the crime, I suppose," Sir Ernest said, "though goodness knows what we can expect to learn from it."

Mr Todhunter looked about him curiously. It was the first time he had seen the ground in full daylight, and he was surprised to find how short was the distance from the hedge to the converted barn which had seemed so interminable and tortuous that night.

They stood on the banked lawn outside and surveyed the structure, with its grey, weather-beaten uprights and its hint, genuine as it was, of something of "ye olde" type of spuriousness about it.

"It's not so big as I thought," muttered Mr Todhunter. "It looked enormous that night."

"Things always look bigger at night," suggested Mr Chitterwick.

They went on looking at it.

"Well," said Sir Ernest, "we don't seem to be getting much forrader. Anyone got any suggestions? All right. Let's reconstruct the crime. I see there's a deck chair or two still here. Where exactly was she sitting, Todhunter?"

On Mr Todhunter's directions, so far as he could remember, the scene was set. Sir Ernest Prettiboy, who seemed to be thoroughly enjoying himself, then made Mr Todhunter go through the motions of his murder.

"I approached, I think, from this direction," said Mr Todhunter, not without reluctance, for he found this play-acting rather horrible. "I came within quite a short distance, and—"

"Without her seeing you?" put in Sir Ernest.

"She gave no sign of having seen me," replied Mr Todhunter drily.

"Yes? And then?"

"And then I fired."

"And she. . . ?"

"She seemed to—to—no, that wasn't the first shot. It was . . . great heavens!" Mr Todhunter clapped his hand to his forehead. "I think I'm going mad."

"Tck! Tck!" clucked Mr Chitterwick in distress. But Sir Ernest had been quicker on the point. "What happened?" he shouted, almost dancing with excitement. "Think, man! The *first* shot? Then you fired. . . ?"

"Yes," said Mr Todhunter in a dazed way. "I fired twice—and I've never remembered it till this minute."

4

"But you must remember in which direction you fired," said Sir Ernest Prettiboy despairingly.

"It was in *that* direction," Mr Todhunter repeated for the tenth time. "But I'm probably not a very good shot," he added.

Sir Ernest groaned.

It was in the middle of the afternoon. Half an hour had been taken up in the morning, following Mr Todhunter's revelation, in an intensive search for the first bullet, without success. Sir Ernest had then carried them back to his house for lunch, despite their polite protests, and had introduced them to his wife, who appeared to accept their presence with equanimity, and to two small Prettiboys of assorted sexes, who showed themselves quite indifferent to it. Now, replete with roast beef and horse-radish sauce, apple pie and, in Mr Chitterwick's case, a more than passable claret (for those who like details it was a Pontet-Canet, 1925, a light vintage, still quite drinkable but just passing its best) , they had applied themselves to the task once more. Bidden to take up the exact position (so far as he could gauge it) in which he had been standing when he fired and point in the direction in which he had aimed, Mr Todhunter had already occupied half a dozen different spots and pointed his finger in a dozen different lines.

"I can't help feeling," ventured Mr Chitterwick, still a little timid in the presence of this great and self-confident man, "that this score on the brick floor may be significant. If that is where the bullet struck, and it rebounded—"

"Ricocheted," corrected Sir Ernest.

"Ricocheted," accepted Mr Chitterwick gratefully, "why it might be almost anywhere."

"But, damn it all, he wouldn't have hit the ground," objected Sir Ernest. "You wouldn't have hit the ground, Todhunter, eh?"

"I might have hit anything, and the ground is certainly the largest," said Mr Todhunter with a mirthless grin.

"Pretty poor shot, are you?"

"Probably the worst in England."

"Humph!" said Sir Ernest and joined Mr Chitterwick in looking in the most unlikely spots for the bullet rather than in the most likely ones.

These tactics met almost at once with success. It was, in point of fact, Mr Chitterwick who actually discovered the shapeless little lump of lead embedded in a tie beam right at the other end of the barn; though to hear Sir Ernest's satisfaction, not unmixed with a suggestion of self-commendation, one would have said that it must have been he who had found it.

It was, at any rate, Sir Ernest who dug it carefully out with his penknife.

"I'm your witness," he announced when Mr Chitterwick expressed a hesitation as to whether it might not be better to leave this important evidence in situ. "That's quite in order. Besides, we want this. I'm no ballistics expert myself, though I do know a bit about firearms, and we shall want a report on this. If it proves to have been fired from your gun, Todhunter, I should say we've got 'em cold."

Mr Todhunter looked doubtfully at the squashed and misshapen fragment now balanced in Sir Ernest's palm.

"Can they really tell what gun that came from?" he asked.

"Well, I'm not so sure," Sir Ernest had to admit, his optimism faltering slightly. "Doesn't look as if it'll carry much marking, does it? That's the worst of these lead bullets. Especially after bouncing off this floor. Now if it had been nickel . . ." His tone conveyed disapproval of Mr Todhunter's remissness in using a lead bullet. It also seemed to suggest that for his next murder, if he wanted it detected without all this difficulty Mr Todhunter had better employ nickel bullets.

"Anyhow," he went on, "we must hope for the best. I know the fellow we must send it to. And that revolver of yours must go with it. I'd like to look at that revolver myself too. I'll get the car out."

"The car?" Mr Todhunter echoed stupidly.

Sir Ernest looked surprised. "We've finished here, haven't we? Well, we'll go round and have a look at that revolver. No time to let the grass grow under our feet, you know."

As a result of Sir Ernest's hustling methods, Mr Todhunter found himself unlocking his own front door less than twenty minutes later. Feeling a little overwhelmed, he invited the other two to follow him upstairs.

In the bedroom Sir Ernest showed interest in the drawer from which the bracelet had disappeared and took the revolver from Mr Todhunter with the easy familiarity of one used to firearms. Mr Todhunter watched him with interest as he squinted down the barrel and up the barrel, sniffed it, twirled the chamber and generally put the weapon through its paces.

"That sergeant's a fool," he pronounced at last.

"What?" said Mr Todhunter.

"That sergeant. Said this revolver had never been fired, didn't he? Well, he's wrong. It has been fired, and pretty recently; though it's been carefully cleaned since."

"Exactly what I told him," said Mr Todhunter, not without relief.

"We're getting on," beamed Mr Chitterwick.

CHAPTER XIII

Mr Chitterwick had been over-optimistic.

The next day was a Sunday, and little could be done then. Vincent Palmer's trial was to open at the Old Bailey on the following Thursday. That gave just three working days for the proving of the case against Mr Todhunter. It was very short.

During those three days Mr Chitterwick worked like a demon. He spent a whole day trying to get on the trail of the missing bracelet and managed to interview every single person whom Mrs Greenhill could name as having visited the house while its owner was away. In each case he not only drew a blank but was able to feel convinced that the person had had no hand in the theft. Nor could he uncover any evidence that an unauthorised person might have got into the house and purloined the bracelet. He questioned and cross-questioned Mrs Greenhill and Edie, regardless of their tears, protests and indignant handing in of notices. And he advanced not one single step.

Mr Chitterwick also inserted a desperately worded appeal in the personal column of every national newspaper to the occupant of the empty punt which had been moored at the bottom of Miss Norwood's garden on the fatal night. No one came forward.

To add to the depression, the report of the ballistics expert on the bullet found in the barn was disappointing. It was too much damaged for positive identification, and all that could be said of it was that it could have been fired from Mr Todhunter's gun. The bullet was then handed over to Scotland Yard, and Chief Inspector Moresby confidentially told Mr Chitterwick that the report of their own man was to the same effect. As a decisive factor in the case the bullet, on which such hopes had been pinned, was a failure.

During these three days Mr Todhunter was equally busy. At first Mr Chitterwick tried to look after him as a hen guarding a chick, for fear that in the rush and scurry Mr Todhunter might wreck the case by bursting his aneurism prematurely, and Sir Ernest Prettiboy was also inclined to act as watchdog over their precious but fragile witness. When, however, Mr Todhunter, irked by his guardianship and feeling himself perfectly capable of safeguarding his own aneurism, had been induced to promise that he would behave as calmly and circumspectly as if nothing was in the air at all, he was allowed to go off by himself in taxis and conduct his own interviews. In this way he again saw Furze, who had to report that the assistant commissioner whom he had sounded had pooh-poohed the whole thing. The opinion at

Scotland Yard was quite definite. They no longer considered Mr Todhunter mad. Enquiries had been made about him already, and the state of his health had been ascertained.

"So what?" demanded Mr Todhunter as Furze paused.

"So they think you're just trying to save Palmer, as a friend of the family, knowing it can't make much difference to the length of your own life."

"The devil they do!" Mr Todhunter remained calm only by an effort. "And they think all the evidence I can produce quite worthless?"

"Quite."

"But—but—"

"You see," Furze pointed out, "they're quite prepared to believe that you were in the garden that night. They see no reason why you shouldn't have called on Miss Norwood yourself. In fact, I gather that they've put you down in their minds as the owner of the empty punt. But they think you arrived there, if you did arrive at all, *after* the woman was shot."

"Damn!" stormed Mr Todhunter. "Damn! Blast! Hell! Blazes!"

"Steady!" implored Furze. "Steady, for goodness' sake."

"Yes," agreed Mr Todhunter grimly, "I'm damned if I'll die just yet."

Mr Todhunter also had another interview with Mrs Farroway, in which a good deal of veiled and careful talk passed. Felicity was at the theatre, so again Mr Todhunter did not see her; if the truth were told, Mr Todhunter had deliberately avoided the meeting. He did not know much about actresses, and what he did know was not encouraging; and he feared that Felicity might carry drama into private life. Mrs. Farroway, on the other hand, was remarkably calm. She did not appear to think it of very great importance that Mr Todhunter's efforts to prove his guilt should have been so far abortive, or indeed that her son-in-law was standing trial for a crime that he had not committed. Indeed Mrs. Farroway went so far as to say that she thought it would do Vincent a great deal of good.

"But supposing, he's convicted?" asked Mr Todhunter.

"He won't be," replied Mrs Farroway with a confident smile.

Mr Todhunter could only be impressed by such optimism. For himself, he had regarded the trial as tantamount to a conviction, though he could not have said why.

On one evening only did Mr Todhunter permit himself a certain relaxation. Taking Sir Ernest and Lady Prettiboy with him (Mr Critterwick was far too busy), he paid a visit to the Sovereign Theatre and witnessed Felicity and the play. To his great indignation there was no box available, and only by great luck were three stalls empty, returned at the last moment. Mr Todhunter, who had not thought to ring up the theatre in advance and arrived with his guests only a minute or two before the certain went up, felt vaguely that there was some mismanagement in this and complained as much to Mr Budd in the interval. Mr Budd, however, was so full of exuberance, of congratulations and (it must be admitted) of whiskey, that it is doubtful whether he ever heard anything that Mr Todhunter mumbled to him.

After the performance Mr Todhunter felt constrained to apologise to his guests. Felicity Farroway had been good—yes, quite good. But the play, in Mr Todhunter's opinion, was the most dreadful trash he had ever seen. Mr Todhunter was genuinely surprised that both his guests should disagree with him and ascribed their protests to politeness.

The next morning the trial of Vincent Palmer opened.

2

The trial was a full-dress affair. The expectation was that it would last ten days. In point of fact it lasted eight, from the ninth to the sixteenth of December.

From the beginning the defence were confident. The case against the prisoner, though one of the gravest suspicion, was felt to be lacking in definite proof. Even the fact that Palmer's revolver had been recently fired was not of particular importance, for there was no bullet to prove that it had been his gun which had killed Miss Norwood. If there had been a bullet, and if it could have been shown that this bullet had definitely not been fired from Palmer's gun, there would have been no real case against him at all (as Mr Todhunter was becoming rather tired of hearing people point out); but even in the absence of such concrete evidence for the defence it was felt that there was not nearly enough concrete evidence for the prosecution.

The question of whether Mr Todhunter should or should not be called was undecided until the last possible moment. Palmer himself was against it. Knowing himself innocent, he could not believe that there was any real chance of his being convicted, and he saw no reason why Mr Todhunter should voluntarily brand himself as a murderer on his, Palmer's, behalf. In other words young Mr Palmer, who unaccountably seemed to have taken a dislike to Mr Todhunter at sight, announced that he did not want any favours from that quarter and would, in fact, be damned if he'd have any.

On the whole counsel supported this view. The police opinion was known, that Mr Todhunter had come forward in a spirit of altruistic idiocy, and some difficult cross-examination could be expected on this point. There was, too, the possible effect on the jury, who might be inclined to think that the defence must feel themselves in a very weak position to rely upon such a fantastic tale. For the unfortunate truth was that Mr Todhunter's tale still sounded fantastic, and Mr Todhunter himself looked like being a most unconvincing witness to it. Moreover neither counsel nor the solicitors for the defence believed it for one moment.

It was finally decided, therefore, in spite of the unofficial urging of Sir Ernest Prettiboy, not to call Mr Todhunter. In consequence that gentleman, not quite knowing whether to be disgusted or relieved, was able to sit in a privileged position on the witnesses' benches and listen to the whole trial.

At first all went well. The opening speech for the prosecution showed clearly the weakness of the case against Palmer, and the attorney general, who was conducting the case in person, spoke with such obvious moderation that the only inference was that he himself was none too convinced of the prisoner's guilt. Right until the last witness had testified for the Crown the odds were strongly in the prisoner's favour.

And then things seemed to go wrong. Palmer himself made an exceedingly bad witness: truculent, assertive and stubborn. The sulky way in which he admitted the rivalry of his father-in-law and himself for the dead woman's favours, the contempt with which he spoke of Miss Norwood and the obvious change of heart that he must have experienced towards her (he spoke as if her memory were repellent to him), the occasional violence with which he met some particularly awkward question—all these could not but have a bad effect on the jury.

There was, for instance, the question why he had first of all denied having been in Richmond at all on the fatal evening. This denial, as Mr Todhunter and his advisers knew, had produced an exceedingly bad effect on the police; for Palmer's story that he had been at home had been supported originally by his wife. Only when incontrovertible evidence was put to him that he had been positively identified at the Norwood house did Palmer retract this fiction and admit his presence; and he had added that his wife had supported his story upon instructions from himself. To the police this naturally appeared in the light of a conspiracy and pointed overwhelmingly to Palmer's guilt.

It was not possible to question Mrs Palmer in court upon her part in this conspiracy since this would be tantamount to requiring her to give evidence against her husband, nor was she charged as an accessory after the fact. Palmer himself however was pressed on the point; and admitted that first of all he had denied being at Richmond in order to spare his wife pain, since she knew of his interest in Miss Norwood and it had made her unhappy; and secondly, when asked where he was if not at Richmond, he had lost his head and said he was at home without realising that this would involve his wife in supporting or denying his statement.

Mr Todhunter, however, when he heard of this explanation, was sceptical. He had expressly asked Palmer whether his wife would be prepared to back up his statement, and Palmer had replied that she would. Obviously there had been a conspiracy between them, arranged probably between Palmer's two visits to the Farroway flat; and if the evidence of the Norwood servants had not burst the balloon, both husband and wife would have stuck to the story. This looked bad.

Then again there was the still more difficult question of why Palmer should have brought his revolver round to his sister-in-law's flat early that morning, directly the news of the murder became known. Was this the action of an innocent man who feared he might be wrongly accused, or was it the action of guilt? Palmer sullenly maintained that it was the former; fearing that his quarrel with the dead woman might have been overheard, he had thought that it might be better that no revolver should be found in his house. Pressed as to how it was that the revolver showed signs of having been recently fired, Palmer rather unconvincingly denied that it had showed anything of the sort. His counsel tried hard in re-examination to smooth these difficulties out, but a bad impression had been made and Palmer's demeanour did nothing to help matters.

On top of all this, the judge, for some reason best known to himself, showed himself definitely hostile; and when he summed up, although his words were scrupulously fair, his own opinion could be plainly discerned between them. Moreover he commented, as indeed he was quite entitled to do, on the unfortunate absence in the flesh of Farroway himself, whose evidence, owing to his continued ill-health had had to be taken in the form of an affidavit. Farroway, observed the judge, might have been able to clear up several points that remained obscure. As he had not appeared to do so, the jury must form their own opinions on the points in question. And the implication was only too plain that, to the judge's mind, Farroway's evidence under cross-examination would have been definitely damaging to the prisoner; and its absence was due to a family conspiracy to protect him.

The jury were out nearly five hours, and they were the five longest hours Mr Todhunter had ever known. When at last they returned, there was hardly a person in court who had not anticipated the verdict of "Guilty" which they returned.

"And what," rather shrilly demanded Mr Todhunter of Sir Ernest Prettiboy as they followed the others outside, "what the hell do we do now?"

"Hush, hush," soothed Sir Ernest. "We'll put your case forward. I knew they were wrong. You'll see. It'll be all right. They can't hang him."

3

It seemed that the home secretary disagreed with Sir Ernest.

In due course Palmer's appeal was heard, on the grounds that the verdict had been against the weight of evidence. It was dismissed, very solemnly, by three learned judges.

Then a petition was drawn up, couched in ancient and magnificent language, and here it was definitely stated that Lawrence Butterfield Todhunter had already confessed to being responsible for the death of the said Jean Norwood and was prepared to submit to all necessary interrogations, pains and penalties for his deed, in view of which fact and the grave doubts at least which it cast upon the guilt of the prisoner Vincent Palmer, the home secretary's petitioner did very humbly beg and pray that a stay of execution be granted while the statement of the said Lawrence Butterfield Todhunter was examined by the law officers of the Crown (the said petitioners knowing very well that once a stay of execution is granted the execution is never carried out). To all of this the home secretary replied, curtly, that the prisoner Vincent Palmer had been properly condemned by a jury capable of estimating the facts, that he had consulted with the learned judge who had heard the appeal, and that as a result he saw no reason to interfere with the jury's verdict.

This news had to be broken to Mr Todhunter with such circumspection and care that it was two whole hours before he realised that the home secretary considered him no more than a deliberate and rather childish liar.

"Very well," said Mr Todhunter with creditable coolness, "On the day they excuse Palmer I will shoot myself on the steps of the Home Office."

"Gad, we'll tell the papers that," cried Sir Ernest Prettiboy with enthusiasm. "Nothing like a bit of publicity in the right direction."

Sir Ernest was as good as his word. In consequence every popular newspaper the next morning carried a banner headline to this effect, while the more solid journals referred to it with some disgust on an unimportant page. It had interested Mr Todhunter to observe that the popular press supported him to a lord, while the other newspapers, although inclined to think that this was a case in which the home secretary might perhaps exercise his prerogative of mercy, professed no doubt concerning the prisoner's guilt.

The banner headlines had no effect. The home secretary was a dry and legal man, full of precedents and the letter of the law, and a popular agitation was quite enough to stiffen him in any unpopular course of action. If the home secretary could manage it, Vincent Palmer should hang.

"We'll save him yet. I swear we'll save him," fumed Sir Ernest. "My God, if we'd only got a *man* at the Home Office instead of this bundle of old parchment tied up with red tape. The very worst home secretary there's been for a century, for our purpose. But we're not done yet. There's still old Powell-Hancock."

Mr Chitterwick nodded brightly. Mr Todhunter looked doubtful. Sir Arthur Powell-Hancock was another of Sir Ernest's "strings."

Mr Todhunter had indeed been astonished at the reliance which Sir Ernest Prettiboy placed on his "strings," as Mr Todhunter termed them to himself. One would have said that Sir Ernest was a man of fairly definite purpose and direct action, but it seemed that according to the rules of the game no one must ever do anything himself. Somebody else always had to be approached, and the more circuitously, the better, to do it for one. These persons Sir Ernest would refer to as "a string to pull." Old This could pull a string with the king's proctor, old That was at school with the attorney general, old the Other knew a second cousin of the home secretary's wife and might be a useful string. Everything must be done on personal grounds, never on the rights or wrongs of the actual case. Sir Ernest knew all these important persons himself, and apparently quite well; but he seemed to think that the home secretary's decision was much more likely to be influenced by an elderly aunt of the permanent secretary's, over a tea table in Bayswater, than by a discussion on the justice of hanging an innocent man in the cold formality of the home secretary's own office. It amazed Mr Todhunter still more that the solicitors, and indeed everyone who might be expected to know the ropes, not merely shared this view but seemed to think that no other view was possible.

Mr Chitterwick, with whom Mr Todhunter discussed this phenomenon, knew better and tried to explain the inert mass of unimaginative bureaucratic dead weight against which any reform or even any measure of plain humanity had to strive.

Sir Arthur Powell-Hancock was Sir Ernest's parliamentary "string." Mr Todhunter's amazement had been deepened on finding that there was a disposition to treat the hanging of Vincent Palmer as a political question. Members of Parliament who supported the government were, it seemed, on the whole disposed to back the home secretary and execute Palmer; members of the opposition professed to regard Mr Todhunter's story as true, or at any rate worthy of examination, and accused the government of persecution, injustice and, probably, simony; while the *News Chronicle,* in a thoughtful, leader, tried to prove that the civil war just then raging in Spain was entirely due to the government's malicious intention to hang an innocent man.

Sir Arthur Powell-Hancock, although a supporter of the government, had almost undertaken to raise the question of the execution in the House of

Commons. (Mr Todhunter gathered that it was expected to win him over finally through some arguments concerning the removal of the tolls on a bridge in his constituency, which did not at first sight appear very relevant but in which Sir Ernest seemed to have considerable faith.)

Exactly four days before Vincent Palmer was due to die Sir Arthur at last succumbed to the argument of the toll bridge and formally gave notice of his intention to raise the question on the adjournment or whatever it is that members do raise questions on; Mr Todhunter was a little bewildered on the point.

Mr Todhunter was indeed a little bewildered altogether during these two weeks. The matter seemed to have been taken out of his hands completely. Although the principal actor, he was to play his part now, it seemed, entirely off stage. Sir Ernest Prettiboy spoke for him, acted for him, agitated for him and almost ate his meals for him. In fact Sir Ernest strongly advised Mr Todhunter to retire to his bed and stay there, for he could do nothing more to help except by remaining alive. On the day that Sir Arthur tabled his motion Mr Todhunter took this advice—after a final visit to Maida Vale, a last interview with Mrs Farroway, whose distress was now beginning to show through her self-imposed front of calm confidence, and a last desperate entreaty to her to do nothing, say nothing and generally keep out of things until 6 a.m. on the day that Vincent Palmer was to die. After that hour, said Mr Todhunter in some despair, anybody could do anything so far as he was concerned.

4

The report of the proceedings in the House of Commons was given to Mr Todhunter in his bed that evening by Mr Chitterwick, who attended in person, and by the indefatigable Sir Ernest Prettiboy, who, having thrown all precedent and procedure to the winds, was scandalising his professional colleagues more and more every day.

Sir Arthur Powell-Hancock rose, in a somewhat apathetic House, to raise the question of Palmer's execution on the motion that the House should go into Committee of Supply. Roughly, members were divided into five groups. There were those who regarded the question as a political one and intended to support the home secretary in his refusal to intervene, and there were, of course, those less tape-bound members who honestly believed in the infallibility of trial by jury. On the other side, supporting Sir Arthur Powell-Hancock, there were those few members who believed Mr Todhunter's story; there were the members of the opposition who were politically minded; and finally there was a large body of opinion which was seriously disturbed by doubts as to Palmer's guilt and considered that there could be at any rate no harm in sparing Palmer's life in order to review Mr Todhunter's confession, whether they had to keep the fellow in prison for the rest of his life or not. It was on this last group that Sir Ernest Prettiboy chiefly relied, and it was towards increasing their numbers that his ardent lobbying had been mostly directed.

Not even Sir Ernest's eloquence, however, nor the fiery articles that had appeared in the press for or against Palmer had done very much to rouse enthusiasm on either side; and Sir Arthur's rather dull speech did not help to increase it. The debate dragged on and gradually developed into an academic discussion from which it was hard to realise that a man's life could be at stake. Indeed about the best help that Palmer received was from the home secretary himself, who spoke with such inhumanity and arid lack of any of the broader warmth or understanding as to alienate even some of his own supporters.

In spite of this small profit to Palmer's cause, it seemed certain, however, that the division must go against him, when Sir Ernest played his trump card. It was an unexpected card, and its existence had been unknown even to Sir Arthur Powell-Hancock himself; nor did Sir Ernest play it until quite sure that the debate was going definitely against him. Then a note was brought by an attendant to Sir Arthur, who stared at it in perplexity for some moments and then fumbled for the Speaker's eye.

Catching it, he rose and said:

"I have just received a note. Its purport is not altogether clear, but I understand that a—hum!—a civil action for murder is actually being brought, or entered, against this Mr—hum!—Lawrence Todhunter. A—hum!—a *civil* action for murder. My legal friends may understand better than I do what that exactly means. But if any action for murder is being brought in the courts against this gentleman—that is, for the same murder under which Vincent Palmer now lies condemned, I think I can hardly be wrong in suggesting that it would be the wish of the House that the execution of Palmer should be delayed at least until the outcome of this trial—if 'trial' is the correct term—has been reached."

Sheer bewilderment, in fact, had prevented Sir Arthur from being as prosy as he preferred, and, on the division being taken at once, it was announced that the motion respiting Vincent Palmer had been carried by the narrow majority of a hundred and twenty-six to a hundred and seven.

"My God!" said Mr Todhunter and ate a grape.

CHAPTER XIV

Mr Todhunter had found himself caught up into great issues. His actions had been discussed in Parliament; precedents had been created in his name; and now he found himself the centre of an almost unheard-of legal crisis. It gave him a curious and irksome feeling of impotence to find that though now the centre of these great and controversial activities, he could no more direct them than he could direct the course of the moon round the earth: he was the centre only, fixed, immovable—and bed was about the best place for him.

The notion of a private prosecution for murder was perhaps the most brilliant flash of genius in all Sir Ernest Prettiboy's brilliant career. The course was, in point of fact, not unprecedented, but it took a legal genius to realise that the machinery for a resuscitation of this curious civil right was still in perfect working order.

Briefly, the essence of the matter is that although, in all criminal cases, it is the Crown which is almost invariably named as prosecutor and has indeed in theory the prerogative of acting in this capacity, in practice prosecution for minor criminal offences is almost always undertaken by the private person who has suffered damage, acting, of course, in conjunction with the police.

"But in this case, my boy," expounded Sir Ernest jovially, "the police not only won't help; if they can, they'll jolly well hinder. And why? Because they've already prosecuted their own candidate for the rope, and to help indict another would only be to make them, as well as the original conviction, look silly. Besides, they're still convinced they've got the right man."

"But this isn't a minor case," objected Mr Todhunter, who liked to get one thing clear at a time.

"You're right it isn't. By the way, we're a wily lot, aren't we? By custom and so forth we've gradually put the responsibility for the repression of minor crime onto the shoulders of the injured parties themselves. Saves the authorities such a lot of trouble, that does. It's a practice peculiar to this country. It would be."

"Yes, but murder isn't a minor crime."

"No, but if they allow it in minor offences, they must in major ones too; though of course it's very rarely done when the authorities themselves aren't willing to act. The private prosecutor has to put up the dibs himself, you see, and there's precious few of us who wouldn't let a criminal get away with anything he likes so long as we don't have to foot any bill for putting him in gaol."

"But you said," Mr Todhunter pointed out patiently, "that in such cases it's the injured party who prosecutes. In a case of murder that can hardly apply, can it? I mean, the person who suffered the damage is hardly in a position to prosecute, being dead."

"Oh, it needn't always be the injured party," returned Sir Ernest glibly. "Haven't you ever heard of a common informer? That's what a bloke is called who prosecutes in any case of felony or misdemeanour in which he himself has suffered no damage."

"Then the person who prosecutes me will be a common informer?" suggested Mr Todhunter with acumen.

"Not a bit of it. A common informer prosecutes in the hope and for the purpose of obtaining for himself the reward, pain or penalty prescribed for the offence in question, or a goodish lump of it, or for any other reason working to his own advantage, such as turning king's evidence."

"Then what will the person who prosecutes me be called?" demanded Mr Todhunter in despair.

"The prosecutor," replied Sir Ernest simply. "He will in fact be usurping the functions of the Crown, and he'll have a hurdle or two to jump before he'll be allowed to do it too."

"Hurdle?"

"Yes. There'll be the grand jury to be argued into returning a true bill against you, the magistrates to be persuaded into committing you, and goodness knows what other merry little obstructions that the hostile authorities won't be able to devise."

"They make it very difficult for a man who only wants to get himself hanged," lamented Mr Todhunter.

"You bet they do," agreed Sir Ernest with great heartiness. "Otherwise chaps like you with these dam' delicate consciences would be getting themselves hanged in rows at 8 a.m. every morning of the week in every prison in the country."

2

Naturally this intricate legal situation required much discussion.

In a way Mr Todhunter enjoyed these conferences. They made him feel important, and also he had taken a liking to the solicitor whom Sir Ernest had brought in on his behalf, a youngish man named Fuller, who was as unlike the usual idea of a solicitor as Mr Todhunter, unknown to himself, was like it. Fuller had a shock of blond hair through which he would run an occasional hand or even, when the situation seemed to demand it, both hands; he had also a suit which seemed permanently a little rumpled and a manner so eager and enthusiastic that when he became excited, as he often did, his words would run so closely together that they could hardly be disentangled.

His knowledge of law was, however, first rate, and he had put all of it at Mr Todhunter's disposal, together with his vast measure of enthusiasm for so entrancing a case. In fact young Mr Fuller entered the chase with such zest that Mr Todhunter felt at times, not without uneasiness, that nothing mattered to him but to get his client well and truly, if quite academically, hanged.

As for the person who was to undertake the role of nominal prosecutor, Mr Todhunter himself had had an inspiration there. It seemed to him that there was only one person to act in that capacity: Furze. With characteristic energy Sir Ernest had at once hurled himself off there and then to the offices of the Middleman's League and put the case to Furze on the spot.

Furze had been delighted to oblige. The idea appealed to his somewhat intricate sense of humour, which had always enjoyed defeating the deficiencies of the law by its own excesses.

Then there was the question of finance. The bill for his own prosecution was of course to be footed by Mr Todhunter himself, and the satisfactory sums rolling in upon him each week now from the Sovereign Theater appeared expressly designed for this purpose—as Mr Todhunter had indeed thoughtfully pointed out to the mother of their chief cause and creator, Felicity Farroway.

And there was plenty of need for funds. Sir Ernest Prettiboy had naturally been instructed—or rather, had instructed himself—for the prosecution, and the matter of fees was not in question there; but there were juniors, there were the solicitors, there were the usual expenses connected with witnesses, there were a hundred and one alleys down which Mr Todhunter's money was scurrying as fast as it could roll. For it was not merely a question of a trial. There were, first, the proceedings before the magistrate; for which, as was to happen at the ensuing trial should the magistrates prove so obliging as to commit him, Mr Todhunter had to stand the expenses not merely of his prosecution but of his own defence against his own prosecution.

The situation was indeed becoming more and more fantastic. In the first place Sir Ernest Prettiboy was almost more worried by the possibility of the magistrates' dismissing Mr Todhunter's case against himself than he was over the chances of a jury subsequently failing to convict. In consequence it had been decided, by him and young Mr Fuller, but not of course by Mr Todhunter, that although the charge against him was that to which he had been confessing so long and so hard, when the thing actually came into court Mr Todhunter was to plead not guilty.

"But I am guilty!" Mr Todhunter had cried from his bed. "What's the good of saying I'm not? I may get off."

"You're much more likely to get off if you plead guilty," countered Sir Ernest. "Don't you understand, if you plead guilty there can't be a trial. You'll never have a chance to call your witnesses, such as they are. I can't thunder against you to convince a muttonheaded jury. They'll just accept your plea, smile and stick you in an insane asylum for the rest of your life—and keep Palmer in clink. That's my view."

"But how can I plead not guilty?" asked the harassed Mr Todhunter.

"You'll plead not guilty to murder, but guilty of manslaughter," replied Sir Ernest glibly. "What you did was to take a revolver with you to that interview with Jean Norwood with the intention of threatening her, which you duly did, but in your excitement and inexperience of firearms the thing went off, and she was killed. Isn't that what happened?"

"Good heavens, no," said Mr Todhunter with disgust. "I intended all the time—"

"*Isn't that what happened?*" shouted Sir Ernest at the top of his exceedingly powerful voice.

"Oh, all right," agreed Mr Todhunter sulkily. "Yes, that's what happened."

"I thought so," said Sir Ernest with satisfaction.

"But don't you get me off on it," ordered Mr Todhunter.

"You forget, my bonny boy," retorted Sir Ernest, "I'm for the prosecution. I'm out for your blood, by Jove—and I'm going to, get it."

"Then who's going to defend me?"

"Ah!" said Sir Ernest thoughtfully. "We've got to think about that, haven't we?"

"What about Jamieson?" asked Fuller. "I'd say he's clever enough to put up a good show and not clever enough to get our friend off."

"Jamieson's the man," agreed Sir Ernest.

"Is he?" said Mr Todhunter in a depressed way.

3

Things were indeed enough to depress him. Mr Todhunter had always found difficulty in grasping details, and the details of his own case were now becoming so complicated that at times he despaired of unravelling them.

Furze, for instance, who sometimes joined these conferences too—Furze had of course instructed solicitors of his own, who had to be in the game, too, and it was under the instructions of these that Sir Ernest nominally was acting; whereas Mr Todhunter, in constant conference with the counsel who was to prosecute him, never even met his own counsel who was to defend him against the best efforts of the man who was putting the case which he himself was trying to strengthen by every means in his limited power. It was all very muddling.

The newspapers found it no less so. Sir Ernest Prettiboy was usually referred to as acting for Mr Todhunter, as indeed he was unofficially though officially exactly the reverse, and Mr Todhunter appeared somehow to be regarded as chief witness for the prosecution and defendant combined; as indeed he was again, in fact if not in legal fiction. The more sober periodicals tried occasionally to disentangle the riddle for their readers, with an air of aloof distaste; the less sober ones, caring nothing for details, continued to serve Mr Todhunter with such a continued roar of publicity as caused Sir Ernest to chuckle with gratification.

"Bound to have its effect on the jury," he would gloat. "Bound to. They'll feel they won't be playing the game unless they convict you. Bound to. You'll see."

In the meantime the preparation of the case went methodically forward. Witnesses were interviewed who could support the fantastic story from its very beginning, which Mr Todhunter fixed as the little dinner party he had given to what seemed now a collection of ghosts a hundred years ago. Fortunately he had consulted so many people and discussed murder in theory with so many others that there was no lack of persons to speak to the idea that murder must have been very much present in Mr Todhunter's mind, while Mr Chitterwick and Furze could both speak to a more particular intention. So far as all this went, things were not unsatisfactory; and with the help of so many witnesses and other witnesses, too, who were prepared without hesitation to give testimony of the kind that Mr Todhunter had "always been queer since a boy," even his own tale might be expected to grow more and more credible in the minds of the jury, if only through sheer repetition.

It was over the question of actual proof that heads were shaken; for here it had to be admitted that, out of sheer bad luck, no doubt, but nevertheless definitely, the proofs of Mr Todhunter's guilt were not nearly so striking as the police case against Vincent Palmer.

"That bracelet," would moan Mr Fuller and look as if about to beat his breast.

It was the bracelet that had caught young Mr Fuller's attention from the start. Under his directions Mr Chitterwick's enquiries were renewed and all the old ground covered once more—but only the old, for no one could find any new ground. The result, as before, was completely negative, but Mr Fuller, alone of the four, refused to give up hope.

"With that bracelet we've got a case," he kept repeating. "Without it, I don't know."

"There's the second bullet," one of the others would remind him.

"Which proves that Todhunter knew of its existence. But nothing more. The police will simply say that he heard two shots when he was in the garden that night, knew that only one bullet had been traced and inferred that the other must be somewhere. That's all."

And Mr Todhunter, who had prided himself a good deal on that second bullet, would feel more depressed than ever.

4

Nevertheless it did not seem as if the loss of the bracelet were to prove an insuperable handicap. For in due course Mr Todhunter left his bed and appeared before the magistrates, and in due course again, much later and after a number of further appearances which he felt to be altogether excessive, Mr Todhunter found himself committed for trial by a completely bewildered bench—just (it seemed) to be on the safe side.

Mr Todhunter disliked these appearances excessively. He was almost mobbed each time he arrived at or left the court, and he was usually cheered too; for what reason he could not quite determine, possibly for having murdered a popular idol whose feet had proved to be composed mainly of clay. He was photographed, sketched and headlined, and the most determined attempts were made to interview him, if it was only to extract a single word from his almost fanatically closed lips. In short, had Mr Todhunter been a lady of rank with a title to sell, the publicity he was getting would have made him almost delirious with delight; as things were, it left his somewhat old-fashioned mind reeling with disgust.

Sir Ernest, leaving nothing to chance, broke with precedent and appeared himself in the magistrates' court. Mr Jamieson, on the other hand, did not (indeed Mr Todhunter had begun to wonder whether such a person as Mr Jamieson existed at all), and the man in the dock, not yet a prisoner nor apparently ever to be one, was defended by his excited young solicitor, happily with the unsuccessful results for which everyone hoped.

Mr Todhunter thanked the magistrates with grave courtesy for committing him and returned from the dock to his bed.

Nor apparently all this time did the Authorities, those nebulous potentates, seek to drop any spanners in the machinery. The police, it seemed, had now folded their arms across their chests and were awaiting the outcome with resignation and a cold aloofness. They would not arrest Mr Todhunter, not even on a charge of aiding and abetting, not even on a charge of loitering with intent; but they would not actively seek to prevent him making this consummate ass of himself. They maintained a legal representative in court, who never rose once, and let things go at that.

Sir Ernest was jubilant.

"Of course they had to, after the announcement in the House," he said, contradicting all the fears he had been expressing for the last month, "but you never know with magistrates. Queer lot of old cusses, and the older the cusseder."

He refilled the glass that was in his hand and toasted Mr Todhunter, the Bench and the case in general with a comprehensive gesture.

"Then you think the grand jury will be equally easy?" asked Mr Todhunter from the bed to which he had been sent, just like a naughty child, immediately on his return from court; for his time was getting short now, and there must be no risk of losing him—and with him (Mr Todhunter could not help feeling) the case of a century.

"The grand jury? Oh yes, I think so. They'll hardly dare to throw out the bill. The whole country's looking forward to your trial. I believe there'd be a revolution if anything stopped it."

"If only we had that bracelet," moaned Mr Fuller and ran both hands several times through his hair.

"I believe I've got an idea about that," modestly chirped Mr Chitterwick from the other side of the bed.

Mr Fuller jumped up with such energy that Mr Chitterwick drew back in alarm, looking just as though he had feared that the young man was going to embrace him.

5

Was there a bracelet at all?

That question, in Mr Todhunter's guilty opinion, was in all minds and had been from the beginning. Not that Mr Todhunter had any reason to feel guilty, for he knew quite well that there was a bracelet. It was just that he could not help it, in face of the doubt that must lurk with the others and had been so very, very kindly never expressed.

Even Mr Chitterwick had no proof that there had ever been a bracelet; yet there was no hint in his voice of any such doubt, except to Mr Todhunter's super-sensibility, as he proceeded to expound his idea.

"You see," he explained, "we've exhausted the possibilities as we know them, and I'm quite convinced that none of the persons whom I've already interviewed had anything to do with the theft. Nor, I'm certain, have our friend's excellent maids. But two days ago, passing the girl Edith on the stairs,

I noticed that she had been crying. In fact she was crying still." Mr Chitterwick paused and beamed round his audience.

"Well?" asked Sir Ernest impatiently.

"Oh, I beg your pardon. Yes, of course. Well, it occurred to me, you see, *why* she was crying." Again Mr Chitterwick paused and beamed.

"Well, why was she?" demanded Sir Ernest.

"I—I don't know," replied Mr Chitterwick, a little flurried.

"Then what the devil's all this about?"

"It was a surmise," Mr Chitterwick hurried on, looking ashamed of himself. "Only a surmise. There is, you see, a well-known expression which is called up when anything happens to a man. Er . . . cherchez la femme, you know. Well, it occurred to me, you see, when one sees a *girl* crying, isn't it equally fitting to observe cherchez l'homme? Er . . . that is to say, seek the man."

"I'm quite capable of understanding French," observed Sir Ernest tartly.

"It was my accent," apologised Mr Chitterwick, going a little red. "I was afraid you wouldn't . . . I was afraid it wasn't quite—er—what you were accustomed to, so to speak."

"Anyhow, what about this homme?" Sir Ernest pursued.

"Well, it's just on the cards," said Mr Chitterwick very tentatively, "that if there *was* an homme . . . a man, I mean, and his conduct was such as to make Edith cry (that is, assuming that's what she was crying about)—well, you see," Mr Chitterwick's voice began to tail off before Sir Ernest's incomprehending stare, "well, he *might* be a bad lot, you see, in which case. . ."

If Sir Ernest was slow in the uptake, young Mr Fuller more than made up. He jumped to his feet and clapped Mr Chitterwick on the back with all the enthusiasm of which he was capable.

"It's worth trying," he exclaimed. "My goodness, it is."

"What's worth trying?" demanded Sir Ernest testily.

His thumb already on the bell, Mr Fuller explained, more or less in words of one syllable.

"Tch!" observed Sir Ernest, annoyed with himself for his obtuseness and therefore with Mr Chitterwick's idea for its brightness. "Girls cry over other things than men, don't they?"

"I don't know," said Mr Chitterwick humbly; and indeed he did not.

"May I conduct this interview?" asked Mr Fuller as the housekeeper's slow tread became audible on the stairs.

Apparently he took the consent of the others for granted, for when Mrs Greenhill arrived he took her in hand at once in the most fatherly manner.

"Sit down, Mrs Greenhill. We just want to ask you a few more questions, though I'm sure you must be getting very tired of them."

"I'm willing to do all I can sir, at this dreadful time," replied Mrs Greenhill sombrely.

"Yes, I'm sure you are. Well, it's nothing of any great importance. Just about Edith and her young man. Let's see . . . I never can remember his name."

"Alfie, sir. Alfie Brewer."

"Yes, Alfie Brewer, of course. They're thinking of getting married, aren't they?"

"Well, Edie is, sir," Mrs Greenhill said darkly. "But as for Alfie—well, it takes a good deal to say what he's thinking, though I've got my own ideas."

Mr Fuller nodded with great energy. "Exactly. That's just it. That's just what I wanted to speak to you about; on Mr Todhunter's behalf of course. He's getting quite worried about Edie, and you know any kind of worry is bad for him. But it *is* worrying, when he hears us telling him that the poor girl is crying all the time."

"Edie didn't ought to cry at her work," agreed Mrs Greenhill with austerity.

"Oh well, girls will be girls, you know. Yes, this Alfie. . . he's a bit of a bad hat, isn't he?"

"Well, he's never been in trouble," answered Mrs Greenhill a little doubtfully. Even Mr Todhunter knew that this phrase stood for trouble of a particular sort; with the police.

"No, but there's always the possibility. Young fellows like him get too easily led astray. Especially living in that neighbourhood, eh?"

"I've always told Edie she was making herself cheap, taking up with a fellow from that Smithson Street," Mrs Greenhill asserted.

"Exactly. But his parents . . . I mean . . . ?"

"Oh, Alfie doesn't live with his parents, sir. They're both dead. He's in lodgings. Family of the name of Guest."

"Most appropriate name," smiled young Mr Fuller. "Yes. Now I suppose Alfie was in and out of the house a good deal while Mr Todhunter was away abroad?"

"No, that he wasn't, sir. I don't hold with him and I won't have him in this house, and I've always said so. If Edie wants to demean herself by taking up with a young fellow of his sort, well, she must meet him outside any house that I'm responsible for. Oh!" Mrs Greenhill's eyes suddenly widened. "It's that bracelet, sir."

"It is," nodded Mr Fuller. "It's that bracelet."

"Oh I don't think Alfie's as bad as that, sir. At least—well, I hope not, for Edie's sake. But I know he was in a very bad state for money just about then. Borrowed all Edie's savings, he did. Borrowed! She might just as well have thrown them into the river, and that's what I told her. Still I hope Alfie hasn't been and done anything so silly as that. Though it'll be a lesson to Edie, that it will. And better soon than too late, as the saying goes."

"So far as you know, then, Mrs Greenhill," resumed Mr Fuller in a slightly more official tone, "this man was never in the house?"

"No, so far as I know . . . but Edie might have brought him in when I was out. I wouldn't put it past her. Artful, that's what Edie's been getting since she took up with Alfie Brewer."

"Yes, that's just what I had in mind." He turned to Sir Ernest. "We know the bracelet hasn't been pawned yet, and I doubt whether one of the fences has it: it's a bit too hot for any of the regulars. If this man did take it, it'll probably be still on his premises. We could go round there and . . ." His voice tailed off in doubt.

"No!" Mr Todhunter gave a sudden cackle. "Ring Up Scotland Yard and tell them to get a search warrant and go and look for it. They've never believed I had it. It would serve them right to find it."

This suggestion being approved, Mr Fuller went off to telephone.

Sir Ernest bent formidable brows on Mrs Greenhill, sitting very much upright on the extreme edge of her chair.

"Not a word of this to the girl, mind."

"Oh, no, sir," Mrs Greenhill shivered. "I hope I know what's right."

"I hope so too," pronounced Sir Ernest,

6

It was exactly four hours later that Scotland Yard rang up to announce, in the blandest tones, that they had discovered the missing bracelet concealed in the chimney in Alfred Brewer's room, and they wished to thank Mr Todhunter kindly for the information.

"Thank Chitterwick," grunted Sir Ernest, making the honourable amend; and Mr Chitterwick looked so pleased that his face became almost incandescent.

"Now we *have* got a case," gloated young Mr Fuller.

"Humph! I'd like to know a bit more about that empty punt," Sir Ernest muttered ungratefully.

7

Only one other incident occurred before Mr Todhunter's trial was due to begin which deserves to be recorded.

Two days before this was to happen Felicity Farroway visited him in the afternoon and made a very painful scene.

Getting into his bedroom without difficulty, she accused Mr Todhunter, at first temperately and then with growing hysteria, of immolating himself upon the altar of friendship. Her contention was that Mr Todhunter never had shot Miss Norwood and very well knew he hadn't and that he was thus blackening himself in the eyes of the world out of sheer nobility and that she, Miss Felicity Farroway, could not bear it and did not propose to bear it.

Mr Todhunter, finding this all very painful and difficult, answered her at first mildly and then with an exasperation that matched her rising hysteria.

When Miss Farroway reached the point of saying that if Mr Todhunter was going to confess in order to save her family she would confess, too, and she would make young Mr Palmer confess anything he could confess, and apparently there was going to be an all-round orgy of altruistic confession—why then the voices from Mr Todhunter's bedroom became so loud that Mrs Greenhill in fright called up young Mr Fuller, who promptly bundled Miss Farroway out of the house.

Mr Todhunter wiped his brow in relief.

"Women," said Mr Todhunter, "are the devil." And he said it with conviction, for he was genuinely anxious that Miss Farroway might put her wild threats into action.

However Mr Chitterwick settled all that. Having heard the story, he paid a visit to Miss Farroway's dressing room that same evening (feeling the wildest kind of dog imaginable) and persuaded her into reason.

No further obstacle cropped up to mar the smoothness of Mr Todhunter's chosen path.

PART IV

Journalistic

SCENE IN COURT

CHAPTER XV

The civil trial of Mr Lawrence Todhunter for the murder of Jean Norwood opened at the Old Bailey on a sunny March morning. Mr Todhunter himself was an interested spectator.

Outside Court No. 4, in which the case was to be tried, Mr Todhunter shook hands for the first time with his own counsel, Mr Jamieson, a tall, stringy man with a wig that gave the impression of being one size too small for him, and a melancholy look. He swept the look over Mr Todhunter and observed merely in a despondent voice and with a marked Scotch accent:

"This is a very strange business."

It was Sir Ernest who, now as earlier, acted as Mr Todhunter's cicerone, let him into the court, indicated the dock and introduced Mr Todhunter to such eminent legal persons as craved the honour. There was no doubt that Mr Todhunter was the lion of the occasion. An impressive hush greeted his appearance; the press, gossiping by their tables below the dais, bent their scrutiny on him as one man; the officials forgot their dignity and stared. There was the usual attempt to get a pretrial statement out of him, but Sir Ernest kept the reporters at a distance with jovial competence.

It all seemed very informal to Mr Todhunter as he stood with counsel and solicitors and discussed the weather.

Then Sir Ernest struck himself on the brow as he remembered his duty and made Mr Todhunter sit down on the witness benches with a solicitude worthy of a trained nurse.

"But I feel perfectly well," protested Mr Todhunter, who did in fact feel better than for weeks, perhaps in relief at having been able to rise from his bed and get into action at last.

"My boy," replied Sir Ernest impressively, "it's my job to keep you alive till this trial's over, and I'm going to do it. Jamieson, ask for a seat for him in the dock at once, will you? You've heard of his condition of course?"

Mr Jamieson agreed to ask that his client must be seated, but in a voice that suggested grave doubt whether the request would be granted.

The hum of low chatter filled the court. Mr. Todhunter, glancing up once, caught sight of a row of heads craning over the balcony rail at him, with eyes on hatpins and mouths open like goldfishes'. He hastily looked away.

By degrees the court filled up. An eminent French lawyer was pointed out to Mr Todhunter and an equally eminent American judge. Evidently his case had roused not merely national but international interest. Mr Todhunter was also surprised to see a number of exquisitely dressed ladies present who were staring at him and whispering among themselves with a lack of manners which shocked his old-fashioned ideas about women and their behaviour in public. Somewhat petulantly he asked Sir Ernest who they were.

"Bitches," replied the gentleman robustly.

"But what are they here for?"

"To gorm at you, my boy, and get a cheap kick out of it."

"But how did they get in?"

"Ah," said Sir Ernest, "you'd better ask the lord mayor and the sheriffs that. They—"

"Hush!" interrupted young Mr Fuller. "Here they come."

There had been three loud knocks which seemed to come from behind the judge's dais, and everyone hurriedly stood up, Mr Todhunter among them. Then, through the door on which the knocks had been made, a small procession entered the court. First the lord mayor, very stout and stately in his robes and chain, then three aldermen, the sheriffs and undersheriffs, and last, tiny and dwarfed, the weazened old figure of the judge himself, Mr Justice Bailey, who never made jokes and ruled his cases without an unnecessary word.

The procession seated itself on the bench, the lord mayor glowing in the exact middle. In a thin voice the judge invited the distinguished French lawyer and the eminent American judge to occupy two thrones there too. The bench was filled from end to end.

"Go on," whispered Sir Ernest to Mr Todhunter.

"Where?" asked Mr Todhunter stupidly.

"Into the dock."

With a rather shamefaced air which he tried to make casual Mr Todhunter sidled into the dock. A policeman politely held the door open for him. There were no warders inside, for Mr Todhunter was not under arrest. Feeling lost in the empty spaciousness, Mr Todhunter drifted to the front and clutched the ledge in a spasm of nervousness, blinking at the judge. He felt exceedingly foolish and a little annoyed in consequence.

Then he became aware that someone was intoning something in a rapid monotone.

"If anyone can inform my lords, the King's justices, or the King's attorney general, ere this inquest be taken between our sovereign lord the King and the prisoner at the bar, of any treasons, murders, felonies or misdemeanours done or committed by the prisoner at the bar, let them come forth and they shall be heard; for the prisoner now stands at the bar on his deliverance. And all persons who are bound by recognizance to prosecute or give evidence against the prisoner at the bar, let them come forth, prosecute and give evidence, or they shall forfeit their recognizances. God save the King."

Immediately on this somebody else popped up, in wig and gown, from just under the dais and addressed Mr Todhunter directly.

"Lawrence Butterfield Todhunter, you are charged with the murder of Ethel May Binns, on twenty-eighth September last. Are you guilty or not guilty?"

"Eh?" said Mr Todhunter, startled. Fog a moment he wondered wildly whether his case had been mixed up with someone else's, for he could not remember ever having murdered an Ethel May Binns. Then he remembered, vaguely, having been told that Jean Norwood's real name was . . . well, it must have been Ethel May Binns.

"Oh, guilty," said Mr Todhunter in some confusion. He caught sight of an expression of consternation on the large face of Sir Ernest, where there was plenty of room for it. The sight shook him. "I mean," said Mr Todhunter, trying to pull himself together, "not guilty."

"You plead not guilty?" said the clerk of the court firmly.

"Not guilty of murder," replied Mr Todhunter, trying to imitate the firmness.

He clutched at the rail, conscious of all those eyes on him and still more conscious that he had made a very foolish start. Would they find him not guilty but insane? he wondered wildly.

Mr Jamieson was making a request in a not very hopeful tone.

"My lord, I appear for the accused. He is in a somewhat delicate state of health. May he be permitted to sit before the jury is sworn."

His lordship inclined his ancient head. "Certainly."

Mr Jamieson looked a little surprised.

A friendly-looking policeman put a chair behind Mr Todhunter, who sat back in it gratefully. Everything still seemed a little unreal to him, like a scene on the stage.

He watched the process of swearing in the jury with a sensation of unreality.

There were no challenges, and Mr Todhunter found himself with a jury of ten men and two women to decide his fate. He gazed at them and then realised that they were all busily avoiding his eye. Mr Todhunter coloured faintly and turned away to the little clerk of the court. He was not used to having his eye avoided.

The clerk of the court addressed the jury.

"Members of the jury, the prisoner at the bar, Lawrence Butterfield Todhunter is charged with the murder of Ethel May Binns, on twenty-eighth of September last. To this indictment he has pleaded not guilty, and it is your charge to say, having heard the evidence, where he be guilty or not."

The jury looked extremely solemn.

"Not so much of the 'Butterfield,'" thought Mr Todhunter testily. He disliked his second name and had for the last twenty years successfully concealed it.

With an informality which mildly astonished Mr Todhunter, Sir Ernest Prettiboy then rose in a leisurely way and, wrapping his gown round him rather like a bath towel, began to speak in pleasant, easy tones.

"May it please your lordship and members of the jury, this is a most unusual case. As we all know, another man has already been convicted of the crime with which the accused is charged and is now in prison awaiting execution; that execution having been postponed until the result of this trial is known. That in itself is sufficiently unusual. To make it more so, this is a private prosecution for murder. My instructions come, not from the Crown, but from a private citizen: a Mr Furze.

"Mr Furze is actuated by the highest motives of public policy in this almost unprecedented course, for, as you will hear from his own lips, he is in a very special position; a position which was able to convince him that the death of Miss Binns was in fact due to the agency of Mr Todhunter here and not to that of Vincent Palmer, who now lies under sentence of death for this crime. You will learn the reasons which did so convince Mr Furze, not the least of which is that several weeks prior to the crime Mr Todhunter announced to Mr Furze, in a private conversation, his intention to commit a murder of some person then undecided, and he actually consulted Mr Furze as to who might be a suitable person for a victim.

"Convinced therefore that it was an innocent man who had been condemned for this crime, Mr Furze has instigated these proceedings in order to rectify what he considered an appalling error of justice; and he instigated them, I may say at once, with the full connivance and approval of Mr Todhunter himself, who is even more anxious to get this error of justice put right and who has, I submit, behaved with the greatest rectitude and propriety ever since the unfortunate deed which he himself so fully admits. For it will be my duty," said Sir Ernest very solemnly, "a rather painful duty but one which I cannot avoid, to emphasise that the proper authorities—I needn't mince matters: I refer to the police and the law officers under the Crown—these authorities, to whom Mr Todhunter unfolded his story immediately he heard of the arrest of Vincent Palmer, attached no importance to this story.

"I do not impugn their motives," went on Sir Ernest, preparing to impugn as hard as he could. "I do not for one moment suggest that the reason why they refused to listen to Mr Todhunter's startling confession was that they had already arrested one man, whom they fully expected to convict, and they would not wish to admit themselves publicly in the wrong. Not for one moment did anything like that occur, I am convinced. Such wickedness—for there would be no other word for it—savours more of other police forces perhaps than ours. No, I am certain that they believe quite genuinely that they had the right man and equally genuinely that Mr Todhunter was an interfering crank. But Mr Todhunter could not accept that nor allow himself to be muzzled when another man's life was at stake. Nor could those who were fully aware of the true facts. That is why this case has been brought in this almost unique way, with the accused in the dock a free man, not under arrest; free, if he liked, to walk straight out of this court and disappear in an instant; for though this grave charge of murder has been sworn against him, the proper authorities are still unimpressed. They have refused to grant a warrant against him. It is my duty, members of the jury, to prove to you that the authorities are wrong and Mr Furze right.

"My lord," said Sir Ernest impressively, "I must ask your indulgence. It is not the practice for members of our profession to make personal explanations concerning the cases in which they are engaged. Nevertheless I feel that in a case so remarkable as this a personal explanation would not be out of place; and with your lordship's permission I should like to say a word or two about my own position. My lord, members of the jury, I will only say this. It would ill become me, as a member of the Bar and having acted many times under the instructions of the Crown, to appear in a case of this gravity, in which the action of the proper authorities must incur severe criticism both from myself and from my learned friend, unless I fully realised my responsibilities.

"I do so realise them. I was brought into the case by chance many weeks ago as a casual witness to certain discoveries tending to establish the guilt of the accused; as indeed you will hear in due course, when you will see the unprecedented spectacle of counsel entering the witness box to testify himself against the accused. Such an action is indeed unprecedented, but I can find nothing to make it impossible; and in a case in which so many features are unique perhaps this conduct, unprofessional as it might appear in any ordinary case, will not merely be condoned but will meet with sympathy and approval. For I feel that I should tell you that it was owing to those discoveries and those incidents which I was called upon to witness that I became a firm believer in the innocence of the man already condemned for this distressing crime; a belief in which subsequent events has still more securely confirmed me. And in consequence I appear before you in this case today, voluntarily and even eagerly, not to serve the ends of man—any man—but those of pure justice. My lord, members of the jury, you will, I hope, pardon this personal diversion, which I felt was owed as much to you as to myself.

"Let me now tell you, in their proper sequence, of the events which led up, in my submission, to the death of Ethel May Binns.

"On the fourteenth of June last Mr Todhunter paid a visit to his doctor . . ."

Sir Ernest then went on to give a brief outline of Mr Todhunter's activities from the moment when he learned that his days, if not numbered, were already in the hands of the Higher Accountant, through the dinner party at which he had received such fatal if unwitting advice, to the actual moment when Mr Todhunter voluntarily entered the dock that morning.

Mr Todhunter considered it an admirable summary.

He wondered sardonically whether he ought to be taking notes of his sensations for an article in the *London Review*. There would be plenty of time to get it written before the date of execution arrived—provided indeed that he were ever found guilty.

Considering the idea to show the true scientific spirit, he whispered a request over the edge of the dock for pencil and paper and, when these were forthcoming, wrote solemnly:

"E.P.'s opening speech for the prosecution more succinct than I would have expected and gave me great satisfaction. His case sounds truly convincing. I think we have a chance."

2

Only one witness was taken before the lunch interval, but he was an important one: Ferrers.

Ferrers's evidence fell under two heads, the conversation at the now notorious dinner party and his own personal relations as editor of the *London Review* with Mr Todhunter. Suave and self-possessed as ever, Ferrers remembered the dinner party perfectly. He agreed that Mr Todhunter had seemed rather to press the question of what a man condemned to death by his doctor might do for the benefit of his fellows. He remembered, too, quite clearly, that the final decision had been almost unanimously for murder.

"In fact, if the accused were seeking advice on this point behind a veil of anonymity, your advice to him at that time was to commit a murder?" frowned Sir Ernest, much shocked.

"I'm afraid the rest of us were not taking the discussion very seriously," Ferrers replied with a slight smile. "Otherwise our advice might have been different."

"But in point of fact you did so advise him?"

"If you put it that way, yes."

"I do put it that way."

"Then," said Ferrers blandly, "I can't contradict you."

"But you never expected the accused to act on it?"

"It never entered our heads."

"Knowing him as you do, would you be surprised to learn that he did act on it?"

Ferrers considered. "Perhaps not."

That brought Sir Ernest to his second head.

"You do know the accused well?"

"Quite well, I think."

"He has worked under you for a certain periodical for a considerable time?"

"He has been a regular contributor to the *London Review* for a number of years, under my editorship," replied Ferrers, seizing a chance of publicity.

"And during that time you have had many opportunities of observing closely not only his work but the man himself?"

"Certainly."

Sir Ernest then elicited the great number of times that Ferrers must have seen, observed and had converse with Mr Todhunter, both in business hours and out of them.

"And during all those years did you form the opinion that the accused was a man fully responsible for his actions?"

"Decidedly."

"You never saw signs of any abnormality about him?"

"Never, in the larger sense."

"What do you mean by that?" asked Sir Ernest scornfully.

"I mean, he had his small eccentricities, as bachelors are reputed to have."

"No doubt we all have that. But outside these small eccentricities common to everyone, you never at any time observed anything in his conduct which could have led you to suppose that he might be in any way mentally abnormal?"

"Todhunter always struck me as one of the sanest men I knew," replied Ferrers with a courteous little bow towards the dock.

"Thank you," said Sir Ernest and sat down.

Ferrers turned with an air of polite and helpful enquiry towards Mr Jamieson.

"Mr Ferrers," said the latter, "you are an editor?"

"I am."

"That means you have a great deal of reading to do, concerned with fact as well as fiction?"

"I have."

"Books of all sorts, no doubt. Have you, for instance, in the course of your duties had to read many books dealing with psychology?"

"Very many."

"Including criminal psychology?"

"Yes."

"Would it be too much to say that as a result of your reading you are perfectly convairsant with the modern principles of psychology, including criminal psychology?"

"I'm no expert," replied Ferrers, so deprecatingly that everyone instantly decided that he must be an expert, "but I have a working knowledge of the subject, yes."

"And have you, in the course of your reading, ever come across such an instance as that of a man who persuades himself that he is going to carry out some great and important action, requiring perhaps much moral courage, and carries all his intentions and preparations up to the very point of action and then his nairve fails him and he recoils at the last moment?"

"That is a very common phenomenon," agreed Ferrers with an expert's air.

"Such a man might even persuade himself that he was going to murder some pairson whom he had taken upon himself to consider obnoxious, and he might buy a revolver with this intention and even visit the pairson fully determined to carry out this murder, and then at the last moment his nairve might fail him and he would content himself with brandishing the revolver in a threatening manner?"

"Quite so."

"You agree that this is possible?"

"Oh yes."

"So that if, in those circumstances, the revolver went off accidentally, owing, it might be, to the pairson's inexperience of firearms, would your knowledge of criminal psychology suggest to you that such a pairson was a deliberate murderer or not?"

"That he was not."

"Thank you, Mr Ferrers," said Mr Jamieson with the air of one who has obtained more than he expected. "That is very illuminating. Now you have told my lord and the jury that you considered the accused one of the sanest pairsons you knew. You made that statement on the basis of your psychological knowledge?"

"Such knowledge of psychology as I have," replied Ferrers rather neatly, "must, I suppose, have contributed to it."

"Exactly. And you still maintain that statement?"

"I do."

"Now in the case of the hypothetical pairson whom we have just been considering, Mr Ferrers, the man who had persuaded himself that he was going to commit murder and bought a revolver for that purpose and even approached his victim with it but at the end did not fire it off deliberately: would you consider such a pairson as that perfectly sane and normal?"

"On those facts alone," said Ferrers carefully, "there is nothing to determine that such a person was not sane."

"Perhaps you could expand that explanation a little for the benefit of my lord and the jury?"

"It would merely be a case of the person's nerve failing," explained Ferrers gently to the judge. "There is nothing to indicate an abnormal mentality in that so far as I can see. The nerves of most of us fail at times. But of course I'm no expert in these matters."

"Yes," said the judge. "Mr Jamieson, I must ask you one question. I am not quite clear as to the drift of your cross-examination. Is it your intention to suggest that the accused was not responsible for his actions?"

"No, my lord," replied Mr Jamieson with much indignation, which caused his accent to become redoubled in vigour. "With the greatest respect, my intention is precisely the revairse. In my respectful submission, my client was fully responsible for his actions."

"Then there is no dispute between counsel on that point, since Sir Ernest also takes that view, so I don't quite see why you need labour it."

"For this reason, my lord: that I understand that the point may be raised in another quarter," said Mr Jamieson darkly, "and that an attempt will be made to throw doubts on my client's state of mind. I wish to bring out such evidence as these witnesses who knew him can give, the point having been already raised by my learned friend, so that the jury may be able to hear the views of those best able to speak with authority."

"Very well," said the judge patiently.

But Mr Jamieson had made his point and cleverly indicated with his early questions what the line of defence would be, and Ferrers was allowed to leave the witness box; which he promptly did, with a courteous little bow to the judge.

3

"I'd never have said old Jamie had it in him," pronounced Sir Ernest with ungrudging admiration. "Dam' clever line to take, that guff about your nerve failing at the last moment, so it's only manslaughter. Dam' clever."

The three sat at lunch in a small restaurant in Fleet Street, for the Old Bailey, unlike the Law Courts, contains no facilities for feeding hungry counsel and witnesses. The other lunchers were obviously gratified to have such a celebrated person as Mr Todhunter among them and scarcely took their eyes off him in consequence, conveying the food to their mouths by a sort of homing instinct.

Mr Todhunter, who was by now becoming more or less accustomed to being the focus of the rude herd's gaze, agreed that Mr Jamieson had evolved an ingenious defence.

"Cunning of him to get his whack in first about you being dotty too," remarked Sir Ernest in an interval between two pieces of steak-and-kidney pie.

"Yes," said Mr Todhunter and looked thoughtful.

He was not looking forward to that part of his ordeal at all. For it had been decided that in order to get the whole matter thrashed out once and for all in open court it would be best to let a representative of the police cross-examine him in the box and afterward address the jury. In this way the police theory that Mr Todhunter was entirely innocent of any hand in the death of Miss Ethel May Binns would receive adequate presentment and would be duly considered by the jury, as indeed it should be. But Mr Todhunter was not at all sure that he would be able to stand up to a hostile counsel, intent on proving his innocence. Like most of us, Mr Todhunter distrusted his own capabilities as a witness; and in addition his memory was now so very poor that he secretly feared that a clever counsel would be able to tie him up into the most hopeless knots.

"In any case, how do you think we're doing?" he asked, sipping his milk.

"Not so bad, not so bad," said Sir Ernest with great heartiness. "The jury are still looking a bit bewildered, but we'll straighten it out for them. You'll see."

4

The jury certainly did look bewildered.

As witness after witness appeared before them during the afternoon and testified to Mr Todhunter's murderous, if, at first, somewhat nebulous intentions, their bewilderment seemed to deepen rather than straighten out. Not one of them looked capable of realising that a man might wish to commit a perfectly altruistic murder, of some person or persons unknown, in order to do a little good to his fellow creatures.

And yet it must be becoming plain, even to such a jury, that Mr Todhunter had once nourished such an intention. Every single member of the dinner party was called to support the evidence of Ferrers (with the exception of Mr Chitterwick, who was to make a star appearance later); and after them came certain selected members of the staff of Consolidated Periodicals Ltd. Young Wilson, for instance, testified to having told Mr Todhunter the whole Fischmann story and described the other's horror and disgust; Ogilvie described Mr Todhunter's interview with him and repeated the latter's indignant exclamation, "The man ought to be shot!", Staithes, young Butts and Bennett gave an outline of the discussion in the office of the last named at which Mr Todhunter had been a concealed auditor, Bennett adding how he had discovered Mr Todhunter in the room after the others had gone—a rather nervous Bennett, though the reason for his nervousness was suspected by Mr Todhunter alone.

Young Butts testified, too, to the fact that Mr Todhunter had asked, when he met him on the stairs, where he could buy a revolver. He added that Mr Todhunter's expression had been set and determined, and he was breathing quickly, like a man who has arrived at a terrible decision. The gunsmith was then called to prove Mr Todhunter's visit to him that same day and his purchase of a revolver, which he now identified as the one produced in court.

In this way and with so many witnesses Sir Ernest was able to prove, to the evident satisfaction even of the jury, that Mr Todhunter undoubtedly had cherished an intention to murder some time before he had ever met Miss Norwood. Mr Todhunter was thankful that the Fischmann episode had taken place, even though it had seemed a fiasco at the time. Its value was now enormous, and without it there was a grave doubt whether a conviction could ever have been obtained.

"The jury was impressed," he confided to Sir Ernest as the latter almost lifted him, with the tenderness of a mother, into a taxi outside the Old Bailey, while Mr Chitterwick and young Mr Fuller tried to keep back the curious crowd. "You bet the jury was impressed," agreed Sir Ernest thrusting his head in at the window. "I meant 'em to be."

Mr Chitterwick scrambled nimbly inside, and the taxi drove off amid the cheers of the crowd.

"Well, what does it feel like to stand in a dock, Todhunter, now you've got there at last?" asked Mr Chitterwick, crossing his plump little legs as he leaned back in his corner.

Mr Todhunter massaged his bony knees with a swaying motion of his trunk. His same disreputable hat was perched forward on his bald head, and he looked anything but a murderer.

"It feels rather like having one's photograph taken," he said.

5

Mr Todhunter was now the most popular man in London.

There was no need for the police to guard his house, if they had ever thought of doing so. It was guarded, from the moment he stepped out of his taxi to the cheers of a second crowd to the moment he entered it again the next morning to the applause of a third crowd, by a whole covey of reporters. At intervals one of them would break away to try some fresh dodge for obtaining an interview, which was invariably unsuccessful; but for the most part they just hung around, ready to record the slightest activity of Mr Todhunter himself, of Mr Chitterwick (who had now taken up residence in the house), of Mr Todhunter's cousins, cook or housemaid, and even of the doctor and nurse who had been installed by Sir Ernest, in spite of Mr Todhunter's indignant protests, to keep watch over his precious life.

Immediately on his arrival Mr Todhunter was seized by this pair and led off, protesting warmly, to bed; but Mr Chitterwick, after a pleasant dinner with the doctor and the elderly cousins at which a bottle of Mr Todhunter's cherished Chateau Lafite, 1921, figured with success, was allowed to spend the evening with him discussing the day's progress and the morrow's promise.

Mr Todhunter also demanded to know what the doctor had said about his prospects of surviving the trial, and Mr Chitterwick was able to report that these were good.

"He said that provided you avoid the slightest overexertion or shock there's no reason why you shouldn't live another couple of months," he said, marvelling slightly that Mr Todhunter and he were able to discuss this question of the latter's approaching death as calmly as if it were a mere visit to the theatre instead of a visit to another world.

"Ha!" said Mr Todhunter with satisfaction.

After that the evening was uneventful, except that at about half past eleven Mr Todhunter insisted upon sending for his solicitor in order to add a codicil to his will, leaving to the nurse (to whom he had taken a violent and quite unreasonable dislike) the sum of five pounds wherewith to purchase a complete set of the works of Charles Dickens, she having failed to recognize a growling allusion to Mrs Gamp which Mr Todhunter had privately considered rather telling.

Mr Benson was quite resigned. There were now over a hundred codicils to Mr Todhunter's will, and it had been redrafted completely just seven times during the last five months.

CHAPTER XVI

The first witness on the second day of the trial was Furze.

Sir Ernest greeted him in the box with an unctuous subservience which Mr Todhunter, from the dock, thought a little overdone.

"Mr Furze, it is you who are bringing this grave charge of murder against the accused?"

"I am."

"Will you tell my lord and the jury what caused you to take so grave a step?"

"It was because I felt convinced that a serious miscarriage of justice had been done and this appeared the only possible way of rectifying it."

"Exactly. You are acting solely out of public spirit and for no other reason at all?"

"I hope so."

"That," said Sir Ernest with a little bow, "is after all only what one would expect from one with your record of public service, Mr Furze; for I am sure there is no need to say anything to the jury of your admirable and unselfish work in connection with the Middleman's League. Now, what was it, Mr Furze, that caused you to form the opinion that a miscarriage of justice had occurred?"

"Two conversations that I had with Mr Todhunter," replied Furze, blinking behind his big spectacles.

"Will you tell my lord and the jury what the purport of these conversations was?"

Mr Todhunter, watching from the dock, approved of Furze's manner, deliberate as it was and evidently sincere. He made a note to the effect that Furze appeared to fulfil all the qualifications of the perfect witness. He answered only what he was asked, and no one could doubt that he was speaking the truth.

"The first conversation," said Furze, "took place at my club about six months ago. I remember it clearly, for it was a very unusual conversation. Mr Todhunter, to the best of my recollection, opened the chief topic by asking me if I knew of anyone who needed murdering. I enquired in a jocular way whether he was proposing to murder anyone I recommended, and Mr Todhunter agreed that he was. We then debated the possibility of his assassinating either Hitler or Mussolini, an idea to which Mr Todhunter seemed much drawn;

but I recommended him not to try, for various reasons which perhaps I need not recapitulate."

"Quite so," purred Sir Ernest. "Now you say that you received Mr Todhunter's suggestion of murdering any nominee of yours in a jocular spirit. Did that jocular spirit remain with you during the whole of the conversation that ensued?"

"It did."

"You did not take the suggestion seriously?"

"I'm afraid not. I see now that I made a serious mistake."

"One that you can hardly be blamed for, Mr Furze. Now you understood of course that Mr Todhunter had only a few months to live. Did you give him any advice as to how he might employ this period rather than devote it to murdering somebody?"

"Yes. I think I told him to have a good time and forget about Hitler and everyone else."

"Very practical. It is only to be regretted that Mr Todhunter did not see fit to follow it. Was anything else said that you think the jury should hear?"

"I think something was said about the possibility of murdering a blackmailer or any other person who was making the lives of several people a burden."

"Ah yes. You discussed with Mr Todhunter the idea of murdering some person, some complete stranger, who could be shown to be a cause of widespread unhappiness and misery?"

"Yes."

"But for your part you did not take the discussion seriously?"

"Not for a moment."

"Nor did you realise that Mr Todhunter was serious?"

"I thought he was toying with the idea, in an academic and idealistic way, but I certainly did not think that he would ever put it into action."

"Precisely. Now you alluded to two conversations. What was the second?"

"The second took place about two months ago; that is, after Palmer's arrest for the murder but before his trial. Mr Todhunter visited me in my office and told me that it was he who had committed this murder. He asked my advice as to what he should do, since the police obviously did not believe his confession."

"Yes, and what did you tell him?"

"I told him in that case it would be necessary to prove his contention, and I advised him to get into touch with a common friend, a Mr Chitterwick, who had had some experience in the detection of crime, and see if he could be persuaded to help detect the murder."

"You mean, Mr Todhunter was to collaborate with Mr Chitterwick in detecting his own crime?"

"Exactly."

"Was anything else said?"

"Yes. I advised Mr Todhunter not to be too much upset, since I considered it very doubtful that Palmer would be convicted. In fact I hardly considered it possible that he could be convicted in view of Mr Todhunter's story."

"The conviction came as a great surprise to you?"

"A very great surprise."

"You felt that a miscarriage of justice had occurred?"

"I was convinced that an appalling blunder had occurred."

"Did you take any steps yourself?"

"Yes. I interviewed a high police official and satisfied myself that the authorities were quite genuine in their belief that they had the real murderer under lock and key."

"But that did not allay your anxiety?"

"On the contrary, it increased it; because this could only mean that the police would prove obstructive to any reopening of the case."

"You kept in touch with the investigations of Mr Chitterwick?"

"Yes."

"Did what you leaned from him confirm or lessen your feeling that a miscarriage of justice had occurred?"

"It confirmed my opinion."

"So in the end, acting with the full approval and co-operation of Mr Todhunter himself, you took this drastic step of filing a private charge of murder against him?"

"I did."

"Thank you, Mr Furze."

Mr Jamieson asked only a question or two, to bring out more strongly Furze's original impression that Mr Todhunter was only toying with the idea of murder; and Furze agreed that a man might carry such make-believe, right up to the last moment and yet never intend murder in his heart of hearts.

2

The stream of witnesses went on.

It lasted for three more full days, and it would be impossible even if it were of any use, to give so little as a summary of all their evidence.

Young Fuller had done his work well. Anyone who could give the smallest corroboration was called. The judge was very patient.

Witnesses were taken more or less in their consecutive order in the story.

At one point Mr Todhunter had a surprise. He knew that Farroway had been subpoenaed, but had never expected him to appear. A doctor's certificate of inability to attend seemed to Mr Todhunter the natural sequence of subpoenaing Farroway. But whether it was that young Fuller's methods were more efficacious than those of Palmer's solicitor or not, when Farroway's name was called, it was Farroway who entered the box.

Sir Ernest spared him as much as possible. His liaison with Jean Norwood was mentioned but not emphasised. It was upon certain conversations which he had held with Mr Todhunter that Farroway's evidence was chiefly required. Sir Ernest questioned him upon them.

Farroway responded nobly. If Sir Ernest was willing to spare him, he was not willing to spare himself. (Mr Todhunter suspected some plain speaking from Farroway's wife.) He was a useful witness in another way, too, for it was clear that he held no doubts about Mr Todhunter's guilt; and the more people who clearly felt that way, the more likely it was that the jury would follow them.

Farroway described his conversations with Mr Todhunter, at lunch in the expensive restaurant when Mr Todhunter had learned the extent of his infatuation for Miss Norwood and how it had broken up his home; and secondly, that long and fatal conversation in Farroway's lodgings.

While Farroway was describing this, the court was completely silent. At times Farroway's voice sunk almost to a whisper, but there was no need to ask him to speak up. The jury and the judge could hear even a whisper.

"I told him," muttered Farroway in so broken a way that Mr Todhunter felt acutely embarrassed in his dock, "I told him, I think, that she was the wickedest woman I knew. I know I told him that I'd often thought of killing her myself but hadn't the courage. I remember saying she was more worth killing than anyone I'd ever met. I loved her then," whispered Farroway with desperate courage, "but I couldn't help knowing what she was."

"Mr Farroway," said Sir Ernest, no less solemnly, "it is my duty to put a very painful question to you. Assuming that the accused was at that time debating with himself whether to kill this woman or not, do you agree that the words you used to him and the attitude you showed to him on this occasion were enough to turn the scale?"

Farroway lifted his head. "Yes," he said, more loudly than he had spoken before. "It's a conclusion I can't escape. I must have incited him to kill her."

Mr Jamieson's few questions, designed to show that Farroway as a novelist and therefore a student of character was quite ready to agree that Mr Todhunter had been incited not to kill Miss Norwood but merely to frighten her by the flourishing of a revolver, came as very much of an anticlimax.

On the whole Farroway's evidence was the most telling that had yet been given. It was obvious that the jury had been deeply impressed by it.

Then came Mr Budd, who no less nobly admitted to having inflamed Mr Todhunter with tales of Miss Norwood's unpleasing behaviour in her theatre. Mr Budd further was able to establish that Mr Todhunter had without a shadow of doubt been making enquiries about Miss Norwood and especially about her less attractive nature; and this, too, Mr Pleydell was able to confirm, with the notable addition of Mr Todhunter's question of whether, taking it by and large, the world would not be a more pleasant place with Miss Norwood out of it. Then came Mrs Vincent Palmer, to drive the point still further home.

Mrs Palmer was asked one other series of questions, which sounded highly mysterious.

"Have you," said Sir Ernest, looking extremely cunning, "have you ever seen a revolver in the possession of your husband?"

Mrs Palmer agreed that she had.

"To your knowledge he possessed a revolver?"

"Yes."

"Have you ever handled it?"

"Yes."

"Have you ever fired it?"

"Yes."

"Why?"

"I don't know. I just thought I'd like to, to see what it was like, one day when my husband was out."

"When was that?"

"I couldn't possibly say. Not very long ago."

"Was it within the last year?"

"Oh yes."

"Within the last six months?"

"Possibly. I think it was one day in the late summer—last summer."

"What did you fire at?"

"I fired it into a bed in the garden."

Like a conjurer Sir Ernest whisked a piece of paper from the desk in front. "Please look at this." The usher took it across the court, and Mrs Palmer duly looked at it. Mr Todhunter gazed at her with admiration. She was acting so well that it might have been the first time her eyes had ever rested on that piece of paper; but Mr Todhunter had learned a thing or two by this time about witnesses and their treatment, before and after entering the box.

"Is that a plan of your garden, Mrs Palmer?"

"Yes, I see that it is."

"The flower beds are clearly marked?"

"Quite."

"Will you show the jury into which bed you fired that shot?"

"Into this one. It's marked with a red cross."

"Thank you, Mrs Palmer. That's all."

The jury studied the plan while Mrs Palmer slipped quietly out of court. It had been an ordeal for her, as Mr Todhunter well knew, but she had carried it off bravely.

Sir Ernest caught Mr Todhunter's eye and very nearly winked. Mr Todhunter looked hastily the other way.

The questions had not been mysterious to him. In fact the whole idea behind them had been his own, and very proud Mr Todhunter was of it.

It had been a point against Palmer, at his own trial, that his revolver had been recently fired. Palmer had denied having fired it himself for years. Either his solicitor had omitted to cover the possibility of someone else having fired it, or else Mrs Palmer had unaccountably forgotten that she herself had done so. In either case Mr Todhunter, while still allowed to make enquiries on his own account, had eluded Mr Chitterwick one day and paid another visit to Bromley where, without preamble, he had bluntly asked Mrs Palmer whether it might not have been she who had fired the revolver; and Mrs Palmer, after a long pause, had agreed that it might.

Mr Todhunter had then ascertained that Mrs Palmer had in fact fired into a certain flower bed, and he had gone back to London to send both Mr Chitterwick and the firearms expert down to Bromley in their turn. The expert had been given a spade and told to dig in the flower bed. In due course he had turned up a lead bullet which could only have been fired from an army pattern revolver; and when the bullet came to be examined, there was no difficulty in proving that it had been fired from Palmer's own revolver. And of course there could have been no hanky-panky about the whole thing, for Palmer's revolver was still in the possession of the police and could not have been borrowed for any such reprehensible purpose as the faking of evidence. By a piece of smart work, therefore, Mr Todhunter had seriously damaged if not destroyed one of the worst points against Palmer.

To clear the matter up, Sir Ernest called the firearms expert next to prove both where the bullet had been found and what revolver it must have been fired from.

Sir Ernest then put the bullet in as an exhibit and produced another cat out of his bag. Showing the expert the shapeless piece of lead that had been dug out of the beam in Miss Norwood's barn, he asked if that could also have been fired from the same revolver. And most obligingly the expert replied that it could not.

"Will you tell the jury how you can be so sure?" suggested Sir Ernest.

"Certainly. In the revolver which is labelled B, there is a barrel flaw which leaves a unique and clearly defined mark on any bullet fired from it. Although the bullet labelled C is so much damaged, the barrel mark of revolver B, it can easily be seen, is definitely missing.

"So that, although you can prove that revolver B did not fire that bullet, that does not necessarily mean that you can say what revolver did fire it?"

"That is so."

"Have you examined the revolver labelled A?" The revolver labelled A was that belonging to Mr Todhunter.

"I have."

"Could that have fired this bullet C?"

"I have made tests with it and undoubtedly it could have done so, but it is not possible to say that it actually did."

Sir Ernest nodded and had the statement repeated in two or three different ways, so that not even the most obtuse jury could fail to understand that Vincent Palmer could not possibly have fired the bullet which lodged in the barn, but that Mr Todhunter could have done so.

With this interesting point established, the witnesses' tale went on.

Mrs Farroway came next, to testify to the good offices of Mr Todhunter, the help he had given her and her family and the distress he had shown on their behalf. She agreed that his feelings towards Miss Norwood had seemed very bitter and that he had expressed them quite plainly. Felicity Farroway was not called, to the disappointment of the spectators. Her evidence could only have corroborated her mother's, and after the scene in his bedroom Mr Todhunter had put down a very firm foot against her being allowed anywhere near the court. An outburst of hysterics would obviously do his case no good.

To compensate for Felicity's nonappearance however, Sir Ernest was able to produce a real thrill in his last witness on this day.

"I now call," he declaimed in his most resonant tones, "I now call Vincent Palmer."

A delighted shudder went round the whole court. Only the judge looked unmoved; but under his wig even he must have experienced a shock. To hear called as a witness the man already under sentence of death for the very murder for which he was now trying a totally different person must cause even a judge to quiver slightly, albeit inside his robes.

Not that young Mr Palmer really had anything very much of importance to tell. Sir Ernest suggested that, in order to save the time of the Court and to ensure that the death of Miss Norwood should be considered from every possible angle, the official report of the examination and cross-examination of Palmer at his own trial should be put in now as evidence. The judge assented, and the jury were bidden to study the typewritten sheets now handed to them, at their leisure.

In this evidence Palmer had admitted having visited Miss Norwood that evening but asserted that he had left her, alive and well, before nine o'clock. It was a fact that Miss Norwood had been seen, very much alive, after this hour, but no evidence had been produced to show that Palmer had left at that time. It had been the police theory that Miss Norwood had left him for a few minutes and then returned.

In response to Sir Ernest's questions Palmer now once again asserted that he had heard a church clock striking nine as he walked down a road at some distance from that in which Miss Norwood's house had lain, in point of fact towards a bus stop; and he was able to remember this because he had unconsciously fitted his steps to the chimes and found that he could take four paces to each stroke. This was interesting, but of course the discovery could have been made at any time, together with its corollary that, in order to have reached this particular road by nine o'clock, Palmer must have left the Norwood premises certainly before 8:55 p.m.

"And when you left, you neither heard nor saw anyone else in the garden?" asked Sir Ernest.

"No one. It was getting pretty dark then, and I was het up in any case. We'd had a row, you see. I doubt if I'd have heard if anyone had been there; I certainly saw no one."

"Most unfortunate, for all our parts. . . . In our submission, my lord," remarked Sir Ernest confidentially to the judge, "the witness must have been leaving the grounds just as the accused was entering them." Sir Ernest was allowing himself a good deal of latitude, but there were no objections to be expected from his colleague on the other side. "Had you, while in the gardens, noticed whether there was a punt moored to the bank at the bottom of the garden?" he continued to the witness.

"No, I didn't go down to the river."

"Let me see." Sir Ernest shuffled hastily through the typescript of evidence. "You have stated that you were not on the premises more than twenty minutes. During the whole of that period you neither saw nor heard nor had any reason to suspect the presence of any unauthorised person in Miss Norwood's grounds that evening?"

"No."

Counsel then went on to ask a few questions concerning the meeting between Palmer and Mr Todhunter at the Farroway flat on the following morning. But here again Palmer had not much to say. He had found his revolver in Mr Todhunter's possession when he arrived at the flat; he could not suggest any reason why it should have been in Mr Todhunter's pocket or why Mr Todhunter should have shown so much interest in it; yet he knew now that Mr Todhunter had a revolver of his own of identical pattern and that Mrs Farroway (as she had stated in evidence) had seen it in its owner's possession before he, Palmer, arrived. Would it strike him, knowing the circumstances, as a feasible explanation if Mr Todhunter had intended to substitute his own guilty revolver for Palmer's innocent one with the feeling usual to the guilty person that he must be the only person whom the police suspect and that incriminating evidence will be safer in anyone else's possession rather than his own? Mr Palmer, somewhat sulkily, could not give an opinion on the point.

Sir Ernest smiled his sulkiness away. He had got the point before the jury so early in the proceedings and that was all he cared about.

In the same way Sir Ernest did not seem worried when young Palmer, after two or three more unimportant questions, left the witness box in the charge of his two warders without having contributed anything of value to his case. He had brought the wrongfully condemned man before the jury and given them a first-class thrill, and he expected them to show their gratitude with their verdict.

3

The next morning it was Mr Chitterwick's turn.

He was examined by Sir Ernest at some length and was able to give evidence of importance, from the occasion when Mr Todhunter had consulted him concerning some person whom he might conveniently murder, to the last discovery of all, that of the whereabouts of the missing bracelet. His modesty and diffidence made an excellent impression on all concerned; and, led very subtly by Sir Ernest, the effect he quite unknowingly produced was that if so charming a person as Mr Chitterwick thought that a thing was so, then it probably was.

After Mr Chitterwick came the sensation of the third day, with the great Sir Ernest Prettiboy himself entering the box to create a precedent in the annals of the English Bar, and allowing himself to be examined by his own junior. With fearful solemnity Sir Ernest corroborated the findings in the gardens which Mr Chitterwick had already described and managed to insert an opinion that it would have been quite impossible for Mr Todhunter to have faked these or even to have known where to look for them, had he not made them himself. Sir Ernest then quickly left the box before the judge or any other interfering person could remind the jury that nobody now, not even the police, disputed Mr Todhunter's presence in Miss Norwood's garden at some time on the fatal evening, and therefore the traces of his entry in no way helped to prove that it had been his finger that pulled the trigger. Sir Ernest's hushed solemnity was worth a ton of dull evidence.

The police officers who had been instrumental in recovering the stolen bracelet, upon information furnished by Mr Todhunter, came next; and naturally Sir Ernest took the opportunity of rubbing into the jury the importance of this testimony. The afternoon was taken up with medical evidence to the effect that the time at which Miss Norwood's death must have occurred seemed to indicate that Mr Todhunter rather than Palmer was probably the cause of it; and this was followed by other evidence, including that of Mr Todhunter's own doctor, of Mrs Greenhill and Edie and of various of Mr Todhunter's friends to prove that he was probably the sanest person walking about London during the past year. The judge did become a little restive under all this testimony, pointing out to Sir Ernest that as no one had questioned the sanity of the accused and as the accused's own counsel had already dealt with the matter there was perhaps little need to emphasise it quite so much.

"My lord," replied Sir Ernest, "with the greatest respect, I understand that the question of the sanity of the accused, on which my learned friend and I are fully agreed may be raised in another quarter, and I therefore feel it my duty to show that he was fully responsible for his actions."

"Very well," said the judge resignedly.

4

Mr Todhunter made a note.

"I am astonished at the strength of our case. I thought, before the proceedings opened, that we should have some difficulty in making it appear feasible, let alone convincing. But it is very different when one hears the evidence marshalled like this from the beginning of the story to the end. I should say now that our case is conclusive. What I can add myself in the witness box will be only a supererogation. This is very satisfactory."

Sir Ernest, however, was not quite so certain.

"Wait till you've heard the police johnny, my boy," he said. "There are some pretty big holes in our story, you know, and he'll know how to tear 'em bigger."

"I wish, we'd never invited him to come and interfere," said Mr Todhunter, alarmed by this prognostication.

"Oh, much better. Otherwise, supposing you were found guilty, the verdict would only be upset on appeal, on the ground that the true verdict had never been put to the jury for their consideration."

"But how could there be an appeal if both prosecution and defence are satisfied with the verdict?"

"The Crown would appeal."

"But has the Crown any right to intervene with an appeal in a case in which it has not acted?"

"Don't ask me silly questions," said Sir Ernest.

5

The next morning the case for the defence opened with a brief statement by Mr Jamieson on the lines which he had already indicated. He then called his one and only witness, and Mr Todhunter shuffled into the box.

Mr Todhunter had passed a very bad night. He had been dreading this ordeal. Not least did he dislike the necessity for committing perjury. It seemed to him most exasperating that, in order to obtain a trial at all, he had to commit perjury. But there it was, and perjury was what he had to commit.

The first part was easy enough, though even with all Mr Jamieson's most persuasive leading Mr Todhunter was not sure that he had managed to put before the jury the exact state of mind which had led him into Miss Norwood's garden that night.

"I... um ... formed my decision on the unwitting advice of many people," he mumbled when invited by his counsel to explain to my lord and the jury just how it was that he had arrived at so drastic a determination as to commit murder. "I knew that if they gathered I was serious, they would not tell me what they really thought. I therefore put to them an ... um ... hypothetical case. The unanimity with which I was advised on all sides to commit murder impressed me. And the more I considered it, the more reasonable I found it. Murder of an entirely impersonal ... um ... nature seemed to suit my exactly."

"It did not occur to you that perhaps your friends might be joking?"

"I'm afraid it didn't. And I don't believe," said Mr Todhunter with some defiance, "that they were. I believe they meant what they said."

"Please explain a little more fully what you mean when you say that murder seemed to suit your case exactly?"

"I mean, I never expected to live to be hanged," said Mr Todhunter simply.

"You did not expect to live as long even as this?"

"I thought at that time that I should ... um ... be dead about a month ago," said Mr Todhunter shamefacedly.

"Perhaps, in the circumstances, it's lucky you weren't," commented his counsel drily.

Slowly, by means of laborious question and answer, Mr Todhunter brought his tale up to the moment of his decision that Miss Jean Norwood must be eliminated.

"By that time," he explained, "I had made the fullest enquiries, and I was unable to evade the conclusion that her death would bring . . . um . . . happiness to a remarkable number of people."

"You formed the conclusion that she was a bad woman?"

"She was a poisonous bitch," replied Mr Todhunter, to the shocked delight of everyone in court.

Five minutes later he was committing manful perjury.

"I think I intended to kill her right up to the moment when I came face to face with her. Then. . ."

"Yes?" prompted Mr Jamieson amid a hushed expectancy.

"Well, I . . . um . . . I suppose I lost my nerve."

"Did you threaten her with the revolver?"

"Yes. And . . . er . . . it went off. Twice. I'm not used to firearms," apologised Mr Todhunter.

"How could it have gone off twice?"

"Well, the—the first shot made me jump. It was . . . er . . . unexpected, you see. And I suppose the shock made me tighten my finger on the trigger. I . . . er . . . um . . . can't account for it in any other way."

"And what happened next?"

"I was a little dazed," said Mr Todhunter, relieved to be back on the path of truth again. "Then I realised that she had fallen back in her chair. There was . . . er . . . blood all over the front of her dress. I didn't know what to do."

"And what did you do?"

"I forced myself to go up and look at her closely. She seemed to be dead. I lifted her forward a little. Than I realised that the bullet had gone . . . um . . . clean through her. It was actually lodged in the back of the chair. I . . . um . . . picked it up and put it in my pocket. Later I threw it into the river."

"Why did you do that?"

"I'd read somewhere that bullets can prove the gun that fired them. I thought it best to protect myself by disposing of it. I realise now that it was an unfortunate action."

"Did you do anything else before you left?"

"Yes. There were two tumblers on a table. I wiped one of them with my handkerchief but not the other."

"Why did you do that?"

"I don't know," confessed Mr Todhunter.

"Did you do anything else?"

"Yes. I removed a bracelet from Miss Norwood's wrist."

"With what object?"

"I'm really not sure now," said Mr Todhunter abjectly. "I was . . . um . . . very confused. I had had a great shock."

"But you must have had some object in mind?"

"Yes, I think it was so that I could prove my . . . um . . . guilt, should the necessity ever arise."

"Do you mean, in just such a situation as has in fact arisen?"

"Precisely."

"Did you anticipate any such situation?"

"Good gracious, no. Such a thing never occurred to me. Dear me, no."

"You never expected that anyone else would be accused of what you had done?"

"Certainly not. Otherwise . . ."

"Yes?"

"Otherwise," said Mr Todhunter with dignity, "I should never have done it."

"Thank you, Mr Todhunter. . . . My lord," said Mr Jamieson impressively, "I have made the examination of the accused as brief as possible, owing to the very precarious state of his health. I have a certificate from his doctor here to say that he is not really in a condition to stand trial at all, if it were not that to have refused permission would probably have agitated him more than the trial itself. In fact the doctor says, very frankly, that he might die at any moment and that strain or agitation of any kind would probably be immediately fatal. I am able to say this in the presence of my client since he knows it perfectly well himself. I propose therefore to end my examination of him at this point. I think I have covered all the necessary ground; but with the greatest respect, if your lordship thinks there is any point which should be made clear to the jury that I may have omitted, I would ask you to put it to my client yourself."

"I don't think there is, Mr Jamieson. Your client admits that it was he who killed the dead woman. The only issue I am trying is whether he did so in wilful murder or whether his action can be held to be manslaughter. I will put this simple issue to him, if you like. . . . Mr Todhunter, did you shoot Ethel May Binns deliberately and, as the law puts it, with malice aforethought?"

"Er . . . no, my lord," replied Mr Todhunter somewhat unhappily. "I did not that is . . . um . . . not with malice aforethought, I think."

"In view of the remarks of my learned friend, my lord, I will not cross-examine the accused."

There was some attempt at applause from the back of the court, which was instantly quelled.

A lean and cadaverous barrister rose.

"My lord, I have the honour to represent the commissioner of police. Mr Jamieson's remarks make my position a difficult one; nevertheless I understand that it is by the accused's express wish that I have been invited to cross-examine him. It is for your lordship to say whether such unorthodox procedure is inadmissible."

"With so much that has been unorthodox already, Mr Bairns, a little more will hardly matter. But I must be satisfied that the accused is willing to answer your questions." He turned his ancient head towards Mr Todhunter. "Do you wish to be given the opportunity to answer any questions that the commissioner of police may wish to put to you through his counsel?"

"In the interests of . . . um . . . justice, my lord," Mr Todhunter replied, "I consider it imperative."

"Very well then, Mr Bairns," said the judge.

The lean Mr Bairns gave a hitch to his gown and then clasped it firmly with both hands, as if afraid that it might run away from him.

"You will appreciate my difficulty," he addressed Mr Todhunter in a quiet, assured tone. "It may be that you will find some of my questions agitating. If so, perhaps I may rely on you to indicate as much at once, and no doubt my lord will give you a breathing space."

Mr Todhunter gave a little bow from his chair in the witness box.

"I apologise for being . . . er . . . um . . . a nuisance to the Court," he mumbled, feeling a little agitated already.

He fixed his eyes firmly on his opponent, nervously determined to be led into no traps. As he very well knew, the crux of the trial had arrived.

"I will make it as short as possible," promised Mr Bairns and fixed his eyes on the ceiling as if seeking inspiration there. "Perhaps, if my lord allows me, I can manage to put a great number of separate questions into one collective whole. . . . I suggest to you, then, that you never shot this woman at all; that when you found her she was already dead; and that out of your friendship for the Farroway family you have taken the responsibility for this crime upon your own shoulders, knowing that it could affect you very little since you never expected to live long enough to suffer the penalty for it."

Mr Todhunter made an effort to speak, his face turned a horrible pale green colour, his hand flew to his chest, and he slumped forward in his chair.

The whole court seemed to surge towards him.

CHAPTER XVII

Mr Todhunter did not die in the witness box.

Within a minute or two he had quite recovered and was testily waving away those anxious to assist him. Nevertheless the judge insisted upon adjourning the proceedings for half an hour to give him more time, and Mr Todhunter, protesting loudly, was carried out by two large policemen, while his own doctor, who had been retained to attend every day, danced nervously in the rear.

"It was touch and go with you that time," he said candidly when he had Mr Todhunter to himself in a large bare room intended for goodness-knows-what legal purpose. "What made you give way like that?"

Stretched much against his will on a trestle table, with the doctor's overcoat under his head, Mr Todhunter grinned feebly.

"It was what I've been afraid of all the time. You see, I can prove that I meant to kill the woman, so far as one can prove that sort of thing; and of course I can prove that I was there that evening. But I don't see how I can possibly prove that I did kill her. Nor does old Prettiboy. Nor does Chitterwick. Nor does Fuller. Nor does anyone. It was my own damned idiocy in throwing away the bullet no doubt, but there it is. Don't you see, with that one question the chap's undermined the whole of the grand case Prettiboy built up? And I'm damned afraid those fools of a jury will go and give me the benefit of the doubt. Or even if they don't the police will take advantage of it to keep Palmer in gaol for a life sentence. It's damnable."

"All right, all right, don't get excited. I can't think why you ever wanted to go and get mixed up with all this murdering business at all," grumbled the doctor. "You used to be a decent fellow once, Todhunter. Now look at all the trouble you're giving me."

"Don't think so much of your damned self," snapped Mr Todhunter.

"Well, you're certainly giving plenty of other people trouble too," agreed the doctor. He concealed a smile. Mr Todhunter was a more satisfactory patient than he knew. He reacted to a small kick in the mental pants as others react to stimulating drugs.

So at the end of half an hour Mr Todhunter was carried back into court (still protesting at the indignity), feeling as well as ever and relieved to know that the worst was over.

Mr Bairns gravely apologised for having caused Mr Todhunter distress.

Mr Todhunter courteously replied that it was nothing.

The judge asked whether Mr Todhunter felt capable of answering any further questions.

Mr Todhunter was understood to reply that he was not only capable but anxious to do so.

Mr Bairns gazed at the ceiling again.

"As a matter of fact, Mr Todhunter, you never answered my original question. I don't know whether you would like to do so now."

"Certainly," replied Mr Todhunter with asperity. "The answer to all the suggestions you made is that they are without foundation."

"You reject them?"

"They are untrue."

"Yet, if I may say so, they appeared to cause you distress?"

"They did."

"Would you care to explain why?" asked Mr. Bairns, scrutinising the ceiling with such obvious interest that one would have said that he had detected a loose piece which might fall at any moment upon some important head.

"I should welcome the opportunity," snapped Mr Todhunter, "if only to obviate any misunderstanding. It was because I can only assert that it was I who killed Miss Norwood; I cannot prove that it was actually my finger that pulled the trigger . . . um . . . inadvertently or not. And it distresses me to consider the possibility of this small loophole being used to save the faces of those who have blundered and to keep an innocent man in prison."

A little gasp went up. This was boldness, to admit the flaw and try to turn it to advantage. Sir Ernest looked worried. Boldness often pays with a jury, but perhaps more often it does not. The judge looked doubtful, as if wondering whether Mr Todhunter were not being allowed too much latitude to make speeches. Only Mr Bairns remained interested in apparently nothing but the ceiling.

"Why did you not go to the police and confess your prime immediately after the shooting then?"

"I saw no reason to do so."

"You preferred to wait until an innocent man had been accused?"

"It never occurred to me that anyone would be accused?"

"Yet you knew the police would make investigations?"

"Investigations, yes; not blunders."

"It did not occur to you that persons with perhaps a more obvious motive than yours would be suspected?"

"I did not think about it. I tried to put the whole thing out of my mind."

"You went for a voyage?"

"Yes."

"With what purpose?"

"I wanted to visit Japan before I . . . um . . . died."

"It was of more importance to you to visit Japan than stay and face the consequences of your act?"

"I anticipated no consequences." Mr Todhunter would have liked to wipe his forehead but was afraid that such an action would be construed as a sign of another approaching collapse.

"You did not set out on that voyage in relief at having had the murder which you had been meditating performed for you, so that you could enjoy the pleasures of Japan with a clear conscience?"

"Certainly not."

"Your conscience did not worry you?"

"Not in the least. My . . . um . . . action may have been unorthodox, but I'm still unable to feel that it was anything but beneficial."

"I wish to allow you as much latitude as possible, Mr Todhunter, but I really must remind you that witnesses are supposed to confine themselves to answering the question asked and not make speeches."

"I beg your pardon."

"Not at all. . . . . It was only when you heard of Palmer's arrest that you considered it time to make a clean breast of what you had done?"

"Yes."

"Yet by that time you might well have been dead?"

"That is so. But I left a memorandum with my solicitor of what I had done, to be given to the police on my death."

"Yes, that memorandum has been put in as an exhibit, I believe. Do you agree that it consisted of no more than a series of bare statements?"

"It was a series of statements of what I had done."

"Statements unsupported by a jot of proof?"

"I considered it contained plenty of proof, and do so still."

"What was the attitude of the police when they perused it?"

"I understand," replied Mr Todhunter bitterly, "that they laughed at it."

"In any case, they took no action on it?"

"No."

"Can you suggest any other reason why they should have taken no action—a body of conscientious public officials—beyond the reason that they considered it a tissue of fabrications?"

"I'm sure they considered it that."

"And yet you thought it good enough to satisfy them in the event of your being no longer alive and able to help them verify it?"

"I did."

"Mr Todhunter, you have been represented to us, by your colleagues on the newspapers and others, as a man of intelligence above the average. I put it to you that, if you had really shot this woman, you would never have remained content with a vague 'statement,' which you must have known was incapable of proof, but would have taken steps to make sure that your guilt was established beyond the possibility of any other person coming even under suspicion?"

"I did not regard my statement as vague nor incapable of proof, and I do not so regard it now."

"Do you not agree that your actions after the murder are more consistent with innocence than with guilt, having in view the fact that, as you assert, you had acted only out of the most honourable motives and had nothing to lose by your guilt becoming known?"

"No, I don't agree to that."

"You think that a man who had planned, mistakenly of course but sincerely, what we may call an honourable assassination, would then run away and leave others to bear the suspicion and possibly, in spite of this 'statement,' the blame?"

"I object to the phrase 'run away.'"

"Let me put it this way. Do you find the actions of yours which followed the crime consistent with the honourable motive which, you tell us, caused you to plan it?"

"Perfectly. I may have been stupid, but. . ."

"I put it to you again—please don't distress yourself—that the defence which has been raised on your behalf in this court is the truth: that you only toyed with the idea of murder, possibly as an interest for your last weeks on earth sufficiently startling to take your mind off approaching death, but that in your inmost mind you never intended to perform it, knowing yourself incapable of doing so when it came to the point; and that when you heard that another person, belonging to a family for whom you had affection and regard, had committed the very murder which you had only academically planned, you saw that the evidence might be so twisted and distorted as to throw a certain amount of suspicion upon yourself, and so as an honourable and very gallant gentleman you accused yourself of a crime you had never committed?"

Those who had expected Mr Todhunter to collapse again before this suggestion were disappointed.

"That is not the case," replied Mr Todhunter with surprising firmness.

His ordeal was over.

2

Mr Todhunter had occupied the box for the whole morning.

His doctor would not allow him to go out for lunch, and a covered tray was brought in for him into the bare room.

Sir Ernest came to him to congratulate him before going out for his own lunch.

"You came out of that well. Turned the tables on him properly. It was risky, but I think it'll pay. Otherwise your collapse might have put us in a bit of a fix."

"What effect do you think his suggestions will have on the jury?" asked Mr Todhunter anxiously.

Sir Ernest looked grave. "Impossible to say. I believe they'd like to find you a gallant and honourable gent by their verdict, rather than a murderer."

"But that would mean condemning Palmer?"

"Exactly."

"Damn it, I'm *not* a gallant and honourable gent," shouted Mr Todhunter passionately.

"Now, now," soothed Sir Ernest and made a hurried exit.

3

The lean Mr Bairns was the first counsel to address the jury after the lunch recess. He did so with a great display of gratitude to the accused and the accused's advisers for their noble-mindedness in allowing him the opportunity. But that did not prevent him from going on to put the case as the police saw it with the utmost frankness and conviction.

His speech consisted chiefly of an amplification of the suggestions contained in his questions to Mr Todhunter, but he made one or two further points. Over the matter of Mr Todhunter's disposal of the bullet, for instance, Mr Bairns made great play.

"The accused tells us that he was responsible for this woman's death, whether willfully or not is of minor importance. Yet there is not a single action of his which is not consistent with his innocence.

"He tells us that he threw away the fatal bullet out of regard for his own safety. At first hearing, that may sound plausible. I submit that it will not stand examination for one moment.

"We have heard a great deal about psychology from both my learned friends, and no doubt one must take psychology more or less into account even in a court of law. Very well, what is the psychology of this act of throwing away the bullet? The accused says it is the crude instinct of self-preservation. But self-preservation from what? Compared with the ordinary murderer, the accused had comparatively nothing to fear from the utmost rigour of the law; or so, as he himself tells us, he thought at that time. Why then destroy this valuable, this one and only piece of utterly convincing evidence concerning the identity of the perpetrator?

"So that he should be free to visit Japan, says the accused. To visit Japan— and leave events to take their own course, innocent people to be suspected and an innocent man to be arrested! No. The only explanation consistent with the psychology which the accused had displayed up to that point is this. He threw away that bullet, not because it came from his own gun, but because it came from someone else's—someone whose identity he knew, someone whose action he fully approved, someone whom he was determined to protect at all costs. That, gentleman, in my submission, was why the accused threw away that damning bullet."

Mr Todhunter cast an uneasy glance at Sir Ernest. The argument had upset him. But Sir Ernest was hunched up into a rotund lump of indifference, and his eye was not visible to be caught.

To Mr Todhunter's increasing discomfiture, Mr Bairns was pulling another cat down from the ceiling.

"I said that there was not a single action of the accused which cannot be interpreted as that of an innocent man, even the most trivial. Take for instance the matter of the exchange of revolvers, which Mr Todhunter intended to effect and which he apparently at one time thought had been effected. What was the object of this exchange? We know what had preceded it: careful questions to ascertain that there was a revolver in the flat at that moment, and that Palmer, the Farroway son-in-law, had brought it thither at a curiously early hour that same morning.

"What did he do then? He asked to see it. And what did he see? That Palmer's revolver was of identical pattern with his own, both old army revolvers of standard make. It would be outside my province perhaps to speculate upon what action the accused might have taken at this point, had the revolvers proved of a different pattern, or to suggest that he would have carried Palmer's away to dispose of it as he had disposed of the bullet. What he did do was to attempt to carry Palmer's away even then by substituting his own for it.

"That is not his own explanation. What the accused says is that his object was to leave his own revolver there. I suggest that it was nothing of the sort; that his true object was to carry Palmer's away.

"Why did he wish to do this? Was it to throw it into the river as he had thrown the bullet? I think not. The revolver, which he still believed to be Palmer's, was left behind in a drawer when he went on his cruise abroad. It could be produced if and when it was needed. What was the object of this manoeuvering? The accused has told us that he knew nothing about firearms.

Is it not then probable that he knew nothing of the numbering of firearms? That he was totally ignorant that every rifle, every revolver carries its own distinctive number, by which it can always be identified without possibility of error or disguise?

"I suggest that the idea in his mind, when he thought he was making the exchange of revolvers, was that Palmer's revolver should be mistaken afterwards for his, and his for Palmer's. Neither you nor I would be likely to make such an error; but I submit that it is exactly the kind of blunder which a recluse, a man of letters, a man totally ignorant of everything that concerns firearms would make.

"What then might have been the reason for this exchange of revolvers that the accused tried to make? If my explanation is right, it would be that there was something incriminating about Palmer's revolver, and equally, something innocent about his own. What could that have been? It could not be anything to do with the markings on the bullet, for that had been disposed of. I suggest it was the damning fact that Palmer's revolver had been recently fired and the accused's had not. That, and that alone, in my submission is the only possible explanation of this mysterious attempt at exchanging revolvers. To suggest, as the accused does, that the object was to plant incriminating evidence upon the very family with whom he was so friendly and whom he wished so much to protect, is simply to strike the word 'psychology' out of the dictionary—it would mean nothing."

Mr Todhunter stifled a groan. This was terrible, terrible. It had been a mistake to let the man come here; a mistake that might well prove fatal. Who could help being convinced by such diabolical ingenuity?

But there was even worse to come.

Mr Bairns was now addressing the judge.

"My lord, as I have explained, I have no standing in this case at all. I am here only by the indulgence of the other parties. In consequence I have not asked for the extended privilege either of cross-examining witnesses other than the accused or of calling any evidence of a rebutting nature. But I think that the object in the mind of every person now in this court—with, I am compelled to add, possibly one exception—is to get at the truth and that only.

"I wish therefore to make a request which your lordship will realise is highly irregular at this stage. I would ask first your lordship's indulgence and after that the permission of my learned friends on both sides to recall one witness who has already appeared, Detective Sergeant Mathers, and then to call two witnesses of my own. I would not make such a request did I not feel that the one or two questions I wish to put to these witnesses would not establish a fact, not yet before the Court, of such significance that it may well solve this baffling riddle by itself."

The judge stroked his lean old cheek. "You assure me that this evidence is as important as that?"

"I do, my lord."

"Very well. What does Sir Ernest Prettiboy say?"

Sir Ernest Prettiboy was in a dilemma, but he could hardly proclaim himself as one not anxious to get at the truth.

"I have no objection at all, my lord."

"And you, Mr Jamieson?"

Mr Jamieson was whispering to his client over the dock rail. He turned back to the judge.

"My client welcomes any evidence that my learned friend would care to bring. Like the rest of us, he is anxious to serve the ends of justice only."

This was not strictly true, for in reply to Mr Jamieson's whispered question, Mr Todhunter had replied with a ghastly grin that he had not the faintest idea what could be in Mr Bairns's mind but would not put it past him to fake a bit of evidence if it suited his book; a suggestion at which Mr Jamison had looked properly shocked.

Amid an expectant hush Sergeant Mathers was recalled to the box.

"When you accompanied the accused back to his house after his visit to Scotland Yard last November, did he show you a revolver?"

"He did."

"Did you examine it?"

"I did."

"What did you find?"

"That it was a brand-new one."

"What do you mean by that?"

"It had never been fired."

"You are sure of that?"

"Quite sure."

"How could you tell it had never been fired?"

"I examined the inside of the barrel. It was coated with oldish, dried oil. Where there was no oil the barrel showed quite smooth."

"How long would you estimate that the oil had been there?"

"It had been there some months, by the look of it."

"What would you have expected to find if the gun had been fired recently? Say within the last few weeks?"

"Oil not so old as that and I should have expected to see signs of striation on the exposed portions of the barrel and possibly lead fouling." This was damning evidence, and Sir Ernest, when he rose to cross-examine, might well have wished that he was in the United States, where a recess of an hour or two would have been granted as a matter of course to enable counsel to consider how to tackle the witness. As it was, Sir Ernest had to rely on a hazy knowledge of firearms left over from the last war and his native wit.

"You are the Scotland Yard expert on firearms, Sergeant Mathers?" he began with a kindly smile.

"No Sir"

"You are not?" Sir Ernest appeared surprised. "But you are an expert?"

"Not an expert. I have a working knowledge of firearms."

"Well, most of us have that. In what way does your knowledge exceed that of the ordinary person?"

"I've been through a course on the subject, as part of my training."

"And that course, though it did not make you an expert, enabled you to pronounce, after a casual examination, just how long ago a gun was fired or not?"

"It enabled me to tell when a gun had not been fired."

"Did you take this revolver to pieces to examine it?"

"No."

"Did you examine it with a lens?"

"No."

"Did you examine it at all, or did you merely glance at it?"

"I examined it as much as I thought necessary."

"In other words, you just glanced down the barrel?"

"No."

"You didn't even glance down the barrel?"

"I looked very carefully down the barrel."

"Oh, I see. So carefully and with such good eye sight that you were able to detect the absence of lead fouling and striatums on the barrel, which a lens is usually required to detect?"

"I was satisfied with my examination."

"No doubt, but perhaps I am not. I want to get this quite clear. Did you really look for such things as striations and lead fouling at all, or did you just look down the barrel and think to yourself, there is dry oil here, so the gun can't have been fired?"

"It was clear to me that the gun had not been fired."

"That is not an answer to my question, but never mind. We will pass that over. Now, I understand you to have said, Sergeant, not 'This gun has not been fired recently,' but 'This gun has never been fired.' The presence of dry oil would have nothing to do with the gun having been fired or not fired years ago. How do you account for that?"

"Enquiries I made showed me that the gun had never been fired."

"Enquiries of whom?"

"Of the gunsmith who sold it."

"These enquiries showed you that, when the gun passed into Mr Todhunter's possession, it was brand new?"

"Not exactly brand new."

"But you told my learned friend that it was brand new."

"I should like to qualify that. It was brand new insofar as it had never been fired," replied the sergeant stolidly, "but it was an oldish gun."

"An old, rusty gun is hardly a brand-new one."

"It was not rusty."

"Oh, it wasn't? We'll come back to that in a minute. It was an old war gun that never saw active service? Is that what you mean?"

'That's what I mean."

"That makes it twenty years old. Yet it was not rusty."

"It had been carefully kept."

"Will old, dry oil prevent rust?"

"I couldn't say."

"But you're the expert?"

"Not on oils."

"But isn't the care of firearms, which involves oils, an important part of the subject?"

"I have no specialised knowledge."

"I should not have thought that specialised knowledge was required to show that old, useless oil will hardly prevent rust. Yet you say there was no rust in this revolver. The barrel, where it could be seen, was quite clean and shiny?"

"So far as I remember."

"Do you agree that a recent firing of the weapon, which would have removed any rust, together with a thorough cleaning afterwards, is a more probable explanation of the absence of rust?"

"No."

"Not so probable as that the old, dried oil had somehow acquired a magical quality and prevented rust even after its oleaginous properties had been dried out of it?"

"I cannot say that the old oil would not have prevented rust."

"Do you agree that, if there is an explanation for the dried oil, there was nothing whatever to indicate that this weapon had not been recently fired?"

"I was satisfied that it had not been."

"Oh yes, by your enquiries. When were these enquiries made?"

"During November last."

"After or before you had seen the revolver—we won't say 'examined' it?"

"After."

"And they showed you that this weapon had never been fired?"

"That is so."

"But did you not make the assertion, in the presence of the accused after your glance at the revolver, that it had never been fired?"

"I may have done so."

"I put it to you that you did so?"

"It is possible."

"That is, before you made the enquiries at all?"

"Yes."

"But if it was the enquiries, and the enquiries only, that convinced you that the revolver had not been fired, how could you assert this as a fact before those enquiries had been made?"

"The presence of the dried oil and the absence of any signs of striation or lead fouling gave me the impression that the revolver had never been fired. The enquiries I made afterwards confirmed it."

"Oh, so it is only an 'impression' now?"

"I was satisfied," repeated the sergeant with a maddening stolidity that made Mr Todhunter want to scream, "that the weapon had never been fired."

"Now I understand that you had an opportunity of examining Mr Todhunter's house. What impression did you form of it?"

"It was quite a nice house." In spite of his training the sergeant showed a trace of bewilderment.

"It struck you as the house of a man who liked to be comfortable?"

"I think I could say that."

"There is no need to be so cautious. You could surely judge by the evidence. Was it for instance a clean house or a dirty house?"

"It struck me as quite clean."

"Well, was it a warm house or a cold house?"

"It was quite warm."

"Did you notice whether there were any signs of comfort—central heating, for instance?"

"I saw that central heating was installed."

"And electric fires in the bedrooms?"

"I only entered the one bedroom."

"Well, was there an electric fire there?

"Yes," said the now unhappy sergeant, who saw the drift at last.

Sir Ernest threw off the mask.

"Exactly. You know the susceptibility of oil, particularly the fine oils used in the care of firearms, to heat?"

"I am not an expert in oils."

"Is there any need to be an expert to know that oil dries rapidly in a warm atmosphere?"

"I couldn't say."

"You tell us that it was not until November that you looked at this revolver. Miss Norwood, as we know, died in September. Are you prepared to assert on oath that the oil on a revolver would not have become dry if left without attention for over two whole months in an overheated room in a warm house?"

"I should not care to assert anything on oath concerning oils," was the best that the sergeant could manage.

"Yet you were ready enough to assert it, apparently, when you were not on oath?"

"I pronounced an opinion."

"Yes. And put it to you that, without the necessary experience or knowledge, you pronounced an opinion that you were not qualified to voice, that you repeated this to your superiors not as an opinion at all but as a fact, and that you now feel compelled to justify your dogmatic and groundless assertion?"

Sir Ernest had got under the sergeant's skin at last.

"That is not at all a fair way of putting it," he said indignantly.

"It is the way I do put it," retorted Sir Ernest and sat down, beaming.

Mr Bairns handled his now slightly flustered witness with care.

"Without going into highly technical and possibly unnecessary details, is it fair to say that your training, even though it may not have specialised in the more peculiar properties of oils, enabled you to recognise at once on examining the revolver that it had never been fired?"

"That is correct," said the sergeant and was allowed to leave the box with a relief that was obvious.

In spite of the indignation with which he had listened to the sergeant's examination in chief (how could the man have had the face to assert as a fact what could have been nothing but the wildest guess?), Mr Todhunter could not help sympathising with him. His own relief was even greater. Sir Ernest had wriggled out of a nasty predicament with remarkable skill.

But Mr Bairns had not finished yet.

He shuffled his papers and looked at the usher.

"Call Miss Julia Fairey."

And who on earth, wondered Mr Todhunter, is Miss Julia Fairey?

He was to be enlightened without delay.

A curious, hunched old person in black crept into the witness box rather like a large snail and took the oath in a mouselike voice.

Her evidence, as reported by the press agencies, ran as follows:

"I live at 86 Hamilton Avenue, Richmond. I am the cook there. The house is next door to that occupied by the late Miss Norwood. I have often seen Miss Norwood walking in her garden. It is possible to see portions of the garden from our windows. I am acquainted with the general layout of the late Miss Norwood's garden. About three months ago I was returning to 86 Hamilton Avenue from the theatre. It was late at night. I think it was just about midnight. I can fix the date from the fact that it was the only occasion on which I have been to a theatre in the West End of London for over a year. The date was the third of December. Just as I was entering the house I heard a loud noise from the direction of Miss Norwood's garden. It appeared to come from near the summerhouse. I was alarmed, remembering that Miss Norwood had been shot there last autumn, and hurried into the house. The noise sounded like a shot. It was a noise like an explosion. I mentioned the incident to my fellow servants the next day. We all looked at the papers for several days. to see if anyone else had been shot like Miss Norwood."

Sir Ernest rose, a little puzzled but undismayed.

"This mysterious noise—you say it sounded like a shot?"

"Just like a shot, sir."

"How many shots have you heard fired in your life, Miss Fairey?"

"I've never heard a shot fired, sir."

"Then how do you know this noise sounded like one?"

This appeared a novel point of view to the witness. "Well, it did, sir."

"Would it not be fairer to say, since you must have heard many fireworks discharged, that it sounded like a firework?"

"Well, it did sound like a firework, too, a loud one."

"Or a motorcar backfiring?"

"Yes, that sort of noise, it was."

"Or a motor launch on the river? Someone trying to start the engine, you know? You must have heard that kind of noise many times? Was it like that?"

"Yes, just like that, sir."

"Let me see," said Sir Ernest engagingly, "this house where you live must be two beyond mine, I take it, so we have about the same sort of view. Now, from where you stood would the summerhouse in Miss Norwood's garden have been between you and the river?"

"Yes, it would."

"So that this noise, which struck you as coming from the summerhouse, might really have come from the river beyond it?"

"Yes, I suppose it could, if you put it like that sir."

"But of course a shot in the summerhouse made a better story to tell the others the next morning?"

"I'm afraid I don't quite understand, sir."

"Never mind. How old are you, Miss Fairey?"

"I'm fifty-six, sir."

"Are you really? Dear me. Faculties getting a bit impaired or not?" asked Sir Ernest, dropping his voice a little.

"I beg your pardon, sir?"

Sir Ernest maintained the same slightly lower tone, which was nevertheless perfectly audible to Mr Todhunter.

"I asked whether your faculties were getting impaired or not?"

"I'm sorry, sir, I couldn't quite. . ."

Sir Ernest dropped another semitone. "I mean, are you getting at all hard of heading?"

"I can't quite make out the question, sir." Miss Fairey innocently cupped a hand to her ear.

"I asked," said Sir Ernest very loudly, "whether you were getting bit hard of hearing?"

"No, that I'm not," retorted Miss Fairey with indignation, "when folks speak up properly." She looked round in astonishment at the laughter which broke from the whole Court.

Amid the laughter Sir Ernest sat down.

Mr Bairns took counsel with the ceiling.

"In any case, Miss Fairey, you have no doubt of what you heard on the night of the third of December. It was a noise that sounded like a shot, and it seemed to come from the direction of the summerhouse in the late Miss Norwood's garden?"

"Yes sir. That's what I said, sir," retorted Miss Fairey, still a little ruffled, and made a snail-like exit.

"Call Police Constable Silverside," requested Mr Bairns.

Police Constable Silverside gave his evidence like a book.

"On the night of December the third I was on duty from midnight to 4 a.m. My beat includes Lower Putney Road. I know the accused's house. I have called there several times on different matters. On those occasions I have often interviewed the accused. Also he has often bidden me good morning or good afternoon as the case might be. I know his house of a nighttime. It is one of the first houses on the beat to put its lights out. The lights are usually out before midnight. On the night of the third of December the lights were on till after 1 a.m. It was a light on the first floor. It was not on when I went first on my beat. I noticed it on when I passed the house about 12.30 a.m. It was on for about half an hour. It made an impression on me because I knew the gentleman wasn't very well. I thought he might have been taken ill. I approached the front door to see if I might be needed to render assistance. The door was locked. I did not ring. While I was standing there, the light went out. I have no doubt about the date, because I made me note in my book. I made the note in case the gentleman had been taken ill suddenly and it was needed later to establish the time."

Sir Ernest was beginning to get the drift of this mysterious evidence, just there was little he could do so far as the present witness was concerned.

"Is it your habit to stand by in order to act as sick nurse to the inhabitants on your beat?" he began with heavy sarcasm.

"No."

"Then why did you do so in this case?"

"I happened to know the nature of the gentleman's complaint and thought it might be necessary to summon assistance in a hurry."

"Did it not occur to you that the telephone might be quicker?"

"I knew there were only women in the house if the gentleman had been taken bad, and they might like to know a man was standing by."

"How long did you stand by?"

"It was only a minute or two before the light went out."

"You say you noticed the light first at half past twelve. You did not approach the house then?"

"No."

"Why not?"

"I did not think there was need. It was only when I passed the house half an hour later. The light was still on then and it surprised me. While I was standing there the light went out."

"What were your hours of duty that night?"

"From midnight till 4 a.m."

"You are on duty every night on that beat between those hours?"

"No, we take it in turns."

"How often would that period fall to you?"

"Every six days."

"So on five days out of six you would have no opportunity of observing the accused's house at those hours of the night."

"That is correct."

"Then you are not really in a position to say whether it was unusual for a light to be on at that time?"

"I had never seen it before."

"You saw the light through the curtains?"

"I saw it between the curtains."

"The curtains were not properly drawn?"

"There was a streak of light between them."

"If they had been properly drawn, you could not have told whether there was a light in that room or not?"

"I can't say."

With a shrug of his shoulders Sir Ernest sat down.

Again Mr Bairns asked his witness only one question.

"You have no doubt that, between 12.30 and I a.m., there was a light in a first-floor room in the accused's house which struck you as unusual?"

"That is correct."

Sir Ernest appealed to the judge.

"My lord, I fear I must trespass on your indulgence again. Matters have been raised which it is only fair that the accused should have a chance of answering. Have I your permission to put him in the box again for a minute or two?"

"I suppose so," said the judge with a sigh.

Mr Todhunter, who had managed to preserve a masklike demeanour during the last half-hour, at grave risk to his life was tenderly escorted once more into the witness box.

"Mr Todhunter," said Sir Ernest in tones of rich commiseration, "can you say whether a light was on in a first-floor room of your house between the hours of 12.30 and 1 a.m. on the third of December last?"

"I haven't the faintest idea."

"Can you suggest a possible explanation?"

"Very easily. I am a poor sleeper. I frequently wake up in the night. When I think I am not likely to sleep again for some time, I turn on the light and read."

"That happens often?"

"Very often."

"What kind of curtains have you in your bedroom?"

"Heavy rep, lined with casement cloth," replied Mr Todhunter glibly. He was not going to be caught out over a matter of domestic detail.

"They would exclude any artificial light inside the room from being seen outside?"

"I imagine so."

"Are they usually closely drawn at night?"

"So far as I know."

Sir Ernest grasped the bull firmly by the horns.

"Mr Todhunter, did you on the night of December the third leave your house, make a journey to Miss Norwood's garden, there fire off your revolver near the summer house for the first time and return to your home about 12.30 a.m.?"

Mr Todhunter stared at him. "Would you mind saying that again?"

Sir Ernest repeated the question.

"Good gracious, no," said Mr Todhunter.

Sir Ernest looked enquiringly at Mr Bairns, but the latter, without taking his eyes off the ceiling, mutely shook his head.

"Thank you, Mr Todhunter," said Sir Ernest.

The court then adjourned for the day—not, Mr Todhunter felt, before it was time. The strain was becoming more severe than he cared about.

4

"So that's what he was getting at?" said Mr Todhunter as, wrapped in rugs, the taxi drew clear of the staring crowd.

"That's it. Damned ingenious, eh? Clever fellow, Bairns," said Sir Ernest ungrudgingly.

Mr Chitterwick ventured to supply the comment that seemed to be called for.

"But you were cleverer. Your cross-examination disposed of the theory altogether."

Sir Ernest beamed. "I fancy I gave it a shrewd knock. But we can't count on it. Juries are queer cattle. This one's going to acquit our friend here if they can find half a chance."

"You really think that?" said Mr. Chitterwick anxiously.

"Well, it just doesn't do to be too optimistic, that's all." Sir Ernest rubbed his rosy jowls. "I wonder where he got hold of that idea? It's really damned ingenious. Suppose you didn't really carry out any midnight expedition along those lines, Todhunter?"

"Don't be a damned fool," snapped Mr Todhunter savagely.

"Now, now," said Sir Ernest in alarm and preserved a subdued silence until the taxi decanted him at his club.

CHAPTER XVIII

The next morning Mr Bairns developed his theory in detail.

There were two major facts, he contended, which the prosecution relied on to link the present accused with the crime: his possession of the dead woman's bracelet and the probability that the only bullet found in the summerhouse had not been fired from the revolver belonging to Vincent Palmer—the inference of course being that it had been fired from the accused's.

But when more closely examined, both these facts were valueless. The possession of the bracelet proved only one thing: that the accused had been in contact with the dead woman. It did not even prove that he had been in contact with her after death, for she might have handed it over to him in life, to have a stone reset or a copy made or for any other feasible reason. Nevertheless the police were prepared to admit that Mr Todhunter might have been on the scene after the death; what they were not prepared to admit was that he had had any hand in it.

As for the revolver bullet—well, really! implied Mr Bairns.

This bullet had been found in a beam in a remote corner of the summerhouse. It must have been an almost incredibly bad shot that placed it there, so far out of the line of aim. Moreover Mr Todhunter had apparently forgotten all about this second bullet (a second bullet only according to his own account), in spite of the fact that he would have been reminded of it by the fact that there would be two empty shells left in the chamber for him to dispose of and not one. He had in fact only remembered it, most conveniently, when two independent witnesses were present to look for it. This alone was striking enough.

To make the episode more striking still, the jury had heard a witness who testified to the fact that she had heard a sound very like a shot coming from the direction of the summerhouse on a certain night and another witness who was in a position to swear that on that same night the accused had a light in his house at an hour which was unusual—which at least meant that he was awake, if not up and about. It was all very well to suggest other explanations for these facts: the facts remained.

What was the inference from them? Why, surely that Mr Todhunter's story of the second bullet was false. It had not been fired so far back as last September. It had been fired in December. By that time Mr Todhunter, who apparently had believed at one time that he had only to go to the police and accuse himself of any crime in order to be instantly arrested, had realised that there was simply no case against him at all. He had therefore set to and manufactured one. The first requisite in such a case was obviously a bullet fired from his own gun. He had therefore gone, at some time just before midnight on the second of December and fired one. And no doubt on the same journey he made those traces of his progress across the gardens which were solemnly discovered the next morning. And on this next morning, too, in the presence of two witnesses, he conveniently "remembered" that second shot. Was not this a far more probable explanation, supported as it was by direct evidence, than the wild assertions of the accused—or the self-accused, perhaps he should be called? It had the advantage, too, of explaining those useful footmarks, broken twigs and so forth duly noted by the two witnesses on the trail across the gardens. For otherwise was it not contrary to all reason and experience to believe that such a trail could persist, in this country of all countries, for months and through the rain and ravage of an English winter? Hardly!

Examine Mr Todhunter's story. It is all assertions. There is no proof of a single item. Take an instance at random. Take the throwing away of the one piece of incontrovertible evidence, the fatal bullet. Mr Todhunter says he threw it away himself. But we have only his word for it. And it is a word upon which, in the circumstances, we cannot rely. We have noted already how extraordinary such an action was, but we only questioned the motive, not the action itself. Question that action and what do we find? Why, that the probability is that it existed only in Mr Todhunter's generous imagination; that he never threw any bullet away himself, but that he did know that one had been thrown—knew who had thrown it—may even have seen it thrown. Proof . . . proof, that was what was needed in a court of law, and that was just what was lacking in this fantastic case of self-accusation—the most fantastic, Mr Bairns ventured to say, that had ever been known in any British court.

Note how the self-accused had changed his story. He admits himself that the story with which he went to the police in the first place was untrue. Why was it untrue? Because he thought it would sound more plausible than the truth. Is that not the clue to the whole riddle? When a plausible explanation is required upon any point, there is Mr Todhunter all ready with it. But that does not mean that it is the truth. And when you ask for proof, the answer invariably is: "There is no proof. You must believe what I say." That is no way to present a case which anyone can take seriously.

And so on. And so forth.

Mr Todhunter had given up listening long ago. His hands held firmly over his ears, he huddled on his chair in the lonely dock, abandoned to despair.

There was no use trying even to keep up appearances. The case was lost. The man Bairns had given it away with both hands. Palmer was doomed.

When Sir Ernest rose to make the concluding speech for the prosecution, Mr Todhunter did not even look up. Sir Ernest was a good man, but not the best man in the world could cope with that kind of thing, with all the weight of police prestige behind it.

2

Sir Ernest, however, did not seem to realise the impossibility of his task. His air as he began was positively jaunty.

"May it please your lordship. Members of the jury. There is no need for me to emphasise the remarkable nature of this case. It is unique in the annals of British justice in more than one respect, but not least in this: that prosecution and defence are substantially at one on the main issue, that is to say, upon the question of whose finger actually pulled the fatal trigger, and are united against an intervening party who has, properly speaking, no standing in this court at all. But it was felt right that the case should be put before you for a verdict for which neither I nor my friend Mr Jamieson ask, that is to say, the verdict of not guilty; and I am bound to add that counsel who has just addressed you put that case as well and as cogently as such a case could be put. His ingenuity must have been as apparent to you as it was to me.

"But it was only ingenuity. He says, for instance, that the case for the prosecution rests merely on the assertions of the accused himself, that there is not an iota of real proof for a single item of it, that every action which the accused admits is open to two interpretations. But apply those same strictures to the case against Vincent Palmer as it was presented in another court. Do they not apply even more forcibly there? You have read the evidence in that case. Was there an atom of real proof that Palmer ever committed this crime? I submit that there was not one single atom. The case against Palmer consisted of nothing but inferences from beginning to end. Would my friend Mr Bairns then say that inferences made by the police are admissible, but inferences and assertions made by a private individual are nothing but nonsense? I am sure he would not. Yet that is, logically speaking, what seems to have been the main plank of his platform.

"But in accusing the man now in the dock of having committed this crime we do not by any means, as my friend Mr Bairns has suggested, rely on his assertions alone. My friend says we have no evidence. I retort that we have overwhelming evidence. You have heard that evidence. It is for you to say whether it was not as much stronger as the weak stuff that passed for evidence against the young man Palmer as champagne is stronger than ginger wine.

"Let me remind you again of the course of events which has brought the accused to this unhappy situation, just as you heard it in logical sequence from the mouths of witnesses who testified to its truth."

Sir Ernest then spent an hour and a quarter in painting the picture again of Mr Todhunter's temptation and fall, and the colours which he laid on it were of the richest.

As he listened Mr Todhunter's attitude changed. Higher and higher rose his little bald head, down dropped his hands, his back straightened, an incredulous smile appeared unwittingly upon his face, hope began to spring once more within his bony breast. For Sir Ernest was wielding the brush of an artist. To hear him, even Mr Todhunter began to realise once more that he was a villain of the deepest dye.

He stole a look at the jury and caught the eye of a fat tradesman in a check suit. The fat tradesman looked hastily away. Mr Todhunter nearly cackled out loud in glee.

Gradually Sir Ernest approached his climax.

"Was it the finger of the accused that tightened round the trigger which fired the fatal shot? That is the real issue of this case. You may feel that the motives which prompted the action were of an intolerable presumption, or you may feel that they were not altogether ignoble. You must pay no attention to either. You are the judges of fact, not motive, and you must deliver your verdict accordingly. It is my duty to suggest to you that his action was deliberate; my friend for the defence will contend that it was, at the last moment, no more than what might be regarded as a culpable accident.

"But you have not to decide merely between us. At this moment another man lies under sentence of death for this crime. You have seen him in the box; you can judge his demeanour for yourselves. You have heard the arguments and the reasons upon which this man was condemned; you have heard the present accused tell what we put to you as the real story of this terrible crime, and you have heard him recount the efforts, the truly desperate efforts he has made to right a great wrong.

"For in the contention that a terrible legal blunder has been committed my friend for the defence and I are united. We would impress it upon you with all the earnestness at our command. We ask you to assess the tortuous arguments and the subtle twistings of fact, which you have heard put forward on behalf of the police, at their true value; we ask you to accept the simple, not the complicated explanation.

"The man now sitting on the dock bears a terrible responsibility. We counsel share it with him. He cannot speak to you for himself; he relies upon us to convince you of the truth. For, whatever may be said of his earlier action, ever since he heard that an innocent man had been accused of the crime which he has told you he committed, Mr Todhunter's conduct has been irreproachable. So vehement indeed have been his efforts to set right this wrong that counsel for the police referred to him as an old friend of the family which he is trying to save. That is not so. As you have heard, they are almost strangers to him. He had met the man who has been condemned elsewhere only twice in his life, and only for a few minutes each time. There is no such altruism here as has been suggested. Mr Todhunter is not trying to lay down his life for a friend. But his aim is no less great. He has only a few weeks—it may be only a few days—to live. Every hour of those weeks, every minute of those days he is devoting to putting this terrible blunder right; do you see that when his time comes to die, he will not have to perish in the dreadful misery of knowing that another man must suffer for the crime that was his.

"Members of the jury, my responsibility has ended. It is passing to you. In your hands you hold the fate, not of one man, but two. May heaven guide you to deliver a true judgment."

Sir Ernest's voice broke as he uttered the last words. He stood for a few moments looking intently at the jury. Then he sat down.

The court adjourned for the midday recess in a silence that was perhaps the most genuine tribute that Sir Ernest had ever received.

3

Mr Todhunter believed Sir Ernest worthy of any tribute that human man could bestow on him.

"That was the finest speech I've ever heard in any law court," he told him as they left the court side by side. Mr Todhunter had never heard a speech in a law court before.

"Ah, but we're not out of the wood yet," twinkled Sir Ernest, quite himself again. "Did you notice the judge? There was a nasty look in the old bird's eye just as I was getting on the jury's soft side. I didn't like the look of it at all."

"I think we're fairly safe now," opined Mr Todhunter, who was not usually given to optimism. "What do you say, Chitterwick?"

"I think," said Mr Chitterwick carefully, "that we've been very lucky in our counsel."

"I'll buy you a drink for that," said Sir Ernest jovially. "Go on back to your private dining room, Todhunter. You know you can't be in on this."

4

The first twenty minutes after lunch were occupied by some gallant efforts on the part of Mr Jamieson to make bricks without straw.

There was little he could say, for he had no case at all; and in the end, after identifying himself with all the pertinent observations of his learned friend for the prosecution and throwing a few stones at the head of the absent Mr Bairns, Mr Jamieson could do little more than appeal to the jury to find Mr Todhunter guilty of manslaughter only and not murder, on the rather inadequate ground that it would be a bit of a shame to hang him.

Then, at last, the judge began to sum up.

"Members of the jury," he said in a voice thin with age but perfectly clear, "it now becomes my duty to go through with you the evidence that has been given in this case; a case which, as counsel have pointed out, is possibly unique in these courts. Another man, as you know, is now lying under sentence of death for this same crime; and it is in order to save this man, believing him to be innocent, that Mr Furze has told us he has brought this action for murder. There is no reason to doubt Mr Furze's motives or to suggest that he has not been actuated by anything but the highest principles; and it is only right to pay tribute to the disinterestedness and public spirit that he has shown. Whether he was right in his belief or not is now for you to decide.

"It makes no difference to you that this case has been brought at the instigation of a private citizen and not, as is almost invariably so in a case of this importance, by the Crown. Nevertheless it is right that you should ask yourselves why the Crown did not bring it and why the proper authorities, although in possession of all the evidence and statements that you have heard, did not see fit to act upon them—or perhaps I should say, saw fit not to act upon them. As their counsel, Mr Bairns, has pointed out to you a mere confession alone is not enough to require action. Instances of false confession are not rare in criminal history. They may be made from varying motives, from insanity to a desire to shield the guilty; and often they are repudiated once the guilty person is safe. You will therefore not be too strongly influenced by the confession which the accused in this instance has made but will decide the case solely on the evidence which has been brought to substantiate that confession.

"I will now review that evidence for you, and in view of the importance of the case, I shall do so in some detail."

The judge was as good as his word. He reviewed the evidence, slowly, methodically and quite fairly, for the rest of that afternoon and at once resumed the task when the Court assembled again the next morning.

As he listened to the ancient voice droning on Mr Todhunter went through a fine range of emotions.

The evidence, heard through this calm, dispassionate voice, somehow sounded far less imposing than when rolled forth in Sir Ernest's robust periods. In fact it sounded uncommonly thin. There was plenty of evidence of intention but none of performance. Mr Todhunter, who had realised this well enough but somehow had persuaded himself that it did not much matter, grew more and more perturbed. It was impossible to say that the judge was minimising it in any way, yet the effect was of minimisation. Mr Todhunter realised, with some disquiet, how much any case owes to oratory in the presenting of it.

One passage in the summing up which occurred fairly early that morning increased his disquiet. The judge had been dealing with the evidence that pointed to Mr Todhunter having been on the scene of the crime after, rather than before, the death. He paused for a moment or two and then added:

"In this connection I ought to warn you that, even should you find the present accused guilty, that is not necessarily to determine that the verdict rendered in the previous case was an incorrect one. There is a possibility which I think has not been put before you at all but which nevertheless you must consider: whether Palmer and Todhunter were not acting in conjunction. There is no evidence to show that they were, but equally there is no evidence to show that they were not. It is a possibility which you must bear in mind, and I mention it lest you might be tempted for sentimental reasons to bring in the verdict of guilty in this case with the idea of perhaps saving the life of a young and vigorous man at the expense of one which is doomed in any case. That would be a most improper feeling, and I am sure you will not allow it to influence you. Nor, as I must warn you, if you did, would it necessarily have the effect intended."

Mr Todhunter was perturbed. Perhaps he had been relying too much on just such a sentiment and its unconscious influence on the minds of the jury. He had certainly been relying on a verdict of guilty in his own case to establish, as an inescapable corollary, the innocence of Palmer. Yet now it seemed that through such a technical and unfair little loophole the authorities would still be enabled to keep their grip on that unfortunate young man.

Mr Todhunter wanted to get up and shout:

"He is innocent! Cut the cackle and come down to truth. I tell you he is innocent—I, who have the best of reasons to know it."

It was true enough that Mr Todhunter, almost alone in the world, had the best of reasons to know that Palmer was innocent; but it was proving a difficult job to convince other people of that simple truth. Mr Todhunter wished that a fact could stand up as hard and solid as a block of granite so that no one could dispute it.

It was, however, not until the judge came to the end of his summing up that Mr Todhunter simultaneously arrived at the end of his tether.

Up to that point the judge had really behaved very well indeed. Refraining from the temptation to tell other people how to live their lives in accordance with the law books, which few judges ever seem able to resist, he had confined himself strictly to the matter in hand. But in the end he succumbed; and, as usual, his last words might have suggested that he was set up in that exalted position to be a judge, not of law, but of morals and ethics.

"Members of the jury, it may be that some of you have had in mind yet another verdict, which has not been suggested to you at all. I refer to the verdict of 'guilty but insane.' It is customary for judges to indicate, when the defence has suggested such a verdict, whether it would be admissible on the facts of the case. In case therefore any of you were meditating a verdict of this nature, I feel it advisable to tell you that in the absence of all evidence on the point such a verdict would be quite inadmissible. It has in fact, quite properly, not been suggested by the defence; and I only mention the matter because you may think that the very nature of the accused's admissions seem to indicate some degree of insanity.

"You may indeed feel that the intolerable presumption to which he has admitted, and in which he seems to glory, of setting himself up as a judge of life and death over his fellow men, may show a degree of megalomania amounting to insanity. But the law defines insanity very closely, and it is quite certain that the accused throughout realised exactly what he was doing or intending to do; and that is the crux of the matter.

"In the same way you must be on your guard against allowing your disgust for him—the disgust which all right-minded persons must feel—to influence your decision. If you feel that the case against him has not been made out, it is your duty to return a verdict of not guilty, irrespective of the contempt and loathing with which his cold-blooded machinations may have inspired you. That he was at one time meditating some kind of senseless, imbecile assassination of some quite innocent person, there is the evidence which I have gone through already; you must decide whether the wild talk in which he seems to have indulged was merely raving to impress his friends or whether there was a sinister substratum of intention

"Nevertheless, as I say, although you may consider him, and perhaps not unjustly, in the light of an inhuman and irresponsible person, with an abominably perverted conception of his duties as a member of society, you must not allow your verdict to be coloured by your indignation any more than you must allow it to be prejudiced by the fact that another man has already been found guilty of the same crime. You are to judge this case on the facts that have been presented to you and those alone."

The judge then concluded with a few illuminating remarks upon murder and manslaughter and what was necessary to produce a verdict in either case and dismissed the jury to talk it over.

5

Mr. Todhunter could hardly contain himself.

"What business is it of that old fool's to call me disgusting?" he burst out almost before he was out of the dock. "I don't call him disgusting to his face, although he cleans his ears in public, I never heard a more gratuitous exhibition of smugness."

"Oh, they all go on like that," returned Sir Ernest easily. "I shall one day."

"Then it's time they were stopped and confined to their proper jobs," stormed Mr Todhunter. "Contempt and loathing indeed? . . . No one has a poorer opinion of me than I have myself, but am I contemptible and loathsome?" demanded Mr Todhunter of Mr Chitterwick with singular ferocity.

"No, no," protested Mr Chitterwick. "Not in the least. Er—precisely the reverse, if anything."

"If anything? I must be something, mustn't I?"

"Yes, I said so," hurriedly agreed Mr Chitterwick. "I said, the reverse."

"And how can I be both imbecile and sane—and responsible and irresponsible at the same time?" continued Mr Todhunter, his indignation unflagging. "Eh? Tell me that. And does it need megalomania to see that an unpleasant person is better out of the world than in it, for the world's own sake? Damn and blast! I never heard such balderdash in my life."

"Now, now," said Sir Ernest in alarm, for Mr Todhunter really seemed to be growing more, rather than less, agitated. And he added in an undertone to Mr Chitterwick: "Where's that damned doctor?"

Fortunately the doctor appeared before Mr Todhunter could actually burst, and led his patient away to work off his tantrum in seclusion.

There was, however, one good result of Mr Todhunter's temper. It lasted him for over two hours and so occupied nearly the whole period of the jury's absence. In consequence the strain of waiting for the verdict was considerably relieved.

The jury were absent for two hours and forty minutes. Then an official brought news that they were returning to court.

"Now look here, Todhunter," said the doctor anxiously, "these next two minutes are going to be a terrible strain for you. You've got to hold yourself together with both hands."

"I'm all right," muttered Mr Todhunter, a little white.

"Fancy yourself in a dream or something, or repeat a piece of poetry," urged the doctor. "*Horatius at the Bridge*. Know it? And be prepared for any verdict. Don't let anything come as a shock. Sure you won't let me give you an injection?" The doctor had already offered an injection to deaden his patient's reactions and slow up the action of his heart.

"No," snapped Mr Todhunter, leading the way. "It's over now. The verdict's been decided on, one way or another. There's nothing more to be done; and if with luck it's guilty, the quicker I pass out, the better. Don't want me to live to be hanged, do you?"

"All right, all right, have it your own way," returned the doctor. "You're the lucky one, either way."

Mr Todhunter snarled.

In court the rapt attention of the onlookers was divided between Mr Todhunter and the returning jury. As always the faces of the latter were scanned, not least anxiously by Mr Todhunter himself, in an effort to read their minds; and as always, their solemn expressions could be interpreted in any way the onlooker chose.

Mr Todhunter held his breath and laid an unconscious hand upon his chest as if to check disaster at least till the verdict should be known. There was no need for him to try to fancy himself in a dream; he felt in a dream. The whole scene seemed fantastic, and not least his own part in it. Was it really himself, in a court of criminal law, being tried for his life? Was it really on him that these men were about to pronounce a verdict? The thing was incredible.

In a kind of trance Mr Todhunter heard the clerk of the court address the jury.

"Members of the jury, are you agreed upon your verdict?"

The foreman, a tall, middle-aged man with an untidy moustache (Mr Todhunter had set him down as an estate agent, for no particular reason), answered firmly enough:

"We are."

"Do you find the accused guilty of the murder of Ethel May Binns, or not guilty?"

The foreman cleared his throat.

"Guilty."

Mr Todhunter stared down at his hands. They seemed an unusual colour. Then he realised that he was gripping the ledge of the dock so tightly as to blanch not only his knuckles but the whole backs of his hands.

He relaxed. The jury had found him guilty. Well, that was all right. Of course. Mr Todhunter had known all along that any sensible jury, like this one, would be certain to find him guilty. There was no strain in that at all.

Mr Todhunter bowed slightly to the jury. The jury did not bow back.

He became aware that the clerk was now addressing him.

"Lawrence Butterfield Todhunter, you have been found guilty of wilful murder; have you anything to say why the Court should not pronounce sentence upon you?"

Mr Todhunter repressed a mad impulse, first to giggle and then to snap at the clerk: "Don't call me Butterfield." He pulled himself together and replied:

"Nothing at all."

More or less master of himself now, he watched with interest a little square of black cloth being laid by an official on top of the judge's wig.

So that's the black cap, thought Mr Todhunter; well, all I can say is that it makes the judge look very silly.

"Lawrence Butterfield Todhunter," came the aged voice for the last time, "it is now my duty to pass sentence upon you, in accordance with the verdict which the jury have pronounced upon you, and I shall do so without further comment. Is there any question of law, Sir Ernest, as to the sentence I have to pronounce? You will understand what I mean."

Sir Ernest bobbed up. "So far as I can ascertain, my lord, no question."

"Then, Lawrence Butterfield Todhunter, the sentence of this Court upon you is that you be taken from this place to a lawful prison and thence to a place of execution, and that you there be hanged by the neck until you are dead; and that your body be afterwards buried within the precincts of the prison in which you shall have been confined after your conviction, and may the Lord have mercy on your soul."

"Amen," said the sheriff's chaplain, at the judge's side.

Mr Todhunter, no longer bearing any grudge, bowed with respectful courtesy to the judge.

"Thank you, my lord. May I make a final request?"

"I'm afraid I can't listen to you now."

"I'm afraid," retorted Mr Todhunter, courteous still but firm, "that you must listen, my lord. My request is that I may now be arrested."

Mr Todhunter was gratified to perceive that his words had caused what would undoubtedly be described in the papers the next morning as a sensation. In the solemn routine of verdict and sentence those responsible had quite overlooked the fact that Mr Todhunter had never been arrested. Now, in accordance with the verdict, arrest was automatic.

The judge whispered to the clerk of the court, the clerk whispered to an usher, the usher whispered to one of the friendly policemen, and the policeman lumbered into the dock and touched Mr Todhunter on the shoulder.

"Lawrence Butterfield Todhunter, I arrest you for the murder of Ethel May Binns, on the night of twenty-eight September last, and I warn you that anything . . . that is . . . and . . . and . . ."

"And about time too," suggested Mr Todhunter.

PART V

Gothic

DUNGEON CELL

CHAPTER XIX

To say that the verdict on Mr Todhunter caused a sensation in the country would be to put it mildly.

Everybody had always told the British (and the British had always told everybody) that their judicial system was the best in the world; yet here were two persons lying under sentence of death for the same crime, and one of them must be innocent. Did the incomparable British judicial system then contain such traps as might catch an innocent man and let the guilty escape?

The Times had a thoughtful leader proving that there was nothing wrong with the system and inclined to deplore the fact that, in spite of the cautious attitude of the judge, Mr Todhunter should have got himself convicted, at the same time equally deprecating the fact that Vincent Palmer had not somehow managed to get himself acquitted. The *Daily Telegraph* had an equally thoughtful leader saying at some length exactly nothing at all. The *Morning Post* was inclined to believe that some subtle Communist propaganda had been at work. The *News Chronicle* was more certain than ever that the civil war in Spain was the indirect outcome of the whole unfortunate affair. The popular press openly and vociferously exulted and called the jury by every flattering superlative it could dig out of its vocabulary. For some reason unknown to him, the popular press had been Mr Todhunter's champion from the beginning.

The public as usual waited for a lead. And the government, equally as usual, waited for a lead from the public.

In point of fact the public wavered for exactly forty-eight hours. During that period opinion was about equally divided between the two alternatives of Mr Todhunter's guilt and his altruistic innocence, with perhaps a tiny balance in favour of the latter as being the more romantically sentimental.

The turning point was characteristic. Somehow, somewhere, from some unknown source the whisper went round: Fascism! Mr Todhunter had decided, all on his own, that someone ought to be killed and had set about killing her. If that wasn't Fascism, what was? Never mind whether he had actually done the deed himself or not; he had intended, and that was just as bad. Anyhow, a jury had said he did do it, hadn't they? What was good enough for a jury was good enough for us. Un-British! Fascism!

The *Daily Telegraph*, in an inspired leader, drew a most interesting parallel between the habits of Fascist dictators in ridding themselves of persons they disliked and Mr Todhunter's action.

In the relieved indignation the slur on the British judicial system was quite forgotten.

The government, with the people now solid behind it, could go on comfortably to hang Mr Todhunter with an easy political conscience.

2

Of all these developments Mr Todhunter knew nothing. In any case, now that his anxieties were over he was far too interested in the routine in which he was now caught up to bother about such trivialities as public opinion. Mr Todhunter doubted whether a really intelligent person had ever had the chance before of observing at first hand the exact procedure followed by a condemned murderer between his conviction and execution, and he realised his responsibility.

It was therefore with an alert interest that he prepared to leave his friends in the dock and follow the warder who had now attached himself. That he was leaving these friends and all they stood for, forever, did not worry him. The novelty, to say nothing of the exaltation, of finding himself a condemned prisoner made Mr Todhunter only agog with curiosity.

There had been a brief scene of jubilation following the end of the proceedings, with Sir Ernest and Mr Todhunter mutually congratulating each other and the beaming Mr Chitterwick congratulating them both; so that one would have said it was a wedding and not a funeral for which Mr Todhunter was bound. The doctor, too, had taken the opportunity of having a word with the warder, to warn him that Mr Todhunter was in a very precarious state of health and was not to be allowed to walk fast, to lift or carry anything or to undergo any exertion at all, or otherwise the warder would find a corpse instead of a live prisoner on his hands; and the warder, impressed, had promised to pass this information on to Mr Todhunter's next guardian. It was all very friendly and informal, and Mr. Todhunter's farewells were no less casual than those of a week-end visitor.

The warder, who was oldish and amicable, led Mr Todhunter through a door with a glass top which led into an inclined passage, or ramp, floored with concrete. A short way down this ramp was an iron gate which the warder opened and then closed carefully behind them. A few yards beyond this gate the ramp led into a long, narrow, stone-flagged corridor. Along the corridor were rows of doors, each with a glass top, and behind them Mr Todhunter could see dim forms and faces which peered at him dumbly.

"Prisoners, I suppose?" he asked pleasantly.

"That's right," nodded the warder. "Convicted or awaiting trial."

"Oh, they keep them here before they're tried too? That seems a little hard."

"There's nowhere else."

"Well, there ought to be," said Mr Todhunter and made a mental note for the series of articles he was planning.

Mr Todhunter himself was then placed in one of these dark little cells and duly locked in. The friendly warder professed himself without knowledge as to how long his stay would be.

Mr Todhunter leant his nose up against the glass of his door and watched the warders, the convicted and the as yet untried, passing and repassing along the gloomy corridor with occasionally a barrister in wig and gown sweeping importantly by.

"Most interesting," observed Mr Todhunter to himself. "Crime does not pay."

In due course he found himself conducted down the corridor once more. At the far end there was a kind of office in which a police official with grey hair was making mysterious marks on a slate with a piece of chalk. Mr Todhunter asked what he was doing and was informed that the marks referred to the various Black Marias waiting in the yard, and their complements.

"Ah, the Black Maria," said Mr. Todhunter, pleased, as he looked out at the shining black vehicles standing ready to convey the convicts to the various prisons.

He became aware that his warder, with a slightly apologetic air, was jingling something metallic.

"Oh yes," said Mr Todhunter. "Handcuffs. That is necessary in the circumstances?"

"I don't know anything about circumstances," muttered the warder. "It's the regulation."

"Heaven forbid that I should offend against a regulation," replied Mr Todhunter pleasantly and held out his wrists. He looked at the results with interest. "Well, well, well. So this is what it feels like. Most interesting.

He was then booked through the clearing office and invited to take his seat in one of the vehicles.

To his surprise Mr Todhunter found that the interior of the vehicle was divided into miniature cells. Locked into one of these, there was just room for him to sit down. He disposed himself as well as possible on the little seat provided and considered the business somewhat barbaric. From the sounds around him it was clear that the other cells were being similarly filled; and after a short wait the vehicle set off. Mr Todhunter knew its designation: the famous prison to which convicts from the area north of the Thames were invariably sent. Had Miss Norwood lived on the other bank, Mr Todhunter would now have been on his way to Wandsworth.

"It's lucky," he ruminated, "that I don't suffer from claustrophobia. The lack of ventilation is disgraceful."

At last the plain van came to a halt. Mr Todhunter, straining his ears, could hear great gates being opened and shut. The vehicle moved on a little further. Then his unseen fellow passengers could be heard disembarking.

Mr Todhunter had arrived.

3

The routine for prisoners condemned to death is rigid. It is laid down in the prison rules thus:

"Every prisoner under warrant or order for execution shall immediately on his arrival in the prison after sentence, be searched by or by the orders of the Governor, and all articles shall be taken from him which the Governor deems dangerous or inexpedient to leave in his possession. He shall be confined in a cell apart from all other prisoners, and shall be placed by day and by night under the constant charge of an officer. He shall be allowed such dietary and amount of exercise as the Governor, with the approval of the Commissioners, may direct. The Chaplain shall have free access to every such prisoner, unless the prisoner is of a religious persuasion differing from that of the Established Church, and is visited by a minister of that persuasion, in which case the minister of that persuasion shall have free access to him. With the above exception, no person, not being a member of the visiting committee or an officer of the prison shall have access to the prisoner except in pursuance of an order from a Prison Commissioner or member of the visiting committee.

"During the preparation for an execution, and the time of the execution, no person shall enter the prison unless legally entitled to do so.

"A prisoner under sentence of death may be visited by such of his relations, friends, and legal advisers as he desires to see, and are authorised to visit him by an order in writing from a member of the visiting committee.

"If any person makes it appear to a member of the visiting committee that he has important business to transact with a prisoner under sentence of death, that member may grant permission in writing to that person to have a conference with the prisoner."

Into this routine Mr Todhunter found himself duly caught up.

He was now a man set apart from his fellows. Not until all the others had been removed from sight was he allowed to emerge from the van. He would have liked then to pause a minute and do justice to his first view of prison walls from the wrong side, but such amenities were no longer to be permitted. With a firm but kindly grasp on his arm Mr Todhunter found himself being conducted across the court, through passages, across an exercise yard and so into his last habitation which, except for brief periods of fresh air, he was never to leave.

"And this is the condemned cell?" Mr Todhunter asked with great interest.

"This is where you'll be," evaded the warder.

Mr Todhunter looked round him. Though not altogether ignorant of modern prison conditions, as with most subjects of social reform, he was surprised at the comparative comfort and spaciousness about him. The place was a room, rather than a cell. A window, barred and set high in the wall but of ample size, admitted plenty of light and air. There were chairs and a fair-sized table, and at one end of the room was a bed which looked comfortable, with clean sheets and pillow cases, blankets and a coverlet. Facing the bed there hung a large picture of the Crucifixion, and other brightly coloured pictures hung on the other walls. In a neat little fireplace a fire was burning cheerfully.

"But this is delightful," said Mr Todhunter.

"The governor'll be along in a minute," said the warder, removing Mr Todhunter's handcuffs.

Mr Todhunter took off his hat and threw his overcoat over a chair before sitting down and clasping his knees.

The next minute there was the sound of a key turning in the lock (Mr Todhunter had hardly realised they were locked in this pleasant room), and there entered a tall man with greying hair and a military-looking grey moustache, a short man with dark hair and a roundabout figure and a second warder. Mr Todhunter stood up.

"The governor," announced the first warder and stood smartly at attention.

"How do you do?" said Mr Todhunter politely.

"Erh'rrm," replied the governor and pulled at his moustache. He looked a little ill at ease. "This is the doctor, Doctor Farthingale."

Mr Todhunter bowed.

"Well, we know all about *you*," said the doctor cheerfully. "I want to have a look at that aneurism of yours. Your man's just been on the telephone to me about it."

"I understand it's in a somewhat precarious state," Mr Todhunter said somewhat deprecatingly.

"Oh, we'll look after it."

Mr Todhunter cackled. "Yes indeed. It would be most unfortunate if it failed to last another month, wouldn't it?"

The governor frowned. "Now, Todhunter, you must understand . . . certain regulations . . . hope you're going to be sensible. . ."

"I shall be happy," replied Mr Todhunter with an old-fashioned little bow, "to conform to all the necessary regulations. Indeed I trust you will find me a model prisoner."

"Yes, yes. Well, first you have to be searched. Pure formality, no doubt, in your case, but there it is. I thought you'd prefer me to do it myself, as the regulations permit. And I must ask you to hand over all personal articles you have on you for inspection."

"I'll put them on the table," said Mr Todhunter obligingly and duly laid out his fountain pen, pencil, notebook and gold hunter watch. "I shall also ask you for permission to retain them."

"That's all you have?"

"Yes. I've already given everything else to my solicitor."

"Very well. You can keep these. Just stand quite still."

Mr Todhunter stood still while a pair of knowledgeable hands passed briskly over him.

"Yes. Well, now, if you'll undress, behind the screen if you like, the doctor will run over you, and then you can get into the regulation clothing." The governor hesitated. "You're supposed really to take a bath on admission, but I think perhaps we might dispense with that."

"I had one this morning," Mr Todhunter concurred.

"Exactly." With a brief nod the governor let himself out.

One of the warders had drawn a white painted screen across a corner of the room near the fireplace. Feeling grateful for this concession to modesty, Mr Todhunter retired behind it.

"Just coat and shirt off first," called the doctor.

In due course Mr Todhunter was sounded gently, thumped and submitted to all the usual processes of a thorough medical examination. His aneurism of course came in for special attention, and the doctor took it with becoming respect.

"I understand it's touch and go with me, at any minute?" suggested Mr Todhunter with the hint of apology with which he always referred to his impending death.

"You're going to bed straight away," said the doctor, briskly putting up his stethoscope. "And what's more, you're going to stay there."

Mr Todhunter suddenly became aware that the idea of bed was not unattractive.

"It's been a bit of a strain," he mumbled.

4

There was one thing that bothered Mr Todhunter a good deal during the next day or two, and really only one thing. That was the constant presence of two warders in the cell with him. Whether he was sleeping or waking, reading or thinking, in bed or in the more private apartment which opened off the cell, there they always were, not watching him obtrusively but never taking their attention off him. Mr Todhunter, who was a solitary by choice as well as through force of circumstances, found their presence at times decidedly irksome.

Not that they were not good fellows; all six of them; for they took duty in pairs on eight-hour shifts. One pair in particular who usually took the midday to 8 p.m. spell of duty Todhunter was always glad to see. Of these, Birchman, the elder, who had conducted him to the cell in the first place, a big, burly man with a bald head and a walrus moustache to compensate, was an excellent companion, not at all self-conscious and always ready to perform any service that Mr Todhunter from his bed might demand. Fox, the second man, was not so easy in his manner and was obviously a little worried by his position; he was of the military type, a shade stiff, and lacked the fatherly friendliness of Birchman; but Mr Todhunter had no fault to find with him. In fact the three of them made an excellent trio, and it was not twenty-four hours before Mr Todhunter's sardonic cackle was to be heard at fairly frequent intervals, followed by an occasional deep guffaw from Birchman and a less frequent subdued bark of a laugh from Fox.

Mr Todhunter indeed came to know all his gaolers very well. He liked them and was touched by the eagerness with which they were always suggesting a game of draughts or any other diversion which might. be calculated to take Mr Todhunter's mind off the immediate present and future.

"It's as hard on us as it is on you," Birchman would say frankly. "Harder in a way, you might say especially in *this* case,"

"No need to be hard on anyone in this case," Mr Todhunter would cackle. "To tell you the truth, Birchman, I'm enjoying myself very much."

"Darn it all, I really believe you are." And Birchman would rub his bald head and look at Mr Todhunter at ease in his comfortable bed with such a comical expression of bewilderment that Mr Todhunter would cackle again.

Then the governor would drop in quite often for a chat. He soon lost his first embarrassment, which Mr Todhunter decided had been caused in equal parts by his own notoriety and by the fact that the two of them came from the same social stratum; and then he would discuss with intelligence and zest the whole question of penal reform, prison conditions and such kindred matters, in which he evidently took a deep interest. Mr Todhunter, delighted to find the man so human and so unlike the unimaginative, reactionary martinet that a prison governor is often pictured, drew him out with cunning and incorporated many of his ideas in articles for the *London Review.*

The doctor, too, came in three or four times a day and could usually be relied on for a chat; and once the chaplain had been made to realise that Mr Todhunter was not interested in dogma, refused to study the orthodox text-books of the Christian religion and would not discuss the condition of his soul (with which he was forced to appear immodestly satisfied), he, too, proved a good fellow, ready to come and talk on any subject under the sun at two minutes notice when the somewhat limited intelligence of Mr Todhunter's gaolers began to pall.

Nor was paper lacking, in unlimited quantities and all neatly stamped with the name of the prison, so that Mr Todhunter was able to cover sheets of it in his small, angular writing for the benefit of Ferrers and the *London Review;* a series of articles, he could not but flatter himself, quite unique in the history of critical journalism.

Finally, as to creature comforts, Mr Todhunter found himself not permitted to smoke (but only by doctor's orders) and had no wish to do so, and was pleasantly surprised by the quality of the food. Enquiring, he was informed that it was based on the standard hospital diet, but the bacon and eggs for breakfast which had so roused his approbation had been specially ordered for him by the doctor.

Altogether, in his comfortable quarters and surrounded on all sides by the friendliest consideration, Mr Todhunter began to regret that his spell in prison was necessarily so short (three clear Sundays from the date of conviction).

It was in fact difficult to realise that he was only being cherished like this in order to be hanged.

5

Of one particular piece of irony Mr Todhunter was acutely aware.

There were two condemned cells in the prison. One was occupied by himself. The other was still tenanted by Vincent Palmer.

For his own conviction had not, as he had somewhat vaguely imagined it would be, been instantly followed by the automatic pardon and apologetic release of Palmer. Nothing of the sort. The authorities had Palmer in the condemned cell, and it looked as if they meant to keep him there.

Two days passed, three, four; and still came no news of Palmer's freedom.

Had Mr Todhunter but known it, he was not the only person to feel agitated on this score. After forty-eight hours the authorities, it was true, had begun to feel that they could now safely hang Mr Todhunter; but it appeared that they could not make up their minds to let Palmer go. On the third day a question was asked in the House.

There had been time for very little notice, but the time had been long enough for a permanent reprieve to be hurried through, which the home secretary was thus enabled to announce, with a slightly injured air, to the House. But he could not announce that the reprieve was accompanied by a free pardon; and to the contention of the questioner's opposition supporters that since a jury, with a fuller grasp of the facts than was available to the first jury, had believed Mr Todhunter's story, therefore Palmer should go free, only an evasive reply was returned. Pressed, the home secretary was understood to intimate that the authorities were by no means satisfied with Palmer's position as a possible accessory before and/or after the fact.

This hedging pleased no one, with the possible exception of the home secretary himself; and the newspapers the next day were for once in their history unanimous in demanding that Palmer should be given the benefit of such a far-fetched doubt and be released forthwith. Whereupon the home secretary, a doctrinaire and obstinate, dug his toes well in and refused to budge. The only result was that Palmer was removed from the condemned cell and placed in the gaol proper, among such burglars, thugs and psychoanalytical cases as happened to be his neighbours.

As for Mr Todhunter, when the governor told him the news, he was seized with such a fit of rage that Fox was despatched posthaste there and then for the doctor.

"It's all right," said Mr Todhunter grimly. "I'm not going to die till I've got Palmer out of here, so you can take that damned syringe of yours away."

The doctor, who was trying to administer a quarter grain of morphia for the benefit of Mr Todhunter's nerves, hesitated. The governor it was, after all, who succeeded in soothing his agitated prisoner.

"It's all right, Todhunter. Perhaps I oughtn't to tell you, but the Press is solid for letting Palmer go, and the country's behind 'em. No government would have the guts to hold out."

"That's more like it," growled Mr Todhunter.

As the door closed behind them the doctor grinned at his colleague.

"Lucky you thought of that. I believe if I'd tried to inject him, he might have resisted; and as little effort as that would probably kill him straightaway."

"We can't have that at any cost," muttered the governor.

The lock clicked behind them.

Mr Todhunter was lying back on his pillows, apparently exhausted. The other two had spoken in low voices, as they passed through the doorway. But Mr Todhunter was not so exhausted that his ears had failed to retain their sharpness. He had overheard, with interest.

6

The result showed itself the next morning, on the tubby little doctor's first visit.

"I want to get up," announced Mr Todhunter after he had been sounded and examined as usual.

"Sorry, I'm afraid that can't be done," returned the doctor cheerfully.

"Oh, it can't, can't it? Mr. Todhunter cackled maliciously. "Why not, eh?"

"You're in no state to get up, I'm afraid."

"And suppose I have visitors."

"It can be arranged for you to see them in here."

The malice in Mr Todhunter's cackle deepened. "I understand of course. You've got to keep me alive, eh?"

"Naturally."

"You've got to look after me as tenderly as a newborn babe. No patient was ever more precious to you. At all costs you must keep me alive—to be hanged?"

The doctor shrugged his shoulders. "You know the situation, Todhunter, as well as I do."

"A bit barbarous, don't you think?"

"I won't contradict you. It's damned barbarous. But there it is."

"So you won't let me get up?"

"I can't."

Mr Todhunter cackled again. "Well, I'm sorry, Doctor, but I want to get up, and I'm going to get up. And I don't quite see how you're going to stop me."

The doctor smiled. "What's the blackmail?"

"You know as well as I do. You can't keep me in bed by force. If you do, I'll struggle. And if I struggle…" Mr Todhunter looked positively baleful.

The doctor laughed outright. "You're too intelligent to be a prisoner. Well, and if I do let you get up, will you behave yourself?"

"I'll make a bargain with you," grinned Mr Todhunter. Like Mr Ramsbottom of immortal fame, he had thought it all out and he'd got his own way; but he was not going to jeopardise things by going on to laugh fit to bust. "I want to look over the prison. If you'll let me do that and sit out in the sun occasionally and stretch my legs when I want to, I'll undertake not to struggle with any officer of the prison in the execution of his duties. (Dear me, execution's an unfortunate word, isn't it?)" Mr Todhunter tee-hee'd horribly. "Well, do you agree?"

"This is a matter for the governor," said the doctor. "Mind waiting till I've consulted him?"

"Not in the least," replied Mr Todhunter amiably.

The doctor vanished.

Mr Todhunter grinned at his keepers. "You know, I've got you all by the short hairs," he said.

Fox looked a little shocked that anyone could have the officers of one of H.M.'s prisons by the short hairs, but Birchman laughed robustly.

"You have, and that's a fact. We've been warned not to handle you. Well, well, you're a smart one, and that's a fact."

"That's two facts," corrected Mr Todhunter pedantically.

The governor frowned on Mr Todhunter.

"It's impossible to grant your request. The regulations lay it down that you're to be kept apart from all other prisoners. They're not allowed even to catch a glimpse of you."

"Dear me, what a pariah that makes one feel. Now, may I speak to you alone, Governor?"

The governor made a sign to the two warders, who filed out of the cell.

"No, you stay, Doctor," commanded Mr. Todhunter.

The doctor stayed.

Mr Todhunter climbed gingerly out of bed, a long, stringy figure in his pale pink pyjamas. He gripped the end of the table.

"I thought we'd better have no witnesses to your discomfiture," he observed seriously to the governor. "Now watch, please. I have hold of the end of this table. If you don't grant my request, I shall lift the table up. The strain will be too much for me. I shall drop dead at your feet. Ask the doctor."

The governor glanced anxiously at his colleague,

"I'm bound to tell you it's true," the latter confirmed. "It'd finish him."

The governor pulled his moustache.

"Look here, Todhunter, be reasonable."

"I won't be reasonable," said Mr Todhunter mutinously and gave the table a little tilt.

"Wait!" implored the governor. "Now look here, I can't possibly take such a decision on my own responsibility. It cuts right across prison discipline. No, wait, man! Will you let me ask the permission of the Home Office?"

"Oh, certainly," agreed Mr Todhunter courteously.

The governor drew a breath of relief. "You stay with him, Doctor. I'll go and telephone at once." He marched out.

The doctor and Mr Todhunter grinned at each other.

"Like to go back to bed while you're waiting?" said the doctor.

"No, thank you," said Mr Todhunter. "I'll sit here." He sat down carefully in a comfortable chair by the fire and began to massage his knees.

The doctor lit a cigarette. It was not his pigeon, and the break in the monotony rather tickled him.

The governor was away from nearly twenty minutes.

Mr Todhunter saw at once from his expression that something had gone wrong.

"I'm sorry, Todhunter," said the governor curtly. "The Home Office refuses to entertain your request. On the other hand they feel there is no need for you to be kept in bed. You may get up, and you may also take exercise at the usual times and in the usual place."

"But. . ." began Mr Todhunter.

"That is all I have to say," the governor cut him short.

7

Mr Todhunter was extremely angry.

He had been outmaneuvered, and he knew it. The Home Office was cunning. It did not want to hang him after all. The Home Office would, in fact, be most grateful to Mr Todhunter if he would kindly go ahead and kill himself. The Home Office would then be free to deal with Vincent Palmer just as it saw fit, without the handicap of Mr Todhunter's execution to tie its hands.

"Damn them," said Mr Todhunter with subdued passion as he crept back into bed again. "Damn them, I *will* be executed!"

8

The authorities still believed Palmer to be the criminal. That was the crux of the trouble.

Mr Todhunter protested in vain. He swore, on any oath the chaplain liked to name, that Palmer was completely innocent. The chaplain allowed him to swear on the New Testament, and believed him. The doctor believed him. Even the governor believed him. But the Home Office remained bureaucratically indifferent. For once not even the popular clamour moved them. Palmer remained in gaol, and the Home Office issued a statement.

"The home secretary," ran the statement, "after fullest consideration, has advised His Majesty to respite the capital sentence on Vincent Palmer. He is now considering the advisability of commuting this sentence to penal servitude for life, inasmuch as, although a jury has pronounced a verdict which exonerates him from having fired a revolver at Ethel May Binns with intent to murder, yet this verdict does not exclude a reasonable doubt that Palmer was a party to this act. The home secretary's decision will be announced in due course."

This statement roused even *The Times* to cynical wrath.

"Presumably," it stated "a commutation of the sentence on Palmer to life imprisonment is designed to satisfy everyone, both those who believe in Palmer's guilt and those who believe that Palmer had no hand in the crime. We can assure the home secretary that it will in fact satisfy no one. Moreover, it is opposed to every canon of British justice that Palmer should suffer life imprisonment on the assumption of the home secretary that he committed an offence for which he has never been tried by the properly constituted authority and of which he has never been found guilty."

Again, where *The Times* led, the rest followed. The *News Chronicle* even had a leader on the topic which mentioned neither Abyssinia, Spain nor the unemployed.

The Home Office, however, appeared unperturbed.

And Mr Todhunter remained resolutely in bed, trying not to fume.

9

The popular agitation of course produced its usual result so far as H.M.'s mails were concerned. A steady avalanche of letters, sometimes totalling thousands a day, descended on the prison for Mr Todhunter, who refused to open a single one of them. There also descended a regular supply of strengthening foods, patent medicines, Bibles, mechanical toys and heaven alone knows what not; but all of these were, in the ordinary course of routine, withheld from him to his considerable relief.

Of genuine visitors Mr Todhunter had few. He refused to see Farroway, he saw Mrs Farroway once, for a few minutes only, and he saw Mrs Palmer; he saw Mr Benson several times for the purpose of making further alterations to his will; and he refused to see anyone else except Sir Ernest, Mr Chitterwick and young Mr Fuller. These three were allowed to visit him in his cell, where they sat, solemnly flanked by the two warders, on the further side of the table and conversed with Mr Todhunter in his bed.

With these he debated the advisability of an appeal, in order to prolong the period for the popular agitation concerning Palmer to have its effect; but it was felt that in view of the attitude of the authorities the danger was so grave of the verdict being reversed altogether as being unjustified by the evidence that the risk could not be taken.

There was now a fortnight left before the date fixed for the execution.

Mr Todhunter did not want to be executed at all, but he hated a job half done; and there was no doubt that the hanging of himself would be the greatest lever in getting Palmer released, whatever statements the Home Office might issue.

"It's like this," Sir Ernest pointed out. "The moment the drop falls, there'll be such a howl that if the government don't let Palmer go they'll be turned out of office. It's a fact. They haven't got a majority in Parliament this minute for keeping Palmer in gaol, and they know it. It's only a question of waiting."

"Damn," said Mr Todhunter fretfully. "I wish to goodness the man could *prove* his innocence."

But every possibility had been long since explored there, and not the smallest piece of evidence could be found to substantiate Palmer's contention that he had left the premises before the fatal shot had been fired.

"That empty punt," fumed Sir Ernest. "Someone holds the key to the secret. I'm convinced of it. Someone was in the garden that night with you, Todhunter."

"I had no knowledge of it," Mr Todhunter said helplessly and with truth.

"Well," said Sir Ernest gloomily, "Chitterwick's still pottering around, but I'm afraid it's useless."

Mr Todhunter did not put in any request to see Palmer himself. There seemed to be no purpose in doing so; Mr Chitterwick had seen him, and so had Sir Ernest; and they could be relied on to obtain any information which it was in Palmer's power to give.

One further visitor Mr Todhunter did consent to see, though with the greatest reluctance.

Ever since his conviction Felicity Farroway had been agitating for an interview. Mr Todhunter could see little use in it, and he greatly feared that Felicity would break down, with consequent embarrassment to all concerned. In the end he agreed to see her on the strict condition that she did not speak a single word during the meeting; she was to be allowed to nod and shake her head, but no more. Felicity sent a tearful message to the effect that she agreed to these cruel terms.

"Well, well," Mr Todhunter greeted her with false joviality when she had taken her seat at the table and was staring at him with huge mournful eyes. He felt extremely uncomfortable and wished the interview over. "Well, well, keeping quite fit, and all that? Play still going well? Good. I—er—I ought perhaps to tell you that I have left you my share of it in my will, so you will be quite free to carry on as your own actress manageress, or whatever they call it. Yes. H'm."

Felicity continued to gaze at him.

"Now look here, my dear girl," said Mr Todhunter irritably, "I know exactly what's in your mind. Do you understand? I tell you I know. So there's no need to say anything about it. You want—dear me, this is very awkward!—you want, I suppose, to—h'm—express gratitude and all that. I understand. I understand perfectly. We both know that your brother-in-law is an innocent man, and I want you to know too that I don't regret—h'm!—well, anything I've done. That woman was a poisonous creature, and it's no good talking about nil nisi bonum. Death doesn't turn a devil into an angel.

"Now please don't think anything more about it. Your mother is very sensible. You must be sensible too. And please waste no regrets on me. I—um—dislike them. You see? And anything I have done, I'm most pleased to have done. Life, you see, means nothing to me either way. Oh, heavens, don't look at me like that, girl! Smile, damn you, smile!"

Felicity rewarded him with a watery smile.

"I—I don't want you to be hanged," she gulped. Mr Todhunter cackled. "I'm not hanged yet. Besides, they tell me it's quite painless. I've no doubt it would be less uncomfortable than my own complaint. It's a race between them. Oh, do cheer up, my dear girl," implored Mr Todhunter. "We've all got to die, you know. And apparently I ought to have been dead a month ago."

"I've signed the petition for your reprieve," whispered Felicity, dabbing at her eyes. In spite of the reputed Fascism, the great heart of the British people had been smitten in its tenderest valve by Mr Todhunter's honourable conduct. There was a strong movement in progress to dispense with his execution and merely keep him in prison till he died of his own accord.

Mr Todhunter frowned. He knew of this movement and deprecated it. To his mind it was merely playing into the hands of the Home Office, which would then find still further excuse for keeping Palmer in prison, too, just to be on the safe side.

"I wish you wouldn't mix yourself up in my affairs," said Mr Todhunter with severity.

"But I am mixed up in them!" Felicity wailed. "We all are. I brought you into it. If it hadn't been for me, you wouldn't ever have—"

"Birchman!" snapped Mr Todhunter. "Kindly remove her."

"No!" cried Felicity and clung to the table.

"You've broken your promise," Mr Todhunter pointed out.

"I—I had to," Felicity sniffed.

"Nonsense! You must learn to control yourself. You're an actress, aren't you? Very well: act. Do you think it's pleasant for me to have visitors crying all over my cell?"

Felicity stared at him.

"That's better," Mr Todhunter chuckled. "Now go home like a good sensible girl. It's been delightful to see you, but scenes are bad for me, you know. The least agitation . . . yes."

Felicity turned to the more benevolent-looking warder.

"Am I allowed to kiss him good-bye?" she whispered.

"I'm very sorry, miss. I'm afraid you mustn't go any nearer to him." Birchman looked as if he really was sorry to deprive Mr Todhunter of the joy of being kissed by this delightful girl.

Mr Todhunter, who had no wish to be kissed, hastily backed him up, "No, no. You might pass me a packet of poison. Regulations very strict about that sort of thing. Just—er—blow me one. Yes. Well, goodbye, my dear girl. I'm glad the play's a success. In fact, I'm exceedingly pleased to have been able to be of service to you—perhaps in, h'm, more ways than one. Yes. Well, good-bye."

Felicity gazed at him, her mouth worked; then she clapped her hand to it and ran to the door. Fox jumped up and let her out.

"Well, thank God that's over," muttered Mr Todhunter, wiping his brow.

10

As the days passed, it was not only the sentimental heart of the public that was touched; its sporting spirit was aroused too. Few people really wanted Mr Todhunter to hang, even among those who had no doubt of his guilt; while those who revered the traditions of the old school tie, in the best accordance with which Mr Todhunter was felt to have acted, signed the petition for his reprieve as many times as they could, in different names (not dishonourable; analogy, cribbing). In fact, everyone hoped that natural death would overtake him before the hangman arrived.

Quick to gather this sentiment, the newspapers naturally gratified it. Every morning they ran some such headline as "Todhunter Still Alive," and extremely eminent persons, from the Bishop of Merchester to a visiting American film star, were canvassed for their views on aneurisms and Mr Todhunter's expectation of life. In the clubs there was a good deal of surreptitious betting on Mr Todhunter's chances of beating the rope, and books on surgery touched phenomenal sales. It had in fact become a great sporting contest of Mr Todhunter versus the hangman, with the odds sentimentally just a shade in favour of the former; and Lloyd's were compelled to issue a statement to the effect that they were unable to accept insurance against either contingency.

This development delighted Mr Todhunter, who had a full share of the sporting spirit himself and was an ardent supporter of Middlesex in the cricket field. He tried once to persuade Mr Chitterwick to lay a bet for him and was prepared to offer 5-4 in favour of his aneurism. Mr Chitterwick, however, had come on a totally different mission and was not in the mood for these frivolities.

"I don't wish to raise your hopes in any way, Todhunter," he said, blinking through his gold-rimmed spectacles, "but I do believe I am on to something at last concerning Palmer."

"Palmer?" Mr Todhunter ceased his infantile cackling and became alert. "What do you mean?"

"Evidence, I mean, concerning the time at which he left Miss Norwood's house."

"Eh? That's good. That's very good," Mr Todhunter commended his detective. "But will it clear him?"

"That's impossible to say. We haven't found it yet, you see."

"Then what the devil are you talking about?" demanded Mr Todhunter.

Mr Chitterwick blinked again and apologised. "But you won't get excited if I tell you?" he asked anxiously.

"I shall get excited if you don't," said Mr Todhunter harshly.

"Well, it's like this," began Mr Chitterwick.

11

The true tale (or more or less the true tale), from which Mr Chitterwick only gave Mr Todhunter, in the presence of his warders, judiciously edited extracts, was as follows.

On the morning before Mr Chitterwick had had a brilliant idea and had hurried all the way down to Bromley with it to lay it before young Mrs Palmer.

The idea concerned wrist watches, and Mrs Palmer was at first somewhat at a loss to grasp it. When, however, she did so, her enthusiasm far outdid that of Mr Chitterwick himself. In consequence she was only too ready to tell Mr Chitterwick all she knew about her husband's wrist watches, including a certain one which Mr Chitterwick was able to mention as having been given to Vincent by Miss Norwood. Further, Mrs Palmer was delighted to allow Mr Chitterwick to search first through her husband's belongings and then through the whole house for this particular wrist watch, which he did very thoroughly and then announced to her, beaming all over his face, that he had been unable to find it. This made Mrs Palmer beam, too (the first time, Mr Chitterwick thought, for months), and she insisted upon his staying to lunch, which he very readily did.

That afternoon Mr Chitterwick, by pulling such strings as he and Sir

Ernest between them could reach, managed to obtain permission for a special interview with Palmer in the prison. There was some attempt at official obstruction, but Mr Chitterwick succeeded in getting his interview arranged for the next morning.

At the appointed time, then, Mr Chitterwick found himself facing Palmer across a table in a barred and boxlike room with a warder leaning in the doorway; a rather less sulky and rather more anxious Palmer, sitting stiffly in his chair with hands on the table the regulation distance apart. The ensuing conversation went something like this.

"I think," Mr Chitterwick opened it cautiously, "that I may be on the track of a piece of evidence which might go a long way to establish your innocence. I've asked for this visit because I want you to clear up one or two points which will help me."

"What piece of evidence?" Palmer asked in a subdued voice and not very hopefully.

"It concerns a wrist watch. The wrist watch that Miss Norwood gave you."

"Miss Norwood never—"

"Please listen to me," said Mr Chitterwick earnestly, "and don't commit yourself to statements that you may regret later. I have already ascertained that Miss Norwood did give you a wrist watch and your wife—your *wife,* mind you—tells me that it had the letters 'V from J' very rudely scratched inside the cover, possibly with a pin. There is no mistaking it, you see. Now, that is our premise, so kindly don't try to deny it. You understand?" And Mr Chitterwick beamed at the young man with a mixture of friendliness, cunning and warning.

The young man smiled slowly. "I'm not sure, but I think I do."

"Excellent." Mr Chitterwick sighed with relief. "I'm sure you do. At any rate, you understand enough not to attempt to deny what I'm telling you. Your wife already knows, you see. Yes, indeed. Well now, let me reconstruct. You quarrelled that evening with Miss Norwood. You left the garden in a temper. Possibly you determined to have no more to do with her; with her or hers. It occurred to you that you were wearing a wrist watch she had given you. You were in such a rage that even this was an offence. You took the watch off and hurled it into the front garden of one of the houses you were passing. Yes, yes, I know all that; don't interrupt me, please. The point is this: *where* did you hurl it?"

"I'm not sure," said Palmer doubtfully.

"Well, I've been at some pains to trace out your route. You passed, I take it, from Riverside Road into Harringay Road, didn't you?"

"Yes."

"And thence into Persimmon Road?"

"I did," said Palmer with a glance at the warder.

"And in Persimmon Road you would have taken a bus. Therefore you must have thrown that watch into a garden in either Riverside Road or Harringay Road. Can you remember which? . . . No, of course not," said Mr Chitterwick hurriedly. "You were extremely upset. You hardly knew what you were doing. Otherwise you would hardly have forgotten all about this watch incident. Or perhaps it did not strike you as important. Never mind. The importance is, you see, that the watch might have struck some hard object when you hurled it and have been broken in its fall. Now do you understand? Assuming that it showed the correct time, it would establish absolutely the exact moment at which you passed that particular spot. If you are innocent, it will be before nine o'clock. If you are guilty, it will be after that hour. You understand now?"

"Perfectly," said Palmer, and he added a slight grin.

Mr Chitterwick deprecated the grin. This was difficult and delicate work.

"Then are you willing to take the risk?" Mr Chitterwick was acutely aware that the warder was listening to every word.

"What risk?"

"Of the watch being found. It may still be there, you see."

"Oh yes. I'm willing."

"Because if found and if it is broken when found, you expect it to indicate your innocence?"

"It must do so, because I am innocent."

Mr Chitterwick took another breath of relief. "That is excellent. This is most important information about the watch. I can't think why you never remembered it before. Still, you've told me now and it isn't too late. I'll have a search put in hand at once, under proper safeguards."

"Yes, do," said Palmer with a slight smile. "I shall be very grateful. It may turn out lucky that I remembered at last. But you know I was almost in a daze that evening."

"Of course, of course," beamed Mr Chitterwick. "Most satisfactory. Exactly. Er—your wife sent her love, yes, and expects you home very soon now. Quite so."

He turned to the warder and intimated that he was ready to go, calling on Mr Todhunter on the way.

12

That very same afternoon Mr Chitterwick, Sir Ernest Prettiboy (determined as usual to be left out of nothing), a detective sergeant and a detective constable began a search of the front gardens in Riverside Road and Harringay Road.

The search began at a quarter past two, and by five o'clock it was completed, in a rough, preliminary way. No wrist watch had come to view.

"He says he threw it into a front garden," said Mr Chitterwick, obviously much distressed. "He's quite sure he did."

"Yes, but where?" asked Sir Ernest acutely.

"He can't remember. He says he was in a kind of daze. Well, we may have missed it. On the other hand . . ."

"Yes?"

"Well, he says he took a bus in Persimmon Road. The bus stop, we can see, is a hundred yards ahead of this corner. The houses here have front gardens too.

"Quite possible," agreed Sir Ernest. "Eh, Sergeant? It's worth having a try in Persimmon Road too?"

"If you think it advisable, sir," agreed the sergeant without enthusiasm.

It was in the third garden from the corner that the watch was found, under the winter leaves, very dirty and grimed and its strap covered with mildew. That it was the watch they were looking for was not in question, for inside the front cover was the faintly scratched inscription "V from J." It was the sergeant himself who found it, and Mr Chitterwick was vehement in his praise of such brilliant sleuthing.

The hands of the watch stood at two minutes to nine.

"You were right, sir," said the sergeant to Mr Chitterwick with respect. "This about lets Mr Palmer out, and that's a fact. Pity it didn't turn up earlier."

"It would have saved many people a great deal of trouble, expense and unhappiness," pronounced Sir Ernest.

Mr Chitterwick said nothing. He was not sure that Sir Ernest was right.

13

As was only fair, Mr Chitterwick was given the privilege of breaking the news to Mr Todhunter the next morning. He was further able to pass on an item of news which he had had from Sir Ernest before leaving home.

Mr Todhunter took the news calmly. "What a damned fool not to have remembered before!" he observed disgustedly. "I might still have been in Japan instead of this bloody hole."

For all his primness in some respects Mr Todhunter was singularly addicted to the use of this foolish adjective.

"And I have it from Sir Ernest," bubbled Mr Chitterwick, "that Palmer's release can now be only a matter of hours. You haven't seen the papers this morning. They have the whole story. I—er—thought it only right to ensure that they should have it. And they've done it justice. No government could possibly stand out against such a storm."

"Well, thank goodness I can have a bit of peace at last," mumbled Mr Todhunter acidly. He relented. "You've done very well, Chitterwick," he added kindly.

Mr Chitterwick looked like a spaniel who has been patted on the head. The ecstatic writhing of his plump little body on its chair was exactly like an attempt to wag a tail.

14

That afternoon Palmer was released, unconditionally. A statement to this effect issued by the Home Office added handsomely that new evidence had completely dispelled any doubts that may have remained concerning his complicity in the crime. (Only one obscure periodical bothered to point out subsequently that the new evidence did nothing of the sort and might have been a cunning plant on Palmer's part to prove the alibi; and in any case nobody cared.)

That same evening the home secretary bowed to the storm and resigned. In a short statement in the House the prime minister, who had quite approved his colleague's firmness in private, administered a final public kick to that colleague's retreating posterior.

When told the news, Mr Todhunter showed no emotion.

"Serves him right," he pronounced judgment. "The man was a bloody fool."

15

In this way Mr Todhunter's last week on earth was a peaceful one. Outside, the agitation for his reprieve had lost impetus and the government, sensing as much, were able to put up a good show of iron determination.

Inside, Mr Todhunter expressed a wish to see no more visitors and said a final and grateful farewell to Sir Ernest, Mr Chitterwick and young Mr Fuller. At last he was able to take things easily, and he meant to do so.

What happened to him now did not matter. Availing himself therefore of the earlier permission, he even got up once or twice to walk in his dressing gown and pyjamas very slowly round the exercise yard in the April sunshine on the arm of a warder. On these occasions no other convict of course was in sight. Mr Todhunter was incommunicado.

He spent many hours writing and was able to complete the series of articles he had planned in the dock upon a trial, sentence and condemned cell from the prisoner's own point of view, and only regretted that he was unable to include an account of an execution from the same unusual angle. There were plenty of interesting and pithy comments to be made upon the working of the British judicial system, and altogether Mr Todhunter felt that he had done an important job not too badly. A note from Ferrers to tell him of the world-wide interest which was being caused by the publication of these articles in the *London Review* made Mr Todhunter cackle with pleasure.

For the rest, he spent his time mostly in chatting with his warders. It amused him that everything he told them even remotely concerning the crime had to be written down by one or the other of them in a notebook; but in return, when Fox was out of the way, Birchman continued to tell him interesting anecdotes about previous distinguished inhabitants of the cell. Both Mr Todhunter and Birchman were sorry that their acquaintance had necessarily to be such a short one.

As the time for the execution drew on Mr Todhunter was touched to see what an object of solicitude he had become. The governor would stay and chat in the friendliest manner, the chaplain was ready to come at any minute and stay as long as wanted, the doctor was determinedly cheerful.

"Does an execution bother you much?" Mr Todhunter asked the governor one day, and received an affirmative reply as emphatic as it was unofficial.

"Loathe 'em! Horrible. Perfectly barbarous, in most cases, though they are sometimes justified. But it's a ghastly responsibility for us officials. It upsets the prisoners, worries the staff. . . . . I dread them. Never sleep for a couple of nights beforehand."

"Please," said Mr Todhunter, distressed, "don't bother on my account. I used to suffer from insomnia myself. I should be most disturbed to hear that I'd cost anyone a night's sleep."

16

On the morning on which he was to die Mr Todhunter woke soon after seven o'clock. He had slept well and, observing his own reactions, was interested to find that he felt quite calm except for a certain mild excitement of anticipation. Mr. Todhunter had in fact by this time arrived at the conclusion that he did not mind dying. In fact he rather looked forward to it. The idea of imminent death had been with him so long that it would be a relief to get the preliminary of dying over and done with. Also, death seemed such a magnificent rest, and Mr Todhunter had grown very tired of his inefficient body. (Mr Todhunter's doctor would have been delighted had he known what his patient had at last come to feel.)

He attended with his usual interest to the last ceremonies; but when the chaplain, hearing that he was awake, hurried over, Mr Todhunter asked him sincerely to keep off the subject of religion. He was ready to die, he was at peace with all men; and that, considered Mr Todhunter, was enough.

He asked in a thoughtful way after the hangman, who, as Mr Todhunter knew, had passed the night in the prison, and expressed the hope that he had slept well. He also remarked that he was disappointed not to have been told when that gruesome official was taking his usual surreptitious peep at him on the previous evening for the purpose of estimating the amount of drop required, for he would have been pleased to stand up and offer him every facility for making a correct guess.

The doctor, who paid a visit to the cell just before eight o'clock, secretly marvelled that his patient was standing the strain so well. He could hardly believe it when Mr Todhunter assured him that he was feeling no strain at all.

By his own special request the warders in charge of him on the last tour of duty were Birchman and Fox. They were a great deal more upset than Mr Todhunter himself.

At breakfast, when he ate his bacon and eggs and drank two cups of excellent coffee, Mr Todhunter remarked with mild surprise:

"The condemned man partook of a hearty breakfast. Dear, dear. So one really does. Well, why not? I enjoyed that very much."

After it he asked for and was given a cigarette, which he smoked with relish, his first for many months.

"They say one loses the taste," he remarked to Fox. "It's not true. This cigarette is exceedingly pleasant."

Soon after eight the governor came, very ill at ease.

"All right, Todhunter?"

"Perfectly, thank you. I'm not," said Mr Todhunter with a sudden cackle, "going to collapse with nerves, if that's what you mean."

"You can have a glass of brandy—er—later, if you want one, you know."

"My doctor's forbidden me spirits," regretted Mr Todhunter and cackled again. "It might prove fatal, you know, and then you'd be responsible."

The governor tried to smile, but it was not a very successful effort. He waved the warders out of the cell.

"Now look here, we all hate this—well, I can't say as much as you do, I'm afraid, but you know how we feel. And I just want to tell you that you must look on it more as an operation than—than anything else. It's absolutely painless, and once the executioner comes in it's only a matter of seconds. I'm sure you'll be brave, and . . . oh, damn it, you know what I mean."

"I do indeed," said Mr Todhunter earnestly. "And I'm exceedingly grateful to you. But please don't distress yourself. I'm not worried at all."

"I really don't believe you are," said the governor wonderingly. He hesitated. "Well, there it is. We all hoped the other thing would get you first, but it hasn't. So we've just got to go through with it. . . . I'll come back with the others, the sheriff and so on, you know, at nine o'clock."

"Certainly," said Mr Todhunter amicably.

He sat down at the table and wondered whether there was really nothing else that ought to have gone into his will. It seemed queer that it was too late to alter it if there was.

"Dear me," said Mr Todhunter, "I feel as if I were catching a train and had got to the station too early. How do they usually fill up the last half hour, Birchman?"

"Well, sir, they often write letters," suggested the warder uneasily.

"That's a good idea," said Mr Todhunter. "I'll write to a friend of mine."

He sat down and wrote a short letter to Furze; but after he had explained that he could not explain his feelings because he had none beyond a sort of expectant emptiness, there was nothing more to say. So he thanked Furze again for all he had done and found that a bare five minutes had been consumed.

"Are all the other convicts locked in their cells now?" he asked suddenly. Birchman shook his head. "No, we don't do that now. They'll be mostly in the workshops and so on, on the other side."

Mr Todhunter nodded and yawned. He had dressed this morning, for the first time for nearly a month. They were his own clothes for a man is not hanged in convict dress.

"Well, we'd better have a game of something," he said languidly. "Dear me, I never expected to be bored this morning, but I am. Just bored. How very odd. Can you explain it?"

"Yes," said Fox. "It's because you're not afraid."

Mr Todhunter looked at him in surprise. "I never knew you were a psychologist, Fox. But you've hit the nail on the head, I think. This waiting is just like any other waiting because I don't mind what's coming. In fact it's not even as bad as waiting in the dentist's room. I wonder if many of the others have felt like this?"

"Not many, I dare say," said Birchman, putting the cards on the table. "What would you like to play?"

"Bridge," said Mr Todhunter promptly. "It's the only game after all. I wouldn't at all mind a final rubber. Can we get the chaplain to make a fourth?"

"Shall I ask him to come back?" suggested Fox, though a little doubtfully. Mr Todhunter had got rid of the chaplain soon after breakfast, afraid that he might become intense if given his head. Mr Todhunter was sufficiently public school to have a dread of intensity.

"Call him," Mr Todhunter nodded.

Fox went to the door and spoke to someone who must have been waiting outside.

Within two minutes the chaplain was in the cell. Whether he approved or not of Mr Todhunter's method of spending his last minutes on earth, he was a good fellow and said nothing. They cut for partners, and Fox dealt.

Mr Todhunter picked up his hand and cackled. There was a grand slam in spades in it.

He got the grand slam.

At two minutes to nine there was the sound of footsteps along the concrete passage outside.

"They're here," said the chaplain in a low voice.

He looked at Mr Todhunter, then suddenly leaned across the table and gripped his hand.

"Good-bye, Todhunter," he said. "I know you dislike sentiment, but I'd like to say this. I'm humbly glad to have know. you. Whatever you've done, you're a better man than me."

"Do you really think so?" said Mr Todhunter, astonished and gratified too.

As the cell door opened he stood up. To his pleasure and somewhat to his surprise, his heart did not seem to be beating any faster than usual. He glanced at his hands: they were quite steady.

A little procession entered the cell: the governor, the deputy governor, the doctor and two strangers. Of the strangers one, Mr Todhunter knew, must be the sheriff; the other. . .

The other detached himself, a squat, powerful man, and came forward at a quick shuffle. He held things at which Mr Todhunter looked with curiosity.

"It'll be all over in a few seconds, old man," said the executioner in kindly tones. "Just put your hands behind your back."

"One minute," said Mr Todhunter. "I'm intensely interested. May I see these—what do you call them? Pinioning straps?"

"Now, don't make things difficult, old man," begged the executioner. "We've no time, and—"

"Let him see them," interrupted the governor abruptly.

The executioner hesitated, and Mr Todhunter had an opportunity to look at the light strap he was holding.

"Much less cumbersome than I'd thought," he commented. His curious gaze travelled up to the executioner's face. "Tell me," he said, "has anyone ever hit you on the chin when you came in here to do this job?"

"Why no," said the executioner. "They usually—"

"Well," said Mr Todhunter, "here's one you won't forget," and with all his strength he drove his bony fist at the other's face.

It caught the man full on the chin and knocked him backwards onto the floor. Mr Todhunter fell on top of him.

Instantly all was hubbub. The warders leapt forward, the executioner picked himself up.

But Mr Todhunter did not move.

The doctor dropped on his knees and felt hurriedly under Mr Todhunter's waistcoat. Then he looked up at the governor and nodded.

"He's gone."

"Thank God," said the governor.

EPILOGUE

Mr Chitterwick was lunching with Furze at the Oxford and Cambridge Club.

It was just a week after Mr Todhunter's death, and Furze was telling Mr Chitterwick of the letter he had received from him.

"He felt no fear, I'm certain. But why should we, after all? Death isn't terrifying. It's only our imaginations that make it so."

"I hope he had an easy passing," muttered Mr Chitterwick, "He was a fine man, and he deserved one, I would like to know just what happened in the cell." It had been stated in the newspapers that Mr Todhunter had never been hanged; he had died from natural causes while resisting the executioner.

Furze, who always knew any official secret, told him.

Mr Chitterwick was delighted.

"How very characteristic," he crowed. "He must have intended it all the time. Dear me, I feel so privileged to have been able to help him."

Furze looked at his guest.

"Yes, you did help him, you and Sir Ernest Prettiboy. But one can't blame Sir Ernest. *He* did it unconsciously."

"Wh-what do you mean?" asked Mr Chitterwick nervously.

Furze laughed. "It's all right. You needn't be alarmed. But I think we'd better have this out."

"Have what out?"

"Why," said Furze frankly, "the fact that both of us know perfectly well that Todhunter never killed the Norwood woman."

It was Mr Chitterwick's turn to stare.

"You know that?"

"Of course. I've know it since halfway through the trial. How long have you known it?"

"Since . . . since he began to manufacture evidence," said Mr Chitterwick guiltily.

"When was that?"

"The day we first met Sir Ernest in his garden."

"Yes, so I imagined. You spotted it then, did you? What made you suspicious?"

"Well," said Mr Chitterwick a little uncomfortably, "he'd said he'd only been there in the dark, but he knew the way far too well. Then the gaps in the bushes were too plain, and the footprints, too; the scoring on the fence was too fresh, and the twigs too newly broken. . .."

"He'd prepared the way?"

Mr Chitterwick nodded. "After I left him the evening before, I imagine, just as the police suggested."

"And that second bullet?"

Mr Chitterwick blushed. "Counsel for the police explained that at the trial, too, didn't he?"

"You mean, the explanation was correct?"

"I'm afraid it was."

"In fact," said Furze, "every single thing that counsel said was correct. The police were right in their ideas about our friend in every single particular?"

"In every single particular," confirmed Mr Chitterwick unhappily.

The two men stared at each other.

Then suddenly they simultaneously laughed.

"But they couldn't convince the jury?" said Furze.

"No indeed, I'm glad to say," said Mr Chitterwick.

Furze took a sip of claret.

"Well, I must say, Chitterwick, you've got a nerve. I wouldn't have thought it of you."

"In what way?"

"Why, faking evidence yourself. And getting away with it. That wrist watch . . . masterly! Did you have much trouble in persuading Mrs Palmer to agree?"

"None," admitted Mr Chitterwick. "She—she'd already been very helpful in the matter of that bullet in the flower bed, you see. Er—Todhunter himself arranged that."

"Fired it, you mean? But no, the police had the revolver."

"Oh, it had been fired right enough, but a very long time before. Mrs Palmer merely dated it later. And the bullet being lead, you see, hadn't rusted; so no one could prove her story untrue."

"Most reprehensible thing, perjury."

"Oh, I'm sure she didn't commit perjury," said Mr Chitterwick, rather shocked. "There would have been a mental reservation."

"And the wrist watch. I suppose you scratched the initials?"

"No, Mrs Palmer did. We thought her hand would be lighter. Er—of course Miss Norwood had never given it to him."

"Of course not. And then you hid it. Well, I repeat, I wouldn't have believed it of you. It was a terrible risk."

"Yes, but I had to, you see," Mr Chitterwick explained earnestly. "The man was innocent. It was terrible. I do believe they'd have kept him there all his life. And he couldn't speak, any more than Todhunter could. Besides, it would have been a shocking thing if Todhunter had had to die with the knowledge that his sacrifice had been largely in vain and that Palmer would have to spend his life in prison."

"Todhunter knew Palmer was innocent?"

"Oh yes. That was what worried him so."

"He knew who really did it?"

"I think he must have done. And I'm sure he admired her for it."

"The empty punt," said Furze thoughtfully.

"Yes, that's how she went. And I think she must have had on a pair of trousers. I believe," said Mr Chitterwick diffidently, "that trousers are quite a usual article nowadays in the feminine wardrobe."

"How many people know the truth?"

"I think only three, besides ourselves. Mr and Mrs Palmer, and of course—"

"Palmer did know, then?"

"Oh, he must have done. From the beginning. There was the question of the revolver, you see."

"Yes, I always thought there was something fishy about the revolver. I still don't see why Palmer took it round to the flat that morning."

"Oh, but he didn't." Mr Chitterwick leaned across the table in his earnestness. "He'd taken it round there several days before. He didn't know he'd done so, though. You see, what happened was that Mrs Palmer began to feel very upset and anxious about the complications with Miss Norwood. She knew her husband was a man of—er—a somewhat violent disposition, and she thought it best to get the revolver out of his way, just in case. So she rang up her sister and asked if she would take charge of it and then did it up in a parcel and sent it round by her husband, telling him that it was some unimportant domestic article. It was only when the news arrived that Miss Norwood had been shot that he looked for it and found it missing. When he heard where it had gone, he hurried round to the flat at once."

"Oh, that's why he went there so early?"

"Yes indeed. And I think he knew then who had shot Miss Norwood. Luckily he didn't lose his head, and just told his sister and mother to hold out at all odds that they had been together in the flat all Sunday evening. As it turned out, the police accepted their story."

"And Todhunter tried to exchange the revolvers in order to get hold of the really fatal weapon and leave the Farroway family with the innocent one, just as Bairns said?"

"Exactly; though of course he could not explain that to Palmer. Dear me, I'm afraid Palmer sadly misjudged him. Naturally he thought Todhunter an interfering busybody. It was not until almost the end that he realized what our friend had really been doing."

"And on that visit Todhunter established some sort of understanding with

Mrs Farroway?"

"Undoubtedly he must have done so. Indeed, she had intimated as much to me. She knew he was trying to help, though of course she did not know till much later that he was ready to go to such lengths."

"Why was Palmer allowed to stand trial?"

"Well, really, no one thought he would be convicted. And it was his own wish. After all, he realised that it was his own foolish conduct which had been responsible for Miss Norwood's death, and he was very properly determined to shield the true assassin well, right up to the hilt, I suspect. . . Not," added Mr Chitterwick, "that she was at all willing to be shielded. I think the family must have had a great deal of trouble to induce her to stay silent. Her one idea was to come forward with the truth. Er—I had a very difficult scene with her myself."

"You?"

"Yes indeed. I visited her one evening. I had to tell her plainly that I knew the truth and that she must let Todhunter do as he wished. I'm afraid I had to put it on very highfalutin grounds," said Mr Chitterwick guiltily, "before I could get her to agree. I—er—I think I said something about his having set his heart on doing more good by his death, in saving a valuable life for the service of others, than he had ever been able to do alive. Even so, it was touch and go." Mr Chitterwick sighed heavily in recollection of that awkward half-hour.

"Well, well." Furze twiddled the stem of his wineglass. "I suppose we shall never know the whole truth of it. That detective sergeant, for instance. I was quite sorry for him in the box. I suppose he was perfectly right? When he examined Todhunter's revolver, it never had been fired?"

"No, of course not. Dear me," said Mr Chitterwick, "there's no doubt that bluff can pay. Our friend put up a quite incredible one; but he got away with it in the end."

"Thanks to a sentimental jury. He wouldn't have done, if I'd been on it," Furze smiled. "By the way, he really did throw away the fatal bullet?"

"Oh yes. That was the only suggestion Bairns made that was incorrect. He threw it into the river that same evening. That action, of course, saved the whole situation. If the bullet had been found, there would never have been any doubt as to which revolver killed the woman. Luckily Todhunter realised that at the time; though he didn't, of course, know then who the killer had been. It was most fortunate."

"You approve then," Furze asked quizzically, "of Todhunter's action? You think it right to cheat justice?"

"Oh dear, but what is justice?" Mr Chitterwick looked very uncomfortable. "They say murder can never be justified. But can't it? Is human life so valuable that it is better to preserve a pestilential nuisance alive rather than bring happiness to a great many persons by eliminating one? We discussed something like that at Todhunter's dinner that night, you know. It's a difficult question. A terrible question. Todhunter did not shirk it. I can't say I don't think he was right."

"But do you believe that he really would have shot the woman himself, when it came to the last, final, irrevocable moment?"

"Who can say? I think myself that he probably might not have done. But it all depends. If one can so believe in the justice of one's intentions as to work up into a kind of exaltation . . . I suppose that's how these things are done . . . for they *are* done . . . Huey Long . . ." Mr Chitterwick broke off, looking much distressed.

"Chitterwick," said Furze, "who *did* shoot Ethel May Binns?"

Mr Chitterwick started violently. "God bless my soul, don't you know?" he asked, horrified. "I thought . . . dear me, I must have given things away . . . betrayed confidences . . . oh dear."

"I won't say I haven't got my ideas," Furze answered slowly. "But no, I can't say I *know*."

"Well, neither do I," Mr Chitterwick answered with defiant untruth. "It would be best not to know, don't you agree? We may have our views of right and wrong, but if anyone ever deserved to die, it was Jean Norwood; if anyone ever did have a right to kill, it was the person who killed her, and if ever a death was justified by results, it was that one. And we are the only people who suspect the truth. Don't you think that's how we should leave it—at unvoiced suspicion?"

"I think," said Furze, "that you're probably right." Mr Chitterwick drew a deep breath of relief. Felicity Farroway's secret must surely be safe now.